The Fortuneteller's Lie

Book One

A. C. Foster

For Gwyn
Thanks for listening

1922
The Golden Horn

PROLOGUE

One of their own was gone. Not gone like killed or left. Gone like where the hell had he disappeared to. The rumors started running up and down the small ship as soon as it happened. Never mind that it was four hours before sunup. As sailors, they were used to waking up at odd hours. Small crews lived odd hours. Standing watch four hours on, eight hours off, twenty-four hours a day every day broken only by the dog watch did that to you. So when it happened, the hour didn't really matter. Before the watch changed, every man aboard was up, listening to one version of the story, then seeking out the next man to hear the latest variation. Rumor was fact, guesses were sworn statements and the only common denominator was one of their own was missing.

The news made its rounds through the gunboat's crew like a particularly virulent type of social disease. Gone, the stories said. He walked right off the quarterdeck while the ship slumbered, tied to the dock in a piss hole part of the world somebody with a bad sense of humor named the Golden Horn.

The crew could forgive a sailor jumping ship. It happened from time to time. You got fed up with things or you found a woman on shore too pretty to part ways with. It happened, especially in the more desirable ports. But this was Vladivostok, and no fool would ever call the place desirable.

Then there was winter. It was just over the horizon and not just any winter. Siberian winter. A kind of winter that made other winters feel inadequate. And if that wasn't enough to discourage a sane man from jumping ship, all you had to do was listen to the thump of Bolshevik artillery. It was almost constant now. Spend five minutes listening to those guns and you knew this wasn't the kind of place you wanted to stick around in.

It didn't wash. None of it. Wash or not, the story spread from stem to stern, port to starboard, keel to crow's nest. A crewman was missing, one of their own, but not just anyone. No. Anyone wouldn't have roused the whole ship's company out of the rack at two in the morning. No sir. Not just anyone could do that. It had to be someone special, someone privileged, someone with a pair of gold stripes on his sleeve and Mister in front of his name, someone like Mister Watkins, the boat's executive officer.

He was missing, gone, disappeared for almost seven hours now.

"I won't have it!"

The shouted voice came from the bridge. The man doing the shouting was the *Devilfish's* captain, Lieutenant Commander Simmons.

"Not on my ship!" the voice yelled.

Every man topside heard him. The line handlers standing on the pier waiting for the order to cast off heard him. So did the handful of Russians walking along the waterfront. The foreigners, if foreigners were the right word for citizens of their own country, glanced at the angry dark blue uniform half seen on the bridge. Maybe one of them stopped for a moment to look at their idea of a foreigner. Maybe they stood there staring for a moment too long.

The sailor standing watch on the pier shifted the rifle in his hands. He was in a mood to do a little shouting of his own. For all he knew, the Russian in front of him might be the one who done it. Clearing his throat, he spat onto the old, gray lumber of the pier.

"Move along," he yelled, emphasizing his words with the barrel of his weapon.

The Russian did just that, leaving ill-tempered foreigners to their own ways.

Past the waterfront's row of warehouses, down the alley where the main road crossed, a file of sailors marching two abreast hurried towards the gunboat.

"About time," the sailor said to no one in particular. He turned for the boat, cupped a hand around his mouth and shouted the words every man aboard had been waiting to hear since it happened. "On deck! Shore party's coming back!"

The whole ship heard the shout. Dungarees came racing out of the below deck's hatch. Line handlers crowded towards the alley's opening to peer down its depth. Sailors standing on the fantail moved to the railing to watch their shipmate's return. Every man aboard counted heads.

Lieutenant Commander Simmons heard the shout like everyone else. So had the lookout standing in the crow's nest directly above him.

"Bridge, they're coming back," the lookout on the tower reported.

"Sir," the ensign standing beside Simmons began, "shore party's—"

"Thank you, Mr. Johnson. We all heard the watch." Like every other man aboard the gunboat, he started counting heads as each man cleared the buildings. Everyone's arithmetic was the same as his.

Fourteen. Not fifteen.

Fourteen men, rifles slung over shoulders, were coming back empty handed. They hadn't found his missing officer. Simmons flexed his jaw with frustration. The high water stain on the wooden pylons was becoming more visible. There was no arguing with the tide. He would have to go soon or wait for the next turn.

The shore party reached the side of the boat. As they came aboard, each man turned to face the stern, then brought their Springfield rifles to present arms. They did it in that casual, just respectful enough way sailors had about such requirements. The last man aboard was the *Devilfish's* bosun. A bare nod of the head from the most senior enlisted man on board told the whole ship's company the news.

"They didn't find him," Simmons said.

The ensign standing beside him, the victim of the captain's most recent outburst opened his mouth to say something then thought better of it. Simmons walked away from the man and went to the stern hatch. As he waited for his most seasoned man aboard to climb the steel ladder, no one on the bridge made a sound. No one moved. To the quartermaster standing beside his chart of Amurskiy Bay, Simmons looked like a caged bear that had been poked once too many times. All four men, one ensign and three sets of dungarees, were doing their best to stay as far away from the cage as they could on the small bridge.

The *Devilfish's* captain didn't have to wait long. The bosun stomped his way up the metal steps. White duty belt still strapped around his waist, he paused before stepping across the threshold.

Simmons waved him forward. "Let's hear it."

"We looked everywhere, sir. Even places where the locals didn't want us. Checked all three hospitals, went to the morgue, and every drinking joint in Vladivostok." The bosun hitched the wide canvas belt to a more comfortable position. "Had trouble with some of the checkpoints. That's why we're late. I had to draw my sidearm once or twice."

"Were shots fired?"

"Shots are often fired in this city, sir."

Simmons thought about that answer for a moment. "Do I need to know something, Bosun?"

"No, sir." The *Devilfish's* bosun was an old time China sailor. He was a man accustomed to telling officers what they needed to know. "Russians are a jumpy lot," he added.

"And what did you discover from the jumpy locals?"

"Nothing helpful, sir. Nobody seen a thing, heard a thing or knows a thing. It's like Mr. Watkins fell through a crack."

Simmons pulled out his pocket watch, pressed the cover's release and sought answers to his dilemma in the roman numerals.

The bosun waited.

The captain's eyes followed the second hand making its measured circumference around the ivory dial. "At oh two hundred hours, the Officer of the Deck tells a seaman he saw something in the alley. He then makes a decision to take himself away from the quarterdeck to go investigate an event that no one else observed. He then walks," Simmons pointed the pocket watch at the alley, "into the darkness never to return. And no one, not a soul anywhere along this rat invested waterfront saw or heard a thing?"

The bosun scratched his chin. "We looked. We offered cash for information. We even tried asking kids in the street, those we could catch. Might of helped if we spoke the lingo, but we made do with sign language, of a sort. We couldn't find anybody who saw anything, or if they did, they weren't saying." The bosun turned to face the rows of flat roofed brick warehouses. "What I can't figure is, when they grabbed him, how did they get past them militia checkpoints? If we had trouble, imagine what it would have been like for a bunch of Bolshevik kidnappers in the middle of the night." The bosun waved an arm in the general direction of the brick buildings lining the dock. "They couldn't have taken him far. He's in one of those. We need to do a door to door. Thump some heads together."

"Taken him?" Pursing his lips, Simmons turned to the ensign, three months out of the Academy and until last night, his missing officer's cabin mate. "Tell the man."

"I looked," the ensign said, "in his personal effects. The Skipper ordered it."

"Tell him what you found," Simmons repeated.

"Everything was there, right where it always is except," the ensign paused.

The helmsman and quartermaster, both enlisted men, had already heard the story. Twice. Both had discussed the discovery between themselves and the duty messenger in a whispered conversation among equals. The messenger had been sent to the wardroom for coffee and by now, every man aboard knew the details. Even the bosun, with barely two minutes on deck, heard part of the report from a gunner's mate standing outside the ladder to the bridge. Such is the nature of small ships. It was the bosun's reaction the two enlisted men wanted to see.

"Here it comes," the helmsman said quietly to the quartermaster. Unfortunately, he said it just loud enough for the bosun to hear.

"You'll shut your mouth, Brockard, when officers are speaking!" the bosun shouted in a volume loud enough to be heard by line handlers on the pier.

Brockard, the helmsman, cringed. The old chief was a fearsome presence on deck, fearsome enough that even the ensign, an officer as new as new could get, knew better than to interrupt when he was screaming at the men wearing dungarees. When he was sure the lesson in naval propriety was over, he finished his report.

"Everything was there except his razor and toothbrush. They're gone."

The bosun scratched his chin again. "Proves nothing. We should put a boat in the water. If some Russian bastards cut his throat and dumped him in the drink, we should at least recover his corpse. It could be any man on this ship out there."

The low thumps of the Bolshevik artillery boomed in the distance. You didn't have to be a gunnery expert to tell they were getting closer.

"Tell him the rest," Simmons said.

The ensign glanced at Brockard. "There's a woman," he said, just loud enough for the bosun to hear. "I've seen them together." He glanced at the enlisted man again. Feeling like he was informing on a friend, he added, "Several times. She's a real looker."

The bosun rocked back on his heels like he'd just heard a talking dog at a carnival show. "Is that so? The XO's got a woman in Vladivostok. I got two, Mr. Johnson. For a ruble or two, they'll do things to a man that'll keep you smiling for a week. Hell, I got a woman in Changzhou can put both feet behind her head." The bosun hitched his thumbs through his canvas belt. "At the same time," he said with a knowing leer at the ensign. "But I wouldn't jump ship for any of them." The bosun pushed his hat onto the back of his head. "You got a point, Mr. Johnson?"

Johnson took a half step backward. "I was just saying, Chief."

Simmons cut off whatever the ensign was going to say. Looking at the water rings on the wharf's pylons, he said, "Quartermaster, note the ship's log."

The man standing next to Brockard unscrewed the cap from his fountain pen. Simmons stared at the gray water lapping along the waterfront's pier. If he stayed for another turn of the tide, for all he knew, the guns thumping in the distance might have the harbor in range. He checked the numbers on his watch once more. Without looking up from the dial, he said, "Oh nine forty-seven hours, September twenty-eight, nineteen twenty-two. Ship's Executive Officer Lieutenant Ashwood Watkins missed ship's movement."

The quartermaster, a smooth cheeked nineteen year old,

bent over the logbook, fountain pen in hand.

"Ensign Johnson appointed temporary Executive Officer," he continued.

The ensign blinked and did a manly job of keeping his mouth from smiling.

"A missing razor and spending time ashore with a woman don't mean he jumped ship," the bosun said. His voice was dangerously close to being defined as loud. "We should search the harbor."

Simmons met his bosun's eyes. "Mr. Watkins walked off the quarterdeck in the middle of his watch because he said he saw something in the shadows. There were no shouts for help or sounds of a struggle and even though he was armed, no shots were fired. You yourself confirmed the local militias report nothing suspicious at the barricades."

The bosun raised a hand towards the quartermaster, freezing him and his pen in his tracks. The chief took a step closer to Simmons. "You can't write that in the log, sir. You know the navy. Even if he was to turn up an hour from now, those words written there would ruin the man."

The artillery somewhere north and west of the city fired another salvo. Simmons raised a finger as if the guns were emphasizing his point.

"The tide is falling as is my opinion of Mr. Watkins. I cannot stay even if I wanted to. I was ordered to sea this morning. Single up all lines, Chief." He turned to his new executive officer. "Mr. Johnson, notify the engine room."

"Engine room, aye." Johnson pointed at Brockard who went to the brass voice pipe to relay the commands below.

The Bosun looked apoplectic. "Another twenty-four hours won't hurt, Skipper. I request we do another search."

A rifle fired in the distance. Gunshots in Vladivostok were becoming as common as firecrackers on the Fourth of July.

"Noted," Simmons said. "You heard my order. I said single up."

"Sir," the bosun said, putting twenty-three years of

experience as a China sailor behind the word. "He ain't jumped ship. Not in this port. Something's not right."

"The discussion is closed, Bosun. We are putting to sea as ordered."

The ship's bosun stood his ground, every inch of his six foot frame showing his immense displeasure for anyone wearing gold braid. Finally, his disagreement broadcast to everyone on the cramped gunboat's bridge, he reached for the speaking trumpet. The chief had a voice that could be heard halfway to Pearl if he wanted it to. Brockard nudged the quartermaster with an elbow. Neither of them had ever seen the chief use the trumpet.

"To your lines! Stand by to cast off!" the bosun bellowed.

The quartermaster's pen scratched its way across the ship's log.

1

I wasn't really asleep. Not completely. More like that in between state when you're just resting your eyes but still partially aware. The woman lying beside me wasn't aware of anything. You could tell by the rhythmic snoring I'd been listening to since the wee hours. When I heard the whistle, I threw off the blanket, pushed the woman's arm off my chest and swung my legs over the side of the bed.

Finally. At last.

That whistle came from the *Devilfish*. I'd heard the sound often enough to know its high pitched gurgle anywhere. The woman stirred in her sleep, half opened her eyes, then pulled the blanket a little closer. Wishing I had something on a little warmer than my underwear, I went to the room's only window. It was smudged and sooty with equal parts grime and coal smoke from a pipe sticking out of the wall on the floor below me. Wiping the pane with my hand didn't help. Not that it really mattered. Even through the grimy smear, the *Devilfish's* mast was just visible through the glass. I was far enough away from the docks to make the mast look like a toothpick sticking up through the flat roof of a building. Her stack had a healthy amount of black smoke pumping into the sky. Someone was shoveling coal into the furnaces. Number Two boiler always needed a half dozen more scoops than Number One to come up to pressure. I had never figured out why. It was one of those things I planned to get around to. Funny the things you think about as you watch your home and everyone you know about to sail away and leave you behind.

The mast began to move. She was underway. Done, I told myself. There was no going back now.

The woman lying in the bed murmured something in a sleepy, not really awake voice. She didn't speak English. I didn't speak Russian. It was a perfect relationship.

"Be quiet," I said to the dingy glass panes. "I'm watching my world sail away."

She said something again. *Krovat*, I think. That meant bed. I found that out last night. Or maybe it meant where's the heat? I wasn't sure. Bed sounded plausible enough. She said it as she patted the mattress. *Krovat*. She wanted me to come back to bed.

I couldn't see the toothpick anymore. Buildings taller than the ramshackle one I had spent the night in were in the way. I turned my back on the yellow haze outside and hoped I had made a fair bargain with the devil. That made me smile. Bargaining with the devil and leaving the *Devilfish*. There was a moral lost somewhere in there.

Last night, after leaving the quarterdeck and slipping into the night, I found a man wearing a long overcoat. No one sees someone walking through the streets of Vladivostok wearing a coat. Everyone sees a uniform. The man was about my size and build, so I gave him a ruble and he slipped out of the coat. Putting it on and buttoning it to the neck, it covered the two gold stripes at my cuffs and the double row of brass buttons. The seller offered me his watch, a pair of shoes I didn't need, and started rummaging through a suitcase for something else

15

he thought I might want. His coat was all I needed. The day before, I bought trousers, jacket, shirt and boots from other men about my size, each item bought on a different street. Yes, I had spent some time with my planning. With my white hat hidden inside my new overcoat and its former owner following behind, I walked a little farther into the Russian night. The coat seller followed me for half a block trying to interest me in neckties and shirts before he gave up.

The room I shared with the woman was small, just four thin walls with two different kinds of wallpaper, all of it old and most of it peeling. You could hear the voices of the hotel's other guests behind the wallpaper. Someone in one of the rooms had a baby. It had been crying off and on since sunrise. It was crying now accompanied by a woman's half heard voice making comforting sounds. An armoire with a door that didn't quite close sat against the far wall. It looked like it was made around the time my grandmother got married. My guest for the evening hung her own coat, dress and underthings on the armoire's only hanger. The navy blues that I couldn't be seen in were piled in a chair; a wooden thing with no arms that wobbled on uneven legs when sat upon. I rubbed my arms, feeling the room's chill, and looked at the iron stove sitting on a little blue square of tiles. A fire would have been nice, but apparently guests of this particular flea bag were expected to furnish their own fuel. I was fresh out. There was a little square table covered by a stained white cloth next to the bed. An oil lamp with a small yellow flame burned behind a sooty mantle.

It was a cold, uncomfortable, shabby little room with no redeeming qualities except the bed. A bed, any bed, was better than nothing and this one, iron framed with rails painted a rust speckled white, seemed to suit the woman curled up in its center.

"Rise and shine," I said to the drowsy woman.

At least she wasn't hard to wake up. She stretched, yawned, scratched something under the blanket, then pulled herself into a sitting position. With her back against the iron rails of the headboard, she looked young, half-starved skinny and typical of waterfront working girls. I found her last night standing under a streetlight outside the hotel. A nod from me, a smile from her and up to my third floor room we went. I didn't really want the company. It was one of those spur of the moment decisions. I thought the girl might make the hotel's proprietor think of me as just another nobody having a night of fun. Maybe I wouldn't look like an American running away from his ship. Couldn't hurt.

The oozing yellow light coming through the dirty window wasn't flattering. She looked tired and worn, still young but fading fast. The old bedsheet of questionable cleanliness and an even older wool blanket were bunched up around her waist. She yawned again, small pale arms stretching out to either side.

"Good morning. You snore like a cow."

"*Dobroye utro,*" she replied.

Probably her way of telling me I snored like a cow. My guest had small breasts, eyes the color of brown almonds, very short straight black hair she kept pushed behind her ears and bone white skin. Some part of every conquering horde that ever roamed the steppes of Siberia was lying in that bed. I had no idea what her name was. I couldn't remember if I'd even asked for it. She said something I still didn't understand, shrugged a shoulder, apparently finished trying to make small talk, then reached for the pipe. Almost a foot long and made of bamboo with a small metal bowl on the end, it was propped against the oil lamp.

Last night, once she understood I wasn't going to partake of her professional offerings, she said something that didn't sound particularly flattering, then walked mother naked to the armoire. I thought she was going to get dressed and leave me and my dirty bed linens to shiver alone. Instead, she pulled the pipe out of a coat pocket and crawled back under the covers, pipe in hand. Like last night, she filled the bowl with something small and dark, raised the globe around the lamp and sucked fire into the bowl. Maybe *krovat* meant opium. She inhaled a deep lungful of the drug, exhaled slowly, then smiled in delirious pleasure before setting the pipe back on the table. She said something else, more Russian words I didn't catch, then rubbed her fingers and thumb together. Sign language for money. The woman patted the mattress.

I shook my head, feeling I needed to keep to the moral high ground. "Still not interested."

The woman, eyes now black glass, threw back the covers, spread naked legs to either side of the bed and made the money sign again. She was subtle like that.

There were footsteps in the hallway outside my door, then a woman's voice shouting in Russian. A male voice answered the shouts. I didn't need to understand the language to know what an argument sounded like. The male voice was making reasonably voiced suggestions. The female's sounded more demanding. I glanced over my shoulder at the dirty window once more. I missed my ship already.

The tan leather holster holding the navy issued sidearm was draped over one corner of the wooden chair. Sidearms were standard issue for officers standing watch in hostile ports. Vladivostok certainly qualified as hostile. What are you planning to do, I asked myself. Shoot your way out of a Russian hotel room and run away? Too late for any of that now. Besides, I recognized the voices outside my door. The male voice belonged to the hotel's proprietor. Last night, I gave him a wad of rubles to remember to forget I was upstairs.

"Time to get dressed," I told the Tartar prostitute.

The door flew open. The hotel's proprietor, a portly man of five feet two or three, stood no chance at holding the taller woman at bay. With the flimsy door no longer a barrier to her and what was inside, she shoved her way past him and stomped into the room. I'm not used to women barging in on me before I've had a chance to put my pants on. Judging by the reaction on their faces, neither were they. I'm not sure which of the two of them were more surprised.

"Don't you people knock?" I demanded with as much righteous indignation as I could muster.

The woman, every bit as attractive as the first time I'd seen her, gave the naked girl a two second appraisal, me a slightly longer one, then turned to face the peeling wallpaper. I'm guessing she preferred the sight of old roses in a tan and yellow motif to me and my night visitor. I needed to say something, something to salvage the situation. I was thinking about how exactly I was going to do that when she spoke.

"Three hours," she told the wallpaper. "You have kept me waiting for three hours." The slightly accented English gave her voice an exotic flavor. Doing her best not to see me, she turned to the Tartar woman displayed on the mattress. Russian flew back and forth between the two women. The girl got out of bed, cocooning herself in the bedsheet as she rose from the mattress, all the while questioning, assaulting or insulting the woman who had barged into the room. There was a pause in the conversation as both sides regrouped.

"I told you," I said, pointing at the yellow windowpanes, "we couldn't leave until the *Devilfish* got underway." Now seemed like a good time to put my pants on, but before I could reach for my trousers, the woman turned her attention back to me.

"You said they would leave at dawn."

The accented English rolled off her tongue in that charming way I remembered so well. Only the words didn't have that playful femininity like they always had before.

"No, I said they *should* leave at dawn."

"Have I bought myself a drug addict?" she demanded, pointing a gloved finger at the pipe propped next to the lamp.

"You didn't buy me, you took on a partner and the opium's hers." I didn't like the way my own voice sounded. I blamed it on the circumstances of my appearance. I would have sounded more convincing if I had been wearing pants. "Nothing happened," I added, realizing as I said the words just how absurd that sounded with a naked, sheet wrapped

19

prostitute standing by the bed.

She raised a gloved hand, palm open, fingers extended towards the ceiling; a simple gesture letting everyone in the room know I was a damned liar.

"I like the outfit," I said, thinking maybe a compliment would smooth some ruffled feathers. I wouldn't have mentioned her getup except that I'd never seen her in anything like it before. For our morning rendezvous, she had on chocolate colored jodhpurs, the kind worn by debutants on polo ponies with the bulging fabric around the thighs. The jodhpurs were stuffed into brown, knee high riding boots that somebody had recently polished. A white blouse, buttoned to the neck, was covered by a nicely fitting red coat. She didn't look anything like the semi destitute refugee I had spent the better part of the last month with. She looked, well, in a word, good. Her red hair, so dark it was almost brown, was pinned up on top of her head under what might have been a man's hat. Military type hats with short leather brims were everywhere in Russia these days. At least the parts I had seen. Except for the hat, she would look perfectly at home sitting on a galloping horse following along behind a pack of hounds.

. Now that the shock of finding me well, as she found me, had settled in, she looked confident in a way I hadn't noticed before. Poised, even. Completely different. I had to admit, the transformation in her appearance was giving me a sense of uneasiness. Five minutes ago, I knew what I was getting myself into. I had it all figured out. This completely unexpected change in her appearance was making me think I didn't know as much as I thought I did. I gave the smeared window a long glance. No ship's mast was waiting for me out there. Not anymore.

Right on cue, the Red artillery started up again. I counted the distant thumps and waited. So did everybody else in the room. Even the baby crying somewhere beyond my walls went silent. When the shells landed, the window rattled as dust drifted down from the ceiling. Closer.

The proprietor said something, looked like a man that had somewhere more important to be, then fled down the hallway, abandoning me to my fate.

"I think you frightened him," I said. I moved towards the chair and the rest of my clothing.

The Tartar girl said something that must have been disturbing to our snappily dressed visitor. More shouting started, this time with gloved fingers jabbing towards the girl wrapped in her sheet. The chair and my pants were on the other side of the argument and I thought it best not to get between them. Both women inhaled. The Bolshevik guns fired again during the brief timeout.

"Countess, if you could wait outside?" I pointed to the chair. "I would like to put on my pants."

"Downstairs," she spat. "I will give you five minutes before we leave without you."

We both knew that was an empty threat. My well-dressed morning visitor couldn't leave without me. I considered mentioning this but thought better of it. Now was not a good time to discuss the obvious. Not while standing in my underwear in a rundown hotel room. Besides, I didn't want to think about what might happen if the verbal war started by the drugged up Tartar girl went physical.

"I'll be right down," I said as diplomatically as I could.

"Strangle the strumpet before you leave," she ordered. "We cannot leave witnesses."

The countess in jodhpurs turned for the door. She paused, put one gloved hand on the jamb, then looked back over a tweed covered shoulder. She nodded her head from side to side, then said, "And I am not impressed." The door slammed closed behind her.

"You think she meant you or me?" I asked the strumpet.

Dressing quickly, I stuck a five ruble note under the lamp then winked at the black haired woman. She tossed the mostly clean sheet onto the striped ticking of the mattress, rested a hand on a too skinny hip then winked back. I do like spirit in a woman.

I had taken the room two days ago, paying extra for a view of the harbor although I suppose one could say every kind of accommodation in Vladivostok cost extra these days. Refugees were pouring into the city. Rooms, even run down shabby affairs like the one I shared with my Tartar friend were getting hard to come by. Even the hotel's stairwell had its tenants. They sat on the bare wooden steps reading old newspapers in poor light, smoked cigarettes and talked among themselves. The stairs thumped with every step of my new boots. I liked my new boots. They were comfortable.

Last night, most of the stairwell residents were asleep. This morning, a dozen pairs of eyes watched my every step as I negotiated my way between them. To the stairwell dwellers, I must have looked like a cheating husband trying to sneak away before the neighbors took notice. No doubt they had understood every word of the shouted argument between the countess and the Tartar. A father sitting next to his wife stared at me with a look of commiseration, his wife one of damnation and their teenaged boy, admiration. A voice whispered behind me and several of the men laughed. One or two spoke to me in Russian. I was careful to answer with only a nod or a smile. I didn't want anyone to remember an English speaking stranger leaving the upstairs room. Simmons might have left somebody behind to hunt for me. I doubted it, but I couldn't be sure.

When I came out of the stairwell, the hotel's owner suddenly found something fascinating to read in the guest registry. I think he was remembering I had paid him well to remember I wasn't here. Looking out the hotel's front window, I didn't see a countess in a riding outfit waiting in the street. The proprietor gave a discreet point towards a bead strung doorway in the direction of the back alley. I nodded just as discreetly, thinking I had seen a villain in a motion picture show do the same thing. Pushing my way through the beads, I went down a hallway and into the kitchen. There was an enameled iron stove radiating heat against a wall and a child of four or five eating her breakfast. Oatmeal it looked like, or whatever Russian children ate for breakfast. Her mother, wearing a pale pink apron with a knitted shawl around her shoulders stood next to the child. She was holding a pottery jug in one hand and I thought about asking for coffee. Before I could say anything, she pointed to a door on the other side of the stove.

"No coffee then," I said, touching the child's head as I went by. The kid started saying something behind me and was quickly shushed by the woman. I really did look like the villain in the motion picture shows. I tried the door. It wasn't locked.

It was chilly outside, but then this was late September on the eastern edge of Siberia. It hadn't turned cold yet, but you could feel winter wasn't far away. The countess was standing beside the open air touring sedan I had glimpsed a few times before. She had company. Two men, one beside her looking as protective as a German shepherd and another on the other side of the car. She said there would be four of us.

The hotel's backdoor swung shut behind me followed quickly by the sound of a bar sliding into place. I don't think my soon to be traveling companion had found a very warm welcome in the flophouse. I suppose that said a lot about who I was choosing to associate with.

The man standing next to the countess was my height, six feet, but considerably older with dark, shadowed eyes. He was bearded, one of those thick untrimmed Russian beards with a good deal of gray in the dark hair. Dressed in a black suit made of thick wool, he wore a shirt that was either gray or a well-worn white, no collar and black leather boots not quite as nice as my morning visitor's. His hair was short, dark and was sticking out from another one of those hats with the leather brim. I once had a painful disagreement with a bouncer in Singapore that looked just like him. Same stocky build. Same big, rounded gut. It's not easy maintaining a stomach like that these days. Not in half-starved Vladivostok. He didn't look friendly, he looked annoyed, like a zoo gorilla that was just told someone was taking away all the rope swings. The lumpy bulge of what had to be a holstered pistol was under his left armpit. Nothing so unusual about that. Not here. Russia had been at war for eight years. First with the Austrians and Hungarians. Then the Turks and Germans and most recently with the Poles and Ukrainians. Vladivostok, the rumors said, would be it. The civil fight between Bolshevik and everyone else was almost over. But not yet.

Our transportation looked a lot like most of the postwar European nobility did these days. Probably something to see in its day, but life had tarnished its former splendor. It was dark green with red spoke wheels, mismatched tires, and a pair of oversized tarnished brass headlamps. There was a long splatter of dried mud down the side and it sported a deep dent in the left front fender. I didn't recognize the make. Probably not American, since its steering wheel was on the wrong side. There was a wooden trunk small enough for a man to carry tied above the back bumper with a couple of canvas packs on top. This being September and the sky gray and heavy with the chance of rain, they had put the top up.

The other man, the one I couldn't see clearly, stepped out of the shadows and moved towards the front of the automobile. He wore a bluish gray suit that looked like it had lived a long life, matching vest, black tie and dark gray shirt. There was nothing remarkable about his appearance except for the biggest mustache I'd ever seen. It was a proud example of facial hair; a dark brown, bushy thing guaranteed to make a walrus start humming love songs. I wondered how he managed to feed himself with a shoe brush like that on his lip. Whatever his taste in lunch specials, there was no pretense about hiding pistols. He laid the long, stovepipe shrouded barrel of a Lewis machinegun across the hood of the automobile, then touched his fingers to the brim of his hat.

"I like your taste in women," he said in accented but decent

English. "She isn't bad looking for the waterfront if you like the skinny ones. Did you check your wallet this morning? That one is known to help herself if the opportunity presents."

I was sure no one had seen me last night. The street was almost empty when I ran into the girl standing under the light pole. I took a step closer. "How do you know about the woman?"

The mustache twitched. "I look. I see. I ask. People tell me things. Your, what is the English, shipmates? They searched for you all morning. Not very well, if you ask me. Still, smart of you to stay hidden."

"Be quiet, Bohdan," the countess said. Her eyes looked at me with something like frustrated contempt from beneath the military hat. "Did you strangle her?"

"Tried to. She held her breath too long. Had to give up."

The countess said something in Russian to the man in black. The man looked up at the window with the dirty glass panes.

"Door's locked. Didn't you hear them throwing the bolt? Your bruiser would have to walk around the block, go in the front door, up the stairs, recover your tarnished pride then come back down again. People would notice."

"She will talk." The countess said something else to the gorilla. "The Bolsheviks will know. She might even be one." Glancing down the alley, she added, "We might be recognized."

"Yes," I said, "because nobody's going to notice an English car in an alley with two armed guards, one sporting a machinegun longer than my leg. Not to mention a Russian noblewoman dressed for a day in the country picking up a man who spoke English." I moved to the car, opened the rear door and slid into the backseat, dumping my rolled up uniform in the floorboard. "Let's go," I told my newest friends. "That artillery's getting closer."

I could hear the driver, the one with the Lewis, laughing. The three of them had a half whispered conversation amongst themselves before the countess joined me on the backseat. If this was yesterday, I would have expected her to slide across to my side. But this wasn't yesterday. Not anymore. The gorilla in the black suit moved to the front of the engine and gave the crank a swift turn. I felt the whole car move when he spun the iron handle.

"Remind me not to arm wrestle that guy." With the engine running, Black Suit made his way to the seat next to our driver. I stuck my hand over the upholstery and tapped the driver on the shoulder. "Ashwood Watkins is my name. Friends call me Stick from the tree in my name. Got stuck with the nickname at the Academy."

The driver reached across his chest to shake hands with me. He was smiling.

"A pleasure," he said, grasping the offered hand. "I am—"

I yanked hard on the hand, pulling the arm across his chest. Before Black Suit could react, the navy issued automatic was in my left hand. Being left handed comes in handy sometimes. Its barrel was pressed against the neck of the man in black. The countess sitting beside me hissed Russian words.

"Before we begin our little adventure, I'll have that retainer we talked about," I said, my eyes on the back of Black Suit's skull. "I gave up a lot to be here and I've done it on a promise and measure of trust. Up until a few minutes ago, I felt pretty trusting. But if you mugs are willing to kill a girl because she might say something that might do something that might lead to something, well, imagine what that makes me feel like. So if we're to get along, I'll need that retainer." My thumb cocked the forty-five. "Right now."

Black Suit growled in Russian. The driver stopped struggling as soon as the pistol had appeared and sat very still behind the wheel.

"You could have asked," the countess said.

Her voice was silky, almost purring. I think I might have accidentally impressed her.

"I always keep my word," she continued. "I am Russian, the Countess of—"

"Save it," I said, cutting her off. "You wanted to kill that girl upstairs. I'm beginning to think maybe I'm seeing the real you." I nuzzled my gun against Black Suit's ear. "Tell the gorilla to keep his hands out of his pocket or I'll splatter brains all over this alley."

"Mr. Watkins," the woman sitting beside me said, "if I wanted to kill the strumpet I would have done so when I was there."

"I doubt you would have won that fight, Countess. She had that wild look in her eyes." I felt a jab just below my ribcage. Not a hurtful jab, just a get your attention kind of poke. I looked down and saw the long blued steel barrel of a pistol sitting against my softer parts. It was a big pistol and there was a gloved finger wrapped around the trigger.

"Oh," I said.

"Please take you firearm away from Ivan's head," she said, pronouncing Black Suit's name like Ee-vahn.

"And kindly release Bohdan's hand," she added. "I believe he may be having trouble breathing."

The barrel of her pistol dug harder into my side.

"Or I will shoot you in the stomach and dump you in this alley."

She has a lovely smile when she threatens to murder you. Medusa should have a smile half as deadly.

"No one is going to shoot anyone in this automobile unless we have to. We need you, Mr. Watkins, and since all of your navy ships have sailed away and left us to the Bolsheviks, I think you need us as well."

"Well," I said, "since you said us. Guess that makes me one of the team." I released the driver's hand, eased the hammer down on my Colt, then lowered the automatic from Ee-vahn's ear. Faster than you would have thought possible for such a big man, he spun in his seat. A Webley revolver was yanked out of his shoulder rig and steadied on a point midway between my eyes. The Russian said something to the countess. I waited for the translation or a very loud bang, my own automatic dangling from a finger.

"Ivan, is it?" I asked, pronouncing the name the same way she had. "Of course it is. This is Russia. What else would a gorilla be called but Ivan."

"You don't like my name?" the gorilla asked. The words were heavily accented, almost muffled like he was speaking them from the back of his throat.

The driver started laughing.

I turned to the countess. "He speaks pretty good American."

"I speak English, some Polish." Ivan cocked the hammer on the Webley. "How many you speak?"

I smiled, or tried to. "We seem to have gotten off to a bad start. But I wasn't going to just sit back and let you kill that girl."

"I was going give her money," the Russian said. "If you stupid Americans spoke anything besides English, you would heard Countess tell me pay her. Instead, you put gun in my ear." He looked at the countess. "I don't like him. Shoot him."

"Don't shoot him," the driver said. "There's no time to find another one."

I was starting to like the man with the shoe brush under his nose.

"We buy another expert," Ivan said. He drew the last word out as if the qualification was in doubt. The revolver's barrel never twitched, never moved.

"Bohdan is right," the countess said. She removed the pistol from my side. It was a broom handle Mauser like those carried by German officers in the Great War. She wore the pistol in a holster on her left hip with the handle reversed for a right hand draw. With her weapon back where it came from, the countess buttoned her tweed jacket, then nodded at Ivan.

"Him first," Ivan said.

I dropped the automatic into my coat pocket, surprised they let me keep it. Like I said, this is Russia. Everyone shoots at everybody over here. Ivan, looking like it was the greatest mistake he'd ever made, stuffed the Webley back under his armpit.

"He doesn't trust us, Ivan," the countess said. "Pay him."

She smiled sweetly at me. Her eyes were as blue as arctic ice. I know. I've seen arctic ice. The smile was dazzling, something designed to make dukes and barons bow graciously when asking if there was any room left on her dance card.

"I see now I was mistaken about you," she said after a moment's consideration. "I don't like you, Mr. Watkins." Her smile was radiant. "Under different circumstances, I would let Ivan pull your arms out of their sockets and break both your legs." She turned her head slightly. "Give it to him, Ivan. Then get us out of this filthy alley before the Bolsheviks stand us all against a wall like they did the czar."

This wasn't the way I planned to begin our partnership. I decided to try to salvage the situation. "Countess, I'm very sorry about this morning, but your driver was right. I had to stay out of sight."

Ivan was digging in his pocket. The countess turned those arctic colored eyes in my direction. She said something but just as she started to speak, the driver gunned the automobile's engine and I couldn't make it out.

"We didn't," I began, but before I could say anything else, she turned away from me to stare at the brick wall opposite her door. Maybe the situation wasn't currently salvageable.

Ivan found what he was looking for, as I considered the pros and cons of reaching for her hand. Pro, I decided, but just as I began to reach for her glove, Ivan dropped something in my lap.

One might wonder what would make a man walk off a gunboat in the middle of the night, straight into a half-starved foreign city; a city surrounded by hostile forces. I didn't do it without reason. I could say I was seduced by a beautiful woman's charms and leave it at that. But that wasn't the reason. Well, not entirely. I got myself in this situation because I decided to stretch my legs one day and go for a walk in one of the better parts of the waterfront. I had never seen the countess before. She was a few paces in front of me, moving the same direction as I was and at about the same speed. She had on an ankle length green dress like women used to wear over corsets, hair pinned up on top of her head, no hat and with a little silver handbag tucked under her arm. She didn't seem to be going anywhere and I was getting the impression she wouldn't object if a gentleman like myself asked her for directions or tea or anything that might come to mind. I was about to do just that when our unseen friends, the Bolsheviks, did what besieging forces do and started firing shells in my general direction. If they hit anyone, I didn't see it, but I did see a lot of panicked civilians running for the other side of the city. The woman I was about to introduce myself to before the artillery started falling stopped where she was and gave the citizens of Vladivostok a disapproving glare. Disapproving or not, one doesn't stand still when artillery rounds are in the vicinity.

"You," I said, "runsky, runsky." I helped her understand my meaning by using two fingers walking quickly across my palm. "Bombs!" I said, adding the appropriate sound effects. "Runsky now." I reached for her arm.

She started to laugh. Not laugh like I told her a joke. Laugh like she was looking at an ass standing in the middle of an artillery barrage.

"If you can tell me where the next shell will land, I will certainly run in the other direction," she said, the words crisp and clean with just that touch of a Russian accent. She looked at the gray clouds above us. "They stopped after three rounds. I hear they are short of ammunition."

Me, being the master of observation, said, "You speak English."

"Better than you, I think. Runsky? What language is that?"

And so our liaison began. Three weeks, twenty-one evenings together in a surrounded city running out of time. We went for walks in the park every day, such as it was with its squatter's tents and marauding children running loose between the trees. We drank coffee in sidewalk cafes when there was coffee to be had. Sometimes, she read the Russian newspapers to me as I admired the way she crossed her legs at the ankles. There wasn't much to do in Vladivostok. The city was short of everything, including privacy. Sometimes we walked for blocks, arm in arm. If we came upon a street musician, I would drop a few kopecks in his hat as she told me the name of the song. We finally settled on a quaintly pretentious cafe with eight or nine tables, waiters in starched aprons and a wine cellar not yet emptied by the confines of a siege. I met her there every evening I could, duty permitting. Me, sitting at our table by the window and she, arriving just at dark driven by someone in a dark green motorcar. The automobile would pull away and she would come into our cafe looking like the kind of woman every man wants to take back to his high school reunion. The car, she explained, belonged to a friend who didn't like her walking the streets unescorted.

Every evening, I hoped seduction was on the menu. The countess never said yes to my menu. Nor did she ever try to bargain her sex for a favor. I confess, I expected her to do just that. I expected it as soon as we met. It was obvious from our first meeting she had no money to speak of and as far as I could tell, her wardrobe consisted entirely of two dresses, one dark green and the other a worn soft blue, one pair of shoes and a small silver cloth pocketbook. Except for the motorcar, she seemed as poor as any other refugee. Where she spent her nights, she wouldn't say, and I had the strong suspicion our dinners together were her only meals. Such is war. I often asked her where she was from and how she came to end up in this backwater of a city but she never said. Just vague generalities that could mean anything.

It was while we were at our table in the pretentious little cafe drinking exorbitantly priced Bordeaux that things between us changed. As the sun inched its way towards the other side of the world, a company of Japanese marines marched down the street, arms swinging in rhythm as their boots stomped the cobblestones in clockwork precision. The occupying Japanese thought it important to show the multitudes there was still hope even though everyone knew Vladivostok would fall before the first bite of winter. When they were past and the normal pedestrian traffic resumed outside our window, I said, "I can get you out." I hadn't planned to make the offer. Until the words were said, I didn't even know I was going to. I put my hand on her knee. "I can." I was pretty sure I could, too, if I set my mind to it. "It wouldn't be luxury but I could probably find you a stateroom on a collier bound for Manilla."

She took a drink of her wine, slowly crossed her legs beneath the table and removed my hand from her knee. Placing it upon the white tablecloth, she smoothed my fingers out flat.

"Maybe Shanghai," I added.

The countess ran a finger down my palm. "Hush, Mr. Watkins. I'm concentrating."

Her fingers moved along a wrinkle in my palm. "You're a fortuneteller now?" I asked smiling. "See any redheads in my future?"

Her finger stopped its tracing. "Blondes," she said, looking at me from under her brows, "in your past."

I took a drink of my wine, remembering a warm evening at the officer's club in Pearl. Esmerelda was her name, Ezzie to her friends. She liked wearing big purple flowers behind her ear. Or was it pink? I had a letter from her last spring. Some destroyer lieutenant had put a diamond on her finger. "Can't imagine who you're talking about," I said.

"Oh no," the countess whispered, desolation in her voice. "This is very bad. This line, you see? It is too short."

"I've got a pocketknife and a high pain tolerance. We can cut a little bit along there. Make it longer."

She shook her head, still paying close attention to the roadmap in my palm. "Scars don't count. How would I pay for this stateroom?"

And there it was. The offer. The thing I expected to hear from the very first day we met. She stopped examining my palm and met my eyes. She didn't say anything else. There was a hotel across the street. Not the kind of place you would ever read about in a travel brochure but one that would suit. She followed my gaze out the window. The countess looked at the hotel's entrance for a moment then back to me. She still held my palm flat against the table, one finger resting on the line that was too short.

"You can owe me," I heard myself say.

She smiled, looked at my palm again then traced her finger along a different line. "This one," she said, "this one is very good."

She released my hand, drank the last of her wine and said, "Mr. Watkins, I'm not trying to find a way out of Russia. I'm trying to find a way *in*."

We finished the bottle of Bordeaux. By now, my chair was next to hers and my hand, free from her necromancy, had grown accustomed to the feel of her knee. It was getting late and most of the cafe's patrons had found other entertainment.

The countess finished her story in a wine flavored whisper, her face very close to mine. It was a good story, too. I ordered a second bottle of whatever was left in the cellar and drank in every word. I'm not saying I believed it. I just didn't entirely *disbelieve* it. Stories from fleeing White Russian nobles were a dime a dozen in this city. Pick the cafe and you could hear anything from plots to restore the Romanovs to desperate confessions that the person sitting across from you *was* a Romanov.

"I know what you're thinking, Mr. Watkins. You think I am lying."

"Not at all" I said as I refilled our glasses.

"I don't blame you. If you told that story to me, I wouldn't believe it either." The countess looked out the window towards the seedy hotel. The setting sun hadn't improved its prospects much. A woman walked by. She had short, dark hair tucked under a veiled hat and a shin length dress that exposed a good deal of skin. The woman stopped by a streetlight, looked through the hotel's window then moved along into the shadows, moving but not really going anywhere. The countess watched her until she was beyond our window before she reached for her little silver pocketbook. Waiting until the waiter was on the far side of the room, she undid the clasp then slid something partway onto the table.

"I never lie," she said very, very quietly.

Four days later, I found myself watching my gunboat sail away. I looked at the thing Ivan had dropped in my lap. Picking it up, I couldn't keep the smile off my face. It was heavier than I expected. Much heavier. Two pounds at least.

"As promised, Mr. Watkins," the countess said. There was ice in her voice. "Your retainer. I fully expect you to earn it or Ivan will ask for it back."

Ivan grunted.

"But I do not think that will be necessary unless you have told exaggerations about your skills."

"I haven't exaggerated anything," I told everyone in the car.

"Well," the countess said, "as promised then. A bargain made, a price paid."

My retainer.

I turned the shiny piece of metal over in my hand. Credit Suisse was stamped in the surface along with the weight. 1 KILO. Gold. Pure, solid gold. I wrapped my fingers around the cold metal. All my dreams come true. Everything I ever wanted. A million possibilities in the palm of my hand.

I dropped the ingot into the inner pocket of my new old coat. I could feel its weight pressing against my heart. "Let's go," I told our driver, "and sorry about the choke hold."

The man named Bohdan waved a hand dismissively. "No hard feelings," he said. "I like a suspicious man. In my business, there are suspicious men and there are dead men." He released the handbrake. "Two hundred million rubles in gold, Stick," he said over his shoulder. "In gold. Just waiting for us."

Two hundred million. A thousand pounds in ingots just like the one I could feel bumping against my chest. Boxes and boxes filled to bursting and I could have all I could carry. That was her offer.

All I had to do was get them there.

2

It's hard to be inconspicuous in Vladivostok when riding in a car. There were only a handful of automobiles in the entire city. All of them, as far as I knew, either arrived with the Allies in 1918 or were imported by the new lords of Siberia before they abandoned Russia to a fate of its own creation. The Czechs had a few cars, but the last of the Legion evacuated two years ago. I didn't think the one we were in now belonged to the Czechs.

"Where do you find the gas?" I asked.

Bohdan answered. "I have someone in—"

"Shut up," Ivan told him. "He doesn't need to know."

Ivan didn't like me.

"You know, Countess, for someone trying to remain unnoticed, arriving at our cafe in a chauffeured automobile wasn't very smart. The whole street paid attention to your comings and goings."

"I wasn't trying to be inconspicuous, Mr. Watkins. I was trying to seduce you. Not literally," she added quickly. "I needed a man of your talents and Bohdan said you had the necessary skills."

So it was like that. I was learning more and more about the woman sharing a car seat with me. She reached across the seat, gently resting gloved fingers on my knee.

"Who's pride is tarnished now?" she asked.

Looking at the back of our driver's head, I told her, "I don't know your man Bohdan. He never contacted me."

"Not in so many ways," the countess said, her gloves now back in her own lap where they belonged. "Bohdan can be very resourceful."

"I know people," the man sitting in front of me said again. "Ashwood Watkins, holds rank of Lieutenant, USN. Engineering officer and second in command aboard the navy gunboat *Devilfish*, a boat currently assigned American flag waving duties here," Bohdan waved a hand at the filth strewn alley, "in the pearl of Russian Siberia. Graduated from the American academy six years ago. Last point of duty, river operations on the Yangtze. Recently in Subic Bay, Manila for recuperation from injuries received. I was unable to find out what injuries. Are you fully recovered?"

"You're very well informed," I told him.

"I have a knack for these things, Stick. Don't take it personally."

"Where did you get your motorcar?" I asked loud enough so the driver would know I was speaking to him and not the smirking female sitting beside me.

"We brought it with us from Irkutsk," the countess answered.

I vaguely remembered hearing the name somewhere.

"It is a long way from here," she continued. "How far, Bohdan?"

"Over two thousand kilometers on the railway."

"Long drive," I said.

"The automobile was shipped by rail most of the way," she said. "Only the last few hundred kilometers were by road."

The railway she was talking about was the Trans-Siberian. Moscow to Vladivostok, the longest train ride in the world. With the war now almost over, the Reds had control of it. But that wasn't always the case. When Russia's European war ended, the Czech Legion wanted to keep fighting. The Czechs were an army unto themselves, sixty thousand strong, operating in a Russia torn apart by war. When Russia bowed out of the Great War, it meant the Legion couldn't continue the fight against the Austrians. Not from their side of the Bolsheviks. Someone got the idea to go east, all the way east, take ship at Vladivostok and sail for still-fighting France. The only practical method for that many soldiers to make the journey was by rail. So the Legion, all sixty thousand of them, took control of whole sections of the line, operating their own armored trains and maintaining their own defenses. Along the way, they won a string of battles against the Bolsheviks, put down partisan efforts to destroy the railway and kept local warlords from becoming too much of a nuisance. It was said if the Legion hadn't been so successful against the Reds, the revolutionaries might not have shot the czar. At least that's what I'd heard.

Back in 1919, too late to fight on the Western Front, an advanced party of the Legion kicked the revolution out of Vladivostok and waited. What to do with them was a primary cause of the Siberian intervention. I doubt the US would have landed troops here otherwise. It took two years, but the last of the Czech Legion were finally evacuated and sent home to their new country of Czechoslovakia. Two years after that, the Reds made it to the outskirts of the city.

"In the middle of a Civil War, you managed to ship a motorcar on the Trans-Siberian. How?"

"That is a story for some other time, Mr. Watkins. Let's just say I had a plan and a very resourceful Czech to help with the details."

"I knew someone," Bohdan added.

I was getting the impression our driver knew a lot of people.

The man with so many friends drove the car down the alley, maneuvering around a horse drawn cart and past a knot of children playing with a ball. The children forgot the ball and ran after us screaming with delight. Like I said, cars are a rare sight in this town. It took three blocks before their enthusiasm or their legs wore out.

The drive was a slow going crawl down a series of narrow alleys. Several times, the three of us had to get out to clear debris out of the alley. Our female passenger kept her seat, serene as visiting royalty while we tossed boards, bricks and the refuse of war out of the motorcar's way.

The main streets would have been faster, but I didn't think the countess and her companions wanted to risk unpleasant questions from curious soldiers. I know I didn't. It wasn't the White soldiers they worried about. Most of those troops had stopped caring. They knew the final battle was upon them. It was the hundreds of non-Russian troops packed behind the defensive lines. Foreign troops standing behind the sandbags, barbed wire and fixed bayonets were sure to stop a car full of armed passengers and ask questions. Those soldiers had an impossible job. There were just too many alleys, side streets and avenues to guard them all. A cautious person could go where they pleased, even in a motorcar.

Most of the foreign soldiers occupying the city were Japanese, with a few French colonials still waving the tricolor. America left with the Legion, the general sentiment being their job was done. So had the Canadians. The last of the French would go next. That left the Japanese. Everyone knew if the city fell, the Empire's puppet state, the Far East Republic, would go next and the Pacific coast would once again be under the control of Moscow. Not that you could tell by looking at the Japanese soldiers marching through the streets. Rumer said they had more soldiers in Siberia than the entire White Army, or what was left of the Whites. I didn't think any of it was going to last much longer.

Our driver brought the car to a stop at the next intersection.

"More junk to move?" I asked, looking over his shoulder at a mud spattered windshield.

"Stay where you are," Ivan told me as he opened his door. He was really taking that whole pistol behind the ear thing seriously.

"We have to be careful here," Bohdan said in a more agreeable voice. "There are sometimes foot patrols."

I had never been in this part of the city before and didn't recognize the street. Ivan got out of the car and walked a little way ahead of us. He spoke to the driver of a wagon blocking our way out of the alley. When he could see down the cross street, he came back to the car.

"He said soldiers were here a few minutes ago," Ivan said. "We can go to the right, Bohdan."

"The left is faster," the Czech answered.

The countess leaned forward to look through the same dirty windshield. "Right," she said.

Bohdan rolled forward, turned right onto the street and joined the wagons, hand carts, men on horseback and general mass of humanity making its way slowly to wherever a hundred thousand people go when you've made it to Imperial Russia's last stand.

The crowds of people made a noise. Not speech, not communication, just a general sound of humanity on the move. Wheels scraped on cobblestones. Horses whinnied. A child cried somewhere. I didn't hear a single word spoken by anyone. Just sound.

"I can walk faster than this," I told my companions.

"We turn just ahead," the countess told me.

Bohdan maneuvered the car past a wagon piled high with barrels, squeezed the rubber bulb of his horn twice, then used his bumper to part the humanity in front of him. There were no lanes and no organization to the traffic. For every person going one way on the street, someone else was trying to get around them to go the opposite direction. After crawling along for another two blocks, we turned left down the next alley.

This one was filled with a forest of beige colored canvas tents. The locals had strung lines between the sides of the buildings and every type of clothing imaginable hung drying in the cool September air. Our car was too big for the alley and its tents, at least for some of them. Half a dozen ropes caught on a fender or snagged on the windshield. Makeshift shelters collapsed into piles of torn canvas. Someone shouted. Ivan got out of the car and stood on the running board. With his revolver in hand, he waved the tent dwellers out of the way. Bohdan never touched his brake.

"There are better ways through the city," I told the countess.

"It is because of you we are taking such precautions," she replied. "We three can explain why we are on the street in a motorcar wasting black market gasoline. We can't explain an American passenger with no pass and no reason to be here."

She had a point. "How much farther?" I asked.

"We have to go beyond the nice part of the city," Bohdan answered.

Nice Vladivostok meant buildings that still had their roofs. Windows were optional. The Czechs might have taken the city from the Bolsheviks four years ago, but the scars of hard fighting hadn't gone away. Some of the buildings had clearly been taken by force. A few had scorch marks above windowsills.

The locals watched us pass. Some pointed. Others, heads down and unsmiling, looked completely disinterested. Looking at them, they had the feel of people trapped in their circumstances. The war was here and there was nothing they could do except survive today. Tomorrow would have to wait.

The car clattered over a cast iron bridge manned by four men wearing various pieces of military uniforms. Each one had a rifle slung over a shoulder. An iron pot hung from a tripod over a cook fire and I was reminded again I hadn't had any breakfast. One of the guards stirred the pot. I thought of the child back at the hotel with her bowl of oatmeal. My stomach grumbled.

"Will they stop us?" I asked.

"Militia," the countess said. "Not soldiers."

"There's a difference?"

"They are Russian, not foreigners," she said. "Today, they are Whites. Tomorrow, they will all be good Bolsheviks."

Ivan spat out his side of the car.

The bridge was a line of demarcation. Once we were over it, we left the residential areas behind us. As the road sloped down towards the harbor, the landscape became more scarred. Bohdan maneuvered around shell craters in the road, bricks fallen from the façades of buildings and a dead cow bloated and rancid in death. The countess held her nose as we passed. On a hillside to our right, shells began falling, exploding in dirt and fire. Men ran for a sandbagged bunker or disappeared into slit trenches. I pretended being a half mile from falling artillery was old news to me. The others didn't seem to be pretending.

Bohdan drove down a sloping dirt road beneath bare limbed trees. We passed a man pushing a wheelbarrow holding a large trunk up the same hill we were going down. A woman in a dark ankle length dress with a shawl over her shoulders and a scarf covering her hair walked behind him. As we passed her, she looked at me sitting next to the lovely countess. Tears streaked her cheeks as she followed along behind the wheelbarrow. A boy of eight or nine walked behind the pair. This one didn't chase after our car.

When the cow was a hundred yards behind us, I smelled the sea. Vladivostok is on a peninsula. Drive far enough in almost any direction, you'll come to the sea. The main harbor where I watched the *Devilfish* sail away was somewhere to the south. We were farther north now, closer to the lines.

The road followed a row of burnt out buildings. In between the black walls and broken bricks, the gray waters of the bay were empty of anything floating. Through a gap in the ruins, I saw three wrecks I recognized. They were sunken hulks all in a row, each grounded along the near shoreline, their hulls slowly rusting away. I knew where I was now. The bridge watch on my old gunboat called them the Three Corpses. A little farther up, and we would be able to see the rail line.

"Are the tracks still in friendly hands?" I asked.

"They were yesterday," the countess answered. "You recognize the area, Mr. Watkins?"

I nodded. "We're close to the lines." It seemed like the right thing to say.

Ivan pointed to the hills less than a mile away. "There," he said. "Other side. They are not yet our side of railway."

"He doesn't really know that," Bohdan added. "A week ago, their guns couldn't reach us here. Now, they reach this far. My contacts tell me they are probing just over there." He pointed to his left. "Our side."

The road turned to the left, still sloping down to follow the course made by the harbor's edge. Bohdan stopped the car at the bottom of the hill.

"Can you drive a motorcar, Stick?" he asked.

Ivan said something in Russian. Bohdan answered. The countess leaned forward and looked through the dirty windshield at a line of trees. I wished they would speak English.

"I can drive."

The two men in front got out. The Lewis followed Bohdan. He wasn't a big man, but he handled the heavy gun easily enough. The countess tapped my arm.

"Be so good as to drive then, Mr. Watkins. Bohdan is worried about those trees."

"You'll have to tell me where to go."

The countess didn't take her eyes off the dirty windshield. "We are almost there."

I got out and slid behind the wheel. Bohdan took Ivan's place on my left, the big Russian taking up a position on the running board.

Patting the barrel of the machinegun, Bohdan said, "If my violin starts playing music, your job is to get the car back over the hill."

"Not a problem. Tell Ivan to hang on."

I can't remember the last time I drove an automobile. In truth, I'm not a very good driver. I don't get a lot of practice serving on a China station gunboat, but I'm familiar with the requirements. Bohdan, the countess and Ivan all jerked backwards as I let out the clutch. Smooth takeoffs are harder than they look. The countess said something in Russian. Bohdan laughed, then balanced his gun on the edge of the passenger door. Ivan grunted. Or maybe he was talking. I was learning it wasn't always easy to tell the difference with Ivan. The trees got closer.

3

The countess wasn't kidding. We didn't go a half mile before someone on my right whistled. Bohdan pointed to a man standing beside a broken masonry wall. The whistler looked a lot like all the other Russians crowding into Vladivostok. A worn, unshaven face, leather brimmed hat and a dark colored tunic with a broad leather belt wrapped around his waist. Like almost every man in this city, he wore his pants stuffed inside his boots. The Russian waved at us.

"Do we know him?"

"Yes, Mr. Watkins, we know him," the countess answered. "We have arrived at our destination. The ship is tied up behind that building."

The building wasn't a building. It was a broken wall with a collapsed roof and an earthen floor. The whole place looked like it would slide into the water if you gave it a good push. As for the ship, the countess and I will have to disagree on the definition of the word. It wasn't a ship. It was fifty feet of floating hulk tied to a ramshackle dock behind a collapsed wall. Made of wood, the hulk had a house on the stern, high prows and a stump of a wooden mast amidship. A rust colored iron stack stuck ten feet into the air. I stopped the car between the crumbled building and the crumbling hulk. Twisting around in my seat to look at the woman in the back seat, I said, "You must be kidding?"

"Do not turn up your nose so fast, Mr. Watkins. Beggars cannot be choosers is the saying, no?"

I wasn't so sure. I killed the engine on the motorcar just as the Bolshevik guns resumed their shelling of the White Army. My companions got out of the car, so I joined them. Bohdan carried the Lewis over his shoulder as Whistler and the countess began to converse in Russian. The Czech walked to a broken wall, set the barrel of the gun on the top, then went down to one knee. With the stock against his shoulder, the Czech watched the tree line. Ivan busied himself unstrapping the bags from the rear of the car. There was nothing for me to do but inspect the boat. After all, this is why I got the invite in the first place.

Black Cyrillic letters painted over mold covered white paint spelled out her name. I started to ask the countess what they said when the automobile started up. Ivan was straightening from the crank handle, the luggage piled beside him. He gave a satisfied grunt then thumped the hood with his fist. I think he enjoyed starting engines. Whistler was sitting behind the wheel. He obviously drove a lot better than me because he lost no time in taking the car around the other side of the collapsed building and back up the hill.

"Hey," I shouted. Nobody tried to stop him.

"It is his car now, Mr. Watkins," the countess said. "When the Bolsheviks take the city, he will sell it to them, he says, and make a fortune. The boat was worth nothing to him. It was a good bargain for us."

"Bolsheviks will shoot him as war profiteer," Ivan said, "and keep car."

"Shot or not, won't we need that when we get back with the

gold?" I asked.

Ivan looked at me, shook his head, and said something under his breath. I'm sure it wasn't complimentary.

"We aren't coming back here with the gold, Mr. Watkins. Vladivostok is a dead end. We three," the countess waved an arm at the other two men, "cannot remain here. Or come back, for that matter. It would be the wall for all of us. You too, I would think."

"You never said anything about not coming back."

"And you never said your ship would sail at dawn." She pointed at the piled luggage and said something to Ivan. "I suppose neither of us has been completely accurate. Fear not, Mr. Watkins. I have a plan."

She may have a plan, but if it was anything like her judgment in boats, I wasn't sure it would be a very good one.

"Now," the countess continued, "let us see if you are worth your retainer." She gestured toward the wooden hulk. "We will leave now."

"We will not," I said. "We will look at a boat now and see if she is going to sink today or next week. Have you even been aboard?"

The countess said something in Russian to Ivan. He answered, also in Russian.

"Stop that," I said a bit too loudly. "We're all in this now, the four of us. Speak English. It's rude."

Bohdan started laughing.

I pointed at the relic they planned to put to sea in. "I'm thinking that stump of a mast was somehow important to the functioning of your new boat." Turning to my trio of partners, I added, "Sails, rigging, all that nautical stuff."

Ivan smirked. "There is big engine. Don't need sail and there is plenty of coal, water and enough food."

I looked at Ivan's bulging stomach. Food wouldn't keep us from sinking. "When's the last time the big engine had steam up? Do you even know if she can hold pressure?"

"That, Mr. Watkins," the countess said, "is why I hired

you."

"You didn't *hire* me. We're partners."

"Semantics," she replied.

Ivan said something in Russian to Bohdan.

"A play on words," Bohdan said, still watching the tree line.

Ivan looked at me. *"Seminicks,"* he said with a nod.

"Make," the countess looked at the Cyrillic letters on the bow, "the *Orca* ready to leave. Do what has to be done, but we must leave. The Bolsheviks are going to attack soon."

"You sound certain," I told the three of them.

"I know some people," Bohdan said. "Today maybe. Tomorrow certainly. They are going to push here along the waterfront and cut off the Japanese troops holding the port. If the port falls, the Japanese will withdraw and the Reds will slaughter the Whites. Us too," he added.

The green sedan was almost over the hill. I turned to look at the hulk named *Orca,* wondering if I should shout something at Whistler or maybe go running up the hill after him. That thing, a derelict that looked like it hadn't left the dock in years, was her plan. I spat into the water and put my hands in my pockets.

"Mr. Watkins?"

"Thinking," I said without turning around. The gold ingot was a solid weight in the inside pocket of my jacket. If the hulk sank under me, maybe the weight of the bar would help me drown faster.

"Mr. Watkins," the countess said again, joining me in my examination of the floating hulk she called a ship. "We are very exposed here. Someone might have seen the car. Soldiers."

"Said I'm thinking." I was, too. I was thinking about pretty women in cafes and idiots who got themselves involved in things they shouldn't have.

Her hand touched my arm. "I'm sorry if you feel I have deceived you. I had no other option. Please, Mr. Watkins. This vessel is our only hope. If you refuse to help, my enemies will find me."

She looked at me as she touched my arm. She didn't smile that medusa smile of hers, the one she had when she jabbed her pistol in my side. Instead, she looked like the woman who had removed my hand from her knee back in the cafe. I sighed.

A wooden plank ran across the gap between the dock and the boat's hull. It bowed under my weight as I crossed, but didn't break. Ivan might not be so lucky. Standing on the deck, I could smell her. It wasn't as bad as the bloated cow, but it was in the same family of odors. Old blood. I guessed her life was spent with seal hunters in the Arctic. There wasn't much in the way of gear. A pile of rope half covered an anchor in the bow. A paintbrush stiff with blue paint lay where someone had dropped it. There was nothing painted blue that I could see. Most of the wood was weathered, bleached gray with peeling white showing in various corners. I gave the brush a kick and sent it sliding across the boards. There was an overturned boat on the deck with a couple of oars lying next to it. The boat looked big enough to hold three people in a pinch. If that was going to be our lifeboat, it would probably sink faster than the tub the countess just swapped her automobile for.

I scraped at a layer of bird droppings with my boot. Most of the lines of black caulking between the deck planks were gone. Bad caulking meant the *Orca* leaked rainwater. I could imagine what it must smell like below decks. She would doubtless be an uncomfortable, damp, moldy ride before she sank and drowned us all. The wheelhouse was on the stern like most work boats so I made my way aft. The hatch to the house was stuck closed, and I had to yank hard on an old brass knob before it would open.

Ivan dropped the motorcar's chest on the deck with a loud bang. The big Russian had managed to make it aboard without snapping the board in half.

"Careful, Ivan," I said. "Drop that trunk on the wrong spot and it might go straight through to the bottom."

The countess said something to him. Again, in Russian. Probably concerned about the welfare of her trunk.

The house wasn't much. Just a little square box with a spoked wheel, a telegraph control for the engine that was missing its handle, a binnacle with two iron balls on either side and a chart table. All the windows were broken. At the rear of the wheelhouse, a ladder went down into the darkness below. There were a pair of small portholes running along each side of the boat, but they were not large and didn't let in a lot of light. Standing over the hole and looking down into the murk didn't show me much. The steps squeaked under me as I went down into the gloom, striking a match against one of the rungs as I went.

I found a gimbaled oil lamp mounted on the bulkhead. Its light helped with the gloominess, but didn't improve what I saw. *Orca's* interior wasn't in any better shape than her topsides. It was dirty, musty, and uncomfortable. Bohdan might be able to stand up straight in the small space, but the rest of us would have to stoop. The galley, with its iron stove was on my right, double bunks on the left, with a drop leaf table and double bench amidships for the crew's meals. You couldn't stand in the small, cramped space with your arms outstretched and not touch something. And I was right about the smell. Perdition.

There was a narrow passageway leading aft. Going past the table, I lit another lamp with my match, then poked my head inside the narrow passageway. It didn't go far. There were a couple of cabins on either side. It was a tossup which one was in the worst shape. Rainwater seeping in from the deck above had caused the overhead to sag with rot. I touched the lowest point over an empty wooden shelf intended as a bunk. Water dripped from the spot. Leaving the passageway and its soggy cabins, I went forward, past the table and to the other hatch. Like the topside house, this one was also stuck closed and required some effort to get open. Beyond it was the engine room. My world. I struck another match and surveyed the gloom.

"Mr. Watkins," the countess called from the ladder. "Bohdan says you should start the engine now. I think that is a very good idea."

"You can tell Bohdan a steam engine doesn't have a start button," I yelled. "Even if I lit the furnace right now, it would be a couple of hours before we had steam up." Stepping into the engine room, I found another lamp, lifted the glass and put the match to the wick. Machinery stretched away into the shadows with white wrapped pipes running between various pieces and parts. I touched the round handle of a valve. It was as cold as dead bones. Squeezing past the boiler, I lit a second lantern.

The engine was a shoulder high, triple expansion three cylinder affair. I didn't recognize the make, but that didn't mean much. The operation would be familiar enough. There are only so many ways to boil water. The cylinders and the long iron push rods were mounted directly over the crank shaft. I followed the line of the shaft, past the jacking gear and on to the propeller shaft. At least everything looked to be connected.

The boiler and condenser were on the other end of the engine and took up most of the space. There was another bulkhead just forward of the tank with a chute built into it for coal. Past that, I assumed, would be the hold where the seal skins were kept back when the hulk was a seagoing vessel and not a floating termite trap.

The door to the firebox was covered in cobwebs. I gave the dogs a kick with my boot and swung the door open. The grate was full of coal ash. I didn't think there had been a fire in there in a very long time.

You have to start somewhere, so I guessed this was as good a place as any. I took off my coat, rolled up my sleeves and took a shovel out of a bracket. After six trips topside with the ash bucket, the fire box was empty. Each trip up, the countess, now perched on the chart table in the small wheelhouse looked at me expectantly. Bohdan and his Lewis machinegun still watched the trees from the shore.

"Don't know yet," I told her on my last trip with the bucket.

The countess remained silent.

Ivan followed me down below. Apparently, he knew how to cook because he had a pot filled with something simmering on the boat's stove before I had finished emptying ashes. I really wanted something in my stomach, but I wasn't about to ask him to feed me. Whatever was for dinner, it smelled amazingly better than the *Orca*.

"Another hour," he said as I squeezed past him.

Good. I knew I wasn't going to ask.

The big Russian was right about the coal. *Orca's* bunker was at least a quarter full. We were lucky in that. If this was winter, I'm sure Whistler would have sold it all off long ago. The sight glass on the boiler showed a full bubble, so I started a fire in the box. It was time to look to the engine.

I've been an engineer for six years. First on coal burners, then fuel oil. I've seen small engines and big engines, but I had never seen one as old as the scrap iron I was looking at now. The seal hunters painted her red. I had a sneaking suspicion the choice in color was so the rusty steam leaks wouldn't show so badly. Wherever this gold hoard was, looking at that engine, I think we would have made a better effort at recovering it if we had kept the automobile. Risking driving through the Red Army's lines seemed like a much more survivable option to me. I kicked around the out of the way storage spaces found on every boat ever built and discovered a tool box. Inside was a basic assortment of things I was going to need. A pipe wrench, plyers, hammer, that sort of thing. I also found a not too terribly musty set of coveralls hanging from a peg. They weren't a perfect fit, but since the only clothes I owned were what was on my back, I was pleased, musty or not.

A couple of hours later, greased to my elbows with water starting to boil and lying underneath the connecting rods, someone kicked my foot. I crawled and pulled my way out from under the machinery to find Ivan looking down at me.

"The journals don't look like they've been oiled this century," I told him.

Ivan blinked. "We have eaten. Carrots and potatoes with cabbage. There is no meat."

My stomach grumbled. I sat my oil can on the deck, pulled myself out from beneath the antique, then knocked ten years of dust and grime off my coveralls. There was no running water on the *Orca* but steam powered vessels, even floating hulks like this one, always had hot water if there was a fire in the furnace. I opened a tap on the condenser and washed as best I could.

I ate my meal on deck, sitting on the overturned dinghy and listening to seagulls scream above me. Ivan had even made tea, scalding hot and strong. Sometime during my inspection, the Bolsheviks stopped shooting off their artillery. Except for the gulls, it was quiet topside. If the Reds had paid attention, they might have noticed the plume of thin smoke coming out of our stack. I cleaned my plate. Every last morsel.

"How much longer, Mr. Watkins?" the countess asked once I had finished eating.

She looked worried. Her plan, whatever it was, didn't plan on sitting in the open within range of artillery while I fooled with a steam engine.

"We have steam up," I said. Ivan came closer. I guess he was getting a little worried, too. "The boiler didn't explode, so that's a positive." Nobody smiled at my comment. Even Bohdan, who laughed at everything, didn't laugh. "I was just about to try the engine when the dinner bell rang."

"We can leave now?" she asked.

"Let's see what happens when I run steam through those pipes. If there's a leak, we aren't leaving. If the engine's seized, we aren't leaving. If something breaks—"

"We are not leaving," the countess said. "Yes, Mr. Watkins. I am aware of things that will stop us from leaving. I need you to be aware that should we not leave, we will most likely die.

Here. On this wretched piece of flotsam."

That last bit hurt my feelings. I'm a sailor and as a sailor, I have an innate dislike for tourist who disparage the vessel I am on, even the ones that are wretched pieces of flotsam. Balancing my empty plate on the dinghy's overturned keel, I got to my feet, slapped a bit more grime off the front of my coveralls and said, "I need to check my gauges," with all the disdain for Russian noblewomen I could muster. Something told me the countess wouldn't be washing my plate.

After my twenty minutes on deck, the interior of the hulk was even more oppressing than before. It also had the additional luxury of being roasting hot. Tying the top of my coveralls around my waist, I went about the business of checking the rusting scrap metal that was *Orca's* heart and soul. The asbestos wrapping on the main steam pipe was frayed and needed mending. That made me laugh. As if insulation was what needed mending down here. Wrapping my hands in rags, I opened the main steam line's valve a quarter turn. Pipes clattered and steam hissed. I opened the valve a little more. When it was half open, I waited. Nothing exploded or scalded me to death. I checked the gauges. They were in Cyrillic and I didn't really know what the pressure readings were, but at least the indicator wasn't in the red.

Good enough.

Setting the jacking gear, I twisted the valve's wheel farther open. The ghost in the steel pipes grumbled. After opening two more blistering hot valves, the engine's crank began a slow motion rotation.

Orca came to life. She did it with a groan and a roar like a giant rudely awakened from a long slumber. The pushrods went up and down, each revolution releasing a disturbing amount of hot steam into the cramped engine room. Still, nothing exploded, and I wasn't scalded to death. I felt the hulk strain against her moorings as the shaft made slow turns. That was encouraging. I shoveled more coal into her firebox all the while keeping one eye on the water bubble in the sight glass and the other on the pressure gauge. The engine clanged and clattered still with just enough steam to turn the crankshaft. I threw a few more shovelfuls of coal into the fire box and watched the needle on my pressure gauge move higher. Just as I scooped up another shovelful of coal, Ivan pushed his way into the cramped engine room. Babbling something in Russian, he jabbed a finger towards the shore.

"What is it?"

Ivan remembered his English. "Soldiers!" he yelled.

Both of us ran for the topside ladder.

4

"You idiot!" the countess screamed. "Look what you've done!"

I did look. I looked up. It wasn't a trickle of smoke anymore. It was a thick plume black as a demon's soul, and it was pouring out of the iron stack. The wind, what wind there was, pushed a black cloud over the ruined buildings and straight towards the tree line.

"They're coming," the Czech yelled.

I ran for the wooden gangplank.

"What are you doing?" the countess screamed.

Her long barreled Mauser was in her hand. I think she was contemplating shooting me.

"Lines," I yelled. "Ivan, grab one of those oars beside the dinghy. Push us off. Bohdan, get aboard or plan on making new friends." Grabbing the stern line, I pulled hard to get some slack, flipped the loop from around a cleat, then ran for the bow line.

Horsemen in long coats and tall hats came charging out of

the trees, all of them riding hard in our direction.

Our side of the tracks.

A drawn saber flashed in the light as I jumped aboard. Ivan leaned on an oar with all his might, brute force driving *Orca's* bows away from the shore. Bohdan ran down the gangplank and jumped to the deck just before the plank fell into the water.

"Get on the wheel," I told him.

"I will drive boat," Ivan said, once more in command of his English. "Shoot horses," he said to the Czech. Dropping his oar on deck, he walked just a little too quickly to the house with its big spoked wheel.

Shoving past the Russian, I flew down the ladder, left a good piece of skin on the crew's mess table, and jumped into the engine room. "Showtime, sweetheart," I told the slow moving pistons. Grabbing a rag, I spun the feed valve all the way open. The crankshaft started to spin with real power as the engine spat waste steam into the air in time with the rising and falling pistons. The engine settled down and seemed to flex itself. Again, nothing exploded, and I wasn't scalded to death. I gave her a few more shovelfuls of coal, watched the needles on my gauges, and pretended not to notice all the steam leaking out of the engine. *Orca* began to move. I listened to the noise of a moving boat waiting for something to fail as water began to slosh in the bilges. We might make it to the deep yet.

The explosion nearly tipped me into the machinery. *Orca* rocked violently from side to side as I made my way to the topsides ladder. Ivan, feet spread wide and both hands on the wooden wheel, looked like he was trying to push the boat forward with arm muscle. We were fifty yards offshore and putting more distance between us and the charging horsemen with every second. The second shell struck the water in front of us and about twenty yards to port. Seawater exploded in a white geyser as the explosion's concussion made my cheeks wobble.

The Red cavalry rode around the ruined building. Some

dismounted by Bohdan's wall while others rode their horses right out onto the dock before bringing rifles to their shoulders. The first shots made everyone aboard the *Orca* duck. Ivan and I both jumped as something hard and moving at man killing speed struck the wooden house. The countess knelt on the deck, her Mauser pointed towards the men shooting at us.

"Don't bother," Bohdan said. "They are too far."

"I am an excellent shot," she told him.

Bohdan balanced the Lewis atop the boat's stern rail as the men on shore continued to fire. Something moving very fast went past my head. When the Czech pulled the trigger on the Lewis, men and horses started screaming. Bohdan swept the gun in a slow arc from left to right. Brick and mortar along the ruined wall of the building exploded into red dust. Horses reared and fell over, kicking and screaming as they died. Soldiers in long coats flew backwards from the impact of bullets before sliding motionless into the cold water. Empty brass shell casings rained down from the Lewis like hailstones from a mechanized thunderstorm. When he stopped shooting, the heat shield of his gun smoked in the cool air as finger length brass shells rolled across the *Orca's* deck. One of the men lying near the water's edge got to his knees. Bohdan fired again, walking a line of splashes across the water, then across the kneeling man. He spun, arms flinging around in a circle as his body slid into the mud at the water's edge. Another Red soldier pulled himself along the ground, one leg trailing limp and useless behind him. Bohdan shifted his aim.

I touched his shoulder. "That's enough."

"One of them is still moving," Bohdan replied as he steadied the Lewis on the boat's rail.

My hand grabbed his shoulder, knotting the fabric around my fist. Pulling him out of his crouched position behind the gun, I said, "That's enough, Bohdan. We don't shoot wounded men."

The Czech yanked his shoulder out of my grasp.

"Sentimentality from a deserter?" He pointed at the

shoreline and its dead and wounded. "They wouldn't stop shooting if it was you or me lying in the mud."

I grabbed the front of his shirt. "Be careful what names you call me, Bohdan." The *Orca's* screw churned the waters of the harbor into a mud tinted white froth behind us. It would be easy to throw the smaller man over the rail, machinegun and all.

"Mr. Watkins," the countess said.

I turned to look at her, my hand still holding the Czech's shirt. The Mauser, barrel pointing at the deck, tapped a slow rhythm against her leg. She tilted her head to one side, as if examining an interesting exhibit at the zoo.

"He meant no insult with his remarks, did you, Bohdan?"

There was no more fire coming from the shoreline. The wounded soldier still dragged himself among his dead comrades. I let go of the Czech's shirt, smoothing the fabric flat as I did.

"My apologies again, Bohdan. I forgot my circumstances."

"Heated moments, heated words," Bohdan said, smiling. "I've experienced such behavior from other men, back in the early days of the Great War." He put his hand to his mouth and shouted, "Watkins of the Navy has spared your Bolshevik life today. Be thankful!"

"I doubt he speaks English, Bohdan."

"No matter. I did it more for your benefit than his."

A shell landed behind us, shooting frothy water ten feet into the air. My cheeks didn't wobble this time.

"Can we go faster, Mr. Watkins?" the countess asked.

"I think we should be happy this old tub is going as fast as it is."

Two more explosions landed far to our right as black smoke poured out of the *Orca's* funnel. The half destroyed brick buildings were between us and the tree line now. There was only a little wind which made the smoke hang onto the land, smearing an impenetrable fog behind us. That smoke had to be playing hell with whoever was spotting for those guns.

I stepped around the small house. "Ivan, come more to starboard. We can blind their aim with our smoke."

Ivan grunted. "What way?"

I turned the wheel. "Starboard. That way." I pointed. "Keep the smoke in their eyes."

"*Da,*" he said. "Make them shoot blind."

More shells landed. The gunners managed to straddle us once, and I thought we were dead for sure but the next salvo flew wide. They would have to move their guns to kill us, which I was sure they would do any minute now.

But sometimes, Fate smiles.

Someone, either the White Army or the Japanese, decided to return fire. Thunder rumbled to our south as, seconds later, the tree line shattered under the explosions. The Reds stopped shooting and *Orca,* the former killer of seals, survived another day.

"You see, Mr. Watkins." The countess was standing beside me. "The boat was worth a motorcar, after all." Her Mauser was still in her hand. I think she might still have been contemplating shooting me for giving away our position to the Red cavalry.

"Where did you get such a big gun?" I asked.

"This?" She seemed to notice she was holding it for the first time. Opening her jacket, she slid the broom handle into its leather cradle on her hip. "I took it from a Bolshevik officer."

"He didn't want it anymore?" I asked with a smile.

"No," the countess replied. "He was too busy trying to pull my bayonet out of his ribs."

Sometimes, there is nothing to say. I think this was one of those times.

"Except for the incredible stupidity with the smoke, you did well," she said. "The boat works and we have escaped the Bolsheviks."

"Again," Ivan added.

"Again," the countess repeated. She said something to Ivan in Russian that made him laugh. He took a flask out of an inside pocket and uncorked it. Saying something that sounded like *zasdarovye*, he took a large swallow. The countess took the flask from the big Russian's hand. Before taking her drink, she looked me in the eyes and said, "Cheers, Mr. Watkins."

Bohdan joined us in the small house after my turn at the flask. The vodka was raw and burned like fire and was absolutely delicious. It went around the four of us twice more before Ivan corked it. I was laughing like Bohdan by then. For a moment, the woman standing next to me reminded me of the attractive, ever so vulnerable redhead I met on a Vladivostok street. The vulnerability I knew now was an illusion. There wasn't anything vulnerable about this woman.

The Golden Horn was mostly empty, anything of a civilian nature that could leave having left before the first Bolshevik shells started to fall. Truth be told, the countess probably made a good deal, swapping her oh so rare green sedan for what had to be the last seaworthy boat in Vladivostok. The old Japanese cruiser *Asahi* sat at anchor in the middle of the bay, so I took our little seal hunter around her stern. The warship took no notice of us as we made our way down the Horn. As the sun sank behind us, *Orca,* her iron stack oozing gray-black smoke into the crisp September air, made a good four knots as she motored into Amurskiy Bay.

"Countess?"

"Mr. Watkins," she answered.

"It's getting dark."

She patted the holstered Mauser on her hip. "I'll protect you," she said smiling.

Nothing like a little vodka to make you and a Russian old friends.

"I don't know where we're going," I told her. I waved my arm in front of us. "The ocean is a big place. Which way to the gold?"

"My father was a cavalry officer," she said.

"Mine was a shipwright, as long as we're sharing."

"In the cavalry, my father said to me many times, you learn

to maneuver. Today, I am maneuvering. Take us up the coast, Mr. Watkins. We need to get around the Red lines first before we get the gold."

"How far up the coast?"

"You are the naval expert here, are you not? You told me you knew this coast. You do know it, don't you?"

I think I detected a hint of a threat in her demeanor. Apparently, vodka induced friendships are a fragile thing with Russians.

"The gold's not on the coast, then?"

"You do not strike me as stupid, Mr. Watkins. You knew that already."

Well, yes I did, but it was nice to hear proof. "We can make for the mouth of the Amur."

"Too far."

"We can turn south, go through China with your maneuver."

"I don't speak Mandarin. Perhaps you do?"

"I'm better at Cantonese."

The countess raised an eyebrow.

"Not a word," I added. "There's a bay up the coast a ways. Saint Olga it's called."

"There will be a way to the interior from the port," the countess said. It wasn't a question.

"Rough country," I added.

The countess reached out and touched my heart. Or maybe it was the gold ingot inside my pocket. "Did you think it would be easy?"

"Saint Olga it is, then. Ivan?"

"*Da?*"

I pointed with my arm. "Take us over that way. Keep us within swimming distance of the shore. I'm going to go shovel coal."

With a touch of nervousness in his voice, he said, "Why swim?"

"Because the old girl might sink when we hit the big water, and I'd like to make it to land if that happens."

Ivan looked nervously at the water.

"He is teasing you, Ivan," the countess said.

"Am I?" I left the countess and my helmsman and went below to find the shovel.

By the time the sun sank below the horizon, we were well away from the last stand of the defeated White Army. Ivan couldn't be pried away from the ship's wheel with dynamite, so I spent the next three hours going back and forth between the boiler and the deck. The countess moved to the bows for a while until the night air got to be too much for her. She came aft to the little cramped wheelhouse, both arms crossed across her chest. Bohdan was sitting on the chart table. Ivan watched the water like he expected sea monsters to attack at any moment. My coveralls were black with coal dust, my hands were blistered, and my back ached.

"Mr. Watkins, I have to," she glanced at Ivan standing at the wheel. She was struggling with something. "I do not know the way to the water closet," she said in a shared whisper.

"Ah," I said. "It's good to be needed by an attractive woman, even if it is just for directions. This way." I went down the ladder into the horribly perfumed galley. The countess, all boots and jodhpurs, followed after me.

"It stinks," she said as the engine thumped away beyond the closed hatch.

"Better than it was earlier. She's getting fresh air below now."

With hands on hips, she surveyed the small space with its narrow table, oil lamp and low overhead. Her hat was somewhere topsides and the pile of dark red hair just brushed the overhead.

"I thought it would be larger," she said

"The boat's mostly boiler, coal bunker and cargo hold." I squeezed past the table and pushed open the hatch to the engine room. The mechanical grind of the engine grew louder. "Not a lot of creature comforts," I shouted over my shoulder.

"What? I can't hear you."

I looked behind me. The countess had stuck fingers in both ears. I motioned her to follow. "Over there," I shouted.

She watched the engine's pushrods going up and down. Each time it completed a circuit, a gout of hot steam blasted into the air.

"Is it safe?" she asked.

"I doubt it. Behind the boiler, over there," I told her.

The countess followed me forward to a small alcove, not much more than a closet behind the iron boiler. Her forehead was beaded in sweat as she stepped over an insulated pipe. The *Orca* rocked on a wave and the countess grabbed for a pipe coming out of the boiler. I caught her hand.

"Don't want to touch that, Countess. That pipe's hot enough to peel the skin off your bones." I held her until the boat's roll settled down and she had her balance again.

"Oh." Taking her hand out of mine, she said, "Thank you, Mr. Watkins. I hate burns."

I pushed a ragged curtain aside and showed her the pail. The countess looked at the grimy bucket, then back to me. It took a moment for realization to set in.

"Dump the bucket over the side when you're finished." I turned to leave, then added, "Just the contents, not the bucket."

5

There were no mattresses on the wooden shelves the builders of *Orca* intended to be used for bunks. I didn't care. After shoveling coal for hours, I was too tired to notice, and if I didn't close my eyes for a little while, I was going to fall over. Bohdan was drafted for engine room watch. He didn't like it, complaining in a very eloquent way he knew absolutely nothing about steam engines. I gave him my best twenty minute orientation class and told him to wake me in a couple of hours. With my Vladivostok coat for a pillow and an antique steam engine clanking a lullaby a few feet away, I crawled onto the lower shelf opposite the mess table. With the curve of the hull touching my shoulder, I stretched out on the hard wood. I think I was asleep before I closed my eyes.

Our luck ran out a little before sunrise. Somewhere deep down in the sleep of physical exhaustion, my brain registered the sounds of something not quite right. I felt it in the wooden boards beneath me. The engine had changed songs. Beyond the closed wooden door between me and the steam engine, something had gone wrong. There was a loud bang like a giant slapping his hands together then a screeching whistle. Before I could open my eyes, the temperature of the air around me shot up to Sahara Desert proportions. The roar came next, and I knew what had happened. The boiler was gone, exploded in blistering steam and no doubt boiling Bohdan alive. A woman screamed. Rolling out of the bunk, I fell flat on my face onto *Orca's* deck. As I began to get up, someone jumped out of the upper bunk and landed on top of me.

"Get off my legs," I snarled. "I need to move." The galley lamp was barely burning, its glow making just enough light to see around the close interior. The countess, hair down around her shoulders and with her blouse pulled out of her riding pants was sitting on the deck. She was holding onto her shin.

"Sorry. Didn't mean to kick you," I said.

Steam hissed and squalled beyond the closed hatch to the engine room.

"Mr. Watkins, are we going to die?"

"Not yet," I told her, "but Bohdan probably copped it."

"I'm here, Stick."

I looked at the square opening in the overhead with its ladder to the darkened wheelhouse. The Czech was peering into the small galley where the countess and I lay tangled on the deck.

"Bohdan!" I screamed.

"I'm not hurt," he yelled back.

Bohdan, my engine room watch, had gone topside.

"The engine? Has it exploded?" he shouted.

"Mr. Watkins," the countess said, "what is happening? What is that sound and would you please let go of my leg?"

"Where's that horse pistol of yours?" The leg removed itself from my hand.

"In my bunk."

"Get it," I told her. "Go shoot Bohdan."

"Stick," Bohdan called from the top of the ladder. "I have claustrophobia. I had to get out of that room. I was just about to come back down."

Untangling my legs from the countess, I climbed over the galley table and made my way to the boiler room hatch. The closed door was warm but not roasting hot.

"Should I come down?" Ivan shouted from the boat's wheel.

"Stay there," I yelled. I didn't need Ivan getting in my way. Opening the hatch a few inches made hot steam blow out in a white cloud. That was bad. I have an innate fear of boilers. It's right up there with my fear of drowning, burning to death and getting eaten by sharks after the boat I'm on sinks.

"We have stopped moving," Ivan shouted down from above. "Bohdan wants know if should I put small boat in water," the Russian said in his thick accent.

"You can put Bohdan in the water," I yelled back. There was a lot of agitated Russian being spoken on deck. "Don't know if we're sinking," I shouted, "and I don't see any flames."

"Can you repair it?" the countess asked.

She was standing behind me. The sweat on her body made her look like she had been caught outside in the rain. "It's too hot here, Countess. You should go up top."

The countess dabbed at her face with a handkerchief. "The engine, Mr. Watkins. Can you repair it?"

"We weren't running fast. I throttled it down while Bohdan had the watch." I tried to see inside the engine room. There was still a lot of steam in there. "If the boiler had burst, we would all be screaming right now. Probably a pipe went."

The countess looked worried. I told them they should have kept the car.

A long half hour later, with the engine's pistons no longer moving and temperatures in the crowded space somewhere north of a hundred and twenty degrees, I stepped through the hatch. Sweat ran down my arms, my neck and my back. Steam does that, right before it cooks you like a breakfast egg. With my hands wrapped in rags, I started closing valves. I couldn't see much. It was too dark, and the sweat kept running in my eyes. I was about to reach for a match to light another lamp when light flooded the tight space. I turned to find the countess setting the glass globe back in place on the bulkhead light.

"Don't touch anything," I told her. "The pipes will scald you."

She held up her hand. "I remember."

"Bohdan," I yelled as loud as I could.

"Yes, Stick?"

"Remember that gauge I showed you? The one with the red colored wedge on the face?"

"The one on the big tank. I remember," Bohdan said from the safety of the ladder.

"What did I tell you about that gauge?"

There was a pause.

"I have claustrophobia," his voice said. "I needed air."

"I told you if the pressure went into the red, things would blow up, didn't I? I told you to vent the steam if it got too close, didn't I?"

"Shall I have Ivan throw him into the sea?" the countess asked.

She said it very low, standing just a few feet away from me. There was no joking in those eyes.

We drifted dead in the water for three days.

6

There were no spare parts aboard, almost no tools and, except for me, nobody had any notion of how steam plants operated. I suppose we were fortunate the sketchy iron monster hadn't exploded the first time she took pressure. Our boiler held, but a relief valve hadn't. When Bohdan's claustrophobia allowed the pressure to go into the unsafe zone, the valve popped open and stayed there. We were lucky. Most of the escaping steam had gone up the stack. If it hadn't, the countess and I would have boiled where we lay. What wasn't vented out the stack leaked through a rusted spot in the pipe allowing just enough hot gas below deck to roast us but not kill us.

After several hours of patient effort and a lot of scraped knuckles, I managed to unscrew the stuck valve and remove the rusted pipe. Some quick work with a wire brush to knock off several decades of rust showed me a crack in the bronze fitting. I didn't have another valve and I couldn't boil water with a hole in the iron kettle. As I saw the problem, it was a question of what could I do without and what did I need. The need part was easy. I needed a plug. For the doing without part, I turned to the condenser. A condenser is basically a big radiator used to cool off hot steam and turn it back into water. It was also the source of our drinking water. Taking it apart might get me the parts I needed to fix the steam plant, but it would also mean we could all get really thirsty really fast.

Ivan and Bohdan took the disaster in stride. The Russian cooked cabbage and potatoes two times a day, once in the morning and once in the evening. The Czech cleaned his machinegun and kept lamenting the fact we had nothing to fish with. He seemed to have forgotten all about red lines on pressure gauges. The countess fumed, telling me more than once she should have let Ivan drown the Czech. Drowned Czech or not, with the relief valve removed, I still had a hole in my boiler.

The good news was *Orca* still floated, sometimes pointing towards the sunset, sometimes towards sunrise. I say floated when wallowed was a better word. Boats without way on them have a peculiar feel when drifting on the ocean. Everything is always moving in every direction. On our second day, a particularly rough day with a strong west wind pushing us out of sight of land, Bohdan crawled into one of the wooden bunks, too seasick to stand. I considered it a small bit of justice. Ivan and the countess seemed to take the rolling little boat in stride although Ivan had his moments. I think he was determined not to show weakness in front of me.

"It is hopeless, isn't it, Mr. Watkins."

The countess said this to me while standing in the hatch between the galley and the boiler room. It probably looked that way to her. I had most of the piping disassembled by then.

"Go away," I told her. I can be as curt as Ivan when I want to. Besides, all the cabbage we were eating was giving me gas and an Academy man never breaks wind in front of a lady.

On our third morning without a boiler, I started putting things back together, rerouting steam lines and hoping for the best. It wasn't neat, and it certainly wasn't pretty, but I had managed to remove one lifesaving threaded plug from the final assembly. Operating a boiler built around the time Lee was leaving Gettysburg with an iron plug for a relief valve was against everything I'd ever been taught.

So was cannibalism.

Our supply of carrots ran out on the second day. We ate the last of the cabbage on the third day. The four of us were down to our last seven potatoes, a half filled tin of tea leaves and a few cans of stewed tomatoes. Ivan, rummaging around in a cupboard, found a couple of mousetraps. He looked at me, me at him, and we both nodded our heads in mutual understanding. If I didn't get things working soon, our mutual nods said, he would have to set the traps. If we didn't die of thirst first. Our water was almost gone.

Dropping the pipe wrench on the galley table, I climbed up the ladder to the wheelhouse. My crewmates were lounging on deck, relaxed and clean. I was bone tired and filthy.

The countess, sitting on the overturned dinghy of dubious condition watched my approach. She didn't look pleased with any of her coconspirators; both of them haven proven to be useless in the current situation. I, however, her face said, had skills. Necessary skills. I think she had almost forgotten about our misunderstanding in the flophouse.

"Mr. Watkins, I don't want to see you on deck again until you have fixed the machinery."

I sighed. So she hadn't quite forgotten.

"Ivan has just suggested eating." She looked at her Russian compatriot and scowled. "I am not going to repeat what he has suggested."

Russian language exploded out of Ivan. It exploded out of the countess, too. Bohdan, having left his bunk for the first time all day and crouching by the downwind rail, shouted the loudest of all three.

"The boiler's fixed," I told them. Instant silence accompanied my words. "Sort of," I added under my breath.

There wasn't a sound on the old tub except for creaking timbers.

The countess rose slowly from her seat on the dinghy's upturned bottom. "It is working again?"

I pointed to the iron smokestack. Thin gray smoke trailed away into a cloudy sky. "We should probably try to find a port before it explodes."

The countess hugged me, an actual arms around my neck hug. I think she was about to say something in my ear when Ivan pulled her away. Then he hugged me and kissed me on both cheeks.

"Men shake where I come from," I told him. "Not kiss each other." The Russian kissed me again.

Bohdan said, "I knew you could fix it, Stick." Then he retched over the side.

The countess, all radiant smiles, said, "Well done, Mr. Watkins. How soon before we reach our destination?"

We reached it seven hours later. I'm sure the countess thought me a wonderful navigator able to find the right port with some internal magic developed by my years spent on the ocean. I couldn't see the harm in letting her think that. The truth was, I turned our limping artifact to Russian seal hunting into the first likely looking piece of coastline we came to. After steaming past some impressive bluffs, the *Orca* limped her way into a sheltered bay that was probably three miles wide and twice that long. As I edged our boat towards the northern end, we passed an outbound schooner whose crew stared at us open mouthed as we motored by. One or two even pointed. If they laughed, at least we were far enough away not to hear it.

The bay itself was lined with tree covered hills growing right down to the water. The shoreline, what I could see of it, didn't look friendly to wooden hulled boats. Boulders, most half submerged, lined the edges for as far as I could see. My passengers on the boat remained silent as I drove us across the bay. Either they had great faith in my navigation or they had no idea where to go. When we were about half way down the bay, I saw what looked like buildings ahead of us, so I pointed the boat towards civilization. An hour later, Saint. Olga, if that was where we were, looked like a town of three or four hundred people. There was a long waterfront with a dozen or so wooden buildings, three docks sticking out into the water and the usual collection of boats either tied up to the piers or riding at anchor. I counted six church steeples with their little round domes and double rowed crosses mixed in among the buildings. Not at all sure what was expected of visitors arriving in floating derelicts, I decided to anchor our boat near where the dock ended and a gravel strand began. The spot I picked had a number of boats pulled up out of the water and several more looked like they were waiting their turn to be hauled out. I didn't see anyone on board any of them. At least no one would point at us.

The countess stood beside me at the wheel. She peered through the broken window at the sights of Saint Olga. Ivan was forward holding our one and only anchor balanced on the rail.

"Is this the place?" I asked her.

The countess nodded. "You have done well, Mr. Watkins. I believe the Avvakumovka River is over that way." She pointed to our left. "And beyond it, the Ussuri and the railway. We will go inland from here."

"How far inland?"

The countess patted my hand where it held the wheel.

We were close to the shore, easy rowing distance with our dinghy. Several townspeople watched our slow approach, probably drawn by the healthy amount of smoke coming out of the stack.

"Don't see any soldiers," I said.

"Bohdan said the Japanese haven't lost this part of the coast yet."

"And if they have?" I asked. "What if there are Red soldiers in the village?"

"Mr. Watkins, I have asked myself that question every day

for five years. But I think we are safe for now." She turned to look at me. "Our Czech friend has never been wrong about these things."

"Now, Ivan," I shouted. The big Russian threw the anchor over the side. "Stop engine," I yelled down the ladder. I had made Bohdan go below, ready to disengage the engine when I yelled. He wasn't happy about the job, saying he didn't know how to operate a steam engine. I don't think he trusted my repairs. The countess had ordered him below. With the Russian looming behind her, Bohdan had skulked away to his post, painfully aware he was still in her doghouse. The steady thump of the engine changed its note as the Czech closed valves. The anchor caught and *Orca* came to a stop.

"Done with engines," I said, mostly out of habit. I patted the wheel. "Thank you for not sinking." Turning to my traveling companion, I said, "We're here."

The Czech made his way up the ladder.

"Bohdan," the countess told him, "help Ivan get the small boat in the water."

"Dinghy," I told them. "It's called a dinghy."

The countess didn't seem to hear. She was staring at a small crowd gathering on the rocky beach.

"Mr. Watkins will row us ashore. Watch for Bolsheviks," she told him. "If I wave my arm over my head, start shooting."

Ivan and I got the dinghy over the side without Bohdan's help. It didn't sink, which I took as a good sign. I went first, balancing in the rocking boat before turning to help the countess down from the *Orca*. As she stepped aboard, I could already see water in the bottom of the small boat. I decided to row fast. Ivan dropped into the boat, then immediately sat on a thwart. He eyed the water with trepidation as the little boat rocked from side to side. The countess in her foxhunting outfit sat in the stern as Bohdan watched over us, his violin at the ready. I put the oars in the locks as Ivan pushed us away from *Orca's* hull. When I rowed us to within easy shouting distance of the shore, Ivan bellowed out something in Russian. The countess touched my knee.

"Stop, Mr. Watkins."

Looking at the water sloshing around my feet, I said, "Sure that's a good idea?"

The countess ignored me. She was looking over my shoulder at the half dozen or so people standing on the shore. A man in a long sleeved blue shirt shouted something at Ivan. The words didn't sound very threatening to me. At least the countess didn't wave her arm. The waves tried to turn the boat, so I used the oars to keep us facing the shore.

"Well?" I asked.

"He is asking questions," she said quietly. "He wants to know where we are from."

I started to ask a question, but she raised a hand, silencing me without saying a word. The countess would have made an excellent schoolmaster. She had a natural way about her for controlling the unruly. I sat on my oars while she listened to the man in the blue shirt talking to Ivan.

"The Japanese have left," she said. "Marching back to Vladivostok before they are cut off."

More Russian words were shouted back and forth. Finally, the countess smiled, then tapped my knee.

"You make continue, Mr. Watkins. The Bolsheviks aren't here yet. Do try not to sound too American to the locals, won't you? It will just make them ask more questions."

"I will do my best, Countess."

She gave me one of those piercingly bright smiles, the one she reserves for cooperative underlings.

Five minutes later, the leaky little boat touched the shore of terra firma. I think all three of us breathed a sigh of relief. I stayed with the dinghy, now pulled safely up on the gravel strand, while Ivan and the countess explored the town. The locals wanted to talk to the new arrival sitting on their shore. I found it best to just nod my head as they talked. I think the general consensus from the town's unofficial welcoming committee was that the stranger sitting in the dinghy was soft in the head.

After a half hour wait, it started to drizzle. An hour after that, my coat soaked through and shivering in the weather, my companions returned. Ivan was carrying two burlap sacks. The countess, jodhpurs and boots walking fast, didn't look happy. They were both as wet as I was.

"Well?" I asked.

"I bought ham," Ivan said, "and potatoes, beets, cabbage and—"

"Three hundred rubles," the countess said, interrupting the menu. "They take me for a fool." She nodded at the boat. "Push us off."

The countess climbed into the boat as soon as it floated and resumed her spot in the stern. Ivan handed me his groceries and cocked a wary eye in my direction. I gave the boat a hard shove, then jumped aboard. This time, Ivan rowed. After he got the oars out, I said, "Three hundred rubles for an armful of groceries?"

Ivan nodded his head from side to side in short, jerky movements, then pulled hard on the oars.

The countess, fire smoldering behind her eyes, spat out her reply with cobra venom sweetening each word. "For *horses*, Mr. Watkins. Three hundred rubles for worn out nags that aren't worth ten. My father was a cavalry officer. Ivan was his groom. We know our business. Three hundred." She kicked Ivan's shin. "You should have let me shoot the thief."

The dinghy bounced against the side of our boat. Bohdan reached a hand for the countess.

"Well?" he asked.

Ivan and I nodded our heads together. The countess exploded in Russian. I don't think her father would have approved of her choices in adjectives.

We went back the next day. I felt much better. I had slept the entire night through and ate a full breakfast thanks to Ivan. The countess said she wanted to try her luck with the horse thief again. I stayed on the beach with our leaky transportation in case somebody came by and mistook it for firewood. The pair came back sometime after noon, still with no horses however Ivan had a dead rooster to add to the larder. At lease we weren't going to eat rats. I didn't ask how things went this time. The countess' face said all I needed to know.

"We try different stable," Ivan said to me after the countess was seated in the boat. "No horses for sale. None."

No one spoke as Ivan pulled at the oars.

The next morning marked our fifth day on board the seal hunter. Either she had stopped reeking of mildew or I had stopped smelling it. My three traveling companions discussed our situation frequently. I assumed it was our situation, anyway. They spoke in low voices to each other, always in Russian. The countess was the spirited one in the group. She was much given to shouting and pointing of fingers towards the village. Bohdan, apparently forgiven for nearly destroying everything, still laughed at this word and that phrase but didn't seem to have any suggestions. Ivan peeled potatoes and drank vodka from his flask. Anchored and with no need of steam propulsion anymore, I seemed to have been relegated to ship's mascot.

Bohdan and Ivan rowed ashore. Out of sheer boredom, I used an old scrub brush and mop to clear away some of the green mold and bird droppings from the *Orca's* deck. The countess watched me through the wheelhouse's broken windows. The Russian and the Czech weren't gone long before they came back with one of the locals. When the two men and the newcomer came aboard, the countess came out of the wheelhouse and touched my arm.

"No English if you please, Mr. Watkins."

Since English is the only language I know, I think that was her subtle way of asking me to keep my mouth shut. Me and the mop stood by the iron exhaust stack and watched the show.

The newcomer stomped his foot on the now partially clean deck. We both saw the boards bending from the blow. He went to the bows and pulled a piece of rotten wood away from the railing then tossed it into the bay. Ivan followed him everywhere, all the while speaking Russian. The newcomer was mostly silent. I caught on pretty fast to what was happening. Ivan was trying to sell our boat. When he gave the stump of broken mast a solid kick, he gave me a long look, like he thought I was somehow responsible for whatever mishap caused the damage.

"I didn't do it," I said, probably with a touch too much defensiveness in my voice. The countess cleared her throat and glared at me. I held my tongue for the rest of the inspection. Unfortunately for my partners, the would be buyer acted like a man who knew his business. He threw open the forward hatch and went into the hold where the seal pelts had been stored. The smell was frightful in there and there was always a half a foot of seawater sloshing in the bilge needing to be pumped out. When he came up for air, he had a sad look on his face. The engine room was next. I followed him down the ladder, thinking he might have questions. One look at my makeshift repairs answered anything he might have considered asking. The stranger threw up his hands and went for the ladder. Ivan followed, explaining, I think, my repairs. I never wished I spoke Russian more than right then. Ten minutes later, Ivan came back from rowing our buyer ashore. The three of us met him on deck as he came back aboard.

"Not good?" I asked him.

"He called ship floating coffin."

"Smart man," I said.

The countess started shouting in Russian. Ivan started shouting. Bohdan slapped his fist on the boat's railing, emphasizing whatever point he was making.

"Just buy the horses," I said. "The price isn't going to change."

The countess rounded on me, blue eyes as cold as a Siberian blizzard.

"With what shall we buy them, Mr. Watkins? Three hundred rubles might as well be three thousand. If we had that kind of money, do you think we would be sleeping on this hulk every night, eating boiled cabbage and potatoes and smelling this stench night and day? If I had that much money, don't you think I might have purchased a change of clothing, or taken a room in that hotel?" She jabbed a finger towards a two story building facing the bay.

I started to speak.

"Yes, Mr. Watkins. We have more gold. Twelve British sovereigns. Solid gold. Enough to buy every horse in this town, with tents and supplies to go with them. I could even hire ten men, twenty, to escort us anywhere I said to go. But I can't, Mr. Watkins. Not one coin. Do you know why?"

I started to speak again.

"I will tell you why," she continued. "Because half of Russia knows the czar's bullion is missing. Thousands of kilograms lost in…"

She stopped herself from saying more. Bohdan was smiling. Just the mention of the secret was enough to bring a grin to his face.

In Vladivostok, the countess told me her story while sitting at our table by the window in our quaint little cafe. Yes, she showed me the golden bar as proof, but there was more to her tale, much more. She had a man, she said, a Czech, one of the Legion's men who, two years earlier, had turned Admiral Kolchak over to the Reds in return for safe passage to Vladivostok. Kolchak was the big man with the White Army. He was the top guy in the Far East Republic; Russia's last stand against the Leninist. The admiral and the rest of the Whites had taken the entire gold reserve of Imperial Russia with them as they were pushed eastward by the tides of revolution. A bank vault full of treasure.

The Legion sent Kolchak to his fate along with four hundred million rubles in gold. But chaos happened as it often does in war. Someone, the countess told me as we sat in our cafe, had some of the gold moved by armored train on the Trans-Siberian. Two hundred million rubles worth.

It would have to be someone high up in the Legion to make that happen.

But something went wrong along the way, something she wouldn't talk about, not then, not in that cafe. The gold disappeared was all she would say. That was the moment she showed me the ingot. Her proof. The countess said she knew what happened to the gold because she knew someone who was there, a man she had known all her life. A man she trusted without question. A man who had brought her the gold ingot.

She had everything she needed to get the gold. Everything but a way to get there.

"The filthy Bolsheviks are turning the countryside upside down looking for it, Mr. Watkins. That pig Semyonov has his Cossacks prowling behind the Bolsheviks looking for it. Even Kolchak's people, those still alive, are trying to find it. So no, Mr. Watkins, I can't use it because if I did, if I started spending gold now, all the hounds would know. All of them. We would all be dead in a week."

The countess crossed her arms and stared at me, daring me to argue with her logic.

"I was going to say, I have a hundred and twenty-seven rubles left and about forty dollars American. Maybe if we showed your horse thieves hard cash, it might loosen their resolve."

The countess looked at Ivan. Ivan shrugged his shoulders.

"I need to think." She turned to Ivan again. "What is for dinner?"

"Cabbage," he said, then he smiled. "And chicken."

"And a little vodka?" the countess asked.

Bohdan started laughing.

The next morning, day six in the charming seaside town of wherever we were, Ivan and I tried to loosen some resolve. We left the countess on the boat. I don't think she was feeling well. Probably too much chicken. Ivan was glad she stayed behind. I think he was worried she might shoot the owner of the horses if the negotiations went badly again.

They went badly.

Two horses. He offered two horses for one hundred and eighty rubles and all my Yankee dollars. Even if we bought the two nags, we still needed money for provisions. Neither Ivan nor the countess were saying anything about the gold's location, but I got the impression it wasn't close.

I let Ivan row himself back to the boat. I didn't feel like facing the she demon's hangover enhanced wrath.

"I want to stretch my legs some," I told him. "See if I can buy a decent slicker." It had rained again while we were at the livery and I was tired of getting wet.

Ivan shrugged. "Don't be fooled, Watkins," he said as he got into the boat. "The village is peaceful now, but if Bolsheviks come, killing will be quick. I have seen it. They shoot foreigners soon as they are found. Boat is safer for you."

I pointed to the sky. "It's going to rain. I'll be along shortly."

He shrugged once more, then went to the oars. "Shout when done shopping," he called as the boat pulled away. "I will send Czech come get you."

I went the opposite way from the livery, turned down the first lane I came to and walked. I had no idea where I was going, but if this part of Russia was anything like the Vladivostok part, as soon as word got around there was somebody looking to buy something, the business would find me. I stumbled upon a blacksmith's shop first, then a bookstore with a few Russian newspapers out front followed by a bakery with no bread to sell. At the end of the street, I found a dress shop. A bell over the door tinkled as I went in. A frightfully unattractive middle aged woman greeted me with a toothy smile. She started talking.

"I don't speak Russian. I'm looking for a raincoat." I shook my dirty coal stained lapels and pointed out the shop's windows. "It's going to rain. I need a slicker." More Russian followed. I pulled some rubles out of my wallet and waved them about me. The woman looked puzzled, then pointed a finger at a manikin in a silvery blue dress with a dark bow around the middle.

I sighed. "Not my size."

I left the dress shop and tried the next street, passed what I think was a pharmacy, then stopped. I didn't mean to stop. He just surprised me, sitting there like that. I started walking, slower than I had before, and looking from left to right. His back was to me, but it was him. I'd recognize the way he held himself anywhere. I'd seen it often enough. Sitting where he was, he hadn't seen me coming yet.

Blue smoke drifted towards me. As if I needed confirmation, I smelled that god awful tobacco he liked. You don't forget a smell like that. My boots thumped on the wooden walkway in front of the building. I was about to tell him he was slipping up in his old age when he half turned and went down the alley between the buildings.

"Try not to look so obvious, Watkins," he said without looking behind him. "In the alley," he added with a bare nod of his fur hat.

I followed along behind, doing my best not to look so obvious. The alley was a narrow gap between two wood framed buildings. Dark and gloomy, bare dirt ran its length a good thirty or forty feet. A newspaper blew down its length, wrapping itself around my leg before disappearing behind me. The man I was following along behind was an inch or two shorter than me, broad shouldered and stocky, with the permanently sunburned complexion of someone used to life in the weather. He carried himself like a prizefighter and, judging by a slightly unnatural angle to his nose, might have been one ten or fifteen years ago. His clothes were inexpensive and crumpled, all in shades of brown and like the person wearing them, looked well lived in. I ran my fingers along the wooden boards thinking if I was going to stab, strangle or otherwise do my best to ruin a stranger's day, I had picked the perfect spot for it.

"Major, can't say I'm not surprised to see you here. What

do you burn in that thing? It smells like scorched raccoon fur."

"Russian tobacco is an acquired taste," a southern accent answered. "I buy it from a Buryat in Vladivostok. Can't find it anywhere else."

"I could probably tell you why."

The major drew on his pipe. "You've led us a merry chase, Watkins. I told my boys you probably drowned on that scow as soon as you hit open water."

"The *Orca's* a fine ocean going vessel," I told him. "Fit for a Fleet Admiral's review."

The major snorted. "Were you followed?"

Was I?

"No," I said a bit too quickly.

"Didn't look, did you." It was an accusation, not a question.

"It's just a village. There are no Reds roaming around. I've kept my eyes open."

"Did you now," the major said with the practiced scorn of a marine officer. "You never saw my boys following you all day, you and that big fellow in black. Bad habits will get you killed in this game, Watkins. I told you that before and I see you weren't listening." The major looked at his pipe. "However, never let it be said I didn't give credit where credit is due. Your disguise is excellent," he said, pointing his pipe stem at my Vladivostok castoffs.

I examined my disguise. The trousers had a tear in one knee and my shirt was so full of coal dust, I could feel it rubbing against my skin. My hands, scratched and burned from tending to an antique steam engine, looked like the hands of a common laborer. Greased black crescents ringed the tip of each finger. He was right. I *was* well disguised. There was nothing about my appearance that looked anything like a naval officer. Not anymore.

"I've had the devil of a time finding you," he added. "I believe I clearly told you to leave a trail."

"I did my best with what I had. She told me she needed someone to run a steam engine. I had no idea what engine or where it was."

"Part of a naval officer's uniform in a hotel isn't much of a trail, Watkins. Cost me five rubles to search your room, by the way. There was some confusion with a drunken prostitute with a tale of a rich woman taking her meal ticket. Then, of course, there was the automobile."

"Green automobile," I said. "Same one I told you about when she met me at the cafe."

"Yes," the major continued. "Our Japanese friends found the motorcar. Your cap was still on the floorboard. I think they're still searching Vladivostok flophouses for our deserter. Probably itching to cut somebody's head off. That part of your trail was well done, Lieutenant. By the way, the owner gave an excellent description of the Countess Irena Obolensky and her three companions."

"Did you let him keep the car?"

The major sucked on his pipe. "Is it him?" he asked, ignoring my question.

"There's no doubt. It's him. It's the Czech."

The major sighed. I think he would have preferred me saying something otherwise.

"Let's hear you report, Lieutenant Watkins. I can't stay here long. The village isn't big enough for strangers."

I told him all that happened since I watched the *Devilfish* leave port, leaving out the part about being interrupted sans pants. I described the ride through Vladivostok, being shelled by Red artillery and my emergency repairs to an antique steam engine. I confess, I was a little proud of that last part. Not everyone can improvise with odds and ends like that. He listened, occasionally asking me to go back and repeat something.

"You've gone to an awful lot of trouble to put me here, Major. I've confirmed your man Bohdan is on the *Orca*. Maybe now you can tell me why he's so important to you."

"Wilhelm Bohdan's really here," he said, shaking his head. "I only half believed it was him. Laughing Billy, we called him. Also known as Colonel Wilhelm Bohdan of the now departed Czech Legion. Laughing Billy was head of their intelligence service," the major added. "It was said he had a network that reached from the Black Sea clear to Vladivostok. I've heard it was his idea to march the Legion east in the first place." The major's pipe bowl glowed cherry red as he inhaled his noxious concoction. He exhaled blue smoke before going on. "We lost track of him after his outfit got tired of Admiral Kolchak and turned him over to the Reds. Bohdan was there for that little dust up, too. Wouldn't surprise me in the least if the whole thing wasn't his idea. It sounds like something he would do."

"The Reds shot Kolchak," I said.

"They did and got a train load of gold from the Legion. Bought their safe passage all the way to Vladivostok with that little deal. Smart thinking on the Legion's part although the late Admiral Kolchak would probably disagree." The major examined the dirt beneath his feet. "I was all set to bring you back to the fleet, Lieutenant, and tell the admiral I told you so but that's not an option now. We've got questions for the good colonel." He examined his pipe's bowl. "I need to think on this."

"Yes sir." Short sentences are best with marine officers when they are thinking. "Bohdan hasn't mentioned anything about his past."

"He wouldn't," the major said. "Laughing Billy has a price on his head. He arranged for the sudden demise of too many Bolsheviks. I remember hearing something about Trotsky offering a small fortune for the man. Interesting study in human nature there, the Reds offering cash rewards from a society that says it's going to ban all wealth. What about the big fellow in black?"

"Ivan. He's the countess' man. She said he was her father's groom."

"What's his family name?"

"I never asked. He doesn't say much and we're not

friends."

The major's pipe was out. Whatever concoction he bought from his Buryat confectioner, it didn't burn well. He struck a match against the wall making shadows sway in the flame's reflection. The smell of roasting raccoon fur made me wince.

"Watkins, you do understand the point of being an intelligence officer is to actually gather intelligence."

Statements like that are the reason why the Navy and Marines never get along. "Yes sir, I do." Another cloud of pipe smoke drifted towards me. I held my breath.

"This could be quite a feather in your hat, Watkins. The capture of such a valuable man. Probably put another half stripe on your sleeve."

I smiled. Every officer's dream. A pay increase.

"The Reds want to shoot Laughing Billy right after they pull out his fingernails and write down a few names. The Japs want to chop his head off for getting their toy admiral killed by the same Reds. And apparently, we hear there's any number of petty criminals, war lords and wartime profiteers looking for a missing boxcar full of gold. The admiral will tell me he was right all along. He isn't, but he'll tell me just the same. And of course, I'll have to agree, won't I Lieutenant?"

"Yes sir," I said again.

"Colonel Bohdan should have left with the rest of the Legion. Now we have to take him and since he isn't likely to let us take him, my boys will have to engage him."

The major strung the word engage out just a bit too long and for an instant, the devil danced in the marine's eyes. "I'd rather not have to do that, Lieutenant. Your pretty countess might get in the way and Russia would lose another member of the nobility. Not that anyone would notice. Shake a stick around here and some Prince This or Duchess That will scramble out of the bushes."

The countess. I thought about what her reaction would be to American marines pointing rifles at Bohdan. "I don't think we should take him yet, Major."

"Why is that, Lieutenant? And don't start up about that gold fantasy. There's no pot of gold at the end of this rainbow."

"I believe her," I said, "the countess. She wouldn't have gone to all this trouble otherwise."

"It's Laughing Billy, Lieutenant. He's riding her like a pack mule to get out of Siberia. Bohdan knows there's a price on his head. His game's up. This is the only play he has left. Billy got careless when he started looking for somebody to run that scow. He should have stayed under whatever rock he was hiding under. There's no gold. I told you. The Legion gave up the bullion and Admiral Kolchak for safe passage to Vladivostok."

"She showed me proof at the cafe. The gold bar."

"She showed it to two more men before you."

The surprise must have shown on my face. The countess had never mentioned anyone else before me.

"Guess the admiral failed to mention that little fact. No, Watkins, you weren't her first target. The other two said no before we could tell them to say yes. Damned unfortunate timing. As for the gold bar, probably given to her by Bohdan himself. I don't doubt the man might have absconded a bar or two. The Legion was leaving Russia, and he was the man in charge of turning all that treasure over to the Reds. So he lined his pockets before he left. Who's to know? That doesn't mean there's a trainload of bullion sitting forgotten somewhere. Gold doesn't get forgotten, Lieutenant. This is Russia for god's sake. Poverty is an institution in this country."

"Yes sir," I said once more.

"There's certainly no buried treasure in this piss hole fishing village. It's too far from the Trans-Siberian. The only way they could have got it here is by mule. You see any sign of mules, Lieutenant?"

"It's not here."

"Of course it isn't here. Bohdan would've had to shoot everyone in the place to keep it quiet. Not that he wouldn't have done it. I hear he had fifty Bolsheviks shot in one day.

That's another reason why the Reds want his scalp."

"The countess knows where it is. The gold, I mean."

"She tell you that, Lieutenant?"

"In the cafe, she told me she knew someone who was there. I'm pretty sure she meant Ivan."

"And when she told you this, did she clasp her hands together, look you in the eye and swear on all the Orthodox saints it was the absolute truth?"

"I'm not a fool, Major."

"I believe I am the senior officer in this alley, Lieutenant. You are what I say you are. She's using you. Why is the countess still here if there's no gold?"

"We are maneuvering."

"You're what?"

"She said she couldn't get past the Reds putting a choke hold on the city so she got the idea to sail around their lines." I motioned with my arms. "Land here, behind them. Maneuver."

"Tactical thinking from a woman. We live in the modern age, Lieutenant." The major chewed his pipe stem. "Can't say I fault her reasoning although I'd be damned if I would have taken that scow anywhere. You diddling the Russian while she tells you she knows where all this alleged missing bullion has gone to?"

I didn't say anything. My experience with marine superior officers has taught me to let them show their extreme displeasure with you through sarcasm and innuendo. It's what they do.

"I have to tell you, Watkins, I was going to end this farce right here and now. You're not the man for this sort of thing. You don't have the training or experience to play in this game. I told the admiral to leave you in a ship's engine room where you belong but he thinks he knows better. Why are they still here, anyway? How many days have the four of you hung around doing nothing? Word's going to get out. I found you, the Reds will too and damn quickly."

"They've been trying to leave."

"For where? Now that would be helpful intelligence, Watkins."

"The countess won't say."

"The countess, the countess. You sure you aren't diddling her?"

"I gave up trying after she stuck that Mauser she carries in my ribs."

The major fondled his pipe. "I wouldn't have given up. I like fortitude in my women," he said, "but then, we marines know how these things are done."

"The navy disagrees."

"Why can't they leave?"

"No horses. Apparently, the countess failed to account for wartime prices. She hasn't got enough cash." I told him about our efforts to sell the *Orca*.

The major touched the end of a finger to the bowl of his pipe. "Do you have any matches on you?"

I patted my pockets, felt the match box, looked at the major's foul smelling pipe and said, "Sorry, no."

"Why am I not surprised," the major said.

He walked to the far end of the alley. I was about to follow him when he did an about face and came back to my end of the lane. He jabbed the stem of his pipe at me as he spoke.

"Alright, Watkins. Since your good friend the admiral would question my decision otherwise, he like you being a believer in leprechauns and pots of gold, I will allow this *maneuver* to continue a bit longer. The problem as I see it is one of logistics so this is what I am going to do. One of my boys will come by tomorrow because he's heard you have a working steam engine. You do have a working steam engine don't you?"

"More or less."

"His story will be he needs that engine and absolutely has to have it."

I scratched my boot in the dirt. "What's he need it for?"

"How the hell do I know why he needs it. Be useful, Lieutenant. Answer your own question. A good intelligence office learns to adapt and respond on his feet."

A villager walked past the front of the alley. The major raised his hand for silence. It gave me a minute to think about the problem.

"Well?" he asked when we were alone again.

"He needs it for a sawmill," I said. "Replacement parts."

"Sawmill," the major said. His chin moved up and down once; a marine officer's version of high praise. "How much money does your woman need?"

"Something north of three hundred rubles."

"Good lord. And she was expecting to sell that tub for three hundred rubles? Does she know it's about to sink?"

"I think she was desperate when we fled Vladivostok. She likes to act like she has this master plan but I think she's been winging it for a while now."

The major put his empty pipe between his teeth. "I've got two hundred and fifty rubles, my discretionary funds. That's all there is. My man will come by tomorrow and offer to buy that derelict piece of driftwood. If the countess won't sell," the major paused, "you make sure she does because if she refuses, I'm taking the Czech prisoner. If she tries to leave on that tub, you make sure that doesn't happen. Break something, understand?"

I did.

"We'll march whoever's left alive after we assault the boat back to Vladivostok. Overland," he added. "I wouldn't sail that boat around this little bay for love of money. Buy your horses, make your plans," the major waved his pipe in a circle between us, "complete your maneuver and find out what Colonel Bohdan's up to. Otherwise, there's going to be gunfire."

"Bohdan's got a Lewis. He shot up some Red cavalry when we left Vladivostok."

The major exhaled through bulging nostrils. "Lieutenant,

when I tell you to report what you know, those are the things you report. A damned machinegun isn't a detail you overlook. Are we clear on the details?"

"Yes sir."

"You ever shoot anybody before, Watkins? I mean up close where it's personal. Not standing behind some deck gun firing at Chinese river pirates."

I could feel the comforting weight of the forty-five in my side pocket. I could also feel the even more comforting weight of my retainer sitting next to my heart. I hadn't mentioned that shiny little detail, either. "No sir. I've never shot anyone."

"Do you still have your sidearm?"

I patted my coat pocket.

The major grunted. "If Billy Bohdan ever, and I mean ever, looks like he's about to point that Lewis in my direction, shoot him. If he finds out your desertion is all a sham, shoot him. Kill him right then, right there. The Colonel may look like your parent's next door neighbor but trust me, he's not. He'll kill you, Watkins and he won't blink an eye when he does it. Shoot him on the spot if you need to. Consider that an order. If you think Bohdan suspects you, forget this gold hunt and that lovely countess we both know you're trying to diddle and put him down."

"Where will you be?" I asked. "How will I find you?"

"Find me? I'm a marine, Watkins. You couldn't find me if your life depended on it. Fear not, me and my boys will be around wherever you go." He pointed his pipe's stem back toward the street. "You're dismissed, Lieutenant."

I almost saluted.

"Oh, Watkins," he called after me as I was just about to step out of the alley, "The word for raincoat is *dozhdevik*. Make sure you buy one before going back to that scow. Wouldn't want to make our friends suspicious."

"How did you know I was looking for a raincoat?"

The major twisted his once broken nose into a scowl before turning for the opposite end of the alley.

"I warned the admiral," he said under his breath.

I resisted the urge to look behind me as I went down the village's dirt street. His boys had followed me all day, the major said. That was both comforting and disturbing at the same time. Everywhere my eyes went now, I saw someone suspicious looking at me; a kid running down the road trying to catch his dog, a woman walking with a baby in her arms, a man coughing into a rag on the corner. I came to the dress shop again and went inside. The same bell over the door tinkled again as I entered. The female proprietor clasped her hands in front of her. She didn't look quite so pleased to see me this time. Now, almost fluent in Russian, I shook my lapels at her and said, *dozhdevik* and showed her my money.

7

The woman caught on pretty fast. With a satisfied smile, I followed her out the door. The dress shop owner stood on the boardwalk, pointed down the street with one hand and gave me a series of instructions in her native tongue. Watching the lefts and rights of her hand motions, I got the idea men's raincoats were available two streets over and to the left. I thanked her for the sign language, gave her fifty kopecks for her trouble and, two streets over and to the left, found a ship's chandlery specializing in all things fishing, seal hunting and whaling. The graybeard owner of the chandlery sold me a slicker, new trousers made for rough handling, two clean shirts and a pair of Russian boots like those worn by my good friend Ivan. The second hand Vladivostok boots bought from a refugee in the city were showing signs of losing a sole. The new boots were more welcome than the raincoat. He also sold me a cardboard box filled with forty-five caliber cartridges. If the major and his marines assaulted the *Orca,* I might need the extra rounds since my pistol only had the seven inside its clip. I changed my clothes right there in the store, leaving my greasy, coal smeared shirt, pants and suspect footwear piled in a corner.

On my way back to the boat, in between glances over my shoulder and scowls at any suspicious looking local who made eye contact, I thought about what the major said, about taking the *Orca* by force. Bohdan and his Lewis had a clear field of fire in every direction. The only way to get to the *Orca* was by rowboat. Bohdan slaughtered a dozen or more Bolshevik soldiers when we made our escape from Vladivostok. The Czech might kill all the major's marines before they even got close. I stuck the box of bullets in my pocket. That wasn't going to happen. I'd shoot both him and Ivan before I let Bohdan get off a single round. Standing on the rocky beach, I thought about just how I would accomplish that while watching Laughing Billy row the dinghy towards the shore.

"Well," the Czech said as the bow of our water taxi touched the gravel, "look at you in your finery."

"You know," I said, "we could move the *Orca*. Tie her up along the dock there. Stop all this rowing back and forth."

"I like the water between us and the enemy. Tied to a dock, the Bolsheviks would take us in minutes. If they try rowing a boat into the bay, I will shoot them all," he said with a smile.

Exactly what I was thinking. Water sloshed in the bottom of the dinghy as he rowed us back to the boat. My new boots were doing a good job of keeping the ocean away from my toes.

"How do you know the countess?"

"I know everyone," he said with a laugh. "I often wonder at how I came to be here. I'm an educated man, you know."

"You didn't seem like you weren't."

The oars dipped steadily. *Orca* wallowed in the bay ahead of us.

"Where were you when the war started?" he asked.

"Which one? The revolution? I don't remember. Probably somewhere on the Yangtze."

"Not this Russian thing. The Great War. The one that

caused so many little wars after it. In 1914, when the Serbs killed that Hapsburg bastard, I saw an opportunity for my homeland. The Czar declared for Serbia after the Hungarians sent in their army and I knew the time had come." He rested on his oars. "I taught economics at the university in Prague, you know."

"Did you?" I tapped the barrel of the Lewis leaning against a thwart. "Didn't take you for the academic type."

"Oh but I was, Stick. I was, but I was also young, naïve for the future and full of nationalism. I knew the Great War was Bohemia's chance to throw off the Austrian oppressors and end their empire. The Russians were going to do it and all because some Serbian shot a man in Sarajevo."

"There were eighteen of us. Czechs like me. We went east together to find the Russians. I remember thinking it would be glorious." Bohdan didn't laugh now. "The trenches were a lot of things, but glorious wasn't one of them." He moved an oar out of his way. "Three years later, we eighteen were five, and I had learned things about myself. Two things really. One," he tapped the wooden stock of the Lewis, "I was very good at killing my fellow man. Two, I was even better at listening to them. People told me things, and I learned how to ask the right questions. Then came Russia's defeat and withdrawal from the war. By then, we Czechs had formed our own unit. Sixty thousand of us, but our homeland still wasn't free of the Austrians. Russia, the country we had fought and died for, suddenly didn't want us here anymore. Where to go? What to do? Then the most amazing thing of all happened. Some upstart from Moscow started preaching a new religion. The masses listened and everything went very badly wrong. All around us, Russians started killing Russians."

"The Bolsheviks," I said.

Bohdan nodded his head. "They didn't like us, these new Reds, and they wanted nothing to do with our Austrian war. We Czechs were cut off from the west so, we went east. We took their prized railroad right out from under them. I'll tell you something, Stick. He who controls the Trans-Siberian controls Siberia. I knew that. We all knew that. So we marched east, killing a lot of Bolsheviks along the way.

"The White Army said they supported us, but the truth was the other way around. The Whites were almost as useless as the Reds. If the Legion hadn't been here, Lenin and that bunch would have ended this war two years ago." Bohdan started to row again.

"I met the countess in Kazan. Does that answer your question?"

The dinghy bumped the side of the *Orca*.

"The countess told me someone diverted a part of the gold train elsewhere. She said she knew the man that did it. That was your work, wasn't it?"

Bohdan smiled, but didn't say anything.

"You must have been someone of importance to do that."

Bohdan laughed. "What do you mean, must have been? Look at me now. I have everything a man could ask for. A place to sleep, agreeable companions, one of whom is quite lovely, stimulating conversation and a promise of a wealthy retirement. What else could a poor Czech want from this life?"

"You never talk about the Legion."

He shrugged. "War stories are for grandchildren. But you are right, Stick. I was important. Two years ago, the Legion came to an understanding with the Bolsheviks. They wanted the Czechs out of their country and we didn't want to be here any longer than we had to. What should have been easy to do wasn't. The Whites wanted us to stay and fight for them. The Japanese wanted us between them and the Red Army. The Legion just wanted to go home. So, we struck a bargain."

"There are men, you read about them in history books, men who, when adversity arises feel a calling. They become great men, leaders, someone to follow. Unfortunately, Admiral Kolchak was not such a man. He was a fool. Believe me, Russia is better off without him. The Reds wanted him and they wanted the treasury back, whatever was left of it. We gave them the admiral and a mountain of gold for safe passage down the Trans-Siberian.

"It isn't easy moving sixty thousand men. Especially when Reds kept tearing up tracks and shooting at boxcars. Kolchak and the gold stopped that. The Legion was allowed to go. But Stick, it was an awful lot of gold. I saw it with my own two eyes." He smiled. "It was my idea. The whole thing. With the help of some friends, I managed to divert part of the payment to the Bolsheviks. Why not? This wasn't our country, and Russia had made peace with the Austrians. They wanted to throw us all out, the Legion I mean, send us home with nothing. It wasn't even hard to do. The Bolsheviks demanded Kolchak and the treasury, but who's to say how much gold remained in the vault? It was what we told them it was. So, I made my decision. My friends and I loaded stack after stack of coins, bars and cash into empty ammunition boxes. Hundreds of them. A fortune, Stick. A real fortune. We put it on a boxcar and attached it to one of our armored trains going east."

"What happened to it?"

"Yes, what happened to it? That is a good question. I spent months, years, trying to find out what happened to my gold. The Legion left for home, but I stayed. Those were desperate times, my friend. I never found my gold, but I found something almost as good. I found Ivan. He was on the train and as far as I know, the only one to leave it alive."

"Do you know where it is, the train?"

"I think that is enough questions about the gold. We all have our parts to play in this game. None of us know everything and that is how it should be," he said with a smile. "Keeps everyone friends."

"Bohdan," the countess said. She was standing in the bows of the *Orca*. "Enough stories."

Laughing Billy climbed aboard. I scooped out a few gallons of seawater with a tin can before climbing after him.

"Good evening, Countess. You are looking lovely." She

was wearing the same chocolate colored jodhpurs and white blouse she had worn since we left Vladivostok.

"I'm sure," she said dryly.

The parcel was wrapped in brown paper and tied up with a string. I held it out in front of me. "For you."

Every woman I've ever known likes surprise presents. The countess was no different. For a moment, the strain of being stuck on a sinking boat left her face and I saw the woman I knew in the cafe.

"What is it?" she asked, taking the parcel from my hands. Pulling the string, she unwrapped the paper.

"It's not much," I said. "Just plain cotton, but I thought you might like a change. I hope it fits. It was the smallest I could find."

The countess shook out the cloth. The old graybeard who sold it to me would have called it tan, the matron in the dress shop, antique ivory or some such flowery name. The countess just called it clean. If you've never had to wear the same clothes over and over, day after day, you can't really appreciate what a clean shirt means.

"Why, Mr. Watkins."

She smiled, that radiant, male hypnotizing smile; the same smile she had shown me when seduction was on the menu. Pulling the shirt to her face, she closed her eyes and inhaled the clean newness.

"Once, men brought me French perfume and flowers." She laughed.

It was the first time I'd heard her laugh since she barged into my hotel room.

"Now, they bring me cotton shirts." Holding the cloth before her, she admired the shirt like it was a new evening gown. "I still don't like you, Mr. Watkins, but I like your gift." Pirouetting a tight circle on the *Orca's* foredeck, the shirt held up in front of her, she said, "I must change for dinner."

As she went by me, heading for the ladder below and its smelly privacy, she paused for a moment then kissed me on the cheek.

8

Dinner was served in the *Orca's* afterthought of a galley. The polite term for four people crowded into the small space is snug. A more accurate term would be uncomfortably cramped. With elbows touching the person sitting next to you and feet stepping on the toes of whoever was sitting opposite, the meal was a constant invasion of personal space. Bohdan was lucky. The countess shared his side of the table. I had Ivan, a man with no concept of personal space.

The big Russian served up the last of his ham, roasted potatoes, more cabbage, and some concoction he created with the stewed tomatoes. He wasn't half bad at cooking. I wouldn't call him a chef, but I've certainly eaten worse.

The countess was in fine spirits. I like to think it was my small gift that changed her mood. Maybe it was the clean shirt or maybe it was the decisions that were being made around that table. Whichever, she laughed a lot that evening, wearing her antique ivory shirt that was two sizes too large for her with the sleeves rolled to her elbows. The galley was warm from Ivan's dinner, so she kept her collar unfastened. I caught myself more than once admiring the display of white skin at her throat.

As for my spirits, I tried to put on my happy face. We all knew we couldn't stay where we were for much longer. It was only a matter of days before some Red foraging party stumbled onto our little seaside getaway. The four of us took a vote. The tally was three to one, me being the one and they being the three. The countess wanted to try our luck a little farther up the coast. Ivan and the Czech agreed.

"It's too dangerous," I told them. "You need to understand. There's no safety on that boiler now. If something goes wrong again, we'll boil. All of us," I said, looking at the two other men sitting at the table.

The countess smiled. "We understand, Mr. Watkins. There is danger. It might blow up. It might break again. We know this. It is why we hired you and paid you so well."

She reached across the table and tapped my chest. Her finger traced a rectangular path around the ingot.

"So very well," she added. "It is decided. Tomorrow you will, what did you call it, get the steam up? I want to be gone as soon as it is light. You will do this."

"Da," Ivan said.

I looked at Bohdan, the master spy. He shrugged.

"I understand we must leave before the enemy discovers us, but," he said emphatically, "I am through with working in there." He pointed a thumb at the closed boiler room hatch. "Stick can do it. Like you said, Countess, we paid him for his expertise in these matters."

"Fine," I said. "In the morning, I'll raise steam." It wouldn't matter, I told myself. One of the major's marines would be here tomorrow to buy this wreck and the countess would have her maneuver. The vote was just play acting as far as I was concerned.

Some previous tenant of our boat had carved a chessboard in the galley tabletop. There were no pieces onboard, but Ivan used bits of this and that from the engine room to make up the players. A bolt with one nut a king; with two nuts, a queen. Washers, screws and other bits of this and that turned into pawns, rooks, knights and bishops. A can of red paint gave color to half the pieces. Our dinner finished, and the armies arrayed for battle, he and Bohdan settled down for their game. The countess and I went topside for air. She brought along Ivan's never empty flask.

The dinghy was on deck. It couldn't be left floating in the water for very long or it would sink. I rolled it over, slapped the bottom with my handkerchief a few times, then offered the countess her choice of seating.

"True chivalry," she said.

My evening companion perched on the keel while I sat on the *Orca's* railing.

"Not what you expected, is it Mr. Watkins."

"I'm not sure what I expected. Except getting rich."

"What will you do after we recover the gold? You can't go back to America. They will imprison you."

"Australia," I said after a moment's thought. "I went there once. Nice country and they speak the same language I do. After a while, you can even understand them."

"And your family?"

The countess turned her very blue eyes on me, almost as if she were inspecting me for some unknown faults.

"What will you tell them, Mr. Watkins?"

"Don't really have much of a family anymore. I've got a brother in Washington State. He builds boats. Gotten pretty good at it I hear, too. Have you heard of the place?"

"Of course. The American capitol."

"Close enough. What about you, Countess? You can't stay in Russia. What are your plans?"

"Russia," she said, a touch of sadness in her voice. "No, Ivan and I cannot stay." She leaned forward, a conspiratorial twinkle in her eye. "Once, I had foolish notions of using the money to restore Imperial Russia. I'm related to the Romanovs, you know. I would be another Catherine the

Great."

She laughed. It wasn't a scornful laugh. It was the laughter one uses when thinking about impossible ideas.

"Irena the Great sits on a rotted fishing boat wearing a fisherman's shirt. I don't think anyone will be calling me czarina anytime soon."

"You have relatives, somebody to go to?"

"I have an aunt. She's a baroness. She and her husband, the Baron, are in Paris now. The last I heard from her was three years ago. She had started taking in sewing. Her husband, the baron, had a job driving a taxi."

The countess uncorked Ivan's flask, took a sip, wrinkled her nose for a moment then handed the flask to me.

"I will not spend my days mending someone else's linen."

I took a drink of the vodka. "No brothers or sisters? Parents you could go to?"

The countess looked very sad for a moment, then reached for the flask. She took another swallow.

"My mother was a gentle woman. Always kind to me and my brother. We were nine years in London. Had I told you that before?"

"Something about the English court. You told me your father was posted there once."

"While we sat in the window of our cafe." She smiled. "I see you were paying attention, Mr. Watkins. He was military attaché to the Court of Saint James for nine years. It's where I learned your language." She held up Ivan's flask. "This, I learned in Russia." She took another drink. "We came home to Saint Petersburg when the Great War started. We had a beautiful home, Mr. Watkins. Not far from the Winter Palace. My father wanted to do his part at the front, but they said he was too old. He was posted to the Ministry instead. When the Bolsheviks started their revolution in seventeen, my father was away. I was at home with a cold. People were shouting and arguing in the foyer. I heard them from my room, so I came downstairs to see what was wrong. They all turned to watch me when I came down those stairs. Every eye. One of our footmen was standing at the base of the stairs. His sleeve was torn." She touched her fisherman's shirt. "I remember that so clearly. The left sleeve. I listened to what he said, then I gathered what men I could, servants and a handful of guards, and went to where the footman said he left my mother and brother. Peter was his name. He was only twelve. The mob had stopped my mother's carriage and drug her and my brother out into the street. I found their bodies hanging from a lamp post. Someone hung a sign around my mother's neck. 'Bourgeois' in hand painted black letters. I didn't even know what it meant."

The vodka was bringing out her Russian accent.

"I'm sorry."

"She was a gentle woman. I never saw her hurt a fly. Peter had only just started wearing long pants."

The countess managed a smile. It wasn't a very nice smile.

"I cut their bodies down, then I tried to shoot the footman." She touched her forehead. "Here. Unfortunately, I wasn't very good with handguns in those days and the man got away. That was the day I started running." She looked about her at the half rotted hulk of the *Orca*. "I've been running ever since." She sighed. "I've talked too much. I shouldn't drink Ivan's vodka. It makes my mornings a misery and my tongue too lose."

She rose from her seat in the dinghy. I stood with her.

"Countess," I began.

"Shut up, Mr. Watkins." She said it softly. "I thank you for my lovely shirt, but I still don't like you." She turned to go, then stopped. "We aren't going to be lovers, you and I, so please stop looking at me the way you do. The promise you saw in the cafe was just a lure to get your help. I am not the woman you think I am. Not anymore."

She left me standing on *Orca's* rotted deck as she went below. Ivan's never empty flask sat on the deck next to the overturned dinghy. It took me half an hour to prove it had a bottom after all. The countess and I would share a headache in the morning. Had I been looking at her like that? I had, of course. She was terribly attractive, after all.

Not going to be lovers, she said. I thought of the major and his marines sitting somewhere out there in the dark waiting to take away the Czech master spy.

Lovers. No, I suppose not.

9

Breakfast reminded me of what condemned men's last meals must be like. All three of my shipmates kept looking at me, no doubt expecting last minute protestations on my part. Ivan and Bohdan picked up our empty plates.

"I'll wash them," I said. "It's my turn."

"No, Mr. Watkins," the countess said. "You agreed last night. Get us ready to leave." She pointed at the boiler room hatch.

I felt like a misbehaving nine year old being sent to my room. Where the hell was the promised steam engine buyer? "I need to dump the ashes out of the furnace."

"Bohdan will help you," the countess replied.

Our master spy's eyes were thin slits of protest.

"You will," she ordered the Czech, cutting off his protest before he could say it.

The countess wasn't a woman to be trifled with. Besides, she was wearing her Mauser again. Probably so she could shoot me in the stomach if I refused to boil water. Someone shouted on the shore.

"What does that fool mean? Are we awake?" Ivan asked.
He went to the ladder and climbed slowly up the rungs. Ivan
was not a man designed for climbing a boat's ladders.

"I'll just go see about getting steam up," I said. I made sure
to look unhappy even though I was beaming on the inside. The
marines were here.

It wasn't long before the countess came into the boiler
room. I was busy wiping a valve wheel with a rag.

"Mr. Watkins!" She looked thrilled. "I think we have a
solution."

"Oh? I'm just about to strike a match." I pointed to the
open grate in front of the furnace and the fresh pile of coal
awaiting the flame.

"There is a man. Ivan has rowed him aboard. He has asked
if our boat is for sale!" The countess clapped her hands.

"He hasn't seen it yet," I said. "Only a fool would buy this
tub. She's sinking at anchor."

"He does not care, Mr. Watkins. He doesn't want a tub."
She pointed at my rusty engine. "He wants that. He needs it
for his sawmill."

Someone was coming down the ladder. The countess
moved to my side. "Don't smile so much," I told her. "He'll
lower his offer if you look too eager."

The smile vanished, replaced by a frown and a wrinkled
forehead. I almost laughed.

Ivan led the way down. A man of maybe thirty years
followed after him. Bohdan stayed topside. There wasn't
enough room for five people below decks all at once. Four
was pushing it.

I'm not sure what I expected to see. A crewcut marine
trying to look like a Russian? Whatever I was expecting, the
man standing beside my engine didn't look like a marine. He
slouched, and he had a limp. His face was pock marked from
either really bad acne as a teen or a mild case of smallpox, and
he had a goatee. His Russian must have been excellent because

Ivan and he were having a lively discussion. The newcomer looked at me briefly, said something to Ivan, who then waved a hand in my general direction. Never mind the expert in the room, the wave said.

"He wants know it works," Ivan said to me.

"*Da,*" I said. My Russian was improving with every day spent in Siberia. The countess snorted, almost laughed, and then made a neutral mask of her face. I must play her in poker someday. Her bluffs were awful.

"Tell him it will take me a couple of hours to get steam up." I motioned to the engine's triple row of cylinders. "Then the little metal parts will go in and out of the bigger metal parts and the shaft will go round and round."

Ivan translated. I think he actually translated word for word. The newcomer pulled a silver watch from his vest pocket, then said something to Ivan.

"He says he doesn't have two hours. He has an appointment," Ivan said.

"Tell him the engine brought us here from Vladivostok," I told the big Russian. "He will get many years of good service out of it once he breaks up the hulk that is holding it."

The newcomer listened to Ivan, grunted something in return, then made his way back to the ladder. Ivan followed. The countess was nearly hysterical with pent up joy. As soon as the pair of men were up the ladder, she squealed something feminine, then wrapped her arms around my neck.

"We are leaving, Mr. Watkins. He said he has cash in his pocket!"

I put my arms around her waist and hoisted her in the air. It was one of those moments. Her face was very close to mine. I think I held her like that for just an instant too long. She stopped moving.

"Put me down." She didn't shout it or make it sound commanding. She said it quietly.

I did.

"We should go up," she said. "Ivan will handle the sale. He

is good with details."

I followed her up the ladder. The major's engine buyer was being rowed ashore by Bohdan. He had left the Lewis balanced against *Orca's* railing. I watched Bohdan as the leaky boat got closer and closer to the shore. Ivan and the countess were talking. Ivan handed her a handful of rubles. They weren't watching the dinghy.

"What is it, Mr. Watkins?" the countess asked.

"Nothing." The few scattered buildings along the beachfront looked the same as they always had. Bohdan reached the shore and our boat buyer jumped onto the sand and gravel. It was the perfect moment. The major could take him now. Even the slouching, pockmarked buyer could take him. All he had to do was pull a pistol and Laughing Billy was caught. I waited. The countess said something. Ivan said something. I didn't listen. Bohdan backed his oars. The buyer even gave the dinghy a shove.

"Mr. Watkins?"

"Yes, Countess."

"You look peculiar."

"Do I? Must be something I ate." Bohdan was rowing hard for the *Orca*. "How much did we get?" I asked Ivan.

"Two hundred fifty."

"How much for a horse?" I asked.

"We have enough," the countess said.

"Fifty," Ivan told me.

I understood. They had enough money to buy four horses, but the *Orca's* sale belonged to the three of them. I wasn't one of the inner circle. Outsiders paid their own way. Reaching for my wallet, I counted out fifty rubles and gave it to the Russian.

"I'll trust your judgment in the purchase," I said. "My luck, I'd buy a plow horse."

Ivan grunted as he took my money.

"You know the ones I want, Ivan," the countess told him.

The Russian grunted again.

"What about the boat?" I asked.

"He will have men here in week to take engine apart," Ivan told me.

"Let's hope she floats that long," I added.

"You are very negative, Mr. Watkins," the countess said. "The boat did everything we asked of her."

"Didn't you call it a wretched hulk yesterday?"

The countess laughed. She said something to Ivan in Russian. He went to the wheelhouse and disappeared down the ladder as the dinghy bumped against the hull. Bohdan climbed aboard.

"I don't like it," he said. "Something is wrong."

The countess waved the bills at him. "You and Mr. Watkins have much in common." Her trunk thumped on the deck followed by a grunting Ivan. "Ivan, take Bohdan with you and if that horse thief asks for more money, tell him I will shoot him. Mr. Watkins, you should pack."

I wiggled my lapels. "I am packed, Countess."

Three hours later, Ivan and the master spy were back with four saddled horses. I rowed the countess ashore for the last time. She sat in the stern still wearing my antique ivory gift. The temperature was cooler this morning, cool enough to warrant wearing the red coat she had on when she evicted me from my Vladivostok hotel room. The leather belt and its holstered Mauser was around her waist.

I don't know a lot about horses, but even my untrained eye could tell the four animals standing on the beach were poor examples of the breed. Two looked underfed. One, a tall brown animal with three white feet and a white spot between its eyes tried to bite the horse next to it. I made a mental note not to ride that one. Ivan's mount was the only one that looked like what I thought of as a saddle horse.

I pulled the dinghy far up on the beach. The countess took my hand as I helped her out of the boat. The surf washed around my feet as she hopped onto the dry sand.

"Thank you, Mr. Watkins."

I smiled.

"You bought packs?" she asked Ivan.

"I bought everything we need."

The trunk was sitting in the bottom of the boat. Ivan tossed a canvas bag alongside it, then dismounted from his horse. Opening the trunk, he started transferring its contents into the pack. There wasn't much. The two dresses I had seen the countess wearing in our cafe rendezvous, a pair of women's shoes that went well with the dresses but not with half sunk boats and worn out horses, some undergarment, her other blouse and a pair of spurs.

"I'll take those," the countess said. She turned to me. "My father's." The countess went to the biting horse and dropped the spurs into saddlebags then swung herself into the saddle. I waited. The horse twisted its head, obviously looking for a leg to chew. But it didn't bite her. Instead, it just straightened its neck and stood there, docile as a poodle. The countess touched her heels to his flanks and walked the biter around in a circle a few times. She seemed satisfied with the animal's circling abilities.

Ivan removed a felt bag from the trunk. Everyone watched the bag. Gold, everyone's eyes said. The big Russian carried the bag to the countess' saddlebag and dropped it inside. I guess the gold reserves went where she went. Bohdan took two flat, round magazine drums out of the trunk, food for the Lewis, and dropped them into his own canvas bag. I was the only one in our party with nothing to pack.

Orca looked terribly abandoned. I suppose she really was. In a week, if no one pumped her out, she would be half sunk. Someone would have to tow her out of the way before she sank in the center of the small harbor.

"Take the mare, Mr. Watkins," the countess said.

I tried to remember the last time I sat in a saddle. I think I was nine. There was a carnival in town and you could go round and round this little corral while an old man in a straw hat walked in front. It was easy. The mare looked at me with big round eyes. I think she knew I had no clue how to work the leather reins running back from her bit. The countess started laughing. Bohdan laughed as well, but he was always laughing at something.

"What?"

"So, our naval expert isn't an expert with horses," she said.

"I know what I'm doing." I didn't, but I wasn't going to tell her that.

The countess pointed at the last horse in the string. "I said the mare, Mr. Watkins. You're scaring the gelding. You do know what a gelding is?" She smiled, then made a scissor motion with her fingers.

"He doesn't know what is mare," Ivan said.

"I prefer geldings to mares," I told them. My foot was in the stirrup. The gelding danced sideways. I had to hop one-legged to keep up. Everyone laughed again.

I should have taken the dinghy when the boiler went and left them all to eat rats.

10

Agony is only a word and after four days sitting in a saddle, I knew it well. My thighs were rubbed raw from straddling a moving horse's body hour after hour and my back felt like I had damaged a dozen vertebrae. The gelding, an evil tempered beast, took great delight in walking under every low hanging tree limb on the road no matter which way I pulled the reins. What was worse than the animal's inability to walk a straight line was its gait. The horse had a bone cracking stumble that was impossible to get used to. I was glad someone had gelded the beast. Even the saddle sold to us by the horse thief was painful. There was a lump in the center of the seat that, after four days, made the part you sat on feel like it was made of cactus thorns.

The rain started on our second day of riding and hadn't stopped for more than an hour since. It wasn't a hard rain, but, exposed as we were, it might as well have been. My companions rode their horses with hunched shoulders and heads down. Only Ivan rode as if we were on a pleasure trip through the forests of Eastern Siberia.

The countess set Ivan to the task of forward lookout. Everyone knew the Red Army could be anywhere and it wouldn't do for the four of us to ride blindly down these muddy roads. So the Russian left us every morning, coming back just before sundown with mud splattered legs and soaked to the skin. He had gone back to his cavalry roots. I think he was enjoying himself.

I found myself missing the comfortable surroundings of the *Orca*. The old tub stank, was rotten to its keel and had a busted engine, but at least it kept the rain off. If the major and his boys were following, and I assumed they were, I hoped they were faring better than I was.

Bohdan rode in front on the mare, his Lewis balanced across the pommel of his saddle. Even though we were all bone weary, the soldier in him kept a watchful eye on the trees. At least the rain made him stop laughing at the world around him. If he hadn't stopped when he did, I think I might have taken the major up on his order and shot him. One can only tolerate so much cheerfulness from one's fellow humans.

The countess rode beside me looking like a natural born horsewoman. She was holding up well. She would be. She was dry. Yes, I had given her my new raincoat. It's what an officer and a gentleman does. They taught me that at the Academy. So we rode, miserable, tired and wet down a muddy lane, doing our best to stay alert for bandits, Bolsheviks and malcontents.

Last night, we all saw flashes of light on the horizon. It was the Red's artillery shelling the defenses around Vladivostok. Or maybe they had turned their guns on the city proper by now. I thought about the Mongol prostitute with the shiny black eyes and the rundown hotel. I wondered if she or it were still standing. Now, after plodding along down the muddy lane for half a day, we could hear the low rumble of distant explosions. They were a constant reminder that we were drawing ever closer to the Bolshevik lines.

"Do you know where we are?" I asked the countess.

"Do not worry, Mr. Watkins. We cannot get lost. The railway," she pointed ahead of us, "is somewhere up there."

It would be easy to get lost in this country. The muddy path we were on followed the natural course of the hills, meaning it meandered according to the geography. There were crossroads, most not much more than trails, every eight or nine miles. Often, the road itself forked left or right. Usually, we took the right fork unless the left looked more used. A few times a day, we would see a group of people coming towards us in the distance. They seldom stayed in sight once they saw us, taking to the surrounding trees until we passed. The countess said this was bandit country. Travelers down these roads avoided contact with people who had a certain look and we obviously had that look. However, a few brave souls either too tired or not noticing until it was too late passed us going the opposite way. Bohdan shouted questions at several groups, but whatever response he got, it didn't seem to satisfy. Bohdan was growing fractious. I don't think he liked riding so close to the Red artillery. I can't say as I blamed him.

An old man somewhere between seventy and death and leaning hard on a cane rounded a curve in front of us. A woman walked beside him with some kind of straw bag on her arm. She had a scarf covering her head, a long dress falling to her ankles, and no shoes on her feet. They both looked like they had about reached the end of whatever road life had them on.

Bohdan shouted something at them as they walked past. The old man waved a hand dismissively and kept walking. The Czech yanked the reins of his horse and trotted farther up the road as the countess dismounted. I stopped my horse and tried to work the latest kink out of my spine. She said something in Russian to the old couple. The gray beard looked distrustful until the countess went to her saddlebag and removed a double handful of potatoes. She dropped them into the old woman's bag, then said something again. The old couple started talking then, pointing behind them and to either side of the forest. The man's voice was low and scratchy. The old lady's was high pitched and sounded almost like a wail. She started to cry as she pointed down the road. The countess said something else to them, then stepped aside to let them pass. The old man gave me a peculiar look as he limped by. I nodded my head as the countess remounted her horse. The old man kept walking, still leaning on his stick for support.

"What was all the pointing and tears about?" I asked.

"She said Comrade Lenin is a few hours walk down the road. The Bolsheviks have set up a checkpoint where the north-south road crosses the east-west. They are stopping everyone and asking questions. If they don't like your answer, they shoot you." The countess paused for a moment. "The old woman said there are a dozen bodies in a ditch."

Bohdan turned his horse around.

"She said there are many soldiers, and they have bought the service of a thousand Cossacks ready to murder everyone in Vladivostok. She also said the czar was seen two days ago on a gray horse coming with the Imperial Guard."

I looked at the two old people hobbling down the road. They looked like every other Russian peasant you see fleeing the joys of revolution.

"Do you believe her? About the soldiers, I mean."

"She started to cry when she talked about the ditch. Bohdan," the countess said. "Ride ahead and find Ivan. He won't be far. Tell him to go west, across country. The old woman said there is another road that way. She said we will come to it by sundown if we hurry."

"Go forward?" Bohdan asked.

I don't think he liked the idea.

"You heard her," the Czech said. "A thousand Cossacks in front of us."

"A Russian peasant sees ten Cossacks and they say there were a hundred," the countess said. "Find Ivan and tell him."

"A hundred of those bastards is a hundred too many. Ivan

is no fool. He can take care of himself. We go west now, through the woods to the old woman's road before they come riding over that hill." He walked his horse closer towards us. "Tell her, Stick. We have to move now."

"I think the old woman might be a bit confused," I said. "The czar is dead."

The countess drew her Mauser. She rested the pistol on the pommel of her saddle as if she always carried it there.

"Bohdan," she said again, "go and find Ivan." Her voice was calm. "Tell him to meet us on the other road. If he cannot find us, tell him I will wait for him at the crossroad."

"What crossroad?" Bohdan asked. "We have passed a dozen in the last four days."

"He will know the one I mean."

"And what happens if I can't find Ivan? What if he is already lying face down in the old woman's ditch? What then? You and Stick go on to get the treasure while I get cut down by Cossacks?"

"If Ivan is dead," the countess said, "there is no gold. You know he is the only one left alive who knows where it is."

I turned my head to look at the countess.

"I'll be damned if I will ride towards enemy cavalry, girl." His hand moved to the Lewis sitting across his lap.

The countess pointed her broom handle at the Czech. Her arm was steady as she sighted down the pistol's long barrel.

"Bohdan, I forgave you once for disobeying orders when you left the *Orca's* engine room. I will not forgive you again."

"I do not take orders, Countess. Not from you and not from him."

He looked at me when he said that last part.

"You forget, the only reason there is any gold is because I engineered it. Me, Wilhelm Bohdan." His hand moved towards the trigger of the machinegun.

"I will shoot you five times before you can lift that gun," the countess said. The Mauser's hammer clicked twice as her gloved thumb pulled it back to the firing position.

117

What, I thought, would the major do in this situation? "Look, let's everyone uncock our trigger fingers and think about this. I'll ride ahead a mile or two and see if I can find Ivan."

Bohdan laughed. "There," he said. "Problem solved. Stick will go."

"No," the countess said. "I did not tell him to go. I told you. Go and show us all how mighty the Czech Legions soldiers are. Impress us with your prowess in front of the enemy."

"I'll go," I said.

"They will kill you before the hour is out, Mr. Watkins. I've seen children who ride a horse better than you."

Probably true, I thought. I put the gelding between the Russian and the Czech. "Bohdan, she's right. I can barely hang on to this nag when he gallops. Besides, I can't leave a woman alone here. Not with soldiers shooting people."

"I go where I please," the countess said.

"Ha," Bohdan spat. "Is that what you were doing when I found you selling yourself to soldiers in Kazan? Going where you please?"

A shot from a pistol is a frightfully loud thing when you are sitting on a horse a few feet from the business end of the barrel. The blast was so loud, it made the gelding do something I wasn't prepared for. I'm not sure I could have prepared for it even if I had known it was about to happen. He reared, throwing his front legs into the air and at the same time throwing me over his rump. The Mauser roared again as my back hit the mud. Cathedral bells echoed around the inside of my skull as my breath left me in a grunt. I laid there for a moment, struggling to make my diaphragm work again. I don't remember the last time I had my breath knocked out of me but the sensation of not being able to breathe was just as unpleasant as I remembered. Horse hooves stomped the mud uncomfortably close to my head. I rolled away from the animal and saw Bohdan hunched over the neck of his horse galloping away down the road. Holy hell, she shot him and I had lost Bohdan. The major was going to explode like a howitzer's shell when he found out.

I put a hand over my ear. I wasn't sure, but I think my eardrum was gone. The countess was staring down at me from her saddle.

"You spoiled my aim, Mr. Watkins. I missed the cockroach with my first shot. The second one was better."

My lungs started to work again. Getting to my feet, I felt the clingy dampness of fresh mud sticking to my back. I managed to suck air into my chest, then cough it out. Bohdan was riding hard down the road. I don't think he was looking for Ivan. The major was going to court martial me if the Reds didn't dump my corpse in a ditch first.

"That wasn't necessary," I managed to say between gasps for air.

"My father taught me to never let an underling disobey a direct order. He disobeyed. So, I shot him." She looked around her. "Where is your horse?"

"And did your father teach you that, when enemy cavalry are near, shoot your goddamned awfully loud pistol a couple of times so they will know where to find you?"

The countess stood up in her stirrups. "There he is. At the edge of the trees, over there." Sticking her pistol back in its holster, she slid her boot out of the stirrup and offered me her hand. "Climb up. You are right, Mr. Watkins. The shots were very loud. We will have to make haste for the other road."

I reached for her hand.

"The machinegun first, if you please."

The Lewis was lying in the mud a few feet away. Bohdan wasn't going to like that. He kept that gun as clean as a clock's gears. The Lewis was muddy but didn't seem to be damaged. We had four just like it in the armory on my old gunboat. It's a decent weapon although heavy. The gunner's mates on the *Devilfish* liked them for their drum capacity. You can do a lot of damage with almost a hundred bullets between reloads. I handed it to the countess, then put my foot in her stirrup. Climbing and pulling, I managed to get myself situated behind her.

"I have never seen a grown man fall off a horse like that before. I'm surprised you didn't break something."

She slapped the reins across her horse and we took off. I wrapped my arms around her waist and held on, vowing that once this was over, to never ride a horse again.

11

The gelding didn't go far. Running was something he might have done in his youth, but I suspected the animal's age was probably on a par with the barefoot Russian peasant. The horse looked at me with malevolent brown eyes as I took the reins again.

"If we starve and have to eat the horses, I'm shooting you first," I told the animal. Swinging myself into the saddle, I felt a fresh pain at the base of my spine.

The countess laughed.

"What's so funny?" I asked. I couldn't see anything at all humorous in our situation.

My riding companion pursed her lips. "Not having a good time, are we Mr. Watkins." The countess waved a gloved hand in my general direction. "I do believe there might be a spot on your left shoulder than isn't covered in mud." She shook her head. "You rolled off your horse like *you* were shot instead of the Czech."

I considered asking for the return of my raincoat. "You didn't need to shoot Bohdan. Have you ever heard the phrase strength in numbers? We might need him pretty soon if that old woman was right."

The countess shrugged. "I did not want to shoot him. He forced me into a corner. He will come back, probably with an excellent story to explain his actions. Our Czech friend always has an excellent story."

"Countess, you just shot the man. Why would he come back?"

The countess rode her horse closer to mine, then handed me Bohdan's Lewis. The gun was heavy, forcing her to use both hands to pass the weapon over.

"I grazed his ear, Mr. Watkins. If I wanted to, I would have hit him in the heart. He will come back. If Cossacks really are about, Bohdan won't like being alone. He's always been afraid of Cossacks. And he loves that gun. His violin, he calls it. I've never seen him without it. But even if there are no Cossacks and he hadn't dropped his prized toy, he would still come back." She stroked her horse's neck. "Because more than anything, anything in all this world, Bohdan wants his share of the gold. Only Ivan knows where the gold is and," the countess turned her horse for the trees, "where I go, Ivan will follow. If Ivan is with me, Bohdan will not be far behind."

"I wouldn't come back," I said, turning my horse to follow behind hers. "How will Ivan find us? For that matter, he should have been back by now. If he was close, he would have heard those shots."

"I do not know where Ivan is, Mr. Watkins. I can only assume he is cut off by the enemy and riding around them. That's what I would do if it were me out there."

Or lying in the old woman's ditch with a nice round hole in the back of his head, I thought.

"As for finding us, that will be easy for my Ivan. He knows where we are going after all. I did not need Bohdan to tell him to meet us at the crossroads. Ivan would have gone there anyway if we became separated."

"Because of the gold?" I asked. The nag walked under a tree branch, forcing me to duck.

"No, Mr. Watkins. Because he and I agreed the crossroads would be our rally point if we became separated." She turned around in her saddle. "Or if we had trouble with the Czech."

"What if you have trouble with me?"

My answer was another one of those smiles she tossed out when it suited her; just a flash of white teeth as if I had said something witty. She turned back around in her saddle and rode into the forest.

We didn't talk again, not for another hour. The countess rode slowly through the trees, then galloped her horse across the open fields too fast for me to keep up. I lost sight of her many times and was forced to follow her by the hoof prints her horse left on the forest floor. The bouncing of my gelding and the falling rain helped shake off most of the caked mud from my soggy clothes. Hauling the damn Lewis meant I only had one hand to hold on to the saddle. More than once, I almost dropped Bohdan's damn gun. I learned a new definition of misery that day.

I stopped the gelding at the edge of a clearing, or rather the gelding chose to stop. The back of the woman I was trying to keep up with disappeared into the trees on the other side. I started to slap the grandfather I was riding, forcing him to run once again when I noticed the tracks. The ground at the edge of the clearing was torn and chewed by the passing of several horses. The tracks could be weeks or hours old. I had no idea, but seeing them made me think of Cossacks. It wasn't a pleasant thought. The countess rode back into the clearing, then waved her arm for me to follow. I think she was getting tired of waiting for me to catch up. If the countess had been born in America in the previous century, she would have been right at home riding with the pony express.

"Let's go, Beast," I told the nag, "and if we see Cossacks, you better run like a race horse."

By the time we made it across the clearing, the countess was gone again.

I gave up trying to guess how many miles we rode. My aching muscles said it must have been fifty although it was probably closer to twenty. Towards sundown, the clouds broke at last and every once in a while, you could see a big orange ball sinking towards the horizon. At least I knew we were heading west. With only about a half hour of daylight left and with Beast starting to stagger beneath me, I came to the road.

The first thing I did was look at the dirt for horse tracks. I only saw one set, not the sign of a troop's passing. I turned the exhausted horse to follow. There was barely enough light to see by when I caught up to her. She was sitting in her saddle waiting for me.

"Mr. Watkins," she said, as if we chanced to meet on a pleasant evening ride.

"Countess," I replied as nonchalantly as I could. I pointed back the way we had just come. "There were Cossack tracks in that big clearing we crossed."

"There were horse tracks, Mr. Watkins. About six animals, maybe eight, and they were going away from us."

"Cossack horse tracks."

"Horse tracks," she said again.

I wasn't convinced.

"Really, Mr. Watkins. I thought America was all cowboys and Indians? You cannot ride a horse and I had to constantly wait for you to catch up. I do believe I would have lost you in the woods if I hadn't waited and you see Cossacks in a hoof print."

She turned her horse and trotted down a grass covered lane. I hadn't noticed it was there until she started riding down it.

"This way," she called over her shoulder. "Not much farther now."

I followed, feeling like a schoolboy who had just been beaten up by the girl in pigtails and braces. If my second grade friends were here, they would never let me back in our clubhouse again.

The lane went about fifty yards before it ended at a small grove of trees. There was hardly any light left, but you could just make out a house or what was left of one. The roof had collapsed on one side and one of the stone walls had fallen over. The windows had no glass left in them and were now just rectangular black holes in the darkness. Knee high weeds grew thick all around the old farmhouse. The countess rode her horse into the thickest part of the weeds, dismounted, then tied something around her horse's front legs. The animal nudged her with his snout and I waited for the yelp of pain when it sunk those big square teeth into soft flesh. Instead, the countess scratched its nose before pulling the bridle away from its head. The animal began to graze in the tall weeds. I rode the gelding into the weeds beside her horse.

"Hobble your horse, Mr. Watkins." She started to unbuckle the leather strap under her saddle. I know it has a name, the strap. I just couldn't remember what horse people called it.

Dismounting, I made sure I was far enough away from Biter to avoid any unpleasantness. He might nudge her for attention and a pat, but I preferred keeping my distance.

"I've never done that," I confessed. "How tight do I tie the knots?"

"Never mind," she said. "Let me."

I undid the leather strap and pulled the saddle off my horse. We spent a few more minutes taking care of our transportation before heading for the abandoned farmhouse. "I'm surprised you saw this from the road."

"Just luck. While I was waiting for you to catch up, I saw the chimney sticking out of those trees."

She carried her own saddle as we walked. I was loaded down like a pack mule with my own saddle, both sets of canvas bags and Bohdan's thirty-five pound violin. There was no door to the ramshackle cottage. The countess was about to step through the dark opening.

"Mind the spiders," I said.

She froze dead still. I nearly ran into her.

"Spiders?"

Uh huh, I thought. Pony express rider you may be but show you a spider and you'll suddenly want a man's opinion on the situation. I pushed past her and into the interior.

Water dripped from the half collapsed roof, the results of the recent rains. The interior was only a little drier than the forest floor outside, but after four days sleeping on that floor, a roof over my head, even a partial roof, seemed like high luxury to me. I dropped my saddle and the bags on the floor. There were a lot of leaves, but underneath someone had laid big square paving stones. Balancing the Lewis across the saddle, I put my hands on the small of my back and tried to stretch some of the kinks out.

"Mr. Watkins?" the countess asked. She was still standing in the darkness somewhere outside. "I can't see."

I fumbled around inside my pocket and came up with a box of matches.

"Just a second," I told her. The match struck and a small glow filled the interior of the cottage. "Better?"

She stepped cautiously towards the light. "I can't abide spiders. Especially in the dark."

"I don't like horses," I told her. "Put your saddle over there." I turned slowly, not wanting to lose the light from my match. There was a thump behind me as the countess dropped her saddle next to mine. I knelt in front of the stone fireplace. "Let's see if we can get a fire going." The roof was still mostly intact on this side of the cottage. Even so, wind and time had blown a tree limb into the interior. My match went out.

Kneeling down beside me, she said, "Do hurry, Mr. Watkins, and I wish you hadn't mentioned spiders when you did."

I broke off a handful of twigs from the dead limb. They felt dry enough. My second match started a small fire in the hearth. The countess helped, breaking off her own twigs until we had enough light to see by. I added larger branches until we had a sizeable fire roaring away. We both squatted in front of the fire, hands out for warmth. I hadn't realized how cold I was until I felt the heat on my skin. "Better?" I asked.

"Much." She sighed, looked at me kneeling beside her, then back at our fire. Rubbing her hands together in front of the blaze, she seemed like a woman with something on her mind.

"It isn't true," she said finally, her eyes watching the fire.

"That you're afraid of spiders?" I saw a flicker of a smile in the semi darkness.

"No, that part is true. I meant it isn't true what Bohdan said. About me, when he found me in Kazan."

"Ah." I tossed another limb onto our small pyre. The flames hissed and spat as smoke made its way up the chimney. "I didn't think it was," I said after a moment.

The countess said nothing. There was an awkward silence in the ruined farmhouse.

"All my jewels were sold by then." She tossed a handful of sticks into the blaze. "The last of my money was finished. There was nothing left, nothing at all. Even my father was gone; killed fighting somewhere north of the Caspian."

"I'm sorry."

She shrugged. "I was told he died charging the enemy. He was a soldier all his life. If he had to choose, it was probably how he would have wanted to go." She motioned at the canvas pack lying beside her saddle. "Ivan brought me his spurs. It's all I have left of him now. The rest is all gone. I hadn't eaten a decent meal in a week. The Reds were always looking for people like me. They killed us when they found us, the old nobility," she added. "They even drug one of the Romanovs out of a nunnery and murdered her. She wasn't political. Just a nun and still, they killed her. What do you think they would have done to me? I had to keep moving, always trying to stay ahead of the hunters. By the time I made it to Kazan, I was finished. That winter, either I was going to starve, or I was going to freeze."

I broke a limb in half and dropped it in the flames. The countess took the other half from my hand and used it as a poker.

"So, I made my decision, Mr. Watkins. I decided I wasn't going to starve or freeze in the snow. Kazan was full of soldiers. I decided to sell myself."

"Look, Countess."

"Do be quiet, Mr. Watkins. Sometimes you talk when you shouldn't. It's very American of you." The makeshift poker jabbed at the flames. "That's when Bohdan found me. I was sitting on a bench in the snow, shivering in the cold. It was so terribly cold. He came towards me." She curled a finger over her lip. "Big mustache. I saw the uniform and knew what I was going to do. I stood up and smiled. Before I could say anything, anything at all, he said my name. My name, Mr. Watkins. Countess Irena. Ivan and I have been looking everywhere for you. Then he placed his coat over my shoulders."

She stopped poking at the fire and looked at me.

"So, you see, I hadn't sold myself to soldiers as Bohdan claimed. Not yet."

I wasn't sure if she wanted me to talk or not, being an American and all, so I didn't say anything. I just watched the flames burn away our small pile of sticks and twigs.

"I would like to change my blouse now, Mr. Watkins. This one isn't completely dry, even with your raincoat. If I change, will you be a gentleman?"

I stood. "Never let it be said an Academy man isn't a gentleman. The kettle's in my bag. I think I saw a well when we were coming in." Digging around inside my pack, I came out with the pewter kettle and made my way into the darkness outside.

The well, a waist high circle of stones, was just a little way from where we hobbled the horses. There was even a rope looped around a post. Tying the kettle's bail to the rope, I dropped it into the darkness, listened for the splash, then hauled it back up. I turned to our home for the night. Across the night darkened yard, the countess was standing in front of the fire. Outlined by the glow, her back was to me as she faced the flames. The fisherman's shirt slid down bare shoulders as the firelight outlined her body. She turned slightly, probably reaching for the white blouse she had worn aboard *Orca*. A gentleman, she asked. Would I be one for her? I sighed, looked away and examined the rump of Beast, the unpleasant gelding. The horse whinnied.

"Yes," I told the horse. "I know no one would ever know if I looked and yes, I am tempted but, she asked me to be a gentleman."

Biter started to pee.

"Is that your professional opinion?" I asked the animal. After a few minutes, my conversation with the horses at an end, I returned to the cottage.

The fisherman's shirt was hanging by a peg from the mantle. She hadn't tucked the white blouse into her jodhpurs and the tail of the cloth fell loosely around her hips. The unbuttoned collar formed a triangle of white skin at her throat, reminding me of our last cramped meal aboard *Orca*. Her soldier's leather brimmed cap was balanced on the pommel of her saddle. It hadn't done a lot to keep the day's rain off, so she had undone her hair and was trying to dry it in front of the fireplace.

"You're going to catch your death," I told her.

"Says the man who gave up his raincoat."

The ever present Mauser and its leather holster were beside the hat. After days cramped and stuffed into a stinking hulk of a boat and four days in the saddle, the countess looked like a disheveled, damp mess. An attractive, disheveled, damp mess.

"There's cheese," she said, pointing to a yellow wedge with a small knife stuck in its center. "Most of our food was in Bohdan's pack. Had I thought, I would have made the cockroach take it out before I shot him."

"Cheese will do," I said, as I placed the kettle on the fire.

"There are tea leaves as well," the countess added.

"Civilization is still with us," I told the fire.

"And I made you a pallet."

She had, too. My saddle was setting on one side of the fireplace with my blanket stretched out in front of it. Her saddle was on the opposite side of the fire. My raincoat was on the ground in front of it with her blanket atop that. She, at least, wouldn't feel the damp stones beneath her.

"Very nice of you," I told her.

We watched the fire burn for a while. I suppose neither of us felt much like talking. There's something about watching a fire burning in a hearth that eliminates the need for speech. Or maybe we had spent too many days together and all the words were said.

The kettle started to whistle. My dinner companion poured hot water into two tin cups as I sliced the cheese.

"Thank you, Mr. Watkins," she said after the cheese was finished.

"For what?"

"For not looking."

"Oh, that. The horses and I needed a word together, man to man."

"I see. The horses."

I picked up the Lewis and set it against a pile of fallen stones with the barrel pointed down the weed filled lane. Unclipping the pie shaped magazine, I blew into the works before fastening the drum back in place.

"Have you shot a Lewis before?" she asked.

"Once, back on my gunboat. Can you shoot it?"

The countess smiled.

"Of course you can. Probably knock silver dollars out of Buffalo Bill's hands at fifty paces."

"Where did you learn to work on things?" she asked.

"Don't really know. I've always liked things with moving parts. When I was a kid, we had this cat."

"I would have thought you more of a dog person."

"It was my mother's cat," I said, continuing. "One day, it got on the mantle as cats tend to do. My mother had this old clock sitting up there and the cat accidentally knocked it off. Or maybe it was on purpose. It was a cat, after all. They do these things."

She yawned and stretched an arm toward the sky then pulled her legs around and leaned back against her saddle. She sipped her tea. The countess would have made a very acceptable cat.

"Anyway, the clock fell and broke apart. My mother was going to throw it out, the clock, not the cat, you understand. She fawned on that cat."

"I understand," the countess said. "Please go on."

"Well, I kept the clock, busted gears and all, and started tinkering with it. After a few weeks, I got it to work. Guess I've been tinkering with machines ever since."

"I should thank that cat then for your ability to put a steam engine together."

I worked the slide on the Lewis, chambering a round, then set it atop the stones. "That steam engine repair was as much luck as skill."

The countess tilted her head to one side before saying anything. "No, I don't think so. And your mother? Where is she?"

"Gone more than ten years now, Countess. It's just me and my brother. He doesn't tinker," I added.

"No cats for him?"

"I guess not. He likes making piles of sawdust. Takes after our grandfather like that." I tossed a few more sticks into the fire. "We're not as close as we should be. Once, when we were kids," I said, turning to look at the countess.

The cup dangled loosely from her finger, the last few sips of tea staining the stones of the farmhouse floor. My audience had fallen asleep.

"I'll tell you the rest some other time," I said quietly. "Goodnight, Countess." Stretching out on my blanket, I covered myself with my wet, still muddy coat and closed my eyes. I don't think I have ever felt so tired before in all my life.

It was the most marvelous dream; somewhere dry and warm. The sun was out, and the countess was there. She was wearing her fisherman's shirt and was laughing in the bright sunshine. Sometimes the blouse was buttoned and sometimes it was falling off her shoulders as she danced and frolicked in and out of a tree filled forest. I reached for the floating cloth, intent on pulling it away when something kicked my boot. My sleeping brain told me it wasn't the first kick. A seminude countess cavorting in the sunshine faded into nothingness as I opened tired eyes.

"Stick!" Bohdan said as cheerfully as if were neighbors bumping in to each other at the corner bar. "You will live longer in this country if you learn to sleep lighter."

He laughed. He would.

I heard the sound coming out of his mouth. I didn't see much evidence of humor in his eyes. Reaching across, I touched the woman sleeping beside me on the shoulder. She didn't move. "Countess," I said, my voice loud enough to wake her up. "Guess you were right."

She stirred, stretched both arms to either side of her blanket, and opened her eyes. My traveling companion awoke with a start, kicked her blanket away and jumped to her feet. Long, dark red hair fell to the small of her back.

I got up a little slower. I've never really been a morning jumper.

We had both overslept. Weepy sunshine made its way through the collapsed roof. Our shelter for the night looked quite dismal after sunrise. Water gathered in puddles making a sticky mess of leaves and mud. Bohdan, I saw, had reclaimed his violin. He held it cradled in one arm like a newborn babe. There was fresh gauze wrapped around his head, and his hat was tilted to one side. Red blood dotted the center of the bandage on his left ear.

Bohdan nodded his head towards the countess. "Katya."

Touching his ear, he added, "you missed."

Katya, he called her. She and I never used first names, but I knew her name was Irena, not Katya. Then I saw the men behind Bohdan. Lots of men. At least a dozen and there were horses outside the ruined wall. The countess said something in Russian.

My coat was in my hand. I could feel the weight of the forty-five in the pocket. "Bohdan," I said. Even I heard the uncertainty in my voice.

The countess looked at the Mauser lying too far away then smiled sweetly at the Czech. "What makes you think I missed? I can shoot apples out of a tree from farther away than I was from you. If I wanted you dead, you would be dead."

Someone pushed past Bohdan and came into the ruined farmhouse. The countess gasped.

The newcomer was younger than me by a handful of years. He wore a black thigh length leather coat belted at the waist and a bandoleer across one shoulder. A pistol was on his right hip covered by a leather flap. The newcomer was trying to grow a beard, but dark brown hair quickly faded into wishful thinking the closer it got to his ears. I don't think he was called handsome very often by members of the opposite sex. He also had something else, something that caused me to take uncomfortable notice. In the middle of his hat, a hat that looked almost a twin to the one worn by the countess, was a red star.

A Bolshevik's star. The Reds had found us.

12

Everyone started speaking at once, all of it in Russian. There was a lot of shouting and finger pointing with the newcomer doing most of the shouting. Nobody bothered translating, so I stood and waited my turn to be told what was happening.

The countess fastened buttons at her cuffs managing to look extremely put out while doing so. Bohdan said something to the newcomer, pointing once at me and then at the countess. Both men laughed. It was a scornful laugh, not at all a friendly sound. The countess didn't join in. I put on my coat, thinking it would be easier to get to the pistol that way. Half Beard unsnapped the leather flap covering his sidearm.

"Don't," I said aloud, wondering if I could pull my automatic out of my pocket before Half Beard could draw his own weapon.

The countess stepped between me and the unsnapped holster, then started in with the Russian again. I'm pretty sure Half Beard could have heard her if he was standing fifty yards away on yesterday's road. He didn't look pleased to be dressed down by a woman.

The man said something that sounded terribly final to me, then turned and walked out of the ruined doorway. The countess grabbed her Mauser and slapped the leather belt around her waist.

Well, that couldn't be so bad. If they were going to dump our bodies in a ditch, they wouldn't let her have a pistol. A trooper came into the farmhouse, his rifle pointed straight at me. Maybe not so good then. The countess turned to face me as she scooped the raincoat off the floor, grabbed the fisherman's shirt off its peg, then stuffed everything into her canvas pack. For just a moment, our eyes met. I saw something in those eyes I had never seen before.

Fear.

I wonder what she saw in mine.

The countess went through the doorway, her saddle and bridle thrown over one shoulder and half dragging the canvas pack behind her. She didn't look at me again. The soldier motioned for me to follow. I did.

"Your saddle and gear," Bohdan said.

"If they're going to shoot me, they can carry it themselves."

"They aren't shooting you. He wanted to. I felt sure he was going to but Katya did, what is the phrase in English? Pulled rank?"

The trooper said something, emphasizing his point with the barrel of his rifle.

"We need to hurry, Stick. They want to ride before they are caught again."

Grabbing the saddle, I hauled it off the stone floor and threw it over my shoulder. "Tell me what's happening."

The trooper hit me in the back. It wasn't a knock me down blow, just a reinforced love tap with the butt of his rifle. Russian soldier speak for move your ass. I got the message. So did the Czech. By the time we got to the gelding, the countess was already in the saddle. She didn't speak to me as

135

she rode away, the half beard with the sidearm riding beside her. More than a dozen Russians watched me as I strapped the saddle on my horse and got the bridle around his ears. Bohdan kept his distance.

As soon as I mounted, the troopers fell into a double column. Bohdan's horse was beside mine. "What's happening?" I asked again.

"No questions, Stick. Not now. Say the wrong word and we're all dead men."

We rode nonstop for three hours. For once, my gelding understood its duty. He followed along behind the horse in front, as if he had done this sort of thing all his life. I was at least glad of that. No one wants to embarrass themselves with magnificent displays of ineptness when captured by enemy horsemen.

The countess was at the front of the double column, riding beside Half Beard. Most of the time, the riders in front of me blocked her from my view. I managed to catch glimpses of a white blouse whenever the double column started to climb a hill. Bohdan and I were two horses from the end, the Czech riding on my left with the Lewis carried balanced across his pommel the same way he had done since we left the boat. His hat now sported a red star in the center of the crown. Always resourceful was our Czech master spy. His knee was very close to mine. I kept my voice just above a whisper.

"You seem to have made new friends, Bohdan."

The Czech winced. "My name," he said, "is Boris Avilov. Never say that other name again in front of my *new friends*."

With lips barely moving and his voice just loud enough to be heard, he explained how he was now a Russian from some unpronounceable place in Ukraine.

"My Russian is excellent, but I am told I speak it with a Ukrainian accent. I've always found that amusing since I do not speak a word of that language." The column followed a sharp curve to the right. "I was worried about you back in that old ruin," he added. "It was touch and go there for a minute while the *komvzvoda* decided if you deserved shooting." He smiled. "Lucky for the both of you, his commander was shot out of the saddle just after dawn. That one would have killed everybody just to be safe."

"What is a *komvzoda?*"

"The Workers and Peasants Red Army of the Russian Soviet Federated Socialist Republic have invented a new order in their military. They elect their leaders now without distinction between officer and enlisted. That's one of their new ranks. No clue what the equivalent rank is in real armies."

The trooper behind us said something.

"He says to be quiet," Bohdan, now Boris said. "They fear another ambush, I think."

An hour later, the *komvzoda* finally called the small column to a halt. A command was given, and all the troopers dismounted in unison. I followed their example a half second later. My legs were stiff and my rump felt like something permanent was broken deep inside. The troopers walked two steps away from their mounts, then unbuttoned their trousers. Seventeen bladders emptied in unison. Again, I was a half second behind them. Small, quiet conversations started on either side of me. Apparently, speaking was permitted while urinating in the Russian cavalry. Several of the troopers dropped their pants and squatted where they stood. The smell of tobacco drifting down the line made me think of the major. Nothing would have pleased me more right then than a squad of leathernecks with fixed bayonets charging out of the brush. I waited. Nothing happened. Bohdan, now Boris started talking.

"Her name is Katya Gavrilov now," he said quietly. "She grew up in Minsk and joined the Revolution in 1919. Are you listening, Stick? Details are important."

"Did you find Ivan?"

"Never mind about Ivan. Trust me, he is very resourceful on his own."

"Why did you bring the Bolsheviks back to us?"

"What was I supposed to do?" Bohdan, now Boris said as he buttoned his trousers. "Tell them I'm not who I say I am and shoot me quickly? They were running full gallop down that damn road same as me. The Whites were somewhere behind them, trying to catch up and finish what they started. You noticed the empty saddles at the rear?"

I had. Five horses were missing their riders.

"Excellent mounted killers are the Cossacks," the Czech said. "They are the only Russian troops I respect on either side of this war. There I was, face to face with a Red patrol, bleeding from where that bitch shot me in the ear. I thought I was a dead man, but before I could think up a convincing lie, the *komvzoda* asked me if I had tangled with the White cavalry. Of course I had, I told him. We got separated, you and the countess going one way, I mean Katya, running for the western road while I led them away."

He laughed. The soldier standing beside us gave him a curious look.

"One thing led to another and suddenly, we were on a rescue mission to reunite—"

Half Beard shouted a command. Troopers reached for bridles and put their boots into stirrups. Bohdan returned to his horse. I followed.

"Katya isn't going to be happy about this," he said. "We only just managed to get rid of the silly bugger before we slipped through the lines outside Vladivostok. She stole his motorcar doing it."

"What silly bugger?"

There was a shout and all seventeen troopers plus Bohdan and I swung into the saddle. I even managed to do it in time with the rest of the men.

"There are a few details Katya hasn't told you, Stick."

"Shhhh," the trooper behind us said.

Bohdan shrugged. The talking break was over.

We rode forever. I stopped noticing the countryside or the line of riders in front of me. I didn't even notice if Bohdan, now Boris was still by my side. I just squinted my eyes half closed and tried to stand just high enough in the stirrups to keep the hard leather seat of my saddle from doing any more damage.

Someone up ahead called an order and the double file of cavalrymen brought their horses to a stop. My gelding's chest and forelegs were covered in white foam. The animal felt like he was about to collapse beneath me.

"He's ruined half these horses," Bohdan, now Boris said quietly beside me.

He had just about ruined me as well. I was too exhausted to bother looking up. When the train blew its whistle, I jumped so hard I almost lost my balance. Even my exhausted nag managed to dance sideways. There was a depot in front of me with an armored train sitting on a siding. A locomotive, red flags the size of bed sheets flapping on both sides, was taking on water. Soldiers were everywhere.

I guess the countess was right. The Trans-Siberian was just a little way in front of us.

13

The color red was everywhere. A large red banner flew from the top of the water tower. Soldier's trousers had red stripes sewn down the sides. Some had red armbands. Even their hats had red bands going around the sides.

"It's an army," I said to the Czech.

"More like a reinforced brigade."

"It's a hell of a lot of Bolsheviks whatever it is," I said. "What happens now?"

"We see if her story is believed or not."

"What story? Bohdan, if you don't start talking I swear I'm going to shoot you myself."

An order was shouted and my escort dismounted, myself and Bohdan included. A row of troughs were lined up beside a stand of trees. The troopers walked their mounts towards the water. More than one of the riders looked just as worn out as I did. Half Beard took the countess by the arm and led her away. Handing my nag's reins to Bohdan, I started to follow. I'm not sure why. It just seemed like the thing to do. One of the soldiers in our escort said something. I recognized him as the one who had planted his rifle butt in the middle of my spine back at the farmhouse. He pointed his rifle at the water troughs.

"He says," Bohdan began.

"I know what he says." The nag and I limped our way to the water. There was a pump beside the troughs and I waited my turn behind a line of tired, dirty Russians. Bohdan started half a dozen conversations with the men waiting in line. It was easy to see he was accepted as one of them. It was just as easy to see I wasn't.

The white blouse disappeared somewhere on the other side of the armored train. A boy soldier worked the handle of a pump as water gushed into the zinc trough. Bohdan set his machinegun against a railing, took off his hat, then stuck his wounded ear under the gushing water.

"She said you would be back," I told him.

He came up sputtering and drenched almost to his waist. "Katya thinks she knows me well. She doesn't. By the way, Stick, when they question you, you will need a convincing story. Think of something simple. Simple is always best."

I took my turn at the water spigot. "Who's going to question me?"

Bohdan raised a hand. I don't think he heard me. He was watching an undersized man in a military uniform coming down the steps from the elevated depot office.

"He will."

"That guy on the stairs?"

"His name is Ivchenko. He is a political commissar."

"Another one of your friends?"

The Czech moved his head slowly from side to side. "One of my hunters."

Bohdan moved his horse, putting most of the animal's body between him and the train yard.

"What does a political commissar do?" I asked.

"Shoots people. I cannot be seen here. I don't think he

knows my face, but I cannot be sure."

He took the reins of my gelding.

"Find me later if you're still alive. I will walk the horses now, cool them down. Remember," he said warningly, "Katya Gavrilov from Minsk. Good luck."

"Bohdan, you're not leaving me alone here. What the hell is going on?"

"My name's Boris. I told you. No time now, none at all. Katya will explain." Balancing the Lewis over a shoulder, he pulled the horses away from the water. "Don't forget, simple stories are best," he said as he left me standing alone in the middle of a reinforced brigade of Red soldiers.

"Boris!" I shouted. My Czech master spy kept walking, all the while keeping the horses between him and whoever this Ivchenko guy was.

The man, Ivchenko, stopped a few steps from the bottom of the stairs. Another soldier came out of the upstairs office. This one was tall and trim in a well fitting uniform with polished knee boots. He came slowly down the stairs in even, measured steps, one gloved hand balanced on the railing.

A troop of soldiers rode by and I lost sight of Bohdan's hunter and the man in the nice boots. One of the Russians we rode in with elbowed me away from my spot at the water trough. "All yours," I told him. My guard, he of the rifle butt, was still watching me. I stepped away from the trough, doing my best to look inconspicuous. The mounted soldiers rode past, heading down the long, muddy road I had just endured. When they were finally out of my way, I saw the white blouse again.

Half Beard was beside her, one hand holding her elbow in a way that said she wasn't quite free to go. The Mauser was belted around her waist. Still a good sign in my book. They talked for a long time. For much of the conversation, the man in the polished boots looked down from his perch on the stairs, hands clasped tightly behind his back. Then he did something I wasn't expecting. He came down the steps, pulled her arm out of Half Beard's grasp then kissed her on the lips, one hand resting on her waist.

"Well, how about that," I mumbled.

Half Beard wasn't done. He pointed towards the water troughs. Four sets of eyes looked my direction.

The commissar started walking. The man in the polished boots followed with the countess walking beside him. Half Beard said something. Shiny Boots dismissed him with a wave.

Keep it simple, the Czech said. Simple is best.

A group of Reds in long coats, shouldered rifles and packs cut off the countess and Shiny Boots, he of the kiss. They weren't marching in ranks and if not for the uniforms, would have looked more like farm boys come to see the fancy train than soldiers. I saw the white blouse trying to get around them as Ivchenko walked steadily towards me.

Keep it simple.

The soldier with the rifle began to make what sounded like a report, but the commissar wasn't interested. He said a quiet word. The soldier came to attention, saluted, and vanished into the crowd of troops.

Bohdan's hunter stopped a few feet away from me. He was shorter than me by at least half a foot, probably somewhere in his mid forties, washed and freshly shaved. Like a lot of the Bolshevik soldiers, he wore a gray pullover tunic with a leather belt on the outside. Wrinkled, lived in black pants were stuffed inside old boots. There was no flashy red stripe sewn down the legs like most of the other soldiers in the depot. Ivchenko, if that was his name, looked terribly ordinary and yet, not a single soldier stepped in front of him as he crossed the train yard. Not even the gawking farm boys. He didn't wear the leather brimmed hat like the one the countess and Half Beard favored. Instead, he wore a soft cap with a tall pointed peak in the center and ear flaps turned up along the sides. A red star as big as the palm of my hand was stitched into the fabric across the front. Almost all the soldiers were wearing one just like it.

The locomotive blew its whistle. Steam hissed as the huge steel wheels spun on the iron rails. The train began to move forward inch by inch. Cars flexed against the motion as the moving locomotive took up the strain of pulling thousands of tons.

The countess and the snappily dressed officer who had kissed her on the mouth caught up to the smaller man, Ivchenko. Shiny Boots was clean shaven like Ivchenko, early thirties, and had an air about him like he expected the world to be impressed with his presence. Unlike Ivchenko, his uniform, a leather coat like Half Beards and black trousers, fit like a tailored suit. The boots shone like dark mirrors. And he was clean. Scrubbed, starched and pressed. Even the pistol belt encircling his tunic was polished. I scratched the stubble on my chin and resisted the urge to run a hand down the front of my coat.

Shiny Boots, hands still clasped behind his back, looked through me, not at me. His expression was unreadable although I would never call it a pleased countenance. The commissar in his pointed hat looked at me behind round, wire framed glasses, his head slightly to one side. He looked at me the way an anthropologist would an undiscovered tribe of headhunters.

"Mr. Watkins," the countess said after a moment. "May I introduce Comrade Commissar Ivchenko of the Revolutionary Military Council?"

The pointed hat never moved.

"And the depot commandant, Comrade *Kompolka* Alexi Gavrilov of the Workers and Peasants Red Army."

"Pleasure," I said, wondering if I should offer to shake hands first or wait for the Comrade whatever she called him to offer.

The countess slipped her arm through the depot commander's as the starched uniform said something that sounded to me a little like a prepared speech. I smiled politely and waited for the translation.

"My husband wishes to express his gratitude to you for seeing me safely back to him."

14

When a boxer takes a hard shot to the head, about the only thing he can do is try to cover up with his gloves and hope the round ends before somebody starts a ten count. Her husband wished to express his gratitude. Bohdan was right. She had left out a few details. Ivchenko looked at me like a vulture trying to decide if my liver was the best place to start the feast. Her husband. I caught myself staring at her hand. And there it was. A little thin band of gold on the third finger. Doing a good job of keeping her face expressionless, she curled her hand into a ball, hiding the proof of her marriage in her fist.

"What is a *Kompolka*?" I asked her. I even said it politely. The pointed hat's eyes blinked behind his glasses. Her husband examined me like I was an insect in need of stepping on.

"It is his rank," the countess said. "I think it might be what used to be called a colonel."

"Well," I said as nonchalantly as I could muster, "hello

Colonel. Name's Watkins. My friends call me—"

"For this you stole Hispano Suiza motorcar?" he said to his wife.

The accent was thick; the words rolling past full lips. I didn't like him. I didn't like him at all. "Where I come from," I said, "we have this thing called community property. Wives can't really steal from their husbands. Wouldn't you agree, *Mrs. Gavrilov?*"

The countess crossed her arms across her chest. "I did not steal it, Alexi. I used it. The antirevolutionaries seized it."

The pointed hat started speaking. His voice was toneless, each word spoken in a modulated, even rhythm. He finished whatever theme he was expounding on by waving a hand towards the train office. Her husband looked me up and down once more, then turned to leave. The countess started to follow. The pointed hat said something that made her stop.

"The comrade commissar would like to ask you a few questions. He has asked if I will translate."

"Fire away, *Mrs. Gavrilov.*"

The comrade commissar walked a slow circle around me. I waited, doing my best to follow Bohdan's advice and think of something simple. The little vulture completed his first loop. I wasn't liking him much either.

"Amerikanski," he said. Then he spat.

"Amerikanski," I repeated, then I spat, thinking the politician would appreciate a little diplomacy.

The commissar started speaking in that same evenly modulated rhythm. I waited for the countess to repeat his questions.

"He wants to know how long you have been in Russia."

"A few months," I told him, "off and on." The countess translated.

"He says the Americans have all left. Why are you still here?"

"There's a few of us still around. A skeleton crew in Vladivostok. Does he understand skeleton crew?"

"*Da,*" she answered.

The pointed hat made another circumnavigation.

"He's making me dizzy," I told her. She didn't laugh. She didn't even smile. The countess looked worried. The politician began to speak.

"He says this is not Vladivostok. Why are you here?"

"Marxism," I answered. "Never heard of it until I got to Russia. I like the philosophy. All that 'from each according to his ability' stuff. I wanted to find out more, see what the revolution was all about."

"And what have you found out?"

I put my hand in my coat's pockets. The pistol was still there. "Russia is a big place. It needs men like me."

"Why does Russia need men like you?"

"Because I can fix things. Machinery. And I can teach other workers, bring Russia into the industrial age, like Marx said had to happen before his vision would work out."

The commissar stopped his circling. Standing beside the countess, he leaned very close to her then whispered something in her ear. Her cheeks blushed scarlet.

"What did he say?"

She shook her head as the commissar continued to lean towards her.

"Translate."

"He said something vulgar, Mr. Watkins. It surprised me for a moment, that's all."

"Did he now?" I took a step closer.

The countess caught my eye, then shook her head from side to side.

"It is nothing to be concerned about."

The Russian, still looking at the countess, spoke for a long time. I waited for the English version.

"The comrade commissar says, on behalf of the Workers and Peasants Red Army, welcome to the Russian Federated Soviet Socialist Republic."

She stopped talking for a moment, probably needing to

inhale.

"They like big names in this country," I said. "He could have stopped with welcome and left it at that."

"The comrade commissar says, if you try to leave he will have you shot."

The Russian waited for a moment, perhaps thinking I was going to do something stupid in the middle of a depot surrounded by hundreds of Red soldiers.

"Understood," I said.

The commissar said something else, then turned away, apparently going about his business.

"He has ordered me to go with him."

"Go where?"

"I am alright, Mr. Watkins. My husband is here."

Husband. Funny how she had never mentioned that little detail before. She said it with a very reassuring smile on her face. Just another Russian girl in the worker's paradise. I could see the fear in her eyes. I wanted to shoot the commissar between the shoulder blades right then and there. Soldiers crossed between us. People shouted and talked. A troop of men rode by on horses. The white blouse never looked back. I watched her until I couldn't see her in the crowd anymore.

"Nasty little bastard, isn't he?" Bohdan said from behind me. "*Kompolka* Gavrilov is a bit of a fool, but Ivchenko, he's cut from a different cloth."

"I'm thinking you two share a history?"

Bohdan sighed. "It is most unfortunate. I knew he was coming east. That is the reason we had to run for Vladivostok in the first place. Katya and her maneuvering with that decrepit boat may have just hastened our demise."

"The countess is married."

"Katya Gavrilov," Bohdan said through clenched teeth. "There is no countess anymore. Not here. I told you that already."

"None of you ever mentioned a husband."

"Should we have?" Bohdan grinned. "Did you think our

lovely Katya was going to warm your bed during the long winter nights?"

"I still have my pistol, Bohdan."

He held up his hands. "I only jest, my friend. I am not a violent man. Not unnecessarily, anyway. I wouldn't be too worried about Katya. It's all smoke and mirrors with her and Gavrilov. It was her idea, a fact that is galling to me on a professional level. I like to think I am the one who has the clever ideas but," he shrugged, "not this time. It was during our first attempt to get the gold that—"

"First attempt?"

"Did you think this was our first try?"

Bohdan, now Boris looked me in the eyes.

"I suppose you would have. As I was saying, we were stuck on the wrong side of the Urals and needed a way east to get to the lake."

"Lake?"

"Baikal. The gold is somewhere nearby. Ivan won't say exactly where. We needed a way east and Gavrilov, he needed a, how do I describe this? The man is," Bohdan now Boris furrowed his brows. "I do not know the English word for it. When I was with the Legion, we kept records on all the Bolshevik officers. The files changed often because the ones we didn't shoot the commissars did. New men arose and so a new file was created. Gavrilov's file had some rumors in it. Interviews from prisoners and others who talked about certain unnatural proclivities."

"Proclivities?"

"It was rumored, strongly rumored Alexi Gavrilov preferred the company of young men. The rumors were growing, and the commissars were talking among themselves. He was heading for the wall unless he did something to squash the rumors. What better way than to bed a captivating daughter of the Revolution such as our Katya?" Bohdan, now Boris laughed. "It was a brilliant plan on her part. I would love to have been in the room when she broached the subject. Can you imagine? The poor man actually thought nobody knew his secret when half the army suspected him all along."

"I see, so the countess."

"Katya," Bohdan, now Boris said.

"So Katya married Gavrilov and in turn, the good Bolshevik gave all of you safe passage east."

"Gave is not the word I would use. Forced is more accurate. Gavrilov is in charge of troop movements along the eastern section of the Trans-Siberian. Where he goes, his beautiful wife goes too. It was a perfect, if somewhat temporary plan. I think the poor fool is terrified of Katya exposing him. One word from her and it would have been *his* corpse dumped in a ditch."

"What did that commissar say to her just now? She wouldn't translate."

"I was too far away to hear. Your answers were quite good, by the way. You thought fast on your feet, like a professional."

"They weren't hard questions."

"Not this time," the Czech said. "The Russian smells something. We had best be on our way as soon as we can figure out how a quick exit can be accomplished. I will think on it."

"The horses?"

"Worn out," Bohdan, now Boris said. "I think that komvzvoda may have a few questions from the commissar of his own to answer. He ran from the counterrevolutionaries. The Leninist don't like that."

"How far is this crossroads Katya talked about?"

"Ask her." Bohdan looked around the depot. "We are running out of time. That troop train is going to the siege. We have to find Ivan if he's even alive while the Russians are still killing each other. Once the shooting stops, things will settle down. Border crossings will become border crossings again. Policemen will start noticing things. Not good for someone with a mountain of gold to move."

A Russian soldier, a boy of fifteen or sixteen with a rifle

over his shoulder and red stripes down the sides of his trousers, trotted his way across the yard. He was coming straight towards us. Bohdan, now Boris stiffened. The boy said something to him then pointed a finger at me.

"He says you are to go with him."

"Why?" I asked.

Bohdan, now Boris shook his head. "I'll find you later. I need to look around."

"I could use a translator."

"The boy said just you, Stick."

Boris, now Bohdan smiled. If he started to laugh, I was going to shoot him in his other ear. Bohdan turned away, elbowing his way past Red troops.

The boy soldier and I started walking across the train yard. There were still a lot of soldiers walking, sitting, laughing and shouting as big crowds tend to do. I think they were waiting for the next train. I've seen the look many times; groups of military men just waiting for something. Many of them had canvas rucksacks either on their backs or, for those with nowhere to go, sitting on the ground at their feet.

The boy soldier said something to me in Russian. I shook my head. "Sorry," I said. "Amerikanski." I touched my chest, feeling the gold bar still setting next to my heart. "I only speak Uncle Sam."

"Amerikanski?" the boy said. He looked genuinely thrilled at the notion. We started walking faster, crossing a double set of tracks, then around the depot office built on stilts with its red banner flapping in the wind and past a row of buildings that looked like oversized storerooms. There were more troops inside the buildings. The white blouse was standing next to her husband at the far end of the yard. Soldiers parted before me as the boy and I approached. Gavrilov was showing his wife a heavy duty truck sitting close to a double row of train tracks. The colonel had both hands in front of him like an architect trying to frame a future vision. The white blouse wasn't paying attention. Instead, she watched me and my teenaged escort approach.

"Mrs. Gavrilov."

"Mr. Watkins," she answered.

I think she was glad to see me. "Colonel," I said to the starched uniform standing beside her.

The truck was a big, black thing with a large wooden platform on the back. Somebody had loaded a field gun on the bed.

"You fix things, Katya say."

I looked at the countess. "Something needs fixing?"

"Fix," the colonel said, waving both hands towards the engine compartment as he spoke.

The colonel made a slow circuit around the back of the vehicle, much like the commissar had done with me. I walked with him, examining the field gun more than the truck. The carriage was missing its wheels and there were signs of damage to the rest of the gun. It had seen hard use at any rate. Someone had stacked wooden blocks under the missing wheels, then strapped the whole thing down with chains.

The colonel pointed a hand at the artillery piece. "Make tank," he said. "Like Britisher." Pantomiming driving the truck, he pointed at the gun, then made an explosion sound. "You fix," he said again.

"He wants to use the lorry to transport his gun," the countess said.

"I got that when he made the steering wheel motion with his hands," I said as I looked under the bed. The wheels were doubled, solid rubber on leaf springs with a heavy linked chain going to the transmission. It was a good, solid truck, but the Russians had badly overloaded it. The springs were barely holding the weight of the gun.

"If he shoots that thing, he's going to be surprised by the results. The suspension won't hold the recoil. He'll have bits and pieces of springs, axels and lord knows what flying everywhere. Probably flip the whole contraption over on its back."

"I told my husband you are good with broken machinery."

Her husband. It was going to take a while to get used to hearing that. The husband said something in Russian. Another one of those conversations started where I got to stand at the side and wait for the translation. Finally, the countess turned to me.

"My husband is leaving on the next train. He will return tomorrow. I have told him when he returns, you will have," she glanced over her shoulder at the field gun, "fixed his tank. He has told the commissar the gun will be a terrible weapon against the Imperialist."

"Ah, well. If it's the commissar."

"Be careful, Mr. Watkins," the countess said softly. "One does not make jokes about such men. Not even in English."

A train's whistle blew in the distance. The colonel turned to look down the track.

"That your ride?" I asked.

The countess said something to him. The colonel turned away, took a tin whistle out of his pocket and started blowing it. Troops began to stir. Gavrilov kept walking, issuing orders in Russian.

"I don't think he likes me," I said to the countess.

"He's afraid, and he's not happy I have come back. My presence here is both a risk and a relief for him. He hasn't decided which yet. You see, Alexi is."

I held up my hands. "I know what he is. Bohdan told me."

"Good. Then you understand the situation. I lie to Alexi so he can lie to the Bolsheviks and neither of us gets shot."

"And I am a new complication."

"Yes, Mr. Watkins. You are a complication."

"What's wrong with the truck?"

"It is broken. I cannot stand here talking to you. Eyes are watching us both. I have to go say goodbye to my husband in front of those eyes."

She left me standing beside the truck. The locomotive's whistle blew again as black smoke rose above the trees.

"*Broken*," I said in a nasally impression of an infuriating Russian countess. "*I don't like you, Mr. Watkins,*" I said in the same voice. "*I'll shoot you in your stomach, Mr. Watkins.*"

I took off my coat, the one formally wrapped in Siberian mud, and threw it across the flatbed. Running my hand along the cab, I felt the solid feel of the truck. "She thinks I'm the complication," I told the wood and iron. Going around the front, I ran my hand over a large letter M embossed in the metal grill. "What's a Mack truck doing at a railroad siding in Siberia?" I asked it. "Did my fellow Americans leave you behind when we pulled out?"

There was a single brass carbide headlamp mounted on the front. The matching lamp on the other side was gone. If that was the only part missing, maybe the colonel would get to kill himself when he fired that gun after all. Grabbing the iron crank handle, I gave it a whirl. It wasn't easy, forcing me to spread my feet and take a double grip on the handle. Nothing happened. Pulling the hood open, I examined the patient. Gasoline engines aren't as simple as antique steam plants, but the principle of ignition isn't hard to follow. There's gas and there's a spark. Get it right, they start. Get it wrong, they don't.

Behind me, the locomotive rolled into the station pushing a sandbag lined flatbed in front with belt fed Vickers machineguns peaking over the bags. I saw soldiers with red armbands sitting at the ready behind the guns. The train's bell clanged away like the mayor's daughter had just got married. Everyone in the whole depot was watching, including me. More red banners were flying from the engine and, like the first train, this one was also armored. Thick steel plates lined the locomotive down both sides. Foggy steam surrounded me as the train slowed to a stop. The engineer blew the whistle for so long I had to stick my fingers in my ears.

Two hours later, loaded to standing room only, the locomotive pulled out of the station on its way to Vladivostok.

15

Two more trains came and went, one stopping just long enough to load more troops for the coming push and one, just an engine, coal car and passenger car, going the opposite way. With the last train gone and no more packed masses of Red soldiers to load, the depot settled down to just another whistle stop on the Trans-Siberian. There didn't seem to be anything for anyone to do except sit on unused flatbeds, walk the tracks, or watch me fool with a truck engine.

Bohdan hadn't reappeared. Neither had Mrs. Gavrilov. As the light began to fade, the soldiers lit scattered fires around the depot. I counted a dozen, each one with a handful of troops drawn to the warmth on a chilly September evening. A few Red troops still wandered about. Some were guards, walking the tracks with slow strides and rifles over their shoulders. A few eyed me suspiciously when they passed. I believe I was the only foreigner in the whole place, reason enough to give me a suspicious look.

It was too dark to do anything else on the truck, so I packed up the toolbox I found behind the seat and washed the grease from my hands with gasoline. The sun was a sliver of light on the horizon when the Red messenger boy, the same one who brought me to the colonel, showed up with a loaf of bread still warm from someone's oven, cheese and sausage. He also brought a sizeable bottle of a clear liquid with a label covered in fancy writing. I had no clue what the writing said. Pulling the cork out, I tried a cautious sip and waited for my eyes to stop watering. The soldier was a boy after Ivan's own heart. I ate all the bread and cheese and swallowed the sausage. With starvation avoided for the evening, the kid and I parked it on the truck's running board. We passed the cleaning solvent back and forth in companionable silence as the night came on. We passed it a few times more than was probably prudent for a man trapped in a train depot with a few hundred hostile troops. After the bottle's fourth or fifth trip, I didn't much care anymore. He pointed at the tank I was building for the colonel and made a few polite enquires, none of which I understood.

"Sure it's fixed," I told him. "What do you take me for, an amateur? Did I ever tell you about the time I rebuilt an antique steam engine?"

I belched.

He gave me the same look I do when Russians are speaking to me; kind of half smile, half say it again a little slower look and maybe I'll understand you this time.

"Tomorrow, I'll take you for a ride around the neighborhood. You ever ride in a Mack truck?"

The boy smiled and reached for the bottle.

"Me neither," I said. "But right now, I need to find a spot where I can curl up."

He handed me the bottle, and I took another sip.

"Last one for me," I said, then I made a pillow of my hands and laid my cheek against them. "Sleep. I'm worn out." Picking up my coat, I decided to try my luck in one of the warehouses. A nice dry concrete floor surrounded by a few dozen snoring men sounded awfully inviting.

The boy started talking as soon as I started walking. He motioned me to follow.

I shook my head and pointed to the closest row of sheds. "Some other time, kid. Thanks for my dinner."

The boy grabbed my arm and started pulling, kept talking and started pointing down the tracks. I tried to pull my arm out of his, but he wasn't taking no for an answer.

"Guess this means I'm not making an early night of it. Quit pulling. I'm coming. If it's that pointy headed commissar again, I'm going to tell him a thing or two," I told the boy.

We went past the warehouses, under a water tower, past the elevated office sitting high up on wooden stilts, then turned down a dirt lane. The kid never slowed. His eyes must have been better than mine because once we left the depot and its campfires, everything got very dark. I couldn't see a thing.

"You aren't taking me to meet my murderer, are you?" I said it in jest, thinking it would sound funny. As we walked farther down the lane and deeper into the trees, my little joke didn't sound so amusing. Sticking my hand in my pocket, I felt the comfort of Mr. Samuel Colt and the Seven Dwarves.

The kid was walking fast, and I tried to keep up. The dirt road dipped into a hollow and the night got a little darker. I had gone just about as far into the woods as I was going to go when a small building nestled in among the trees came into view. It was a cottage about half the size of a boxcar. There was a door with a little peaked gable over it, a glass window on one side, and a chimney. I could just make out little wisps of smoke twirling away between me and the starlight. I didn't see any light coming out of the window. I didn't see any light anywhere.

The kid stopped walking and looked at me.

"The commissar in there?" I asked my tour guide.

He offered the bottle.

"Not me. I'm damn near seeing double."

The boy shrugged, then went down a little stone walkway. I followed along behind. He knocked three or four times on the door, said something I didn't understand in a voice loud enough for anyone inside to hear then offered me the bottle again. I shook my head and said in a voice almost as loud as he did, "Ivchenko!"

The kid put a finger in front of his lips. "Shhhh."

"You shush," I told him. "You did it louder than me."

The curtain over the window moved. An old woman's face peered at me from behind a little square pane of glass. The curtain fell back into place. We waited a good minute before the door opened.

The face from the window belonged to a woman thick at the waist, heavy at the breasts and toothless at the mouth. She had to be seventy or eighty years old. Holding a candle the size of a can of beans, she looked past me at the darkness.

"He brought me," I said, turning to point at the boy. He wasn't where I was pointing. The kid was halfway down the stone path, rifle over his shoulder and bottle in his hand. I turned back around. "Evening," I said, straightening my shoulders and doing my best to look presentable. "Where's Mr. Pointy Head? I intend to speak to him about a vulgar statement whispered in a lady's ear. Man to man. Tell him Watkins of the Navy is here." That last part made me smile.

The old lady looked me up and down, seeing nothing that impressed her, then spat out a dictionary's worth of Russian words. I gave her my usual don't have a clue what you're saying face.

She waited for my answer.

I did my best not to sway.

With a sigh, she stepped aside, inviting me in with gestures.

As soon as my boots touched the rug, the words started flowing again. Grandmother objected to my muddy boots marching through her parlor. I could tell by the way she was jabbing a pudgy finger at my feet. She had a point. The boots were caked in mud. My grandmother would have been mortified if I had worn them inside her home.

"It's been raining a lot," I said.

The old woman sat her candle on a little hall table then, showing surprisingly good knees for a woman of her age, dropped in front of me and started lifting my leg. She had a lot of strength in those arms. I lost my balance and stumbled into the table. Nothing broke, but I did knock her candle to the floor. I heard it rolling off into the darkness. She hissed something, made an exasperated sound that didn't need translating, and finished pulling off my boot.

"I'll do it," I said, before she could grab the other leg and toss me onto my back. Hopping around on one foot, I managed to get the boot off without slamming into anything fragile. It was so dark in the hallway, I couldn't tell if the old lady was still squatting in front of me or had given up and left me standing where I was. "You there?"

She mumbled an answer, took the boot out of my hand then started pulling at the shoulders of my coat. The old gal must have had eyes like a bat. "Here," I said, sliding out of my overcoat. I waved an arm in front of me, trying to feel my way out of blindness. The front door opened and I saw a silhouette of a fat woman holding my boots away from her like they were made from a dead cat. She dropped them outside the door, then made a dusting motion with her hands. When the door closed, I found myself standing in a cave without a flashlight. A hand touched my chest.

"I can't see a damn thing," I said. "Where'd you stick my coat? There's a box of matches in—"

The hand pushed. It was a no nonsense kind of push. I took a step backwards as the bat eyed grandmother twisted me around and pushed me again. She screeched something, probably Russian for move your drunken ass.

"I'm moving," I told her. My arms were out in front of me doing that side to side, up and down thing you do when you're being made to walk and you don't have a clue what's in front of you. My hand found the wall on my right and I used it as a guide as I slid along down the hallway. I stopped when I hit something, a picture frame it felt like. I managed to not knock it off the wall.

"You know," I told her, "electricity is a wonderful thing. Lightbulbs could do wonders for the place." The hand on my back pushed again. I took a few more cautious steps. My fingers touched the wood of a door sill.

The grandmother screeched again.

"We turning here?"

More Russian words. I heard a drawer slide open and the sound of somebody rummaging around. She made what I took to be pleased sounds, then I heard a scratch. Light flared from the tip of a match. A gnome's face with a broad, toothless grin touched the match to another candle. This one was a about the size of my finger and about as big around. She saw me looking her way. A wrinkled hand curled protectively around the flame like she was afraid I was going to knock this one over, too. She made a shooing motion towards the door.

I raised a hand preparing to knock. The grandmother snorted. Maybe it was a laugh, but it sure sounded a lot like a snort. Glancing over my shoulder, I saw her make a sweeping arm motion towards the door. There was a glint of something in those old eyes.

"He really doesn't scare me," I told the wrinkled face behind the candle. To hell with being polite. Opening the door, I went straight in. "Commissar," I said in my best I'm not taking any crap from you voice. I expected to find myself in an office or maybe some kind of library, the kind with overstuffed chairs and the smell of cigars. There was none of that. It was a bedroom. I could tell because there was a bed, a heavy wood framed thing with corner posts thicker than an elephant's legs that were taller than me. It sat high off the ground with a foot thick feather mattress, the whole thing covered by a dark colored quilt. The front of the quilt was turned back from a row of white pillows piled against a carved headboard. It was the first real bed I'd seen since leaving my hotel back in Vladivostok. The room was almost as dark as the hallway, the only light coming from a pile of logs burning in the fireplace and a couple of long yellow candles sitting on either end of the mantle. I've gotten used to being constantly cool in Siberia. This room wasn't cool. It was warm.

Someone had drug a zinc lined horse trough into the room and parked it in front of the fire. The thing looked bigger than the dry docks back at Pearl. A woman was pouring water into it from a metal pail. Judging by all the steam rising from the surface, damned hot water.

"That's a horse trough," I said, pointing at the huge container, proving my outstanding powers of observation were still intact. The water pourer was dressed in a long blue skirt with a lined pattern in it, a white blouse with sleeves to the elbows and a dark colored shawl over her shoulders. Brown hair peeked out from under a scarlet colored scarf. An unremarkable but not unattractive young woman's face looked at me with neither a smile nor a frown. It was just an expressionless stare. There was no acknowledgement to my pointing out the obvious, so I lowered my finger. Collecting myself, I said, "I'm looking for the fellow in the pointed hat." I held out my hand about shoulder high. "About this big, wears glasses and likes to whisper vulgar comments. He and I are going to have words."

Three steps into the room and the horse trough turned into a bathtub with handles on each end and a wooden filigree rail along the edge. The dry dock was almost three quarters full. It must have taken the girl in the skirt a dozen trips with her pail to get it so full. Seeing the bathtub made me very aware of just how long it had been since I'd washed in anything bigger than a bucket. When the pail was empty, the woman sat it on the floor, then wiped her hands on her skirts. The expression on her face was hard to interpret. I stuck my hand in the steaming water.

"I don't think you will find him here," a voice in the shadows said.

I spun, feeling the messenger's potato juice twirl me a half step too far.

"Countess. I thought this?" I pointed at the open door behind me. The toothless grandmother came in after me, her candle lighting the way in front of her. There was a little square table by the bed and she headed towards it. She lit a second candle with the fire from the one in her hand sending a soft glow across the pillows. It was still very dim on the far side of the bed.

"Where are you?" I asked the shadows. A dark outline moved. She was standing on the other side of the bed behind one of the elephant's legs where the room's shadows were the deepest.

"My apologies for the darkness, Mr. Watkins. I'm told there isn't a drop of paraffin in the house."

"I didn't expect you to be here," I told her. "There was this kid and." I let the words trail off. "Skip it. Doesn't matter."

"It's my home and my bedroom, Mr. Watkins," she said from her side of the post. "Where else would you expect me to be?"

The countess said something in Russian. The girl beside the tub did a kind of half curtsy, picked up her bucket, then left by the same door I just stumbled through, giving me a very frank, very appraising look as she passed. I've seen looks like that before from other women in a dozen different ports of call. Worldly is a polite way of describing it.

"Didn't mean to disturb you," I said, as I tried to process the situation. "I should have knocked. Her fault." I waved an arm at the grandmother who was ever so slowly walking with her candle, one hand still guarding the flame. She muttered something as she went by me, heading for another table on the far side of the bed.

"We shall call it even, Mr. Watkins. I seem to remember walking in on you once without knocking."

She finished the words with a giggle. I scratched my head. I've found that alcohol, especially too much alcohol, slows my reasoning processes.

Giggles.

I'd seen this woman seductively sharing golden secrets in a cafe, furious in a flophouse and melancholy on the *Orca's* deck. I had never heard her make such a noise before.

The countess stepped out of the shadows. She did it slowly, like a leopard stalking a gazelle. I blinked. Maybe I even gasped a bit. Shadows danced in the room as amber light won and lost a war with the darkness. The countess moved slowly away from the oversized bedpost. As she moved closer, the light from the fire flickered up and down wonderfully naked legs. The grandmother, the room's last candle lit, shuffled towards me in that way old ladies do. Pointing a wrinkled finger at me, she started in on the second volume of the Russian dictionary.

"She wants your clothes," the countess said. "She says she's never seen a grown man so filthy before."

"Pitched my boots out the front door," I said. "You uh, you look interesting, Countess."

She giggled. "Interesting? I hope that was a compliment."

"Lovely, I meant to say."

"Thank you. Have you eaten? There's—"

"I ate earlier."

"Oh, good." She came another step closer, her fingers lightly touching the bedpost.

She was wearing her white blouse. I could see that now. The same one I'd seen her in half a dozen times before, the one with buttons at the cuffs and buttons all the way to the neck. It still had the buttons. She just hadn't bothered fastening half of them. The tail of her blouse ended just above the middle of her thighs. "Should I step outside?" I pointed to the bedroom's door.

The countess pursed her lips as if the question needed deep pondering. "No, I don't think so. You're here now."

The old woman was talking to me again.

"I still don't understand you," I told her.

"She's asking if you are a pig farmer," the countess translated. Very slowly, she placed one bare foot in front of the other, every step a delicious provocation as she came closer to the fire.

"I fell off my horse," I told the old woman. "It was wet."

She gave me a blank stare.

"I remember that," the countess said. "I really must teach you to ride someday."

"Pass," I said.

"How is Alexi's project coming along?" She stepped a little closer to the fire. Her hair was loose, part of it falling down her back, part of it running down each side of her half open blouse.

"The magneto needed attention, and some fool had screwed up the spark advance."

The countess tilted her head to one side and smiled.

"Running," I said, giving her the abbreviated version.

"I never doubted it wouldn't be."

She spoke to the grandmother. The old lady sat her candle on the mantle and started unbuttoning the front of my shirt.

"Stop that." I pushed the old fingers away from the buttons, but that just made her reach for my belt. "Will you stop," I said again. I needed a moment to collect myself. Honestly, I was feeling highly confused by the situation. Blame it on that messenger boy and his damn bottle. The Russian grandmother had another one of those one sided conversations. "What is she saying now?"

"She says you smell like goat piss, and that you fidget worse than a six year old. Give her your clothes."

"Why would I do that?"

"I told her to wash them."

The countess stepped between the tub and the fire, releasing a button with each step. The younger female in the blue skirt came back into the room carrying a fresh bucket of steaming water. The old woman tried her best to hold a conversation with me. The girl with the bucket started pouring as the grandmother grabbed at my belt buckle.

I pushed her hand away.

"No reason to be shy, Mr. Watkins. By the looks of her, she's been a camp follower since the Crimean War."

Another button was undone. Her blouse was a deep v of bare skin from neck to navel.

"It took longer than I expected to heat so much water. Have you ever seen a bigger bathtub?"

"Made from a horse trough, I think," I heard myself say.

"Is it? I had no notion."

The last button was undone. The blouse bared her shoulders. She paused for a moment, one naked shoulder shining in the flame's reflections. It was only a moment's pause, like she was considering her options before making up her mind. The white cotton slid down her arms. There was nothing underneath it.

She ran her hand along the wooden filigree. "How clever of them. Where ever do you think they found it?"

"Who?" I asked. It seemed like the proper response to make to her question although I wasn't really following the conversation. The countess, naked from head to toe, seemed completely unconcerned by my presence hardly an arm's reach away. The old lady was still talking. My head nodded in deep understanding.

"The stationmaster," the countess said. "This was his house before it was confiscated for the greater good of the Soviet. He and his shrew of a wife have moved into the office on stilts." She twirled a fingertip through the water. "Devine," she sighed, then handed the discarded blouse to the maid.

The veteran of the Crimean War pulled at my jacket.

The countess stepped daintily over the edge of the tub, one hand covering her more private parts as she lowered herself into the water.

"Oh my, that's hot," she said. "Far too hot."

It might have been far too hot, but it didn't stop her. She sank neck deep in one fluid motion. Her eyes closed in rapturous pleasure as steam rose around her. "I have found paradise," she said as she stretched her legs out in front of her.

The trough was almost long enough for her to straighten them all the way out.

"The look on your face, Mr. Watkins, is priceless."

The old lady started to unbutton my shirt.

"Wait," I said.

The countess raised a leg and balanced it along the rim of the tub. The skin was pink from the heat and shimmering in the fire's reflection. Running a sponge along her skin, she said, "You're weaving."

"There was this kid," I said, waving my hand in the general direction of the train yard.

"That's what you said before." The sponge made a slow progression back and forth.

"Never mind," I said. The sponge moved to her neck.

A dark bottle of something was sitting on the bedside table. It looked like alcohol to me and I was feeling extremely thirsty. I went to see what was in it, the sounds of a woman luxuriating in a hot bath behind me. There was a pottery jug filled with water sitting next to the bottle. Two glasses, one clean, the other with a splash of something in the bottom sat next to the jug. I poured two fingers of a pale green colored liquid into the clean glass. I'd never drank anything green before. Absinthe, the label said.

She splashed and I drank.

"Delicious, isn't it," the countess said. *"La fée verte,"*

The green fairy, some forgotten French lesson translated for me. It wasn't bad. Not sure I'd call it delicious, but it wasn't bad. I turned for the tub. The countess had her arms half draped over the side watching me.

The naked stranger giggled again, then resumed her position leaning against the tub's back. Two bright pink breasts floated just above the level of the water. Tiny wisps of steam rose from each of them. I swallowed the rest of the contents of my glass. This was the woman who wouldn't let me touch her knee? She looked at me, looked at her breasts sloshing around in hot water, then back to me.

"What is the saying?" she asked. "Penny for your thoughts?"

"Steam engines."

She frowned, looked puzzled, then looked at her steaming anatomy. She smiled, then sank her engines beneath the sea.

I wiggled the bottle. It was more empty than full. "Had much?"

"I adore absinthe."

She drew the words out into one long breathy whisper, the Russian accent stronger than I had ever heard it before.

"But you did it all wrong. There's a spoon somewhere. You're supposed to put a sugar cube on it and poor water over it. Just a little. Not too much."

There were no spoons or sugar cubes on the table. Not that it mattered. I poured another ounce into the glass and took another swallow. Green fairy in hand, I observed the woman bathing in her horse trough. The girl in the red scarf was holding long strands of hair outside the tub as the countess sank nose deep. The old lady was smoothing the discarded blouse, still holding her one way conversation with anybody who cared to listen. Slipping the ingot out of my pocket, I slid the gold bar under the nearest pillow. My audience didn't notice. Setting the rest of the green concoction on the table, I went back to the fancy horse trough. Tonight was definitely going to beat sleeping in a warehouse.

The old lady shook her head, still lost in her one way conversation.

The countess scooped both hands in the tub, then let the steaming water run down her face. "I think you have failed to impress her, Mr. Watkins. She says she can find me a much better lover."

The countess reclined in her tub and gave me a very appraising look. The bathwater was dark in the candlelight, but not so dark that it hid the outlines of female skin beneath the surface.

"You sure about this?" I said. Her maid had most of her

hair hanging behind her, outside the tub. A few strands floated on the opaque surface. Her breasts were just beneath the level of the water, darker circles that danced and moved among tiny waves.

"Aren't you?" The surface of the trough rippled and moved.

Talking away, the grandmother pointed at my pants.

"She says if you want your filthy clothes back by morning, she needs to wash them now or they will never dry."

"Can she at least turn around?"

The countess translated. The grandmother replied. All three women laughed, the old lady loudest of all.

"What did she say?"

"Trust me, Mr. Watkins," the countess said, still laughing. "You really don't want to know. Give her your clothes."

This isn't something I do every day and I was decidedly uncomfortable with the entire proceedings, but I had the courage of the green fairy to help me through it.

"Fine," I said. The jacket and shirt went first. Three pairs of female eyes watched. I dropped my pants, tossed them to the old woman, slid my drawers down my legs and managed to get my socks off without falling. The old woman held my clothes away from her the same way she had my dead cat boots. The girl in the scarf gave me a head to toe appraisal before going back to smoothing long strands of red hair. This, I thought, is how eunuchs in the sultan's harem must feel.

"You've got a bruise, Mr. Watkins."

She pointed at my thigh.

"Right there. And there. And another one over there. Turn around."

"No."

"Don't be shy. Turn around."

I did with my hands out at my side.

"Oh my," the countess said. "Your bum is blue."

She said something to the audience and all three women laughed again.

"I hate horses," I told the room.

The old woman pointed at the bath and began another of those long conversations.

"She's told you twice to get in, Mr. Watkins, before the water gets cold."

"Are you getting out?"

The countess drew up her knees. "Do you want me to get out?"

Water sloshed over the sides as I sat. The temperature felt like it was just below the level of unbearable. I think I moaned. When I stretched my legs out down each side of the tub, the countess laid hers over mine. My hands were on her knees. Sitting at our little table in Vladivostok, I wasn't allowed to hold her knee. Looking down at the opaque water of the tub, I didn't think those old rules applied anymore. The Crimean camp follower and the red scarfed maid left us, whispering something to each other as they closed the door behind them. The countess leaned sideways to see around me, watching the two women leave.

We were alone. My hands slipped along glistening pink thighs. "You have lovely breasts, Countess." As soon as I said the words, everything changed. It was like I had flipped on a light switch. The naked female with steaming pink skin and appraising eyes vanished. My hands stopped their slide down her thighs. She hissed something in her native tongue, knocked my hand off her thigh, then pulled her leg back so far it touched those just mentioned lovely bosoms. The kick hit me square in the middle of my chest. A lot more water sloshed onto the floor. It was no love tap. The countess had a kick that could make a mule nod with appreciation.

"Do you think I'm sitting here for your entertainment?" she said between clinched teeth.

Doubling over, I groaned, "You damn lunatic. I think you cracked something." My bathing partner looked at me like she wanted to kick me again.

"Keep your voice down."

Her words were somewhere between a loud whisper and a

soft demand. The prowling cat look I fancied myself seeing when she stepped around that bedpost was completely gone. She was staring with focused attention at something over my shoulder.

"He'll know if we fight."

I twisted around to see who was standing behind me. There was nothing there but a closed door. "Who will know?"

The countess looked at me like I was a simpleton and pointed over my shoulder. I looked again.

"Do you see someone there?" I asked cautiously.

The heel of her palm hit me in the forehead.

"Sober up," she said through clenched teeth.

I was sobering by the second. "That's it." I started to stand.

"Sit down," she said, pushing on my thighs. It wasn't a request.

I sat.

The countess crossed her arms over a pair of naked breasts, then leaned her body outside the tub. She couldn't take her eyes off the door. "Excite yourself."

"Come again?" I asked.

She pointed at the water between us. "They will expect it. Do," she whirled her hand in front of me, "whatever is necessary."

I moved my hands to the bathtub's wooden rim. "They're going to what?"

The doorknob rattled behind me. We were about to have company again.

"Too late." The countess chewed her lip then looked at the water between us. "It will have to do."

"What do you mean, have to do?"

A hinge squeaked and I felt a breeze on my back. The countess reclined against her side of the tub.

The light switch flicked again. Once more, I was looking at demur sexuality. Her kick and my reaction to it had dumped a sizeable amount of water out of the tub. She couldn't sink neck deep anymore. The water wasn't coyly hiding her breasts now.

She noticed my eyes and I braced for another kick. Instead of planting her heal in my chest, she laid both arms along the rim of the tub. I rubbed my sternum. Right then, I figured the odds were fifty-fifty I was getting out of that tub in one piece because one of the occupants in this fancy horse trough was crazy.

"By any chance, Countess, we're you recently bitten by a rabid dog?"

The woman standing behind me spoke. The countess nodded. Scalding hot water poured over my head. I gasped. Fingers started to rub soap into my hair. I closed my eyes as lather covered my face. If she kicked me now, I wouldn't see it coming.

"Was she trying to cook me or wash me? That water was damn near boiling." More water poured over my head, rinsing the soap off my face. The woman began to soap my shoulders and chest.

"Countess," I said.

"Enjoying your bath, Mr. Watkins?"

A voice in the marginally sober portion of my brain, the part that wasn't luxuriating in a hot bath while staring at a woman's naked body was sounding an alarm. "What are we doing?"

"Play your part, Mr. Watkins. Look at me as if we were lovers. I told you," she glanced at the maid, "they expect it."

The Russian girl who my slow thinking brain identified as the referenced "they" soaped my chest. She did this while looking at a spot south of my navel.

"What's in that green concoction you've been sipping?" I asked.

The countess closed her eyes, drew in a deep breath and lifted her chin. I braced for another kick.

"La fée verte," she said with a sigh. "I do enjoy that green concoction as you call it." Her words ended with that disturbing giggle. "It makes me feel so," she opened her eyes and looked at me, "you know."

I knew. Rabid dog crazy. The Russian girl pushed me

172

forward and ran the sponge down my back, all the way to the bottom of the horse trough. "You've got a good leg, Countess. We could have used you when we played Army."

The red scarfed girl, her soapy sponge done with me, went to the countess. I've never watched a woman being washed before. I got the impression it wasn't all that unusual for a Russian noblewoman. The countess looked every bit the noblewoman now, raising one arm and then the other as the girl did her work. When she leaned forward so the maid could scrub her back, her face was very close to mine. I caught the odor of absinthe in the air between us. The maid said something to her. The countess leaned closer as the girl worked the sponge back and forth across her back. The ends of her long hair floated in the water around us. Her lips drew closer to mine and the odor of *la fée verte* grew stronger. The rubbing of the sponge was making her body sway just a little. She came closer, she moved back. She came closer again and she moved back. With each stroke of the sponge, her breasts swayed in a rhythm I found absolutely mesmerizing. When I looked up, the look the countess was giving me was anything but mesmerizing.

"Enjoying yourself?"

"More than you'll ever know," I said, my eyes once more watching the rhythmic sway in front of me.

The maid looked at me like she did this kind of thing every day. She probably had the same look on her face when she washed dishes.

The countess leaned forward, all the way forward until her lips were next to my ear. I waited for her to whisper a secret only she and I would ever know. There were no whispers. Instead, I felt her teeth clamp onto my ear. I thought about the day Ivan arrived with the horses, when the mare bit the gelding. "Mother of—"

Her teeth let go.

"That's for enjoying yourself too much," she said softly.

Her hand came out of the water and patted my chest. The

countess reached for the sides of the tub and began to rise. Aphrodite never looked half as good rising from the sea. I felt my ear as water dripped off the tips of her breasts, ran down a smooth stomach, then curled itself in her sex before sliding down bare legs. As she stepped out of our horse trough, the girl wrapped her in a towel. Covered in white cotton, the countess went to the bedside table. Wet footprints trailed after her on the wooden floor.

"Get out of the tub, Mr. Watkins."

For the first time, I noticed her Mauser hanging by its leather holster. She had it draped over the corner of the headboard. Still holding my ear, I thought this is the moment when she shoots me. But she didn't reach for the pistol. Instead, she poured pale green absinthe into a glass, added a splash of water from the pitcher and sipped her adored concoction.

"I think I would rather just sit here for a moment if you don't mind."

The Russian girl was standing beside the tub, a second towel at the ready. Her dress was soaked across the front from all the washing. She saw me looking at the wet fabric and smiled. Worldly, a voice in my head said. Certainly no teacup and saucer lady.

"Get up, Mr. Watkins. The sooner you are out, the sooner she will leave and we can talk about our escape."

The countess added something in Russian. The girl spread her towel and waited.

"I'm a little biologically impaired at the moment," I said.

Half empty glass in hand and with the towel tucked tightly around her, she came back to the tub. Running fingers through my hair, she said, "I am aware of the biology. I think I might have had something to do with the impairment."

The old lady opened the door just as I was about to stand. Perfect. More witnesses. She was carrying a silky white garment draped over her arms. The towel fell to the floor and I thought again of Aphrodite. Taking the gown from the old lady's hands, she pulled the silk over her head. Falling to her ankles, the cloth glued itself to not quite dry skin. Where there was moisture, the fabric looked as thin as a moth's wing. She smoothed the silk across her hips as the old lady ran a brush through her hair.

"It was a gift. From Alexi's troops on my wedding."

"Did they expect him to wear it or you?"

She laughed. Not the disturbing giggle sort of laugh. A genuine laugh. "Out of the tub, Mr. Watkins."

I sighed once then stood up. The Russian maid wrapped the towel around me after waiting just a moment too long for decency's sake. Stepping out of the bath, I left my own set of watery footsteps as I went to the fire. With the towel wrapped tightly around my waist and my back to the women, I raised hands to the fire. I wasn't at all cold. I just didn't feel like turning around. The countess spoke. Behind me, a trio of Russian women squealed with laughter. I didn't ask what was so funny. A moment later, I heard the bedroom door open and close.

"You're safe now," she said. "I doubt they will come back tonight."

Putting my back to the fire, I said, "I'm not sure what just happened here."

The countess reached for one of the elephant's legs, missed, and stumbled against the feather mattress.

"I think you've drunk too much of the green fairy," I told her.

"As if I could do this sober," she said back to me.

I think my feelings were just hurt. "Which part?"

"He said you would go along with it."

"Ivchenko?"

The countess closed her eyes for a moment, exhaled in what looked like a tremendous effort to master herself then said, "Imbeciles. I am surrounded by idiots and imbeciles." She sighed. "Not Ivchenko. Bohdan."

"I haven't seen Bohdan since I left him with the horses."

She stood there for a moment, slowly breathing long, deep breaths through her nose, one hand resting on the bedpost. After a moment, she nodded her head. "I understand now. That bug eyed little cockroach didn't tell you. He did that on purpose. He likes his little games does our Czech friend."

She crossed her arms. I think she was trying to look like a woman in charge of the situation. If she was, a paper thin negligee draped across her better parts in a most flattering way spoiled the effect.

"I see I need to explain things to you, Mr. Watkins, and I would prefer you not stare at my breasts while I do."

"You tell me to look at you then you tell me not to. You tell me to 'do what's necessary' then you try to bite my ear off for enjoying myself too much."

"It performed well enough," she said. Her mouth fell open then her cheeks turned a dark shade of pink. She spun around to face the bed. "I can't believe I just said that." With a determined step, she marched to the bedside table and set her glass next to the pitcher. Picking up the cork, she put it on top of the bottle then thumped it home with her hand. "No more ever again."

I saw her make the sign of the cross like a good Orthodox. Forehead, stomach, right shoulder, left shoulder.

"I swear."

The silk negligee started to pace the floor. The room wasn't very large, forcing her to turn around after four steps and go the other way. She swayed when she turned, one hand reaching for the wall to steady her balance. "Tonight was a charade, Mr. Watkins."

"Was it now," I said, watching the white silk marching across the room.

"Bohdan's idea to deceive Ivchenko," she added. "He suspects. Me, you, Alexi, everybody. It is what he is here for. He watches, looks, listens to the whispers of his informants then passes his judgment." She touched a finger to the side of her head, mimicking a pistol. "Bang. That's all it takes.

Suspicion." Still barefoot and armored in damp silk, she went to the table and gave the corked bottle a long look. She paused for a moment, placing one hand on her stomach before going on. "It had to look real. The whore will report everything to Ivchenko." Temptation mastered, she turned away from the absinthe and came back to stand by the foot of the bed. The silk plastered itself to her every curve.

My head was swimming and I felt slow and dull. The whole thing hadn't been any more real than the giggle. "Who's a whore," I asked.

"It was Bohdan's idea," was her answer. "He's clever like that. It was also his way of getting even with me for notching his ear."

Moving away from the fire, I touched my own ear. I needed to sit down but there was nowhere to sit except on the bed so I stood, wrapped in my towel and doing my best to appear sober as a judge.

"Ivan, myself and that bug eyed cockroach managed to escape him once."

"Ivchenko?"

"No, you idiot. My husband."

"Call me an idiot again and I'm walking out that door." I pointed at the just mentioned door.

She looked me up and down. "Just you and your towel?"

I looked me up and down. "That might be an issue," I admitted.

"Mr. Watkins, don't you understand what is happening?"

"Do I look like I understand?"

She raised her hands, palms towards me. "We cannot fight," she said, "you and I. I am sorry for my choice of words. You are not an idiot. Do forgive me."

"Better," I said.

She waved a hand in the direction of the train yard. "I will explain. When Semyonov attacked the bridge—"

"Semyonov?"

"General Semyonov. Someone Bohdan had dealings with

when he was still in the Legion."

"He's part of the White Army?"

"Semyonov is a part of Semyonov's army. My husband went chasing after him, taking most of the available troops with him and we took his motorcar. There is a road that runs all the way to Vladivostok. Not a very good one but good enough." She gestured around her. "I had to leave almost everything I owned behind." She sighed. "Unfortunately, Bohdan had to use some of the coins as bribes to get us past the checkpoints. Too many of the coins. I knew if we used the gold, the hunters would know but Bohdan said it was worth the risk. None of us ever planned to come back here again. I think you know the rest."

"Why did you just," I motioned towards the bathtub. The water was smooth with a film of yellow white suds on the surface. "All that."

The countess closed her eyes and exhaled a long breath. "Because you were early."

That seemed like a pretty thin reason to me. I think it seemed pretty thin to her, too.

"Will you *please* stop staring at my breasts?"

Looking up, I said, "I wasn't staring. I was trying to concentrate. I've had a lot to drink tonight."

She made an exasperated sound then turned her back to me.

"Do you have any idea how long it has been since I have seen a bathtub?" she told the nearest elephant leg. "I've endured the company of men for weeks, eating with you, sleeping beside you, looking the other way when you relieved yourselves on the nearest tree." She looked at the ceiling for a moment. "I just wanted a hot bath before you showed up. But there you were, pounding on the door right as I was about to get in."

"I didn't pound."

She spun on her heel, facing me again.

"What was I supposed to do? Tell Ivchenko's spy to go tell my lover to go away. Come back when Bohdan said you would arrive."

"I could have waited until you finished," I suggested. "With your bath, out there in the front room."

"Yes, you could have waited, but you just walked straight in with Ivchenko's creature standing right there." She pointed at the spot where the Russian girl had stood with my towel at the ready. "You still do not understand. I couldn't risk the suspicion of something not being what it seemed. You remember the old lady on the road, the one who said she saw a ditch full of bodies?"

I nodded.

"We're standing on the edge of that ditch right now. The commissar shoots people like you and me because," she gestured with both hands at the room, "who knows, we might do something counterrevolutionary. There are ditches full of bodies from here to Moscow. When Alexi's man found us together in that wrecked farmhouse, you heard the argument. I told him I had gone to Vladivostok to bring you out."

"He didn't ask why?"

"Of course he asked why. I told him to ask Alexi, that I couldn't tell him why. The whole ride here, I thought about what I would tell Alexi, how I would explain who you are. I could only think of one thing. I told him you were my lover and if he did anything to you, I would expose him."

"And telling him I am your lover, it didn't occur to you he might just have me shot on the spot?"

"I had to risk it," she said very agreeably.

It was my turn to cross my arms. "How fortunate for me your plan worked."

"It was a small risk. Alexi has never once shown any interest in me in that way. He wouldn't care if I slept with the entire Red Army so long as his secret stays a secret. The commissar won't shoot him for having a promiscuous wife. But for the other thing, he would be dead in an hour. Alexi has no choice. Ivchenko is a different matter. He has told his whore to watch and report."

"The maid with the scarf?"

"Maid," the countess said in a voice filled with derision. "When she isn't under Ivchenko, you can find her in the soldier's tents."

"So I played the other man and you, the promiscuous wife."

"I needed her to believe we are lovers. Ivchenko will believe what she tells him. Bohdan agreed it was our only plan. You were supposed to play along."

"You're the one who told me to get in the tub."

Her cheeks turned strawberry red. "The old woman told you to, not me. Among other things I shall not repeat."

I looked at the boards in the floor. They were still stained dark from spilt bathwater. "I thought you—"

"I saw what you thought, Mr. Watkins."

Clasping my hands behind my back, I asked, "So what happens now? You and Bohdan seem to have it all figured out."

"You leave in the morning. I've ordered breakfast."

I looked around the dimly lit bedroom. "I'll sleep on the floor. Spare a fellow conspirator a pillow?"

"Very gallant of you, but we can't take the risk of someone coming in. There's no lock on that door. The charade goes on for a few hours yet."

"We're sharing the bed?"

"I'm afraid we must." She went to the little table, glanced at the bottle of her adored concoction then said over her shoulder, "Left or right?"

"What?"

"Which side do you want, left or right?"

"The one closest to the door. I may have to run from a jealous husband before sunrise and that window's too small to jump through."

The countess crawled across the feather mattress, blew out the candle, crawled under the covers then pulled the quilts to her chin.

"You do remember the old woman took everything I was

wearing," I said.

She nodded, then turned her back to me. I doused the two candles on the mantle then walked slowly towards the elephant's legs. In the nearly dark room, I dropped the towel on the floor, pinched out the last candle then slid between velvet smooth sheets. The bed felt softer than a mother's kiss. Until I stretched out on that mattress, I don't think I was really aware of just how sore and worn out I was. As I sank deeper into the feathers, my weight caused the mattress to slope. The countess, her back to me, had to adjust her position on her side of the bed to keep from sliding against me.

We laid there for a long time, neither one talking. Neither one moving. Lying on my back, I crossed my hands behind my head. The gold bar was a hard lump under my pillow. A slow minute went by then another.

"Do you want to talk," she said in a quiet voice.

"I do not," I said, staring at the ceiling. More minutes ticked away. The only sound in the room was the logs being consumed by fire.

I felt her roll over, twisting around to face me in the darkness. With her head propped on an elbow, she was a shadowy outline beside me.

"I had to make it look real. Don't you understand? If there was any hint of anything besides passion between us, it would be our lives."

"You made it look very real. Everyone was fooled." I listened to the crack and pop of the fire. The room was almost completely dark now. Our fire was fading. The room would be cold before sunrise.

The feathers moved.

"You aren't going to be difficult about this, are you?" she asked.

"Nope."

"Mr. Watkins?"

"Still here."

"I can only imagine what you must think of me."

"Not thinking about you at all," I told the darkness above my head.

"I've never behaved like that before."

"You explained the whole thing. Would have been nice if you explained things before you started squirming all over me, naked as a French painting and covered in soap suds."

We lay there for a long time after that, neither of us moving, neither speaking, both awake. After a very long time, she whispered into the darkness.

"The old woman was right. You did smell like goat piss."

It was a long time before anyone fell asleep.

16

Soft tapping on the bedroom door woke me before the sun was up. My eyes opened to almost complete darkness, the fire having burned down to embers in the night. Still languishing in the luxury of clean sheets and a feather bed, my fingers touched the woman beside me. For the second time in as many mornings, I was waking up next to her. The female body inside the silk gown moved.

"Countess," I said. "It's morning. Your maid is here." I touched her shoulder.

"Not a maid," she mumbled sleepily. "Bolshevik camp follower."

My sleeping partner pushed unruly hair away from her face before she opened her eyes.

"One last charade, Mr. Watkins, and then it will be over."

She slid closer to me, laying her head on my shoulder and draping an arm over my chest. "They will expect to find me in your arms."

Her leg touched mine under the quilts as I put my arm

around her shoulders. Charades, she said. Just a carnival show for Ivchenko. The maid tapped on the door again, then opened it a crack.

"We're ready now," I said a bit too loudly for such an early hour. It was the young one, still in the same clothes she had on the night before, still with the same uninterested look in her eyes, still with the red badge of the loyal Soviet in her hair. Ivchenko's spy carried a tray with a single burning candle. I smelled food.

"What ungodly hour is this?" the countess murmured into my chest.

I looked at the room's only window and saw a dark curtain. "Early."

The toothless grandmother followed Ivchenko's camp following spy into the bedroom, a pile of clothing in her arms. I recognized my trousers.

The maid sat her tray on the bedside table, used her candle to light the one beside our bed, then went to the mantle and lit the two sitting on either end of the wooden beam. The countess was a pile of dark hair tucked in beside me.

"Time to wake up," I told the pile.

She mumbled something unintelligible.

There were eggs on the tray. I saw toasted bread swimming in butter and a pot of tea. "Breakfast is here."

A hand scratched at the mop of hair. "Don't want any." Rising slowly, she touched her forehead and groaned. "Pour me tea, Mr. Watkins. Is there milk and sugar?"

I looked at the tray. "Just milk."

"Barbarians," she groaned, then collapsed onto her pillow.

The maid filled a chipped mug with tea, added a splash of milk and handed it over. The fumes roused her. My bedroom companion sat up, blinked her eyes, then pulled herself into a sitting position. Taking the mug from my hands, the countess inhaled the steam coming out of the cup before taking a dainty sip of the hot brew.

"Tell them to give us a moment," I said. "I need to get

dressed."

"They won't care," the countess said between sips.

"I need to get dressed," I said to the maids. I spoke the words very slowly, separating the English into clearly distinct words. That's supposed to make it easier for people who don't speak my language understand what I'm saying. The young one handed me another cup of tea.

"I told you. They won't care."

"Perhaps I do."

She made a dismissive sound. "You do understand the nature of a camp follower's trade, don't you, Mr. Watkins? They won't notice and I, for one prefer to keep my eyes closed."

The countess was right. Neither of them batted an eye when I got out of bed. They just poured more tea, chittered among themselves, and fluffed pillows. Keeping my back to the countess, I reached for my drawers. The clothes were warm and smelled fresh as new cut hay. The grandmother must have hung them over a stove while we slept. Dressing quickly, I drank very hot tea, put my respectably covered torso between the two maids then slid my golden ingot into its customary place in my pocket.

"Nicely done," the countess told me.

"I should have been a magician."

"There's still time," she said smiling, then put her hand to her forehead. "Dear god, it hurts to smile. Go find our friend. If he's done his part, we leave before the commissar knows a thing."

"His part?"

"The cockroach will explain." She made a shooing motion with one hand that was eerily similar to the same one the toothless grandmother did last night. "Go, before the camp wakes up."

"Can I have the toast?"

"I see you are cruel in the morning, Mr. Watkins." She placed a hand on her stomach. "I couldn't touch food. Take it all. Just leave the tea if you please."

I left, stopping at the front door to pull on my boots. A miracle had happened in the night. The mud had disappeared and the leather was freshly shined. My coat was hanging from a rack beside the door. Someone had taken a brush to the dirt and grime. The old cloth looked cleaner than it had when I bought it.

Opening the door, I felt the first hint of things to come in Siberia. The autumn morning was cold, crisp and as still as a photograph. Buttoning my freshly cleaned coat, I stepped into a brand new day as Venus shined down from a still dark sky. It was a fine morning to be alive. I felt much better than I had a right to considering the amount of alcohol consumed the night before. As I left the cottage, a female's voice began shouting behind me. The countess, it seemed, wasn't feeling quite as refreshed as I was.

The east was showing hints of sunrise as I walked down the forest path and past the warehouses. A soldier coughed as he stirred a fire. My nose caught the smell of freshly baked bread drifting in the air. I started to hum a song as I strolled along with my hands in my pockets. Even in the morning, with her hair nearing bird nest proportions and foggy from too much of that green concoction she was drinking, she was still a beautiful woman. It would be a long time before I forgot the sight of her walking out of the shadows last night. All a charade, she said. Play acting. A hoax to fool Ivchenko's spies. Bohdan's idea. I laughed in the chilly darkness of a Siberian morning. Giving a rock a kick with my freshly shined boots, I started to whistle.

I needed to find Bohdan and find out what our next move was now that Ivchenko's suspicions about me and the countess were satisfied. Unfortunately, I had no idea where to look. The man hadn't reappeared since that boy fetched me to go look at the comrade colonel's tank. The depot wasn't very large. There were only so many places he could be. He wouldn't be hard to find once the sun was up. I decided to go to the truck and wait for daylight.

The Mack was still where I left it, still with the ridiculous field gun on the back. I thumped the bed with my fist.

"So I was right all along, Lieutenant," a southern accent said from the other side of the truck. Rancid pipe smoke reminiscent of an open sewer drifted along an unfelt breeze.

"Major?" I whispered to the surrounding darkness. Once again, the marine had managed to surprise me. I was glad he couldn't see my face.

"Around this side, Watkins. That Russian walks by every five or six minutes. No need to let him see you talking to me."

I hadn't seen any Russians walking anywhere in the darkness. There was hardly any light at all except for the grays and blues on the eastern horizon. Moving around the front of the truck, I put the big vehicle between me and the train tracks.

Shadows moved. The major stepped out from behind stacked railroad ties and a pile of about a half dozen knee high metal cans. He walked like he was just another Russian coming back from relieving himself in the bushes. The marine was still in the same clothes I had seen him in before. Same fur hat and with the same awful smell coming out of his pipe. The only thing different was the pistol strapped around his waist and the sling holding his left arm.

"Something wrong with your arm, Major?"

"Never mind my arm. Found any misplaced piles of gold yet?"

In the darkness, I could just make out a bandage wrapped around his hand. The major sagged slowly onto the truck's running board.

"That as bad as it looks?"

"My grandmother, the Good Lord rest her soul, always said Cossacks were Satan riding a horse." He moved his arm, wincing as he did so. "Semyonov's got his boys out. They've been chasing me for two days." Slowly and with a face twisted against the pain, he pulled his bandaged arm out of the sling and held it up before him. "Damn Cossack with a saber ruined my favorite shirt. Had to cut the sleeve off to wrap up my arm."

"I've heard the name."

"Well, Lieutenant, our mission is a success. You've identified the name of a local warlord. I suspect his days are numbered. Soon as the Bolsheviks finish their business down in Vladivostok, they'll find a nice shallow grave for the general. Good troops, he had. Just not enough of them." The major slid his bandaged arm back into the sling. "Got a few less now."

"Major, I—"

"Quiet Lieutenant. I haven't given you leave to speak. Had to send my boys east, pull some of them away so I could come get you."

"Come get me?"

"Get you out. Made it just in time, too. Be sure and remember me to your offspring in the years to come." The major tried to flex the fingers of his wounded hand. He couldn't move the little one at all and could just wiggle the one next to it. The pain felt like he'd accidentally grabbed the wrong side of a hot iron. "It's over, Watkins." The major stood up, sliding his back against the truck as he rose. "I've got three horses tied up about a half mile that way." His good hand pointed into the trees. "At least they were there last night, right about the time you went for your little walk down the lane there. I see you and our lovely Countess Irena have become the best of friends."

"It isn't like that," I said defensively.

"I don't give a good god dammed what it's like, Lieutenant. This little adventure you and the admiral cooked up is over. I'm pulling the plug."

"The admiral's orders said—"

"The admiral and his orders are sitting on their shore duty ass in Subic Bay. I am your superior officer, Lieutenant, and I am giving you a direct order. I gave you your chance and all you've done is get you britches washed and force me to rethink my extraction plans. It's over. We are leaving right now while these green boys playing soldier aren't looking. Where's Bohdan?"

"I lost track of him, sir."

"Of course you did, Lieutenant, because you don't belong here. I told the admiral that very thing and believe me, it will be in my report. He never should have taken you out of the Yangtze. I'm sure you'll do fine back on the gunboats." The major tapped the pipe against the sole of his boot. "Bohdan's asleep in that second building over there, the one with the wheelbarrow beside the door. He's been there since he watched you go for your stroll last night." The marine looked at the sky. "We don't have much time. Twenty minutes at best I would say."

A train's whistle blew in the distance. This one was coming from the direction of Vladivostok.

"Until sunrise?"

"No, Watkins. Until they attack. There's at least two hundred men in those trees. I told you, Semyonov's boys are out. They smell blood. This depot is about to be overrun. Half an hour, it will all be over. Nothing left but the bodies. My bet, they're waiting for—"

The locomotive's whistle blew again. You could see its headlight shining in the darkness down the tracks.

"—the train," he said, pointing towards the approaching light. "Whoever's in charge of this backwater needs to be cashiered. If he had put a few pickets in those woods, he would have known he was about to get his men slaughtered."

"Two hundred men are waiting out there," I said. The trees were a wall of darkness running down both sides of the Trans-Siberian.

"Saddled up and waiting for the order. This is what you are going to do, Lieutenant. You are going to walk into that shed, find the man you were supposed to be following, and bring him out. Quickly. Make up an excuse. If for some reason he doesn't buy it, pull your sidearm. You do still have your sidearm, don't you? Or did you lose track of that, too?"

I didn't bother answering.

"If he starts to yell, slap a good solid piece of navy steel alongside his jaw. I suspect he'll come peacefully after that. Pretend for a minute you are a marine and move quickly with force and determination. Get him back here to this spot. I'll cover you as best I can from that pile of lumber. If any Red soldier tries to stop you, shoot him. By the time they figure out what's happening, the killing should be well underway by the fellows in the woods. Get Billy here and we'll head for the trees in the smoke and confusion. You understand your orders, Lieutenant? I would go over them again to reconcile any operational confusion on your end, but I believe the show is about to start. Best you get started."

The locomotive was a football field's length away from the siding. The engine clanked and clattered as the giant iron wheels rolled slowly down the tracks. The major grabbed my arm with his good hand just as the engineer rang the bell.

"Not that way, Lieutenant. Over there, that one." He pointed his damaged hand in the direction of Bohdan's shed.

I pulled my arm out of his and started walking.

"Lieutenant," he hissed.

The locomotive arrived, steam screaming from the engine and bell clanging. The train was pulling empty flatbeds and a few boxcars. I didn't see any troops onboard.

Overrun, the major said. The show was about to start. She was at the far end of the depot sipping tea and arguing with her maids.

"Lieutenant!" He yelled it this time.

Pulling my pistol out of my coat pocket, I pointed it at the predawn sky. "Alarm!" I shouted. I shouted it so loud the strain hurt my throat. The gun jumped in my hand as I pulled the trigger. Then I started running.

17

The major was right. They were waiting for the train to roll into the station. The echo of my warning shot didn't have time to die away before a bugle's brass roar screamed out its signal. Semyonov's horsemen charged the depot. They swarmed across the open ground, rode their horses into the tents and yelled their battle cries. A few Red soldiers, seeing death pouring out of the forest, grabbed bolt action rifles. A few, not nearly enough, managed to get a shot off before the sabers found them. Most of the defenders were exposed. Caught in the open, they were killed where they stood. It was like watching wolves herd sheep. Confusion was everywhere. Only the raiders seemed to know what to do. The depot troops fled, or tried to. Running for the safety of the far side of the station and its wall of oaks, they ran straight into a second assault coming out of the darkness. Green boys, the major called them and the boys were caught, jammed between twin charges of Cossack horsemen. Half the depot's troops were killed in that first wild charge.

I heard Russian voices shouting, whether friend or foe I had no idea. Guns fired, their muzzle flashes like giant sparks in the night.

"It's this way," I shouted over a shoulder, expecting to see the major following me. He wasn't. No one was there. "Major," I shouted. Was he dead? Fighting? In the dim light, I could just make out the stack of ties, the truck looking like a shadowy mastodon and men running in every direction. I didn't see the marine. Turning around, I ran along beside the train, trying to keep myself as close to the flatbeds as I could. They hadn't come from the direction of the cottage, but a running horse would get there in seconds, long before I could. Rifles fired from a warehouse's doorway, each shot sounding like a small clap of thunder in my ears. None of the attackers were knocked off their horses.

The Cossacks, never still, hunted the running men, slashing their bodies with curved blades as one of the warehouses caught fire and began to burn with bright orange and yellow flames. A black bearded man rode past me, one hand holding a severed head high in the air, the other waving a bloody sword. He was laughing, spurring his horse into the steam and noise of the locomotive. I watched him go, crouching under the edge of a railcar until he was out of sight before sprinting down the length of the train. I had a long way to go.

A horse came charging out of the confusion. The raider saw me, yanked hard on his reins, and waved a saber over his head. Shouting a challenge, the cavalryman put heels to his horse's flanks. Man and beast thundered straight at me.

Satan on horseback, the major said.

I fired too quickly. My aim no doubt was rattled at the sight of mounted death coming for me. The second shot wasn't any better. With my life a half second away from ending, the third bullet struck the horse. The animal went down in a heap thirty feet away, throwing the rider over its head as it rolled. The horse screamed and kicked as its lifeblood colored Siberian dirt.

He almost had me. I was watching a dying horse kick its life away and not what it was carrying. The Cossack, a giant of a man, was on his feet, four feet of steel in one hand. The swing from his saber ripped the air in front of my stomach. When he pulled his arm back for a second swing, I shot him. The bullet should have put him on his back to kick his own life away. It didn't. The Russian grunted, half turned away, then lunged for me. Arms wrapped around me, pushing, pulling and twisting. The forty-five went off again when the Cossack tried to yank the pistol out of my hand. The slide locked open. My last round was gone.

We fell, the two of us wrapped in a hand to hand struggle that only one was coming out of alive. It wasn't the kind of fighting young men did in boxing rings in American gyms. It was brutal, ruthless, and desperate. I held on to the arm holding the saber, punching when I could and straining with all my strength to push the bigger man off me. If not for my bullet, he would have killed me easily, but there was a forty-five caliber hole somewhere in that body and I could feel his strength beginning to fail. I just wasn't sure if it would fail before or after he killed me.

We rolled on the ground, each trying to best the other in the most personal kind of combat there is. I took the major's advice and hit him with navy steel. If I couldn't shoot him, I would beat him to death with the pistol. The first blow struck the side of his head. The second smashed open his cheek. The third would have ended it, but the giant caught my arm in an iron grip, then slammed it against the train track. The pistol flew from my hand as fingers clawed at my throat. In the end, it was my bullet that made the difference. The Russian's great strength left him, and I wrapped my hands around his throat. He fought still, legs kicking as he tried to throw me off. I held on, squeezing his neck with every ounce of strength I had until death glazed his eyes.

A gun fired. Not one of the slow firing bolt actions. This

gun fired in steady bursts of six or eight shots, then a pause followed by another short burst.

Bohdan.

I don't think the fast moving Cossacks had planned on trying to ride down a man with a machinegun.

The dead Cossack and I were under one of the railcars. I didn't see the pistol. It was gone, lost somewhere in the dirt and gravel. I crawled away from the corpse, back to where the horse had fallen. How much time had I lost? How much was left? I had no idea. Bohdan's Lewis fired again. A dozen voices shouted as a second warehouse began to burn. More horses galloped past, most without saddles or riders. The Cossacks had helped themselves to the depot's remounts. The rider's attentions were focused towards the sound of the Lewis and the dozen or so animals running before them. None of them noticed a single unarmed man crouching in the dark beside a flatbed. Once they were past, I started running across the train yard. Red soldiers were lying everywhere, some struggling to drag themselves away from the battle. Most weren't moving at all. I stopped beside one, a teenager whose front was sliced open from collarbone to crotch. The barrel of a rifle was sticking out from beneath his body. Dragging the gun free, I started running again.

Behind me, the boxcars went up in flames. Orange fire reached towards the sky as thick gray smoke stung my eyes. A horse came charging out of the darkness, its saddle empty. In its eyes, I saw the animal's fear of fire and death. Waving my arms, I shouted something and reached for the reins. The animal wasn't having any of it. It jerked away and disappeared into the smoke. I almost ran after it. The flames were a roaring heat behind me now. I could hear men shouting as rifles fired from every direction. Had I passed the lane to the cottage? I coughed in the smoke and rubbed watery eyes. Making myself as small as I could, I ran across the yard, hoping I was going in the right direction. When the air cleared, I saw the office built on stilts. I ran towards it, trying to orient myself with the stilts and the flatcar at my back. The cottage was somewhere to my right. I remembered that much, but there was more than one path leading into the woods. Last night, I was drunk and not paying attention. This morning, I was humming songs and thinking about silk gowns that left nothing to the imagination. Which path was the right one?

A chair shattered the office windows and came crashing down into the train yard. A woman screamed as a man came tumbling down the stairs. He landed in an unmoving pile of pajamas ten feet in front of me. I needed to go find that damn little house in the woods. The woman screamed again. The countess said the stationmaster had moved his family into one of the buildings. This one.

I took the stairs two at a time. Male voices shouted inside the small office. Something heavy enough to make the stairs shake crashed to the floor. I went through the door with the rifle at my shoulder as one man smashed the butt of his own rifle against a telegraph key. His partner threw an oil lamp against a wall. Flames licked up the side of the wood as thick black smoke crawled its way towards the ceiling.

A woman in a long nightgown stood against the far wall. She was shielding a child behind her. The two men turned to face me. I'm better with a rifle than a pistol. I must be, because the first shot took the nearest man square in the chest. The bullet knocked him off his feet as the rifle he was using to smash the telegraph clattered onto the floor. The second man pawed at a leather holster. Working the bolt as fast as I could, I fired again. The bullet drove the Cossack into the flames from the shattered lamp. He didn't get up.

The woman looked at me, looked at the two dead men, then at the burning wall. Scooping the kid into her arms, she ran for the stairs. I followed her as fire consumed the depot office.

Fear must have put wings on her feet because by the time I got to the bottom of the stairs, she was nowhere in sight. Working the rifle's bolt again, the empty brass shell went sailing into the air. There were no more rounds in the magazine. Once again, I was unarmed. Another one of the sheds went up in flames. With the office above me burning like a lighthouse beacon and the fires from the warehouse making a too bright glow on my left, I felt terribly exposed. Anyone could see me silhouetted by the flames. I needed to get out of the light. Seconds I couldn't afford to lose ticked away, but I simply could not remember which path was the right one.

The one to my right was the farthest from the glow. At least I wouldn't be silhouetted by the flames. Still trying to make myself as small as I could, I ran down the barely seen path through the trees. There were no Red soldiers. No marauding cavalry, either. The fight was behind me. Nobody seemed interested in a twisty, turning trail running directly away from the train. That was fine by me. I ran, an empty rifle in my hands and the sound of hell and death behind me. I went as fast as I could, still not knowing if this was the path the messenger boy and I had stumbled down last night.

The fires were just a glow in the sky behind me now. There was no moon and the thin light coming from the predawn sky wasn't making it through the trees. Everywhere and everything was shadowy darkness. I tripped over something and went sprawling like a man trying a face first slide into second base. As I picked myself up, I heard it before I saw it. It was a horse, heavy hooves thumping into the ground somewhere in front of me. It sounded like it was moving fast. I was about to jump for the cover of the nearest tree when I heard the yell. It was a woman's voice; a high shriek coming out of the darkness in the direction of the unseen horse. A long heartbeat later, I saw her. She was running towards me; a formless shadow barely seen in the darkness. But she wasn't fast enough. Not nearly. The horse caught her. Its rider leaned far over in the saddle to scoop the running woman up and off her feet. He swung her belly down across the front of his saddle while his horse thundered down the path. She yelled again. The rider laughed. It was all a game to him. A prize.

His reward for being in the right place at the right time. If he looked up, he would have seen me standing in the middle of the dirt path, but he wasn't interested in what was in front of him. His attentions were on his prize; a kicking, fighting woman in a dark skirt and white blouse with a red scarf around her hair. It was the maid. The one who hauled water for us last night. The girl who spied for Ivchenko, or so the countess said.

The horse was huge. In the twilight, it was all power and strength. The animal was a darker shadow galloping out of the night. I saw a white forelock as the animal tossed its head. Maybe it was laughing, too.

I was too late. If they had the maid, where was the countess? Too late and too far away and now I was about to be killed by a laughing Cossack. The major was probably watching my last moments on this earth from somewhere in the forest, no doubt with that told-the-admiral-so look on his face. Any second now, the Cossack would look up and see me standing in front of him.

It all happened so quickly. The woman managed to throw herself half off the saddle. She almost made it. Almost. I think one of her feet might have made contact with the ground before the Russian hauled her back across his saddle. I reversed my grip on the empty rifle. Holding it by the barrel, I raised the heavy stock shoulder high. The Cossack was slapping his hand on the girl's rump. The horse galloped towards me, tossing its head in the shadowy predawn light. The rider raised his hand about to pound another slap down on the woman when he finally saw me standing in the road.

I dropped to one knee and swung the rifle as hard as I could.

The hard charging horse's front legs folded beneath him. The Cossack bellowed an indignant shout as the horse began to cartwheel.

I lost the rifle. It spiraled away to land somewhere among the trees as a tangled mess of kicking hooves, whirling skirts, and yelling Cossack tumbled past me. Something hit me. I think it was one of the horse's rear legs. Whatever it was, it knocked me flat. When I stood up, the Bolshevik girl was on hands and knees a few yards away. The Cossack wasn't on hands and knees. He was sprawled on his back and was trying to roll over onto his chest. He wasn't making a lot of progress in the attempt, having just had a thousand pounds of horse roll over him.

The horse whinnied in pain as it struggled to its feet. The rider wasn't laughing now. He was groaning. As he rolled onto his side, his hands grabbed at his leg. The fall must have snapped the bones beneath the knee because the lower half was bent in the wrong direction. When he saw his leg sprouting a second knee, the groan turned into a scream.

The Bolshevik girl rose slowly from the ground. Her hair was loose; the red scarf no longer holding it. Pushing long bangs away from her face, she looked stunned and disoriented. Favoring her hip, she saw me in the middle of the road. It took her a moment to understand what had just happened. With a quick nod of recognition, she looked at the broken legged Cossack before dropping to all fours in the dirt. Her hands searched in the darkness like she had lost something valuable. Now was not the time to look for a missing earing and I was about to tell her to get up and run when she found what she was looking for. She had to dig around the edges for a second before she had it free from the dirt. She wasn't looking for a lost earring. She was looking for a rock. The one she found was about the size of a football and must have weighed twenty pounds. The Bolshevik girl took a step closer towards the man with three knees. I thought she looked worldly before. It wasn't worldliness I saw in those dark eyes now. She didn't look anything like the maid who quietly hauled buckets of water. The mask of passive docility was gone, replaced by something cold and merciless.

The Cossack saw it too.

He stopped slapping the dirt around him and grabbed for the hilt of a long saber belted around his waist. The girl limped closer. It took both hands to lift the rock over her head.

Six inches of steel slid clear of the Cossack's scabbard. I moved. If he got that sword free, he was going to skewer the girl, shattered leg or not.

The Bolshevik shouted something in Russian. The Cossack, still trying to pull his saber free, threw up a protective arm. It didn't help. With a grunt, the girl slammed the heavy stone down. Ivchenko's spy had a good aim. Her football hit the unhorsed cavalryman square on the top of his skull. I heard a crack and something that sounded squishy and wet. The Cossack's head bent to one side as twenty pounds of rock rolled into his lap. He wasn't reaching for his sword anymore. He wasn't going to reach for anything ever again. The Russian girl kicked the dead man's mangled leg before spitting out her opinion of Cossacks.

The horse, now lamed in one leg trotted away into the darkness.

The Bolshevik knocked dirt off her fingers, rubbed her hip then turned to me.

"Too late, Watkin."

I think I heard a touch of satisfaction in her voice.

"Men in dacha got her now."

It hit me then. Her words. English words. Christ above, the whole time the countess was putting on her bathing beauty act, the girl understood every word we said to each other. She even heard me call her countess. Bohdan warned me. Call her Katya, he said. I hadn't, and now this girl knew the truth.

"You speak English?"

She nodded, then waved a hand down the dirt road. "Too late for her. Come with me." Pointing into the trees, she added, "You safe me. I safe you."

A scattering of shots went off in the direction of the depot. We both looked towards the sound. There was nothing to see but darkness and a fire lit sky.

"Watkin."

She drew my name out in a long, whispered hiss. Still

looking towards the sound of the shots, she reached for the sleeve of my coat.

"Come with me. With me, live. With her, die."

I needed to go. I had already stayed too long. Pulling my sleeve out of her grasp, I said, "I need a gun."

We both looked at the dead Cossack. Trying not to see the mush that was the man's head, I pulled the soldier's coat open hoping I'd find a holstered pistol. There wasn't one. When we boarded junks on the Yangtze, officers were required to wear a cutlass. I had boarded many a suspect pirate, but I had never once used a sword in a fight. Still, it was better than nothing, which was what I had right now. I pulled the half drawn saber free of its scabbard. It made that swishing, sliding sound long sharp steel makes. The blade was curved and heavy and felt solid in my hand.

The girl took a step backwards.

"I'm not going to hurt you."

Her eyes said she wasn't convinced.

I pointed the long blade at the forest. "Find a place to hide until this is over."

I left her standing by the dead Cossack. The cottage couldn't be much farther. The messenger boy and I hadn't walked that far. There was time, I told myself. I wouldn't be too late. With the heavy blade swinging a lethal counterbalance beside me, I started to run. The Bolshevik girl's words repeated over and over inside my head with every step. Too late.

The sky was turning a washed out pale gray. I could see individual limbs on the trees now, dips in the road, and puddles of water here and there.

The cottage.

There it was at last, straight in front of me along with a pair of horses tied to a rail. I looked at the piece of steel in my hand, sucked in my courage, and ran straight at them.

18

The front door was splintered and torn, hanging by a single remaining hinge. Bits and pieces of painted wood lay scattered in front of the ruined entrance. I grabbed the broken door with my free hand and ripped it out of the way. There was a man standing in the close interior. He turned, probably thinking I was another of the raiders come for the looting. Like me, he held a long, curved saber in his hand. As he turned, the look on his face changed from welcome to violence.

A gun fired from the bedroom; three shots going off as fast as a trigger could be pulled. The blasts coming from the other room surprised the man crouched for the attack. He looked towards the second smashed door, the one to her bedroom. He should have kept his eyes on me. With the blade sticking straight out in front of me, I lunged.

The Cossack was quick. His own blade swept around in a quick arc and knocked the point of my saber to one side. My opponent retreated farther into the home, putting distance between me and my jabs at his midsection. The surprise attack and the distraction of the gunshots were over. In just those few moments of contact, both of us knew he was better at playing with long knives than I was. He was going to kill me. The Cossack put a foot behind him and backed farther into the room. I saw him getting ready for his counterattack, and I wondered which body part I was about to lose. Then he fell. His leg just seemed to roll out from under him as a round, fat bean can sized candle went skittering across the rug.

The steel of my saber made a butcher shop sound as it chopped through his collarbone. The blade sank deep. The man on the floor screamed in agony as his hand grabbed for the steel. When I put my boot on his chest and pulled, the razor sharp saber ripped the flesh from his fingers. His hand fell away and landed next to the leg of the veteran of the Crimean War. The old woman's eyes, glazed and dead, stared up at nothing. Her last moments in this life had ended cruelly. The axe they used to break through the front door was still in her chest. The Cossack slumped across her body. The countess said she wasn't impressed by me. At least I killed her killer.

Another man staggered out of the bedroom. One hand grabbed at the wall as the other tried to stop the blood from pouring out of his chest. He stumbled forward as I swung the saber in a backhanded arc. The tip of the blade hit him just below his chin, slicing clear through his throat before slamming into the wooden doorjamb. Bright red arterial blood sprayed out of the gash. The man gurgled words no one would ever understand, reached for his neck then stumbled backwards into her room. I followed him, stabbing his body twice with the point of my sword before he stopped kicking.

The horse trough was on its side, a bucket lying next to it. A wooden chair that hadn't been there when I left this morning was lying beside the tub, two of its legs broken. She was barefoot, standing by the bed we shared together less than an hour earlier. She was still wearing the wedding gift; the white silk that last night clung so seductively to her body. A hairbrush was on the floor by her feet. I thought of the

Bolshevik girl with the red scarf. The maid must have been brushing her hair when the raid started. Her prized broom handle Mauser was in her hand, its slide locked back on an empty magazine.

"Countess," I said.

"Mr. Watkins," she whispered.

"You alright?"

She nodded, then looked at the empty pistol in her hand. "Yes, I am alright."

I looked around the room. "Any more of them?"

She shook her head. "The old woman?" She pointed at her bedroom wall. The front door was on the other side.

"Dead."

The countess glanced at the bedside table. The remains of our breakfast were still there.

"She went to get more tea," the countess said. "Why would they kill her? She was just an old woman."

Something exploded. The floor of the cottage shook beneath my feet and the single window rattled in its frame. The sound reminded of the shells falling outside my Vladivostok flophouse, but this blast was a lot closer and much louder. The countess was in my arms, both arms around my neck and hanging on like the floor was falling away beneath her.

"You're alright," I said. "That was something in the depot. Not here."

She looked at me and I saw in those eyes a reflection of the way she looked when it was just she and I at our cafe. I reversed the grip on the saber and slammed the point into the nearest elephant's leg. Sunk deeply into the bedpost, the steel quivered as Cossack blood oozed down the blade. I pulled her close. She didn't resist. She fell against me as the Mauser clattered onto the floor. I could feel her, all of her, as she pressed her body against mine. I wrapped my arms around her and felt her fingers touched the back of my neck. She kissed me as rifles fired in the distance and a train depot burned.

When the kiss was over, she pushed away from me. I let her slide out of my arms.

"You shouldn't," she paused, then started again. "We shouldn't have done that."

Her eyes settled on the man we both killed. The woman from our time in the cafe disappeared and I saw the countess once more.

"The whore went to go see what was happening," she told me.

"Cossacks attacked the morning train," I told her as I went to the bedroom's single window and pulled back a thin curtain. There was nothing outside but a wall of leafless trees bathed in blue gray light.

"Semyonov," the Countess said, a touch of satisfaction in her tone. "The bear hasn't lost all its teeth."

"They caught the guards flatfooted," I said as the curtain fell back into place. "It's a bad time to be a Red soldier." I looked at my hand. My fingers were shaking. Five men were dead.

"When they smashed the front door, I went for my pistol, but they broke through before I could get it. I blocked my door with the chair."

Yanking the saber out of the bedpost, I said, "I got here as fast as I could." The tip of the steel blade scratched across the boards on the floor.

"And the Czech? Where is he?"

Scattered among the distant rifle shots, Bohdan's Lewis fired another burst of automatic fire. I hooked a thumb towards the window. "That would be him."

"We need to go, Mr. Watkins. This is our chance to get away."

"In the smoke and confusion," I said, quoting the major. "Put your clothes on, then pack some essentials."

The countess ran her hand down the side of the negligee. "The old woman told me to put it on."

She looked at me.

"Last night."

"Quickly, Countess," I told her. "I don't want to be here if another pack of raiders comes down that road."

The countess straightened her arms by her side, clenched small hands into fists, lifted her chin, then said with serene formality, "Thank you for coming back for me, Mr. Watkins."

Formality isn't easy while wearing a negligee not much thicker than a foggy day. I found myself straightening my posture and wishing I had sorted out my appearance after my wrestling match beneath a flatcar. "Wouldn't have done anything else, Countess." A memory of the major's orders echoed inside my head. He wasn't going to be pleased with me.

19

We stood there for a moment longer. Me, scruffy from my fights, a borrowed saber in one hand and hoping I looked as calm on the outside as she did. The countess, barefoot, wrapped in silk and hair hanging loose down her back. Bohdan's Lewis fired again. The automatic's rattle was followed by a scattering of rifle shots, whether from the Reds or the Cossacks it was impossible to tell. I wondered how long before the defenders regrouped and drove off the raiders or the Cossacks overwhelmed however many Reds were left. Whichever outcome, I didn't think the fight would go on much longer. "Do you have any more ammunition?"

"In there," the countess answered, waving a hand towards the closet.

I yanked the door open. It wasn't a big space. Just a rack with an assortment of women's dresses, an impressive pile of shoes, the boots she had worn since we left the city and the travel worn canvas pack.

"The bullets are in the pack," she said from behind me.

Throwing it on the bed, I grabbed a handful of various fabrics, pitched it all onto the feather mattress, then kicked the riding boots after the clothes.

"Get dressed," I told her, "and hurry, Countess."

Shoving a fresh strip of bullets into her Mauser, she worked the slide, then laid the loaded weapon on the bed.

"I'll wait outside," I said.

"That would be appropriate, Mr. Watkins."

A rifle fired followed by another burst from our Czech friend.

"Yell when you're done." I turned for the front room.

"Leave the door open, won't you? I'll just be a minute."

Her voice sounded as calm as if she suffered through the occasional Cossack attack on a regular basis.

"Quickly, Countess. The Cossacks are killing and burning everything in sight. Us too, if we don't head for the woods."

"I shall only be a minute."

I had to step over the dead man lying sprawled across the floor. The cut in his throat yawed open as dull eyes watched the ceiling. The first dead Cossack was still piled across the corpse of the murdered grandmother. I grabbed him by the shoulder, the one I hadn't sliced open with my saber, and pulled the body away from her. As I was dragging the corpse, one of the horses still tied to the post outside the cottage whickered. I had forgotten all about the horses. Our little hideaway couldn't be seen from the train yard, but two dead men still found it. Anybody riding by could see those horses and might wonder where the owners had disappeared to.

Stepping through the shattered front door, I untied first one and then the other. The big black one didn't seem to understand. It just looked at me with that I'd love to bite you look in its eyes. Waving the Cossack's saber in the air did the trick. The black horse turned and ran for the trees. The brown one was a bit more stubborn. I had to hit it across the rump with the flat of the blade. Both horses gone, I hurried back inside the cottage.

"Countess!" I yelled, "we have to go."

"I'm hurrying. Don't leave me."

Leave her? I disobeyed a direct order to get here, killed five men in the process, and she was afraid I was going to leave. I wasn't going to leave, but I *was* going to drag her out of that bedroom, dressed or not, and run for the woods if she didn't hurry.

The old woman's body was stretched out on the cottage's blood stained rug. I couldn't just leave her lying there. Not with an axe in her chest. My stomach rumbled and I almost lost my breakfast before the heavy iron pulled free from the dead woman's body. I threw it out the destroyed door, straightened her arms and legs, then covered her with the dead man's coat.

"Countess." It wasn't a yell but it was pretty damn close. "We have to go."

"Almost," she said from her bedroom.

The dead man in the hallway didn't have a weapon other than his saber and a long wicked looking knife stuck in his boot. I didn't need a knife. I already had the four foot version. What I needed was a firearm. There was one more body to check, the one whose throat I cut.

"I'm coming in."

She made some reply that could have been anything. I waited for half a second then went through the door. The countess, sitting on the feather bed in gray jodhpurs and a very white brassiere was pulling on a second boot. Her hair was pushed up into a pile under the same man's leather brimmed hat she had worn since Vladivostok. The Mauser was lying on top of her red coat.

"I'm hurrying." Rising from the mattress, she strapped the gun belt around her waist. "You're staring at me, Mr. Watkins."

"I'm not."

"You are." She picked up her pistol and waved the barrel

at the dead man lying on the floor. "See if he is armed."

"That's why I came in."

"And you were staring."

The dead man's dark blue wool trench coat was a mess of blood from the gash in his throat. I'm not usually squeamish but, I really didn't want to touch the gore. Using the saber's tip, I pushed open the lapels, hoping to see a pistol belt. There wasn't one. Just a scabbard for another saber. Looking at the countess, I said, "No gun."

"Pity. Are you ready?"

"I think I am," I said dryly.

"We must hurry, Mr. Watkins. More horsemen could be here any minute." She grabbed a cranberry colored blouse from the pile of clothing on the bed. "We shall take their horses and circle around, find our Czech friend and see—"

"There are no horses."

"But," she pointed towards the front of the cottage.

"You might outrun a Cossack fox hunt, but I wouldn't make it half a mile. I ran the horses off before someone saw them."

"On foot then," she said, a not so slight touch of exasperation in her voice.

The hinge holding the remains of the front door squeaked. Someone was coming. The saber in my fist felt medieval to me, like something from another age, but it was all I had. There wasn't time to think about it. I set my feet, pulled back the curved steel like a batter waiting for a fastball, and got ready to swing as hard as I could. Behind me, the countess cocked the hammer on the broom handle.

The Bolshevik girl, a red headdress covering brown hair once more, stumbled into the room. She was breathing hard from running up the lane and was half doubled over from the effort. Behind me, the countess said something in Russian. Even I could hear the relief in her words.

"They come," the girl said breathlessly. "Run, Watkin!"

The countess gasped, either at the English being spoken by her camp following maid or at the implication of more

Cossacks coming to finish what the first group had failed to do.

"She speaks English."

"One problem at a time," I told her.

"But she heard everything. Last night. She knows."

"We'll sort it out later. Is there a back door?" I asked the girl.

She nodded, leaving us standing in the bedroom and running towards the back of the small house.

Grabbing the countess by an arm, I shoved her towards the door. "Run!" I yelled. She pulled out of my arm, the cranberry colored blouse still clutched in her hand.

"Wait. My father's spurs," she said, pointing at the canvas pack. "It's all I have left of him. I want them."

She wanted a pair of spurs while killers were riding up the path from the train yard. The pack was buried under a pile of dresses, blouses, wool slacks, a powder blue corset like those worn by women before the war, and an assortment of hats, bottled concoctions and shoes. Hurry, I'd told her. Our lives were in immediate danger of ending and she was packing dresses.

"They're in the pack. Bring it along, won't you?" she said from behind me.

Knocking everything that wasn't already stuffed into the bag onto the floor, I slung the canvas pack over my shoulder and turned for the door. "Go!" I yelled it this time. I even brandished the saber. If she didn't start moving that instant, I was going to slap her across her rump with the flat of the blade like I did the Cossack's horse.

Still holding the blouse in one hand and her Mauser in the other, she stumbled towards the door as I shoved and pushed from behind. We ran through the cottage like a pack of panicked hounds. The countess sent a chair tumbling out of her way. I slammed into some kind of hutch when my boot caught on the edge of a rug. Pottery hit the floor and exploded into shards.

"Run!" I yelled. "Fast as you can." We ran down a short hallway and into the kitchen area where an iron stove radiated heat. A wooden door stood open on the other side of a mud room. I caught a glimpse of the girl with the red scarf running across the small cleared space behind the house and into the shelter of the forest beyond. Pushing and shoving the countess in front of me, we headed for the back door. I stopped just long enough to slam it closed behind us.

20

The countess didn't seem to understand the concept of running for one's life. The second time she stopped to try to put on her blouse, I grabbed her by the arm and started half dragging her along behind me.

"Mr. Watkins, wait. I'm not decent."

"Don't care."

"It's just a blouse, Mr. Watkins. Half a second, please," she said with a voice full of righteous protest.

I didn't slow down and I didn't let go of her arm. There were shouts behind us. The enemy was in the cottage. We had made it outside with seconds to spare.

"Keep up," I told her. "So help me, I'll drag you if you stop again."

"Mr. Watkins, I can't run this fast. Slow down, please."

I ran faster. In a fair standup fight, I didn't think I would last long swinging a borrowed saber back and forth like I knew what I was doing with it. If the riders came around the back of the house, I was dead for sure. I didn't want to think about what would happen to the woman I was pulling along behind me.

Just inside the trees, we half slid into a shallow gully. Our Bolshevik rescuer was standing in the deepest part, bent over with hands on her knees and breathing hard.

"Hurry, Watkin," she gasped before she ducked under a fallen tree. Almost on all fours, she scrambled through fallen leaves and Siberian mud. The red scarf and blue skirt disappeared down the gully.

Ducking under the log, I pulled the countess after me. She fell onto her knees halfway beneath the tree.

"Mr. Watkins, wait a moment," the countess pleaded.

I didn't wait. If a Cossack soldier stepped through the cottage's back door, the real chase would begin and it wouldn't end well for any of us. Throwing my arm around her waist, I lifted her off the ground and ran. Slashing at limbs and brush with a saber, a grown woman under one arm and a canvas pack on your back isn't the fastest way to make one's escape. I didn't care. I just needed to make it to the thicker parts of the woods and away from that back door.

"Put me down! I'm not a sack of turnips," the countess protested.

Looking behind me, I couldn't see the cottage anymore. We might make it yet. Letting go of my turnip sack, I grabbed her by the arm and ran after the fast moving Bolshevik. The woods got thicker with every running step.

"Far enough, Mr. Watkins. I can't breathe."

She stumbled again, going down on one knee before I hauled her back to her feet.

"Keep running," I told her.

"Leave her, Watkin," the Bolshevik said over her shoulder.

"Stop, please," the countess said. "I can shoot them if they come. You're hurting my arm."

The low dip we were in snaked its way between massive oak trees. We ran down its length, crashing our way through overhanging limbs, both of us bent over at the waist and me praying with every step we weren't running straight towards more Cossacks.

After what must have been a quarter of a mile of hard running, the countess had gone as far as she could. My own legs were aching and I had a razor sharp cramp in my side.

"Catch your breath," I told the women. It would have to be far enough, however far enough was. The shallow dip in the forest had grown steadily deeper the farther away we got from the cottage. It was poor cover if someone was searching for us, but it would have to do. The countess was on her hands and knees breathing in ragged gasps. The blouse was still clutched in one hand. The Bolshevik collapsed onto her back, breathing just as hard and holding her hip. I wasn't doing much better. Dropping the half empty canvas pack on the ground, I followed the Bolshevik woman's example and stretched out on a carpet of mostly dry leaves. My lungs felt like there wasn't enough air in the world. I don't ever remember running that far, that fast before. After a few minutes of hard breathing, I tried to get my bearings. The Cossack's first wave rode into the train yard from the other side of the tracks. The second wave came from the side we were on now. I had no idea which direction they would go when they retreated, but if it was on this side, all three of us were sure to be seen. Most of the leaves had fallen and you could see a long way into the forest. A mounted man would see even farther. All I could do was hope they left in a different direction from where we were.

Behind me, the way we had just come, black smoke rose into the air. The secluded little house that had been confiscated for the greater good of the Russian Soviet was going up in flames. Smoke mingled with the haze from the burning warehouses.

It started quickly. First a quiet word, then a lot of not so quiet words, then shouting. The countess pointed her pistol at the Bolshevik girl.

"Quiet," I hissed. She turned to face me, still pointing her

Mauser at the girl.

"The whore knows," she said in a half whispered breathless pant. As she rose from the ground, her thumb cocked the automatic. "I'm shooting her."

The Bolshevik girl, still lying where she fell, tried to crawl away from the pistol's barrel.

Looking at me, she said, "I safe you. Came back, warn you, Watkin."

"No shooting," I said far too loudly. I pointed the saber at the smoke coming from the house. "It's not over. You'll bring them straight to us."

"She knows!" It was almost a scream. "If—"

She didn't finish her sentence. We all heard them at the same time.

Voices.

Mounted men a stone's throw away were marching a group of Red prisoners through the woods. The Bolsheviks, bits of red worn here and there, walked dejectedly through the forest. No one looked our way. Not yet.

I tackled the countess harder than I intended. I just wanted to get her down on the ground before someone on one of those horses looked in this direction. I think my tackle almost took the wind out of her. Before she could scream, yell, or shoot someone, I put my hand over her mouth.

I waited. We all did, afraid to move or look over the edge of the shallow ground we were lying in. I felt damp earth beneath me as the countess started to squirm. Someone barked an order in Russian. I crawled off of her back. "What did he say?" I whispered.

"Line up," the countess translated so softly I barely heard her.

"We even, Watkin," the Russian girl said almost as quietly. "No more debt. I safe you." She made a dusting motion with her hands.

"Quiet," I whispered. "They're right over there."

"I leave," she said, the words barely loud enough to make it past her lips.

The countess twisted around, the Mauser still in her hand. "Move out of this hole," she whispered, "and I'll kill you." The broom handle's barrel steadied on the Bolshevik.

"Shoot," the girl told her, "and they come. You they enjoy. Watkin they cut."

The girl started to crawl out of our hole.

"Yelena," the countess hissed. "Yelena."

The girl didn't look back. She just kept crawling.

"Stop her," the countess said to me.

I reached for an ankle just as the shots rang out. It was a volley of a dozen or more rifles all firing at once. The countess and I both looked towards the sound, but we were too low in our sanctuary gully to see anything.

Yelena, the Bolshevik girl, never stopped moving.

"The saber," the countess whispered. "Kill her with the blade before she gets away. I can't shoot."

"I'm not—"

"Give it to me," she commanded. "We cannot let her get away. Ivchenko will—"

I pushed her flat against the earth, my body once again over hers. A rider was coming our way. You could hear the horse bringing the Cossack closer. He or someone near him was talking. Leather creaked as the man shifted his weight. I didn't know where Yelena was, if she was still visible or hiding in the brush.

"Mr. Watkins," the countess said, "get off of me."

I put my hand over her mouth, smothering whatever else she was about to say. Teeth fastened on my finger. "Again with the biting," I said in her ear.

The horse and rider came closer. The countess heard them now. Her body froze beneath mine as I took my hand away.

"He's very close," I whispered in her ear. "Don't make a sound."

She nodded as I slid slowly off her. The countess rolled onto her stomach, the Mauser gripped in both hands and pointing towards the sound of the horse.

The rifles fired another volley.

"They're shooting the prisoners," she said very, very softly.

We heard the rider dismount somewhere just beyond our hiding spot. I gripped the handle of the saber.

"How many rounds does that thing hold?" I whispered, motioning at her pistol.

"Ten."

"Get ready to shoot him. One shot. Save the rest for his friends. I'll grab his horse and we'll ride for the hills."

She nodded. I think she knew as well as I did there was no chance I could grab a horse once she started shooting. The animal would be halfway to the Pacific before I caught him.

The man sighed. There was a sound like falling rain hitting the carpet of leaves.

"He is peeing," the countess whispered.

21

The unseen Cossack, the call of nature finished, climbed back into his saddle. The countess tensed beside me. I readied myself to run for the horse's reins the instant she started shooting. One of the horsemen from the firing squad shouted. Whatever was said, it made the raiders laugh in that comfortable way humans have after the need for killing has ended.

"They told him to stop playing with it and hurry up," the countess whispered beside me.

Our Cossack visitor made a loud reply.

"He said," she paused. "I do not know the English word. To put their mouths."

Raising my hand, I whispered, "I don't need a translation."

The countess nodded.

We waited, the countess holding the automatic just below the rise in the land. I gripped the handle of the saber ready to lunge should the rider come towards us. Without being able to see him, it was hard to tell what was happening just beyond our hollow. The sounds of man and beast slowly faded until there was nothing to hear but the wind blowing through the trees.

"I think he is gone," the countess said softly.

I think she was right. Flat on my stomach, I crawled to the edge of the hollow and peaked over the lip. Everything was bare branches and gray tree trunks. Thick leaves in crumbling browns and old yellows covered the forest floor. A bird hopped from branch to branch. I didn't see any horses. The countess crawled up beside me.

"Are they gone?" she asked quietly.

"Can't see anybody."

"I don't hear anymore shooting at the train," she said. "I think the battle is over."

"Who do you think won?"

The countess shrugged. "Someone will have to go see."

Someone, I thought. The smooth steel of my saber gleamed in the early morning light. It wasn't a fancy sword. Not something to be worn for show or admiral's inspections. Just a solid length of metal honed to a fine edge and made for old world style killing. The blood of the men I killed still stained the blade. "Wish I had my forty-five."

"Did you leave it somewhere?" she asked.

I showed her my wrist. There was a bluish green bruise from where the Cossack I had strangled before sunrise banged my hand against the train track. "Something like that. Ivan the Terrible tried to break my wrist."

"I wondered why you used the saber on those men. I thought you were trying to be noble, fighting them armed as they were."

"You kidding? I would have come through that door with guns blazing if I had one. Wouldn't have mattered if I did have it. It was empty."

"Do *you* have more bullets?" she asked, jabbing me in the ribs with her elbow.

Narrowly escaping death always seemed to put her in a good

mood. I was going to have to learn how to make jokes and remain so calm when running for my life. "In my saddlebags. Bohdan has them if he's still among the breathing."

"I wish Ivan was here," the countess said softly. "If they have killed him, all is lost."

I hadn't thought about our missing Russian partner in a while. "I'm doing pretty good in the save the day department, aren't I?"

"You were until you let Yelena get away. How that fool with the full bladder missed seeing her is a small miracle."

"She can't go far," I said.

"I have to find her, Mr. Watkins. She is Ivchenko's creature. When the commissar returns with my husband, she will tell him everything. They will shoot us both before half the words are out of her mouth."

"Ivchenko left? I was sort of hoping he died valiantly defending a boxcar."

"He went with Alexi to inspect the bridge at Khabarovsk. His whore, Yelena, was supposed to watch me. Us," she added.

"Well, at least your husband is safe."

"You are worried about Alexi?"

"He *is* your husband, *Mrs. Gavrilov.*"

The countess gave me one of those feminine looks. She was good with her looks. This time, her look said she knew secrets and problems I couldn't possibly understand.

"We said some words in front of a Bolshevik apparatchik. I signed a false name. It isn't a real marriage. There wasn't a priest and he didn't, we didn't."

She made a rolling motion with her hand.

"The English word is consummate," I told her. She blushed. Not a lot, just a slight coloring to her cheekbones. It was gone almost before it was there.

"I told you," she said in a low voice. "Back on the *Orca.* I was not the woman you thought I was."

"I thought you meant you didn't know the difference

between Bordeaux and Burgundy."

"I meant I had done things you would not understand."

We laid there for another ten or fifteen minutes, the two of us side by side, staring at tree trunks and watching smoke slowly curl its way into the sky. There were no more sounds of battle coming from the depot.

"May I have my blouse? I'm cold, and your knee is on it."

Moving my leg, I said, "Sorry."

The countess scooped the cranberry colored affair off the ground and started shaking it free of leaves and forest debris. When she noticed me watching her, she covered her chest with the cloth.

"You are still going to be a gentleman, aren't you?"

"Are we back to that again?" Rolling over, I faced the wall of gray trees. Behind me, I could hear the sounds of a woman making herself decent.

"Despite what has happened between us since last evening, I do not normally run around without my blouse on in front of men."

"I forgot to grab your coat," I told the trees. "Too stunned at the sight of all the things you were trying to stuff into a knapsack."

"It was right there on the bed. All you had to do was pick it up after you shoved me out of the room."

I nodded, keeping my eyes on the mostly silent forest surrounding us. "Had a lot on my mind, Countess."

Shoving her pistol into its holster, she began knocking bits of muck off her pants.

"If Ivchenko and your husband are both gone, judging by all the bodies I saw this morning, Yelena hasn't got anyone to run to. She knows we'll be looking for her. If I was her, I'd lie low, find a tree and hide behind it until the train from Kharbara-wherever comes in."

"Khabarovsk and I know what you are thinking, Mr. Watkins."

"I was thinking about the bridge at Khabarovsk. Is that the

long one over the Amur?"

"You have a conscience about these things. About what must be done with Yelena."

"It's new, isn't it? A trestle bridge."

"It would be an admirable quality, your conscience, were we social friends having tea and biscuits in Saint Petersburg, but this isn't Saint Petersburg, Mr. Watkins. She intends to see me shot, so I must find her and silence her."

"Kill her you mean," I said, looking over my shoulder. The countess was buttoning her cuffs.

"Yes, Mr. Watkins. I mean to kill the Bolshevik before she gets to Ivchenko. I was weak earlier. I hesitated when she came into my bedroom. I should have shot her then and there as soon as she spoke the English words."

"Or maybe it isn't so easy to just gun somebody down."

Shoving the tails of her blouse into her pants, she continued. "I will not make the mistake of weakness again."

"She came back to warn us."

"She came back to warn *you*. I saw it in her eyes when she looked at me. She thought I was as dead as the old woman and I would have been if not for you. I have not forgotten that."

"We're not going to kill her."

"Just because we shared a kiss," she paused, "and other intimacies I'd rather not speak of again do not presume things have changed between us. I hired you for your expertise with a steam engine. The rest of our involvement has been an unintended accident."

"You didn't hire me," I said dryly. "We're partners."

"If you say so. Now, one of us needs to go to the depot and see which side killed more of the other. Find Bohdan if he's still alive. He had a job to do last night. It is why he has my gold coins."

My hand touched the ingot still sitting next to my heart. Her gold coins. British sovereigns.

"The whore has a half hour's head start." She pointed into the wall of bare trees. "That way. I think I can follow her."

Swiping her boot through the thick leaves, she said, "The ground is wet. There will be tracks."

"Done a lot of tracking in that boarding school you grew up in?"

Anger flared in her blue eyes. "Mock me if you want, but if she gets to Ivchenko before I find her, the commissar will hang you by your feet and beat you to death. He will do it in front of the good Bolsheviks as a lesson to the rest. I have seen it done. If you have a suggestion about how I can silence her other than with a bullet, please share your insight."

"Shoot Ivchenko instead," I suggested. "Whisper something vulgar in *his* ear, then put a bullet through it."

"If we don't find her, that might be the only plan left for us. While I am gone, you should think about replacing your pistol. I think a gun is more suited to your talents."

"It isn't like I haven't tried."

The countess stepped out of our hollow and peered around the trunk of the nearest tree. The forest seemed to go on forever.

"I have no idea how to track someone," she admitted. "Truth be told, I have a terrible sense of direction."

I pointed to the smoke rising from the depot. "Think of that as the North Star. Just walk towards the smoke and you'll hit train tracks sooner or later."

"No doubt Yelena used the same trick. I always knew she was too clever to be a camp follower. She is probably a Chekists informer."

"The secret police?"

"They are the real hunters in the new Russia. Bohdan mumbles about them in his sleep. He claims their eyes are everywhere." The countess knocked damp earth away from her knees. "Our Czech friend is a man who would know."

"I'll go with you. I don't want you roaming around these woods alone. We don't know if the Cossacks have gone away or just gone for lunch. There could be a hundred men over that hill."

"And you would hold them off with your saber, would you, Mr. Watkins?" She smiled when she said it. "No, go and find Bohdan. We will never get a better chance to leave than now. My home has been burned to the ground and the old woman is dead. Who is to say I wasn't carried off by the raiders? Ivchenko isn't here, the depot must be in chaos and my pretend husband can pretend to be in mourning. Only Yelena knows the truth."

"I'm still coming with you."

"No," she said again. "You will not do what needs to be done, and if you are with me, you will try to prevent me from doing it. You are soft in these matters."

"Ask those men back at that cottage how soft I am."

"That was different. I do not doubt your bravery, not anymore. But you would not silence the Chekists. You would look for a solution as if she was some broken bit of machinery needing fixing. But I will ask a favor of you before you go."

"There has to be a better way."

The countess smiled. She looked like she was indulging me the way a woman would a neighbor cursed with a particularly ignorant child.

"What's the favor?"

"I am cold. May I borrow your overcoat?"

This, I thought to myself, is how I lost my raincoat. "Of course," I said, handing the wool coat to her. "Freshly cleaned last night. A bathing beauty arranged for it while I slept." I meant it to sound funny, but thinking about my laundered linens reminded me of the old woman and the axe.

"Thank you," the countess said. "I'll give it back to you."

Just like the raincoat.

She turned for the trees and began following along the path taken by Yelena. "We need travel papers, Mr. Watkins. Bohdan was supposed to arrange it yesterday. He knows someone," she said over her shoulder. "I will meet you at the depot office in an hour. Two at the most."

"It was on fire the last time I was there."

"By Alexi's tank then."

"And if the other guys won the battle?"

"Find me on the Amur. It has a new bridge, I hear."

"That's not funny," I told her as she stepped deeper into the trees.

"Two hours, Mr. Watkins. We will need three horses, provisions if you can find them and Bohdan's papers. Can you manage it?"

"This is a bad idea," I said to the back of my borrowed overcoat.

She waved a hand in dismissal over her shoulder.

"By the tank," I heard her say again.

I stayed where I was until I could no longer see the back of my coat weaving in and out among the trees. Turning for the depot, my saber hacked through half a dozen bare tree branches. "This is a bad idea. Bad idea," I told the tree in front of me just before I sliced off a limb.

The tree, like the countess, ignored me.

22

Walking through a forest after a hostile attack, armed only with a curved piece of sharpened steel gives one a peculiar feeling of constant vulnerability. Some might call it fear. I preferred to think of it as constant vulnerability. Fortunately for me, the Cossack raiders had either left as quickly as they came or they were poor scouts. No one challenged me, chased me like a rabbit into the brush, or stood me in front of a hastily assembled firing squad. In truth, I was in no hurry to get back to the depot. If there were Cossacks still roaming the area, the countess, despite her notions of tracking down the girl named Yelena, was going to need my help.

I swished the long blade through knee high weeds. Me and Excalibur, freshly pulled from the wooden leg of an elephant sized bedpost, would defend the redheaded noblewoman to the death; an event which was sure to occur about five minutes after I showed up. The countess was right about one thing. I needed to go find my twentieth century pistol and leave playing with long knives to the Russians.

After making a slow walk towards the source of the smoke, and still no sounds of broom handle Mausers shooting up the woods, I reached the top of the last hill between me and the depot. Making the crest, you could see just how effective the Cossack raid had been. It was no wonder the raid was over. There was nothing left to raid.

Yesterday, tired, sore and miserable, I rode into a depot full of red banners and massed troops waiting for something to do. There were no waving banners now. Not a single one. If it hadn't been for the burned remains of a freight train sitting on the tracks, I'm not sure someone climbing the same hill I was on would know it was a depot. Every wooden structure was burned to the ground. All except one. The single remaining warehouse looked like the same one the major singled out as Bohdan's sleeping quarters. It looked like the Czech and his Lewis had taken a toll on the predawn raiders. There were nine dead horses and nine dead men lying in the dirt in front of the wooden building.

The locomotive, whose dawn arrival signaled the start of the attack occupied center stage in a tableau of destruction. Its flatcars still looked serviceable but the five wooden boxcars were burned down to wheels and frames. Even the water tower, the lifeblood of a train's steam engine, was gone. Its smashed remains were a pile of broken timbers lying across the locomotive. The elevated office where I shot two men had collapsed into a pile of smoking timbers and scorched pylons. The stairs were still there although now they were just a walkway of wooden steps leading into empty air.

The raiders hadn't succeeded in killing everyone. A few men stirred here and there. Some poked at the remains of torched buildings. A scattering of soldiers moved among the fallen, occasionally waving for a comrade to help. Some pointed rifles at the surrounding trees while shouting for others to point their rifles at whatever they had seen.

The open ground in the center of the depot where the two pincers of the cavalry attack swarmed into the Reds was a grisly mess. I counted thirty-seven soldiers lying in the killing ground. Not a one was moving. Two soldiers laid a corpse beside a long row of blanket covered dead men. The thirty-eighth by my count.

The colonel's flatbed truck was still there. The field gun, looking like a child's discarded toy, was lying in the dirt beside it. The Cossacks must have tied ropes around it and drug it off the bed with horses. Pieces of broken glass reflected sparkles of sunlight on the Mack's hood. If the windshield was all they broke, Comrade Alexi might get his motorized gun yet if the artillery piece was serviceable. Something told me the raiders did more to the gun than just dump it in the dirt.

It took another ten minutes for me to make my way to the depot. I took my time as I got closer to the Reds, stepping from tree to tree and avoiding the open spaces. I didn't want to get shot by one of the surviving soldiers after managing to stay alive through a Cossack dawn attack. I needn't have bothered. There weren't enough soldiers left alive to watch a third of the station.

Stepping out of the trees, the first person I saw was the woman from the train office. With her night dress hidden by a soldier's trench coat, she was tending to a group of wounded Reds. Fourteen men, some with blood soaked bandages around wounds, sat, laid or crawled in the dirt around her. Soldier by soldier, the woman dipped a tin cup into a pail of water and let each man quench his thirsts. When she saw me, she left the circle of injured men she was tending, then offered me the cup. I drank cool water, not realizing how thirsty I was until I started drinking.

"Glad you made it," I told her as I gave her back the cup. "Thanks for the water."

The woman placed her hand on my arm before she kissed me on the cheek. She said something that sounded like kind words before I turned away.

Walking down the tracks, I came to the first destroyed boxcar. The fire that consumed it was gone. Now it was nothing but steel wheels, blackened boards and ashes. I kept going, retracing my steps to the flatbed where I fought my battle with Ivan the Terrible. When I came to the dead horse, I bent down to look under the flatbed. The Cossack was lying where I left him. Dropping the countess' pack, I stuck the saber's point into the dirt, then crawled under the train car. On hands and knees, I started scrounging around in the gravel.

"Did you drop something?"

Bohdan, bent over at the waist with hands on knees, peered at me beneath the flatbed. His beloved Lewis machinegun was balanced on its wooden stock giving him a three legged appearance.

"I see you're still alive," I told our Czech master spy. "My pistol. I lost it in a wrestling match with the big guy over there." The automatic was lying next to one of the rails. Picking it up, I blew dust out of the action then worked the slide back and forth a few times. When I crawled out from under the flatcar, I shoved the gun into my waistband. "It's empty."

"Looks like we both ran out of bullets," Bohdan said.

"Are my saddlebags still with us? I bought a box of shells back in the village."

"Hello to you too. I thought you were dead for sure," the Czech said. Then he hugged me. "I've been looking for a corpse when I should have been looking for a ghost. How did you get away?" Releasing me from his bear hug, he added, "Just terrible about the countess but now that she is dead, we need to find Ivan and be on our way. It's just the three of us now. No time to mourn the fallen."

"She's not dead, Bohdan. She's out there," I said, pointing at the tree covered hills. Shouldering the canvas pack, I pulled my saber out of the ground and started walking.

"But I went to her residence," Bohdan said as we walked along the train. "I saw her body lying under some roof timbers. The Cossacks burned the place down around her."

"Did you see my body, too?"

He waved an arm in the direction of the destroyed cottage. "I just assumed. There isn't much left of the place."

"It wasn't her body." I thought of the grandmother and the way she had fussed about my muddy boots. "It was an old lady. Cossacks broke down the door and killed her."

"They didn't kill you?"

Bohdan stroked his enormous mustache and seemed to be looking at me with a fresh appraisal of my worth.

"Wasn't there," I said. "I left before sunup. I was here, looking for you when the train pulled into the depot." I pointed at the dead man lying beneath the flatbed. "If he hadn't delayed me, I might have saved them all."

Bohdan touched the gauze patch covering his ear. "They must have used our fair countess very badly. I guess you killed them for that. Is that where you found your saber?"

"Nobody used anyone, Bohdan, and try to hide your disappointment a little better. I got there before they finished their business."

"You cannot blame me for being overly concerned about the woman's wellbeing. She tried to kill me." Bohdan scratched his wounded ear. "Still, I suppose if she were incapacitated or worse, dead, Ivan would be difficult."

"Not to mention only she knows where he is," I added.

Bohdan wagged his finger in the air. "Not so, my American friend. I have been busy while you were off snuggled up beside the she wolf. You see that cart over there?"

Bohdan pointed to a two wheeled farm cart flipped over on its side. One wheel spun a slow, wobbly circle. A dead horse was strapped into the cart's harness.

"What about it?"

"The owner, he is around here somewhere, swapped a sack of potatoes with a large, fat man in black yesterday."

"There are a lot of large, fat men in black. Doesn't mean anything."

"He swapped his potatoes for six cans of stewed tomatoes. You remember our meals aboard that famous seal killer, *Orca,* don't you?"

We both stopped walking. I remembered the stewed tomatoes.

"Where is he?"

"Well," Bohdan mused, "now two of us know where Ivan is. I know and the she wolf knows."

"You aren't going to tell me."

"In this business, compartmentalization is the key to survival. Did I pronounce the word correctly?"

"Survival? Yes, Bohdan, you said it just fine."

The Czech laughed.

"Do you know a young woman with brown hair who is working for that Ivchenko character? She might be a prostitute following the troops or she might not."

"You mean Yelena Ilyinichna," the Czech said, nodding his head. "I warned the countess about her yesterday when we were making our plans. I was hoping the Cossacks had hauled her away."

"Plans nobody included me in."

"A hundred eyes were watching you, the new foreigner in camp. Nobody cared about me. It was safer not to involve you."

We started walking again. A few soldiers passed us, some going one way down the length of the train; others going the opposite direction. Bohdan stopped at a dead body. Rolling the corpse onto its back, he started unbuttoning the man's coat.

"I didn't take you for the grave robber type, Bohdan."

"I've done worse things. In the trenches, you learn a different set of morals. But I'm not looking for a few kopecks in a dead man's pockets." He pulled a leather bandolier away from the body. "A Lewis is a hungry mistress." Opening pouches, Bohdan started dumping loose cartridges into his coat pocket. "If there is a second attack, things will go badly for us."

That made me uneasy. The countess was out in those woods doing whatever she thought she was doing. "Do you think they will attack again?"

"It is doubtful." The Czech waved an arm around him. "There's nothing left to attack. Cavalry don't stay in one place. They attack, they disappear then they attack somewhere else. Red reinforcements will be here soon." He dumped another handful of cartridges into his pocket. "Still, I have not lived this long by not being prepared."

The body stripped of its bullets, we continued our walk down the side of the train.

"You sent that messenger boy to find me yesterday."

"I did. Speaking of empty stomachs, you're welcome for the bread and sausage. You see? I was looking out for you all along."

"You didn't tell me I was supposed to play the romantic lead with the countess last night. She said you did that on purpose."

He smiled. "If I had warned you beforehand, would you have enjoyed the surprise half as much?" He nudged me in the ribs. "I thought you would be thanking me. A night with the prettiest female in the province. That doesn't happen very often. Besides, we both know you want to bed the wench. I was giving you your chance."

He looked me up and down.

"You did bed the wench, didn't you?"

"Careful, Bohdan. This thing's blade is very sharp."

"Clothes washed, too," he added. "I don't remember you bringing your pajamas along last night."

"If I stabbed you," I told the Czech, "do you think any of these Reds will notice? I can make it quick. I've discovered I've got a knack for using long, sharp pieces of steel."

He laughed. "After surviving a skirmish that killed almost everyone alive I am to die, struck down by my only friend."

"I bet I could take your head clean off your shoulders with one good swing. I've had a lot of recent practice."

Bohdan laughed. He laughed for a long time. "Have I played Cupid? Tell me the truth. Is she smitten with you now?"

I moved the saber to my other shoulder. The Czech danced away beyond the reach of the blade. Men groaned in pain and bled their lives out into the dirt of an unnamed depot somewhere near the Amur River. Many would soon bleed to death and Bohdan laughed like an angel was tickling his ribs with her wings. Laughing Billy was a good name for him.

"Nothing happened between us. It was all a charade for the girl Yelena's report. Unfortunately, there was a complication." I told him about our discovery of Yelena's language skills.

"The countess was right, Stick. You should have struck her down with the saber before she got away. This complicates things in the worst way. You have set a clock to ticking on our lives."

"That clock started ticking a long time ago, Bohdan."

Our little stroll along the train ended at the locomotive. Lying next to the big driving wheels was another row of corpses. What looked like the train's engineer and his fireman were stretched out shoulder to shoulder. There were three other corpses in the row, each one with a piece of red cloth sewn somewhere on their uniform. The last one was Half Beard, the man who wanted to shoot me outside the ruined farmhouse.

"The *komvzvoda*," Bohdan said. "He was left in charge by Alexi Gavrilov."

Bohdan spat into the dirt. "I don't like Reds, but I dislike incompetence even more. Boys from an orphanage could have taken this depot. Without my gun," he slapped the heat shield of the Lewis, "they would all be dead now. They made them back it up first."

"The train?"

Bohdan nodded his head. "Just far enough to block the, what do you call it in English, the part where the track goes two ways. They wanted to block the tracks so another train couldn't get past them." He pointed at the man I thought looked like the engineer. "Then they shot the crew."

"Won't delay them long," I said.

"If the Legion still held the trains, an hour or two. But then, if the Legion still controlled the Trans-Siberian there would be dead Cossacks laying everywhere and not these green boys."

Green boys. The same thing the major called them.

"These Bolsheviks will take a day to clear the tracks. Maybe two." He tapped the locomotive with a fist. "This, they ruined. The cab's been dynamited."

"The countess said she wants to leave as soon as she gets done with her hunt for Yelena."

"Of course she does. We will have to run now. Ivchenko will put all the pieces together."

"You were supposed to be getting some papers."

Bohdan tapped his jacket. "Four sets of passes on the Trans-Siberian plus identity papers. The owners won't be needing them anymore. They died from cholera last spring. All stamped and approved by the depot master. Poor man was killed in the raid. His widow was tending to some of the Red wounded earlier."

I thought of the man lying at the base of the stairs.

"Fortunate, that. If I had waited until today to bribe him, he would be dead and we wouldn't have the passes. Lucky us."

"Unlucky him," I said.

"By the way, you're Greek now. Do you speak the language?"

"Why am I Greek?"

"Because that's who the cholera killed last spring, Theologos Kokkinos. That's Russia. If war doesn't kill you, the shits will. We have another problem. We need horses and there isn't a single one fit to ride left in the depot. I've looked."

"The countess said Ivchenko is due back later today. He went with Gavrilov to inspect the bridge over the Amur."

"A golden opportunity," Bohdan said, "to escape our captors, but how to take advantage of it?"

We both turned to look at the truck.

23

"It's called a Mack," I told Bohdan. "A good, serviceable truck."

"Well, that is called a Putilov," Bohdan said, pointing at the overturned artillery piece. "A good, serviceable gun."

"Not anymore," I told him.

"No, this one has fired its last salvo I think. The breech is damaged."

The body of the man who had damaged the Putilov was draped across the gun.

"He was unfortunate," Bohdan said. "I had a clean line of fire from the doorway of my quarters. Alexi Gavrilov should give me a medal. Without my Lewis, the Cossacks would have destroyed both gun and truck. Lend me a hand with this dead bastard, Stick."

I drove the point of my saber into the earth between the gun and the truck. I don't like touching dead bodies, especially ones killed by a machinegun. Fortunately, Bohdan didn't seem to share my squeamishness. With me pulling at the man's shoulders and Bohdan leveraging dead body parts away from adjustment wheels, sights and all the other little parts that catch in clothing, the corpse eventually sagged into an unnatural looking pile of meat. I tried not to look at the blood splattered face of the Cossack. Some things you just don't need to remember seeing. The Czech knelt beside the soldier and started rooting through his pockets.

"I thought you said you don't loot the dead?"

"This is different," Bohdan answered. "He's a dead enemy killed in battle." The Czech looked up smiling. "My kill, my loot, to use your word. Spend a few seasons in a muddy trench. You will understand, my friend."

The Cossack had a few rubles inside a leather wallet. Bohdan counted quickly, then stuffed the bills into his trouser pockets. Leaving the Czech to his looting, I gave the Mack a quick examination. Aside from a few scattered bullet holes from the Lewis and a shattered windshield, the truck looked the same as it did last night. I tossed the canvas pack onto the floorboard.

"The Red Army will not look kindly on the destruction of their depot," Bohdan said. "Alexi Gavrilov will have bigger worries than a lost gun. The colonel should have been here. Better he died with the *komvzvoda* defending the worker's paradise than off inspecting a perfectly fine bridge." Picking up the sledgehammer the cavalryman used to destroy the gun's breech, he tossed it onto the bed of the truck. "Still, your Cossack over there may have saved a lot of Red lives with his hammer. The colonel is a fool to think that truck could take the recoil of a three incher."

"I tried to tell him that yesterday."

"I do hate amateurs," Bohdan mused. "We should be on our way now. You fixed it, yes?"

"The magneto needed a little attention. Do you think Ivchenko is on his way back?"

"That, my friend, is anyone's guess. If the telegraph operator sent out a distress signal when the attack started, he could be halfway back by now."

"I don't think a signal got out. I was in the train office this morning. They smashed the telegraph key and the only person who might have sent a signal was killed early on."

Bohdan hopped onto the bed of the Mack. Taking a seat on the wooden platform and with his legs dangling in the air, he started to remove the pie shaped magazine from the Lewis. Holding the drum in one hand, he began adding bullets out of his coat pocket.

"Warning or no warning, our window of opportunity is closing." The Czech loaded a second handful of bullets. "Have you considered our position here? And by our, I mean you and I. We are a four man partnership, but surely you have noticed the countess and Ivan are one half of the organization and you and I, well, do I need to spell it out? We are the expendable half of the team. The countess and Ivan don't really need either of us anymore. You, they stopped needing once we left that decrepit boat. Me," Bohdan tapped the pocket of his tunic, "they stopped needing as soon as I arranged for the travel documents."

"You have a suspicious mind, Bohdan." I thought of the two dead Cossacks in the burned cottage. "I think I'm still playing for the varsity."

"You are making a mistake in perspective, my friend. It isn't what you think your worth is. It is what the countess thinks. And I can assure you, whatever the countess thinks, Ivan thinks." The Czech loaded the last of his bullets. "We have an opportunity before us, you and I," he said as he snapped the magazine onto the top of the Lewis. Running his hand along the stovepipe shaped heat shield of the gun, he said, "What if I told you, hypodermically speaking, we had an opportunity to split the treasure three ways instead of four?"

"Hypothetically."

"What?"

"The word is hypothetically, not hypodermically."

"Are you certain? I am sure I have heard hypodermically

used."

"Get to your point, Bohdan."

"The countess and Ivan don't need us anymore and if you think that hasn't occurred to her, you haven't been paying attention. But," he continued, "in an interesting turn of events, it is you and I who do not need *her* anymore."

"I don't think I am liking your hypodermic question, Bohdan."

The Czech looked to his left and right, then leaned towards me. In a low voice, he said, "Thanks to a can of tomatoes, I know where Ivan is and thanks to the Cossacks, we have an opportunity that deserves consideration. Right now, I am sitting on the only functioning transportation in the whole depot."

"I think I might have known that before you, Bohdan."

The Czech rapped his knuckles against the Mack's wooden bed. "And thanks to Ivchenko's spy, the countess is off chasing shadows in the forest. For all we know, Yelena has cut her throat or some Cossack is humping her behind a bush."

"No."

"No what?" Bohdan asked.

"The answer to your hypothetical question is no. I won't double cross the countess and neither will you." I didn't like the look in Bohdan's eye. The saber was a half a step too far away for me to reach.

"Ivan is the only man alive who knows where a boxcar full of gold disappeared to. If we leave now in this truck, we can be at the crossroads in a few hours. We tell Ivan the countess was killed. It isn't really a lie. If Yelena hasn't already killed the bitch, Ivchenko will shoot her before the wheels on his train stop moving. You know we cannot wait. Ivchenko and the colonel are on a military express train. If they get here before we leave, our chances of getting away are nonexistent. We cannot wait and we cannot ignore opportunity."

"You know," I said as I stepped closer to my saber, "I think that is a possible outcome." The saber was within reach.

Bohdan worked the cocking lever of the Lewis.

"We should have gone to the warehouse and got your bullets first, Stick. If we had, your pistol would be loaded and you wouldn't be reaching for a saber stuck in the dirt."

The Lewis swung in my direction.

"Always remember, Stick, I gave you the choice."

Raising my hands, I asked, "Are you going to shoot me?"

Bohdan seemed to ponder the question. I could see him weighing the pros and cons. I weighed a few myself. The saber was too far away and even if I managed to grab the hilt, Bohdan would put a half dozen rounds in me before I could manage a swing.

"I should," he said. "A year ago, I would have without blinking an eye. If this was Legion business, I would have shot you the moment I knew the truck was undamaged. I am growing soft, I think."

The Czech hopped off the bed of the truck. The heavy Lewis never stopped pointing at my chest.

"I like you, so I am not going to kill you unless you force my hand. And Stick, you wouldn't want to force me. I have shot many people I liked over the years. It became a necessary function of my former profession." He waved the barrel of the gun towards the front of the truck. "If you don't mind, would you be so good as to start my transportation? Time is pressing, and I want to be at the crossroads and on my way with Ivan before the Bolsheviks regroup."

"Just like that, you're going to drive off and leave us here?"

Bohdan touched the bandage on his ear. "As children in the schoolyard say, she started it. Besides, I gave you the opportunity. Now, if you please. Go to the front of the truck."

I did. There wasn't much else I could do. Bohdan climbed behind the wheel, then shoved the barrel of the Lewis through the shattered remains of the windshield.

"Now would be a good time," he told me.

Bending over and setting my legs against the compression, I gave the iron handle a firm yank. Nothing happened.

"Once more," Bohdan yelled, "and keep turning this time."

I spun the crank again, hoping the Mack would prove stubborn to start, but Bohdan knew how to coax fire out of the ignition. On the third revolution of the iron handle, the Mack's engine caught and began to idle.

"Step away," Bohdan shouted. The Lewis was across the hood of the truck. Shards of broken glass vibrated and slid off the sloping engine cover. Engaging the gear, the heavy truck pulled forward as Bohdan drove a slow circle around the siding. Bumping over the rails, he pulled the Mack to a stop not far from where I was standing. Down the length of the yard, several of the surviving Red soldiers were walking towards us. Bohdan moved the Lewis until the gun was sitting across his lap with the barrel once again pointing at me. The Czech reached a hand inside his tunic.

"Because I like you," he shouted, "I will give you a fighting chance." Two thick envelopes sailed out of his hand to land a few yards away. "If I were you," the Czech jerked a thumb over his shoulder towards Vladivostok. "I would start walking. Two days, maybe less, you should reach the next depot." He pointed to the envelope. "The pass might get you on a train if Ivchenko hasn't figured it out yet. Go home, Stick. Tell your navy some story, take your gold bar and go back to where you came from. What is the worse they will do? Throw you out? Better than what Ivchenko will do, no? If you want, take the countess with you." He pointed at the second envelope. "I wouldn't, and she will get you killed if you try but, we both know you will try, don't we? Who knows? Maybe you will make it. Stranger things have happened in this war. If you do, put a baby in her stomach. Maybe that will calm her down and make her behave like a proper lady and not shoot people in the ear." Letting out the clutch, the Mack pulled away at a slow walking pace. "Look me up in Prague," he shouted. "I will be easy to find. Just ask for the richest man in the city."

The sound of the Mack's exhaust pipe wasn't quite loud

enough to drown out the sound of his laughter.

Bouncing over the rails, Bohdan steered the slow moving Mack towards one of the forest roads. Stooping over, I picked up the envelopes. They were made of heavy brown paper and coated with something to keep rainwater away from the contents. Opening the first one, I found a very official looking piece of high quality paper with a red star watermark and an unreadable signature. The freshly inked scrawl was next to an embossed stamp. Putting the pass back into the envelope, I looked past the ruined gun to the stack of railroad ties that had shielded the major from view last night.

The Mack rounded a bend in the road and disappeared from my sight. The stack of metal cans still sat beside the ties. Three of the cans had holes in them, probably hit by the same burst from the Lewis that killed the hammer swinging Cossack. The other three looked untouched. I couldn't read the Cyrillic letters on the cans, but my nose didn't need language to know what gasoline smelled like.

"I know something you don't know, my Czech friend. Never take a road trip without first filling up the tank."

24

One hour, she said. Maybe two and she would meet me by the truck. I didn't have a watch, but I was pretty sure three hours had come and gone and still no countess.

Or Yelena.

My canvas pack, rescued from Bohdan's warehouse, sat on the ties beside me. The forty-five, fully loaded and with half a box of loose bullets in my pocket, was once again ready to be called upon if needed. Several of the surviving Red soldiers, all twenty-three of them by my count, came and went. A few looked my way, but either preferred not to mess with the unhappy looking foreigner with the bared saber in his hand or had other more pressing business.

At the end of the fourth hour of waiting, I went to stand in a soup line with the rest of the survivors. The woman who gave me a tin cup full of water was now serving weak stew and yesterday's bread to the shell shocked troops. Her son, the boy she had shielded from the raiders, raced up and down the train yard in that hopelessly energetic way boys do. It looked like he was carrying messages between two groups of soldiers trying to guard the ends of the ruined train.

Hindsight is a beautiful thing. The train didn't need guarding now.

My stew finished and still no countess, I decided to go check the burned cottage. There was no good reason why she would go back there, but I didn't know where else to look. The rear wall with the back door was still standing. The rest had burned. Some of the big roof timbers remained along with a few iron odds and ends. I didn't spend a lot of time there. The grandmother's body was in there somewhere and I didn't wish to see it again. It wasn't the dead I was looking for. I needed to find the countess. Where the hell was she? For the first time in my life, I wished I had a horse. I went back to the hollowed out piece of ground that had saved us from the urinating Cossack. Following along the direction she had gone when she set out to track down Yelena, I made a wide circle through the forest. Seeing no trace of her anywhere, I went back to the railroad ties hoping she would be waiting for me there. She wasn't. Another hour passed. And another. Twice more, I made circles through the surrounding woods. When I came back to the ties, the Red soldiers were beginning to line up for their evening meal. I wasn't hungry.

With the sun hanging in the western sky, a voice in the back of my head began to whisper unpleasant possibilities. The image of the Cossack riding hard down the lane with Yelena thrown over his saddle kept worming its way into my imagination. By letting her go after the girl, had I doomed the countess to the same fate? I didn't think so. She wasn't the type to give up. If the horsemen found her, the crack of her pistol would have echoed for a half mile or more through the quiet woods. She said she had a poor sense of direction. Maybe she was lost. It wasn't hard to do, especially in thick timber on hilly ground. When you're not used to the forest, the trees all start to look the same. To make things worse, the smoke that spiraled into the sky from the wrecked depot was long gone. The last of the fires had burned themselves out hours ago. She had lost her north star.

Bohdan was off hunting Ivan, the countess was missing, Yelena had knowledge that would doom us all and Ivchenko could show up at any time. It was a difficult situation. The countess was hopelessly overdue.

The sound of a locomotive's steam whistle sounded from somewhere far down the tracks. A train was coming, and it wasn't coming from the battlefield around Vladivostok. It was coming from the direction of the Amur. The commissar was making his appearance at last. When he walked his slow circles around me, he said he would shoot me if I left the depot. After Yelena told her story, he would shoot me if I stayed. How much time did I have? Hours or minutes?

The Bolshevik girl was the wild card. My eyes watched the trees. Was she out there or was she off grunting her trade under a new set of Cossack customers? The voice in the back of my head said she was out there. The countess didn't find her. She was probably watching me now, waiting for Ivchenko. The way she had crushed that raider's head with a stone told me the Bolshevik girl in the simple blue dress could give lessons on how to survive in almost any situation. She said we were even, no debt. I believed her. She would sell me to Ivchenko without a moment's thought.

A saber is a poor carving tool. The steel was sharp enough, just not designed for digging letters into the side of a railroad tie. Still, it did a fair job. The English letters carved and scraped midway up the stack of ties were legible enough.

> *Our friend took truck*
> *No gas*
> *Going to get it*
> *Go to Ivan*
> *Watkins*

With the saber driven point first into the ties, if she came back here, she might get the message. If she did, at least she would know where I was. The train's whistle blew again. I couldn't stay any longer. My time was up.

Slinging my canvas pack over my shoulder and carrying two cans of gas, I started for Bohdan's road. If the train coming from the Amur had horses, I doubted I was going to get very far. The gasoline sloshing in the can said Bohdan wouldn't either. Even if there weren't any horses, Alexi might send troops after me. How fast could Russian troops march? If it was anything like the endurance of the cavalrymen that found us in the ruined farmhouse, they would catch me in an hour. If Alexi sent troops, I would just have to deal with them when they showed up. There was only a half hour or so of light left in the day. Maybe the colonel would wait until morning or maybe the commissar would think I wasn't worth weakening the defense of the depot. A second locomotive sitting beside the ruined freight train would require protection.

My bigger problem was just how far the Mack would go before it ran out of gas. I checked the tank yesterday when I was trying to start it, but I didn't really pay close attention to how much gas was inside. I just remembered seeing enough fuel to start the engine. It wasn't full. I remembered that much. Not nearly. There couldn't have been much more than a quart. Ten miles, I told myself. Ten miles and Bohdan would be on foot.

In the dark, how fast could I hike ten miles down a dirt road carrying a canvas pack and two cans of gas? Three hours? Maybe sooner if the truck ran dry before it made ten miles. Before midnight, certainly.

No one paid any attention to me. Everyone in the camp was much more interested in the approaching train coming down from the Amur. The depot troops heard salvation in that train's whistle. One foreigner slinking away into the forest in the fading light of a Siberian evening didn't even draw a questioning glance.

Once I hit the tree line, I started to hurry. I didn't go nearly as fast as I had when I drug the countess through the forest, but I made good time. Call it encouraged hurrying. By the time Ivchenko's express pulled into the depot, I was well out of sight. A half hour later, the noise of the locomotive and the depot's troops couldn't be heard any longer. An hour after that, with an orange and maroon sky on the western horizon, it was just me, the forest and a narrow dirt road disappearing into the darkness.

The moon was still somewhere on the wrong side of the sky when I walked into the stream. It wasn't much of a stream. Really just an ankle deep wet spot in the road. Still, the sound of me splashing through the water sounded very loud in the quiet darkness of the forest. Walking onto the dry road on the other side, I stopped. A rosy glow suddenly appeared next to one of the ink dark trees in front of me. The glow was followed by an all too familiar and all too unpleasant smell.

"Lieutenant," the major said, "I'm going to assume that, due to the effects of wild exuberance on the eve of your first real battle, you misinterpreted my orders this morning."

"It's about time you showed up," I said.

"And that your evening stroll to try and catch up to Laughing Billy is your attempt to get back in my good graces." The major kicked a shadowed lump sitting at his feet. "Wouldn't you agree, Billy?"

The shadowed lump sitting on the earth at the major's feet moved. "Hello, Stick," Bohdan said tiredly. "Is that ear shooting bitch dead yet?"

25

The twin gas cans plopped onto the ground. Flexing my fingers, I said, "Well Bohdan, guess Prague will have to wait for its next millionaire." My pack slid off my shoulders to join the cans.

"A small setback," the Czech said.

I tried to stretch a kink out of my back. It had been a long hike and my muscles were glad it was over. "Don't suppose you have any water on you?"

"With the horses," the major answered.

"There is a canteen on the truck's seat," Bohdan said. "Help yourself, Stick."

"By all means, Lieutenant. Help yourself to Billy's water. Lord knows if I told you to walk ten feet in the trees to the horses, you'd probably be lost till sunrise."

I didn't answer. I was too tired to answer. I saw the truck now. It was right there in front of me. If I hadn't been walking with my head down and hauling two damned heavy cans of gas, I would have seen it when I stepped in the stream. I drank half the canteen.

"Is that's gas you are hauling?" the major asked.

"It is. You should have checked the tank, Bohdan. The truck was on empty."

He didn't laugh this time.

"Wasn't sure how far he'd get, but I wanted to have transportation available when I caught up to him."

"That's the first nearly useful thing you've done since you joined this mission," the major said.

"The machine took me far enough," Bohdan said from somewhere in the darkness. "If not for this imbecile, Ivan and I would be having caviar and champagne by now. Now, if you would be so kind, shoot him and you and I shall discuss renewing our partnership like gentlemen."

I heard a thump and a groan.

"That's for calling me names," the major said, "and now you've gone and made me hurt my hand, Billy. Do that again, and next time, I won't tap your skull so softly."

A wind that felt like it was fresh from an arctic vacation came slithering out of the night. It curled and twisted among bare tree limbs and sighed its way past my ears. The clouds opened, letting a half moon make a brief appearance in the night sky. It was gone again before I had a chance to locate the voice. The cold steel of the navy issued sidearm was in my hand.

"I'd rather you didn't discharge your weapon, Lieutenant, if it is all the same to you. I think Semyonov's boys are headed for the next depot but I can't swear it for a fact. Gun shots might bring unwelcome visitors."

"I thought the prisoner was going to start trouble," I said as I dropped the Colt back into my pocket.

"Oh, he's going to start trouble. You can count on it. Tonight, in the morning, all week. He'll whisper words and make promises and do everything his training has taught him to do because my friend here knows his business."

"Major," the Czech began, "if I may just—"

Something thudded in the dark and Bohdan grunted again.

"See what I mean, Watkins? He knows all he has left is words. I'm not having it."

That ice cold wind whistled past my ears again. The major's pipe engulfed me in a nauseating miasma of odors.

"Weather's coming. Rain by sunrise," the major said. "Going to be a cold night and a long ride."

A horse whinnied from somewhere in the darkness. I crouched, my hand going to my sidearm. The Cossacks hadn't gone after all.

"At ease, Watkins. That's my horse. The beast doesn't like this wind. Probably smells a wolf." The major cleared his throat, then spat. "Or Cossacks. Billy here was in quite an agitated state about the failure of his mechanical contraption when I eased up behind him. Never liked those infernal motorcars myself. Nothing but a fad, if you ask me. Mark my word, Young Watkins. A decade from now, they'll all be piles of rust in a scrap yard. There's nothing one of those things can do that a string of mules can't do better. Mules don't run out of gas, either, do they, Billy?"

"Am I free to answer that question?"

"No, you are not. As I was saying, it's going to be a cold night and a long ride. There's a road to the east about twenty or thirty miles down that way."

I assumed his arm was pointing in the direction of that way. I couldn't see a thing.

"But before I give you your orders, by any chance, were you planning on explaining why you are just now arriving at my location? I do believe, Watkins, you are a man destined to try my patience."

I was tired and in no mood for the marine's sarcasm. "*I believe*, Major, you are aware of where I've been. You seem to always know where I've been."

"I am and I do, however, that does not excuse you from making your report."

"I've been searching for the countess. She missed our

rendezvous by some hours."

"How you managed to miss finding her is a naval mystery destined to be debated in the austere halls of Annapolis. You practically walked right over her and that other one."

"He means Yelena," Bohdan quipped.

"Quiet Billy," the major said. "Your talking privileges are at an end. I want that road far behind me by the time the sun comes up. Fortunately, I still have my three mounts and their tanks are completely full. If you're finished sipping that canteen, we'll be on our way now."

"Where was she?" I couldn't see where the major was standing. It was too dark.

"About a half mile east of the dacha." The pipe's bowl seared the darkness. "You walked a circle around them."

"They're going to kill her."

"And I'm truly sorry about that, Lieutenant. She was a feisty woman and damned kind on the eyes but, she isn't our fight, this isn't our country or our war. Even if it was, what would you suggest we do? Ride back into a hostile camp and demand they release her into our custody else we attack in force?" The major's glowing pipe pointed at some undefined spot. "He is our mission. That is why we are here."

I picked up the gas cans.

"What are you doing?" the major asked.

"Going to move the truck," I told him. "There's a snappy dresser back at the depot that's sure to come looking for it. I'll drive it off into the bushes far enough to get it out of sight from the road. It might buy us some time once the sun's up."

"I believe they might just follow the tracks, Lieutenant."

"Not if it rains hard enough. And the tracks don't look that much different than the ones made by wagons and carts."

The major puffed his pipe without comment. After a moment of careful consideration, he said, "Approved."

I poured both cans into the tank, saving a few ounces for the fuel bowl.

"Hurry up, Watkins. We need to get a move on."

Setting my feet in a wide stance, I grabbed the crank. "No trouble out of you. I'm in enough hot water and I don't need attitude from you. Be nice. I brought you gas." The iron bar spun a three hundred and sixty degree circle. The engine started for a moment, tried to idle, then died. Spinning it again, the Mack backfired louder than one of Bohdan's Putilov cannons.

"You are aware of the possibility there are unknown numbers of enemy hostiles in our vicinity, Lieutenant."

"Quiet, now," I whispered. "Don't misbehave. You heard the jarhead in charge. There are things in the woods." On my the third try with the crank, the engine started. Pulling myself into the cab, the first thing I saw was Bohdan's machinegun. Leaving that gun sitting in the cab was going to haunt Bohdan for a long time.

I sat there, staring into the darkness. The moon, a half circle of silver brightness, decided to burn another hole through the night sky's clouds. Trees appeared. So did the major. He was leaning against the nearest tree, a foot resting on a log. The log moved and I recognized Bohdan lying on his stomach, arms behind his back. The forest, I saw, looked thinner on my right. It was more brush and waist high bushes with a handful of bare branched saplings mixed in.

I patted the wooden bench. "Don't let me down now," I told the truck. The transmission clanked and rattled as I shifted it into gear.

"Just pull it over there," the major shouted.

I didn't look at the marine and wasn't sure where his over there was. I was looking at the thinnest spot in the forest about fifty or sixty yards in front of me. There might be enough room. I looked at the moon. More clouds were coming. My light would be gone in half a minute. I gunned the engine and rolled the Mack down the road. With enough speed and enough luck, I thought I could make it.

Nobody would ever call the Mack fast, but it did have a lot of mass once you got it rolling and if the ground was firm enough, it had power. When I reached the spot where I judged the trees were the smallest and the thinnest, I twisted the wheel around and slammed my foot down on the pedal. The Mack went off the road, bouncing and tearing into the brush. The engine screamed as it was begging to be shifted into a higher gear, but I kept it in low. The truck kept rolling forward. A sapling five or six feet tall hit the front end. The whole truck shook and almost stopped me where I was. I yelled at it, sounding like Ivan when he was trying to make his horse run a little faster. The tree bent, limbs snapped, but the truck kept rolling. Pushing out of the brush, the Mack made it all the way around and I was back on the road facing the opposite direction from where I started.

"Lieutenant!" I heard the major shout.

"Here it comes," I told the steering wheel. The moon abandoned me to my fate, slipping behind her clouds. The night, once more dark as death, closed around me.

"Lieutenant, are you trying to make me hate you? Perhaps you've failed to notice you've driven that damn contraption around in a circle and are now back on the road."

"Yes, sir," I said. "I did indeed notice just that."

The major was lost to me again. He was somewhere on my right out there in the darkness.

"Did I not speak clearly enough when I told you to put this scrap iron over there? I am not going to bother mentioning your profound lack of understanding of the situation we find ourselves in. Let me be brief, Watkins. Why have you turned that truck around?"

"Major, you aren't going to like this."

"Lieutenant, I haven't liked this since the admiral saddled me with this foolishness about lost treasures."

"I'm going back."

There was a long silence.

"Repeat your last," the major said. His voice had a dangerous calmness about it.

"I said I'm going back, sir."

"I see I have misjudged you, Stick," Bohdan said from somewhere out in the darkness.

There was a thump followed by a groan.

"Billy, if you want to survive this night, I suggest you keep your comments to yourself and not interrupt my communications. Now, Watkins, shut that engine off and get out of that truck. You're not going back for that pretty little Russian gal."

"Shoot him, Stick," Bohdan's voice drifted out of the darkness again. "We will go back together and kill them all. You have my word as—"

There was another thump in the darkness and a louder grunt from Bohdan.

"Shut up, Billy!" the major screamed. "So help me, I'll rip the tongue out of your mouth if you say another word."

"I am, Major."

"You aren't, Watkins, and that's an order. No misunderstanding my intentions this time."

"Yelena will kill her," Bohdan said, the words coming out in a half groan.

The major kicked him. "Last warning, Billy."

"Alright, Major," I said, "this is what's going to happen."

"Watkins, do not ever presume to tell me what is going to happen. What *is* happening, however, is you are going to climb your ass out of that truck like I told you, get on that horse and the three of us are going to rendezvous with my boys. There's a junk waiting for us at Khabarovsk to take everyone upriver to Harbin. We take the Chinese railway from there to Port Arthur. A week, maybe ten days and we're back with the fleet. Can I make my intentions and plans any clearer to you, Lieutenant?"

"The Amur River it is, sir. I'm your man."

"Outstanding, Lieutenant, now—"

"But I have to go back first," I said, interrupting him.

The major came around the front of the truck. He was just a dark outline and I thought this is what the angel of death must look like to a man standing at the gallows.

"You even think about standing up, Billy, and so help me I'll hamstring you," the major shouted into the night. "Watkins, you seem to have become confused about who gives orders and who obeys them."

"The Manchurian railway is controlled by the Japanese south of Harbin," Bohdan said softly. "The Empire has a price on my head. Better you kill me here. We will never make it so far."

"I am not a man known to make idle threats, Billy," the major said warningly. "Lieutenant, you move one inch down that road and the best possible outcome for you is Portsmouth Naval Prison."

"The admiral's orders were clear, Major. Confirm the Czech was Wilhelm Bohdan. I did. Capture him if possible for questioning. He's right over there. And determine if the bullion was real or not."

Bohdan started laughing.

The Mack tilted as the major climbed onto the running board. "Son," the major said

His uninjured hand touched my arm.

"I believe the phenomenon you are presently experiencing is known as good intentions. Unfortunately, good intentions won't keep you alive. What *will* keep both of us alive is remaining undiscovered. Nobody's looking for either of us and as long as it stays like that, we'll be drinking beer in Port Arthur in a couple of weeks."

"It has been called Royjun for the last twenty years, you imbecile," Bohdan said. "You have not thought this through. May I suggest going to Chita instead?"

"Shut up, Bohdan," the major and I yelled together.

"Or downriver towards Sakhalin?" the Czech added, ignoring both of us. "A longer journey, but we might actually get there with my head still attached to my shoulders."

"Forty-eight hours, Major. That's all I need and I'll either meet you at the bridge or Ivchenko will have done for me."

The major didn't move. He just stood there looking at me in the darkness outside the cab.

"In this hypothetical rescue mission you believe you are capable of accomplishing, have you thought about what happens when you get there? What I'm asking is, and I will speak slowly so as not to confuse you, just what the hell do you think you're going to do? It's an armed camp. Reinforced, no doubt, by that sundown train."

"They're going to shoot her."

The moon peeked out from behind her blanket and I saw the major's face staring at me. He put that infernal pipe of his between his teeth and inhaled. The bowl glowed red and the fires of hell reflected in the marine's eyes.

"You go back, Watkins, and they're going to shoot *you*." Wisps of fragrant smoke accompanied each word. "The best you can hope for is his and her poles when they put you in front of the wall. You'll die. Simple as that. You can't save her."

"What do you care, Major? You've got Billy. Isn't that why you volunteered me for all this? I'm not needed anymore."

Just before the last of the moonlight faded, I saw the pipe stem jabbed in my direction.

"Lieutenant Watkins, that's the first truly intelligent observation I have heard you make since this mission began."

The truck rocked again as the major stepped off the running board. He took a step backwards and became indistinct with the forest shadows.

"You miss that junk at Khabarovsk," his voice said, "and you really will have missed ship's movement this time. Am I clear?"

"As a crystal, sir. Two days, and we rendezvous at Khabarovsk."

I put the big truck in gear, let out the clutch, and let it find its own speed. As the front wheels hit the shallow stream, I heard the major shouting behind me.

"You do realize, if the situation was reversed, going back

for you would never have crossed her mind."
   I did.

26

The Mack powered down the narrow dirt road at something marginally faster than a hurried man could walk. It wasn't so much because the truck couldn't go faster as it was my inability to see more than a few feet past the hood. The moon, that guiding light in the sky, turned shy after an hour's appearance and hid behind ever thickening clouds. My Siberian forest road, never more than eight or nine feet wide, twisted and turned in a long series of snakelike curves up one low hill and down the next. Every few minutes, the cab's roof would hit overhanging branches from the surrounding trees sending loud screeches and squeals into the darkness as wooden fingers scraped along the roof.

The major was right. Going back for her would serve no purpose. Yelena had her, which meant Ivchenko had her. What did I think I was going to accomplish by going back? I should have left the truck sitting in the middle of this forest, climbed aboard the major's hay burner and ridden for the Amur with Bohdan tied to his saddle. That's what a sane man would have done. But if I did that, I knew for the rest of my days I would second guess myself. Years from now, I would eat my soul to pieces for abandoning the countess to the firing squad. Maybe there was nothing I could do to save her. Maybe it was all vanity, a bandage for my future conscience, but I had to at least be able to tell myself I made the attempt.

The wind whistled past me, making towering trees sway and twist in the night. Limbs twisted and turned as autumn leaves swirled along the dirt road. It was a spooky night in Siberia. No wonder the major's horse was nervous. All that was missing was an iron cauldron bubbling over a burning fire and three old hags in black hats to make the picture complete.

I needed a plan, one that didn't end with me standing in front of a brick wall with a half dozen indifferent Russian soldiers pointing rifles at me. The problem was, I didn't have one.

The Mack started to climb a steep hill. I remembered this hill. It was the tallest one I walked over on my outbound leg of this trip. I had rested at the top, catching my breath before half sliding down the opposite slope. Working the shifter, the truck slipped into its lowest gear. That's when the threatened rain began to fall. It started with a few splatters hissing on the hood. Then a light drumming on the cab's roof. A moment after that, the clouds opened up and rain poured out of the sky like Niagara Falls. The double set of solid rubber tires on the rear of the flatbed began to lose traction. The Mack stopped its slow climb up the steep hillside and began to slide. The major said vehicles like this were a passing fad; that mules could do anything this mechanical beast could do and do it better. As the truck began to twist in the narrow road, I could see his point. The Mack did a very ungraceful corkscrew to my right then slid into the side of a tree. Water poured through the shattered windshield as I buttoned my jacket against Noah's flood. Somewhere along this road trip, I distinctly remembered buying a raincoat. Where it had ended up was anyone's guess. It was probably sheltering a Russian Cossack fifty or sixty miles away.

I gave the Mack a little gas, felt the rear tires slip in the mud, then slowly pull away from the tree. Straightening the machine with the road, I made my second attempt at climbing the mountain. This time, I hit the slope at a dead run, going nearly as fast as a man can run. The Mack made it about thirty or forty yards up the steep slope before the wheels lost traction. Once more, the truck started to slide backwards.

The third attempt wasn't any more successful than the first two. The Mack wasn't going to climb that hill, not when it was slick with fresh mud. My jacket soaked and my teeth starting to chatter, I reversed the truck in between two trees. I don't know why. Something in my inner mechanical brain told me one doesn't intentionally park a vehicle in the center of a road. Not even in the middle of Siberia. The truck safely out of the way of traffic, I turned a switch on the dash and grounded the engine's spark. The motor's low clatter was replaced by hard blowing northern winds driving their way through the forest. That same wind now had a knife's edge to it. I think I was in for a very cold night.

The faraway echoing boom of a gunshot came drifting through the woods. My first thought was of Bohdan and the major, but the sound hadn't come from that direction. It sounded like it was from the other side of the hill. Another shot echoed through the night, then a volley of a dozen or more. Grabbing Bohdan's Lewis, I shoved it through the broken windshield and pointed it in the general direction of the gunshots. I knew Bohdan hadn't fully reloaded the drum magazine. Whether I had twenty rounds or fifty in the gun was anybody's guess. Not that it really mattered. If whoever was out there came this way and it turned into a gunfight, I wouldn't last long. The major was right. The point was to remain an unknown until the last possible moment. A Lewis shooting at Russians in a pitch black forest didn't sound like a good way to stay unknown for very long.

I waited for more shots as the wind continued to blow a gale outside the truck's cab. Excited soldiers at the depot, I reasoned. Who wouldn't be trigger happy after what they had gone through? It probably wasn't the first nervous shots at ghosts in the darkness. The sound of the Mack's engine would have hidden the distant bangs from my hearing. It did tell me one thing, though. I was close.

It took the better part of two hours for the clouds to rain themselves dry. When it finally stopped, the wind ripped a clear slice into the night sky and once again, the moon made her appearance. Silvery light danced in and out of shadows as Siberia dripped and the wind screeched. Sometime during the respite from the rain, fatigue finally caught up to me. It wasn't a very restful forty winks. Dreams of witches mumbling incantations into bubbling cauldrons haunted my sleep. That and a general inability to get anywhere close to comfortable in the soaked cab meant I woke up cold, cramped and wishing the countess had won her wrestling match with Yelena.

Sliding out of the cab, I shoved Bohdan's favorite toy as far under the dash as I could. It was tempting to take the machinegun along with me but, at a good thirty-five pounds of extra weight to haul around and a single half full magazine, I wasn't sure what good it would do me. It wasn't like I was planning on an armed assault although if the major and his missing leathernecks were here, that's exactly what I would be planning. I couldn't shoot my way to the countess. I could see light blues and soft grays to the east. Sunrise wasn't far off. I needed a different strategy and I needed it before the sun turned the night into day. Something told me if I didn't have a plan by then, it would be too late.

I started walking.

The hill wasn't nearly as hard to climb as I thought it would be. I only slipped once in the mud before I made the crest. Standing in the moonlight, I gazed down the dark slope towards the depot as the wind pushed against my back. Maybe I stood there a little longer than necessary staring down towards a faint glow below me. Maybe I was having second thoughts about what I was doing. Maybe I even thought about turning around and going back to the major and his infernal horses. I've never laid any sort of claim to foolish bravery or youthful invincibility. The major was right. If I went down there, Ivchenko was sure to kill me. Go back, the voice inside my head said. Not your war, your country or your fight. Nobody would blame me for turning around.

The walk down the hill towards the faint glow went much faster than the uphill climb.

27

There wasn't any reason to hurry. With the night's weather turning into one of those evenings that give pneumonia a bad name, it was doubtful the Reds would be shooting a captured countess before things dried out a bit more. Besides, the same trepidation that caused me to be so cautious about walking into the depot after the raid was even stronger today. Ivchenko's express train was sitting nose to nose with its destroyed sibling. I caught sight of it every now and then through the intervening tree limbs. Three hundred yards out, with the wind still blowing a gale force out of the north, I was close enough to hear the occasional voice drifting in the morning air. Fifty yards out, the Reds finally saw me walking down the muddy road, hands over my head and the wind whipping my clothes around me.

"Morning," I said in a loud, clear voice. "Don't shoot me. Am I in time for breakfast? I'll take two of whatever's on the menu."

The Reds had improved their defenses while I was away. A

sandbagged semicircle sat dead center in the middle of the road. Four heads, each with the tall peaked hat like the commissar wore with ear flaps down against the wind, peered over the edge of the bags. So did four rifles with fixed bayonets. I stopped moving. That seemed the best way to stay alive until those barrels were pointing a different direction. In addition to the sandbagged circle, the fallen water tank had been pulled away from the wrecked locomotive. A handful of soldiers swarmed between the two engines. It looked like they were getting ready to reverse the express and try to drag the freight train clear of the station's junction. By the looks of the effort, Bohdan was right. They weren't going to clear the track any time soon.

A few makeshift canvas shelters had sprung up overnight. They looked like cold, sodden and miserable places to spend a wet night in. One of the tents that looked like it was made of tied together blankets blew apart in the wind much to the distress of two men inside. There still didn't seem to be a lot of soldiers. Ivchenko and the colonel mustn't have had a very large bodyguard with them on their bridge inspection.

"Amerikanski!" a voice behind the sandbags shouted. It was followed by a string of Russian, most of it from the three other heads pointing rifles in my direction.

"Amerikanski," I replied, wondering if I should spit again. A familiar face rose shoulder high above the sandbags. "Well, if it isn't the adolescent alcoholic in training. Don't suppose you've got any more of that sausage, do you?"

The messenger boy, the kid who got me half soused, then walked me to the countess and her bathtub rose from behind the barricade. Grinning like we were old friends, he stepped over the bags. A very spiffy green raincoat caught the wind and sailed out behind him.

"That's mine, you little bastard," I said. "Wondered where it disappeared to."

The kid swung his rifle over his shoulder, made a vroom vroom sound and pantomimed holding a steering wheel.

"Yeah, vroom vroom big truck. I'd love some eggs and bacon and a quart of strong coffee. My bones are freezing. How about it?"

The kid said something to the three men behind the sandbags then slipped the rifle off his shoulder. With well-practiced hands, he worked the bolt.

"Easy there, Doc Holliday. I'm a friendly, remember?" I didn't get an answer. All I got was the business end of a rifle pointed at my chest.

The kid spat into the mud.

"Guess this means Alexi heard about where I slept while he was away. Don't suppose it would do any good to tell you I was ambushed by a Czech with a funny sense of humor, would it?"

The grin disappeared behind a soldier's face.

"Didn't think so."

He waved the barrel of the gun towards the depot's last remaining building with a roof and four walls.

"That the way to the breakfast buffet?"

The other three soldiers rose from behind the sandbags. Their rifles still pointed straight at me. Lowering my hands very slowly, I opened the front of my coat. "You might want to disarm me," I suggested. My Colt pistol was stuck in the front of my waistband. Better they find it now and not after they searched me. No point in getting beaten with rifle butts if it can be avoided. The kid stepped forward quickly as I expected he would, pulled the pistol out of my waistband then waved it in the air for his companion's benefits before sticking it through his belt.

"Don't lose that," I told the boy. "I had to sign that out and if I misplace it, the navy will dock my pay."

The teenager motioned me forward.

"How do you say 'Ivchenko' in Russian?"

The kid froze. Even the three soldiers standing behind the sandbags stopped moving.

"Guess I said the magic word. Don't everybody piss down

your legs at the same time. Just follow along quietly and maybe he won't put the evil eye on you."

My new friends and I were about to start marching towards the warehouse when we heard a woman's scream. Everyone stopped whatever they were doing. Even the men working to untangle the broken locomotive stopped and looked towards the wooden building. I started walking. By the time I reached the boardwalk, I was almost running. The kid and his bayoneted companions followed along behind me.

The warehouse had a soldier standing guard at the door. This one was fully grown and with a face that looked like it had seen true misery in this world. He barred my path with another bayonet tipped rifle. The kid and his companions were a few steps behind me, their boots stomping in time along the boardwalk. "Ivchenko in there?" I asked the hard faced soldier. "Tell him the Amerikanski needs a word with the beady eyed little bastard."

The messenger boy started talking. So did the hard faced veteran. I waited, praying that scream I just heard didn't mean what I was afraid it meant. The veteran opened a door and disappeared inside.

"Don't suppose I could have my pistol back?" I asked the messenger. His answer was to again point his rifle at me. "To think, yesterday I was worried the Cossacks had cut your grubby little throat." The door opened. A second later, the stone faced guard grabbed the front of my jacket and yanked me through the opening. My escorts from the sandbags stayed outside.

The warehouse was never meant to be used as anything but an oversized storeroom. There were no windows inside. It was just a big empty box about forty feet deep and twenty wide, with a scattering of crates and barrels stacked mostly along the walls. Heavy wooden beams ran crossways from one side to the next with half a dozen wooden posts supporting a tin roof. The eves were open and most of the interior light came from daylight making its way between the roof's overhang and the wall. Most of the light, but not all. At the far end of the building, someone had improvised some kind of table made from a pair of sawhorses and planks. Sitting on one of those planks, a kerosene lamp added a yellowish glow to the interior. The commissar sat in a chair behind the makeshift desk. Scribbling away on a pile of papers, he didn't look like the kind of man whose name could cause soldiers to stop dead in their tracks. He looked like a bookkeeper.

The veteran put the butt of his rifle against my back and shoved. It was a hard, solid shove and almost put me on my knees. Stumbling forward into the center of the warehouse I saw two more people. Only one of them was still alive.

28

On my left side, not too far from the wooden wall, a man hung lifeless from the roof beams. His body had an almost imperceptible movement to it like a clock's pendulum slowly ticking down from the moment of his death. His right hand was caught up in a rope tied around his neck. The left hung at his side. The wooden keg they stood him on was a couple of feet away. They hadn't dropped him from a height. Instead, his executioners had kicked the barrel out from under him and left him to strangle. Alexi Gavrilov had died slowly.

On my right, Yelena leaned against one of the roof supports, arms crossed over a cranberry colored blouse. Gray jodhpurs were stuffed into a pair of knee high riding boots. I recognized the outfit. It was the same one the countess was wearing when we parted company. Yelena didn't quite fit in her new ensemble. The blouse was a size or two too small. If she wasn't careful, she was going to pop something. The maid's outfit might have been swapped for trousers and a tight shirt, but she had kept the loyal Bolshevik's red scarf. Only it wasn't tied around her hair anymore. She had it wrapped around her neck in a loose knot. It was like I was looking at a different woman. She didn't look like a woman capable of bashing a man's head in with a rock. She looked civilized.

"Yelena," I said as pleasantly as I could. "The problem with living in a small town is, everywhere you go, you keep running into the same people."

"Watkin," Yelena said. "Told you, we even."

She pointed a finger first at me, then at herself.

"No debt now, you and me."

I glanced at Gavrilov hanging from the ceiling, then back to Yelena. "Got it. Clean slate between us."

Stepping away from the timber post, Yelena moved closer to the lamp's halo of yellow light. "Like me better now. I have new clothes. Much nicer."

She fussed with her red scarf, then ran a hand down the front of the cranberry blouse. There was a gleam in her eyes. The last time I'd seen it, she was about to bash in a man's head. I was about to say something, but the soldier behind me stuck something sharp and pointed into the small of my back.

"Easy with the steak knife, chief," I said as I stepped closer to the sawhorses.

Yelena met me half way, smiled like we were old friends and put her arm through mine. She made a tisk tisk sound as the soldier with the bayonet prodded me in the back again.

The warehouse wasn't empty. There were a few crates here and there, a row of barrels with labels I couldn't read and a long row of shelving. With Gavrilov swinging in the breeze on my left, Yelena cheerfully pulling me forward on my right like she was bringing me home to meet her folks and the sharp point of a bayonet uncomfortably close behind me, I kept my attention focused on the desk and oil lamp. My escorts and I had just passed a shoulder high stack of wooden boxes when I saw her. She was barefoot and sitting on an armless chair with legs that were a bit too tall for her. Only her toes touched the floor. Her arms were penned behind her, forcing her shoulders into that posture people have when their hands are tied. Head down, her dark red hair spilled around her shoulders. They had her in some sort of sack dress that looked like it was made from mattress ticking. A shapeless thing, it covered her from neck to shins. Her head rose slowly.

"Mr. Watkins," she said in a soft, flat voice.

I tried to say something, something that would let her know everything was going to be fine, but when my lips moved, no sound came out. Yelena spoke instead. Not to me. She said something in her native tongue. The words were aimed at the countess. She patted me twice on the chest then spun out of my arm. Yelena went to the countess, still speaking soft Russian words until she was standing behind her chair. She pulled her hair away from her face and gathered it behind her head. The countess tried to pull her head away. Yelena's soothing sounds were making gooseflesh stand up on my arms.

"I see you and I have something in common," Ivchenko said from behind his makeshift desk. "We are both early risers."

The soldier didn't stick me in the back, so I supposed he had decided I was standing at an acceptable distance for conversation. "Sometimes."

Ivchenko was scribbling away with a fountain pen on a long sheet of paper. Not bothering to look up from the page, he continued. "My father was a baker. It was my responsibility to start the fire in the oven every morning. No fire in the oven, no bread to be made. No bread, no kopecks in my father's pockets." The commissar finished with whatever he was writing, picked up the long sheet of slightly yellow paper by the edges and sat it onto a small stack on his right. "I don't believe I have managed to sleep past four since," Ivchenko paused to think, "well, in a very long time."

"Didn't know you spoke English. Good. I was afraid your camp follower was going to have to translate." I regretted the words as soon as I said them.

"So pretty," Yelena said as she ran her fingers through the countess' hair. "Pretty, pretty." Stooping over, Yelena placed her face next to the countess. "You think she pretty than me?"

The countess looked at me but didn't say anything. Yelena yanked hard on her hair. The countess tightened her jaw.

"Answer, Watkin."

"You both look very much alike. In the right light, one could hardly tell you apart."

"Yelena," Ivchenko said. The commissar motioned with his fountain pen. The Bolshevik girl went back to running her fingers through her hair.

"I seldom get the opportunity to use my language skills these days," Ivchenko said. "I had a few books around here somewhere, probably burned now." Ivchenko exhaled slowly. "I used to read them when the snows came. To pass the time," he said with a soft smile.

"When snow come," Yelena said.

"Snows," Ivchenko corrected. "I also teach English."

"Got a lot of students?"

The commissar removed his high peaked cap. I hadn't realized how gray his hair was until he took off the hat. Adjusting the wire rimmed glasses sitting on his nose, he shuffled through the pile of papers on his desk. Without looking up, he began to speak.

"Thank you for coming in, Comrade Watkins. You saved me a good deal of trouble hunting you down, especially now that we find ourselves so shorthanded. I have just finished hearing the most amazing confession." The commissar selected a long sheet of paper then held it up to the light from his lamp. He read it quickly, shook his head then repeated the same selection process again. "Yes, this is the one. I was trying to capture my impressions, get them down while they are still fresh before I make my report to Comrade Trotsky." Looking away from the paper in his hand, he gestured towards the hanged man. "We just concluded our first trial of the morning. The second trial," he nodded his head towards the countess, "was just about to commence when you came calling. I suppose now we will have three trials before breakfast."

"What was the charge?" I asked.

"Whose?" Ivchenko asked with a politely raised eyebrow.

"The man swinging in the breeze."

"Have you seen this station?" Ivchenko shuffled more papers before selecting one from the stack. "Six warehouses complete with the people's war materiel destroyed, a water tower destroyed, five permanent dwellings destroyed, thirty-one horses stolen, five boxcars burned, three flatbeds heavily damaged, and an irreplaceable locomotive ruined beyond repair. Not to mention forty-nine soldiers killed or missing and seventeen wounded. All while the *Kompolka* was off examining a perfectly safe and heavily fortified river crossing."

"Does your report to this Trotsky fellow mention you were also off inspecting the bridge with Colonel Gavrilov?"

Ivchenko's face took on that vulture eating my liver look I remembered from the day I first arrived here.

"Never mind," I said. "Stupid question."

"Then there was his marriage."

Yelena snorted. The commissar used the end of his fountain pen to spear a small band of gold on his desk. He held the pen balanced between his fingers as he examined the ring. With the tip of his finger, he spun the wedding band around the pen's shaft. "Of course, you knew the marriage was just a cover for Gavrilov."

"If you're going to hang men for bad marriages, you're going to need a lot more rope."

Ivchenko sighed, dropped the wedding band into his hand then pitched it towards Yelena with all the emotion of a man feeding bread crumbs to pigeons. She caught it in the air. The countess twisted in her chair and said something in Russian. Indifferently, without so much as a glance at her, Yelena swung her arm in a backhanded slap that nearly toppled the chair onto its side. Ivchenko's creature slid the wedding band into the pocket of her stolen trousers.

"I regret hanging the man now," Ivchenko said. "He was a soldier of sorts. The Comrade *Kompolka* should have been given the dignity of the firing squad." Ivchenko shrugged a shoulder. "I lost my patience."

"Lost temper," Yelena said. She tilted her head to one side, stuck out her tongue, and made a gagging sound.

"Yelena," the commissar said with exaggerated slowness.

"Why did you remove her clothes and why are her hands tied?" I asked.

Ivchenko read from the page in front of him. "The counterrevolutionary, formerly known as Countess Irena Obolensky was restrained for the protection of Comrade Yelena whom she physically attacked during her late husband's trial."

I felt the skin on my face tighten.

"Oh," the commissar said. "I see you thought I was in the dark about that additional bit of deception. Comrade Yelena is quite skilled at finding answers once she has the scent."

"Countess," Yelena said, drawing the word out in one long hiss.

"No matter," Ivchenko continued. "We will come to that in a moment. As to the prisoner's clothes, Yelena." Ivchenko twisted in his chair. "What happened to the prisoner's clothing?"

Yelena touched a small tear on the shoulder of her cranberry blouse. "Tore when we strip her."

Ivchenko laid the paper he was reading from on his desk, took up his fountain pen again and began to dictate as the pen scratched out the words. "The prisoner's garments were damaged beyond salvage during the search for weapons, contraband and concealed items known to be on her person."

"Were her boots torn as well?"

Ivchenko raised that polite eyebrow again. This time he pointed its unspoken question towards Yelena. She bent at the waist, giving me, Ivchenko and the Russian guard a prolonged view down the front of her blouse. The woman ran a hand down the length of her boots.

"Leather like new," she said. "Fit is good like glove."

Ivchenko waited until Yelena straightened from rubbing her new boots before continuing his monolog. "The counterrevolutionary imperialist traitor," he began, once more scratching his pen across the paper. "Wished footwear extorted from Russian workers be reissued for the good of the Soviet. I like that last part. Makes the bourgeoisie sound contrite. Moscow will approve."

The countess stiffened in her chair, then began to shout in her native tongue. Yelena slapped her again.

"That's enough of that," I said.

"You do not give orders in this place, Comrade Watkins," Ivchenko said warningly.

"My apologies, Comrade Ivchenko. I've had a long night. May I request the court dress the accused in a decent set of clothes? That's a sack somebody stitched together."

"It is not a sack, Comrade. It is a dress issued to the prisoner so she may cover herself. We are not barbarians. We do not hang naked women."

The countess groaned. Yelena had a double handful of her hair and was using it to force her to look at the hanged man.

"Stop pulling her hair. Ivchenko, tell her to stop mistreating the colonel's widow. Even here, the accused have rights."

Ivchenko peered at me over his wire framed glasses. "Even here," he said slowly.

Without taking his eyes off me, he spoke quietly in Russian. The guard who had marched me into the warehouse came forward. Standing by Yelena, he unsnapped the bayonet from his rifle's muzzle, then handed it over.

"Ivchenko, Comrade Ivchenko," I said quickly. "I came here for a reason."

Yelena took the bayonet in one hand, then pulled the countess' hair straight back. She began to saw the sharp steel back and forth through her hair. The wooden floor beneath the chair began to look like a well-used barbershop.

"Why is she doing that? Tell her, may I ask she stop doing that?"

"Comrade Yelena, why are you cutting the prisoner's hair?" Ivchenko asked.

"*Vshey,*" she answered. The bayonet continued to saw back and forth.

"Disgusting," Ivchenko said, turning once more to his list. "The prisoner was discovered to be infested with lice," he said aloud as the pen scratched.

Handfuls of dark red hair fell as Yelena continued to slice with the blade. When she was done and the remaining hair was no longer than my finger, she put her face next to the countess' again.

"Still pretty now, Watkin?"

"Mr. Watkins," the countess said. A tear ran down her cheek. "I told you."

My fists were clenched into tight balls. The countess dropped her head to stare at the floor as the soldier snapped his bayonet back onto the barrel of his rifle. When he was finished, he resumed his position behind me. The warehouse's tin roof rattled and snapped.

"Listen to that wind," Ivchenko said. "I think the ice will be early this year.

"How much, Ivchenko."

"I beg your pardon?"

"Bail for the prisoner. How much?"

The commissar laughed. "Are you such a fool?" He said something to the soldier with the handy blade. I didn't bother looking over my shoulder. A moment later, Gavrilov's corpse crashed onto the warehouse floor.

"There is no bail here, Comrade Watkins." Turning to face the countess, he said, "Irena Obolensky, I find you guilty of counterrevolutionary activities, murder, adultery and," he twisted a scrawny neck my direction, "giving shelter to the enemies of the Russian Soviet. Sentence is death to be carried out as soon as I am done with my questioning of your lover.

Try not to urinate on my floor when you feel the bite of the rope."

"Tell Yelena and the guard to step outside," I said.

"And why on earth would I do such a thing?"

"Because if you don't, after I tell you what I'm about to say, you will regret it more than you know."

"Comrade Watkins, you are going to tell me everything you know regardless of whether the guard is in the room or not. I have found there is an art to extracting information. It is always easier if there is an apparent weakness. I know yours." He said the last words while looking at the bound woman in the chair.

Ivchenko moved piles of paper on his desk. He found what he was looking for beneath the third stack. Picking it up, he tossed it towards Yelena. There was a loud clatter when it hit the floor between her feet. It was a set of iron pliers.

"The prisoner was complaining of a toothache. Unfortunately, the depot is without a dentist. Comrade Yelena, please be so kind as to pull the tooth giving her trouble. Start with the ones in front."

Yelena picked up the pliers, then started to kneel on the countess' lap.

I took a step towards Ivchenko. The commissar reached a hand towards his waist. When he brought it back up, he was holding the long barreled broom handle Mauser.

"One step closer, Watkins and the prisoner will witness her second execution of the morning."

"Comrade Ivchenko, have you asked yourself why am I here? Here, in some backwater hole in Siberia. Have you thought about that?"

"It is all I have thought about ever since you came riding into my depot. The real question is how many teeth does Yelena have to pull before you tell me the story? Not the desperate lie you will begin with, but the real story. The one I truly want to hear."

"All you had to do was ask. It's why I stopped by this

morning."

Ivchenko raised his hand. "Yelena." The Bolshevik stopped with one hand around the prisoner's throat and the other holding the pliers.

Leaning forward, ever mindful of the Mauser pointing at my chest and the commissar's finger curled over the trigger, I said just loud enough for him to hear, "How would you like a boxcar full of gold?"

29

Ivchenko started laughing. He sat back in his chair and howled like he had just heard the best joke in his life. With the Mauser held casually in one hand, he slapped the planks of his desk with the other. Piles of neatly stacked papers began to tilt. Resettling his glasses on his nose, he nudged the papers back into columns with the barrel of the pistol.

"Really, Watkins, I thought I had heard all the amazing stories I was going to hear this morning. I do wish you would have cooperated and just told me what I am going to find out anyway. It is so tiresome listening to a woman scream and I'm afraid she will look quite horrible afterwards. Completely unrecognizable. Yelena," he began.

My retainer had sat in the inside pocket of my jacket next to my heart for so long, it almost felt like a part of me. It seemed a shame to surrender it now. But it was the only chance she had. The gold bar landed between the stacks of freshly ordered paper columns. The sound was very similar to the one made by the pliers when they landed on the warehouse floor. Only it wasn't a piece of common iron making the noise this time.

Ivchenko's eyes were staring at the gold bar sitting in the center of his desk. The Mauser's barrel drifted to one side, no longer pointing at anything. Out of the corner of my eye, I saw Yelena climb off the countess' lap and crane her head towards Ivchenko's desk.

"Last chance," I whispered, "to keep it just between us."

Yelena took a step towards the table. I couldn't breathe. Turning my head slowly towards the countess, our eyes met. Her head gave the briefest of nods.

Ivchenko was still looking at the ingot lying between his paper columns. He hadn't moved.

Yelena, pliers in hand, came another step closer.

"Comrade Yelena," Ivchenko said just before she made it to his desk. "Bring me some tea." Slowly, nonchalantly as if nothing special had just happened, he slid a single page of paper over the gold bar. The commissar looked past me at the soldier standing beside Gavrilov's corpse. Something was said in Russian.

"Tea?" Yelena asked.

"Go with Yuri," Ivchenko told her. "Tea. I am thirsty."

"But," she gestured behind her at the chair and its waiting victim.

I don't know what Ivchenko's shouted Russian words meant, but Yelena certainly did. Whatever he said, it made her take a step backwards.

"Da, Komissar," she said, once more looking like a docile housemaid, fancy new clothes or not. Pausing by the soldier, she said something to him. I didn't make a sound. Not until I heard the door opening.

"Yelena," I said loudly, "the countess and I will have some as well, and don't forget the sugar this time."

Ivchenko waved his hand. He was good with that hand waving trick. The door to the warehouse must have been well made. You could tell because it survived the impact after Yelena closed it behind her. I turned to the countess.

"Stand where you are," Ivchenko warned.

The Mauser was once again pointing in my direction. He might pull that trigger, but the odds were on my side. I had momentum. Now was not the time to start obeying threats.

"Relax, Ivchenko. You'll hear the whole story in a second." Reaching around her, I fumbled at the knots. Her hands were tied with some kind of coarse cord. The knot would have been easy to untie if I stepped around the other side of the chair, but I didn't like the idea of her body between me and that Mauser. Accidents happen.

"Leave the prisoner alone," the commissar said.

"What are you doing, Mr. Watkins?" the countess whispered softly. She sounded weary, like a person operating on the last remains of her strength. "He will shoot you."

"Let's hope not," I said, my voice just loud enough to be heard over the windstorm howling away outside. The knot unraveled in my hands. Pulling her arms around in front of her, I laid them in her lap. The sack they had her in really was made from an old mattress cover. It wasn't much more than a bag with a hole for her head and two more to stick her arms through. The knuckles of her hand were scratched and there was a long bruise down one arm. "If you plan on getting in anymore wrestling matches, let me know. I'll show you a few maneuvers I learned on a playground's battlefield."

The countess touched her head. "My hair."

Pulling her hand away from the butcher job Yelena had done, I said, "Long hair is out of fashion these days. All the women are going for the short look since the war ended."

"Has the war ended?" she said as she dropped her hand into her lap. "What a lovely peace we are having."

"Watkins, turn around now or I will kill you," Ivchenko shouted.

He was probably telling the truth, so I turned around. There wasn't another chair in the warehouse and I didn't feel like standing in front of the commissar's paper columns while he waved a confiscated pistol at me.

"Where did you get this? Tell me this instant," he said, the gold ingot grasped tightly in his left hand. The right was still holding the broom handle.

The only thing in the place to sit on was the keg that had been under Gavrilov's very shiny boots. Feeling like I was breaking some primeval taboo, I used my boot to roll the keg closer to Ivchenko's desk. I didn't really want to touch it with my hands, but there was no other way to stand it on end. When it was right side up, I parked my behind on it, crossed my leg at the knee and cleared my throat.

"Now," I began, "where were we?"

"Tell me about this or I will kill the woman." The Mauser swung towards the countess.

"I wouldn't. Do that and we'll lose part of the map."

"Map?"

"To Kolchak's gold. Kolchak was this admiral in charge of the Russian treasury."

Ivchenko's thumb cocked the hammer on the pistol.

"But you've heard that part." The countess rose from her chair and walked to my side. She moved slowly, like someone hurting. "You should sit," I told her. I started to stand, but she put a hand on my shoulder.

"I will negotiate with the Bolshevik, Mr. Watkins. It is my fortune you are giving away."

"This is not a negotiation, you bourgeoisie cow," Ivchenko screamed. "It is an interrogation."

"That, Comrade Ivchenko, is a title that means more to me than countess. Please, use it often."

Afraid to gloat in front of the gun waving commissar, I smiled on the inside. That was the woman I came back for.

The door to the warehouse opened followed by a blast of wind so strong the fire in the commissar's lamp flickered as the tin roof rattled. The ingot vanished into the side pocket of a well made, if too large for him leather coat. I recognized the coat. The last time I'd seen it, the late colonel was wearing it.

Yuri the stone faced guard, carried a wooden platter with a

pewter tea pot and three fist sized enameled cups on it. Yelena didn't make a return appearance. If Yuri was surprised to see the countess standing beside me with one hand resting on my shoulder, he didn't show it. Yuri had the kind of face that didn't understand the need to express oneself. Ivchenko said a few Russian words then did that hand wave thing again. No one made another sound until the soldier left the building. This time, the door wasn't slammed hard enough to shake the walls.

"The prisoner may pour the tea," Ivchenko said in a disdainful voice.

"Pour it yourself," the countess shot back.

"Allow me," I said in my best diplomatic voice. I handed the countess a steaming cup. For a moment, it looked like she was going to throw it at the commissar. "Drink your tea," I said quietly.

She smiled at me. It was a very condescending smile, but at least all her teeth were still there. Ivchenko sipped his own cup.

"What map?" he said at last.

"I have a piece of it up here," I said, tapping my temple with a finger. "She has her own piece. An unnamed partner you don't know about has the final piece."

"Who is this supposed third partner?"

"The one that is keeping you from shooting me."

"Shall we call for the dentist? You've made Yelena very angry. I can assure you, she won't be gentle."

I remembered the stone football. No, she wouldn't be gentle. The fingers resting on my shoulder tightened. "We both know I can't stop you, Commissar, but it won't do you a bit of good."

"More than a dozen grown men," he glanced at the countess, "have said similar things."

"Told you, Ivchenko, I'll answer every question. There's no need for violence. I walked in here of my own free will. A smart guy like you should have known I was coming to make a deal."

"Who is the third man, then? Answer me this instant."

"Sure. No problem." I added a fresh splash of tea to my cup. As I sat the pot back on Yuri's tray, I said, "The third person is a man named Bohdan, Colonel Wilhelm Bohdan. I believe he was the head of the Czech Legion's intelligence section."

Ivchenko spilled brown tea across freshly compiled notes for Comrade Trotsky.

"The Countess and I rode in with him with those Russian troopers the day before yesterday. Didn't you see him watering the horses? He damn sure saw you. Told me himself you came here looking for him. Something about British sovereigns used to bribe their way into Vladivostok. Admiral Kolchak's sovereigns I was told."

The countess patted my shoulder. She did it very softly. Ivchenko sat his cup onto the planks of his makeshift desk. The vulture was looking at my liver again.

"Colonel Bohdan," I continued, "was the man responsible for diverting part of the gold payment the Czech Legion made to you boys when they turned over Kolchak."

The wind ripped and tore at the metal roof of the depot's last remaining shack.

"Still find my story funny?"

30

"You're lying," the man with vulture's eyes said.

"Czech professor from Prague," I told him. "Taught economics. Stands about a head taller than you and a good bit heavier. Speaks Russian with a Ukrainian accent."

Ivchenko inched slowly forward as graceful as a lizard about to eat a fly.

Reaching for the teapot, I asked, "More tea?" Before Ivchenko could start asking questions, I started talking. I thought it was better to keep someone like the commissar on the defensive.

"Here's the situation, Ivchenko. Wilhelm is waiting a few miles from here with the horses."

"There are no horses."

"Go tell the three dead Cossacks that. The countess here was supposed to meet me a little way down the road."

"Which road?"

"Thanks to her little mishap with Yelena, she didn't make the rendezvous, so I told our Czech partner I was going back to find her. Wilhelm didn't want me to go. Said it was too dangerous."

"Which road?" Ivchenko said again.

"There are five different ways in and out of this depot not counting the tracks themselves. If you want to go hunt him down, you've got a twenty percent chance of picking the right road."

"I could make you tell me easily enough, Watkins. It wouldn't be advised for you to try me."

Small, delicate fingers tightened their grip on my shoulder. "Very true, however, there's my insurance policy."

Ivchenko raised an eyebrow.

"The colonel thinks the game is up. He says if I'm not back by the time the sun hits high noon, he's heading for some place called Sakhalin. Said he would tell his grandchildren all about the boxcar full of gold he never got."

Ivchenko drummed his fingers on his desk. The countess and I sipped our tea like thirsty manikins.

"It's true," she said, finishing her tea. "Wilhelm needs us just as much as we need him."

"You take me for a fool," the commissar said. "I will have the road out of you before my tea is cold. Then I will have the Czech."

"Did I say I wouldn't give him to you? I knew I was giving up my shot at all that gold the minute I walked in here. The man's nothing to me now." Reaching for the hand sitting lightly on my shoulder, I said, "I like redheads. We'll call it a fair trade. You get all three pieces of the map plus a man wanted by every Chekists in Russia. The woman and I take a long walk in any direction you point."

The countess leaned against me. I felt her pulling me closer. It was a simple thing to do and it conveyed a mountain of intimacy to the watching commissar.

"Trotsky," I said. "Was that his name? I bet he's one of the big shots in this revolution. Living in a confiscated palace. Warm fires. Best food in the city. Ballet in the evenings. Plus, the power a man like that must have. While you, you get stuck out here in Siberia freezing through the winter." I looked around the warehouse. "Making do in a drafty shed reading old books to Yelena and writing reports nobody's going to read." Putting my hand on the countess' bare calf, I added, "All I want is the woman. You can have the Czech and spend a few hours making him tell you where the gold is buried."

"Which road?" Ivchenko asked for the third time.

Letting go of her leg, I stood up slowly. Ivchenko covered me with the Mauser. "Let's go. We'll take you straight to him."

"You will tell me and I will send my men."

"You've got two, maybe three hours before Colonel Bohdan gets on his horse." I raised my hands. "I'm making you a fair deal. If he sees me and the woman coming down the road, he'll wait for us. The treasure will make him wait. All you have to do is hang back forty, fifty yards until he steps out of the bushes, shoot his horse, then run him down. Trotsky will send a private train to come get his new deputy commissar of the revolution. A deputy commissar with more gold than a pharaoh."

My heart was beating so hard against my chest I was sure he could hear it. If it hadn't been so cold in the unheated shed, no doubt beads of sweat would be running down my temples. I drank the last of my tea and tried to look like I was negotiating a claim with an insurance agent. The wind screamed and the roof shook.

"Yuri!" Ivchenko shouted

The warehouse door opened almost before the sound of the shout died away. The stone faced soldier stepped into the room. Ivchenko started talking as I ran my tongue around the inside of an ash dry mouth.

"He says to gather twenty men," the countess said next to me. "With weapons and rations for the day."

The soldier spoke.

"He says there aren't twenty men," the countess translated.

"Shut up, cow!" Ivchenko screamed. "If this is some scheme to make a fool of me, things will not end well for you." The commissar stood, then shoved the broom handle into the holster on his belt. It was the same one the countess had worn every day since Vladivostok. "Now," Ivchenko said as he came around the sawhorse desk, "show me the road before the Czech leaves. You've wasted enough time."

"Return my clothes," the countess said, "and my boots."

I wasn't fast enough to stop it. The slap struck her cheek with hard force. I grabbed for her but only caught the sack cloth she was wearing. The thin fabric ripped as she fell.

"Never, ever make a demand of me." Spittle flew from Ivchenko's mouth. "On your life, if you do it again, I will hang you on the spot." He turned for the door, pulling on a pair of gloves as he went. "While you spent the winter wrapped in sable, thousands of Russian peasants wrapped rags around their feet. It will be good for you to understand the plight of the Russian worker. Bring her Watkins or leave her where she lays. It makes no difference to me."

"What have you done?" she asked quietly as I helped her to her feet. "Where is Bohdan, and why are you betraying him to Ivchenko?"

"Bohdan's long gone. I'm buying us time."

"Ivchenko will never let us leave."

"One problem at a time, Countess."

"Watkins," Ivchenko shouted from the doorway.

The countess tried to walk. She almost fell again.

"My foot. The whore stomped on it."

"Can you walk?"

"A horse stepped on the same foot years ago. It gives me trouble." She tried a cautious step. "How far are we going?"

"About a mile. Maybe a little more," I said low enough that only she could hear.

The countess stopped walking. I put my arm around her waist to help her.

"I will not be able to keep up. Ivchenko will make me stay

here and force you to take him to Bohdan."

"You're damn well going to try," I told her. "Walk the soreness out."

She nodded. "I will try. They made me watch, Mr. Watkins. When they hung Alexi. I had to sit there on that chair and watch him strangle. He was just another Bolshevik and I felt nothing for him, but I didn't want to watch him die. Yelena made me. I don't want to die like that. Make them shoot me. I don't want to strangle."

"Nobody's going to hang you, Countess."

By the time we made it out of the warehouse, she was leaning harder than ever on my arm. Four Russian soldiers waited outside. Each one had a pack on his back and a bayonet tipped rifle over a shoulder. One was Stone Faced Yuri. The reins to a horse were in his hand. The teenaged messenger, still wearing my raincoat, hitched his shoulders to settle his pack better, then smiled at me.

"Vroom, vroom," he said.

The other two, both big rawboned boys looked like they should be milking cows and bailing hay on a farm. All five men wore the high pointed uniform cap with the red star on the front. Wind caught the mattress sacking dress and whipped the thin material around the countess' legs. The Russian boys smiled in appreciation. One of them elbowed his companion and grinned. Yuri didn't move.

"What is wrong with her?" Ivchenko demanded. "Can she not walk?"

The countess gripped my arm.

"Don't leave me behind."

Ivchenko took the reins from Yuri's hand and swung himself into the saddle. The horse shied sideways and lifted a foreleg. The animal's hoof barely touched the ground.

"She doesn't need to walk," I said. Letting go of her arm, I went past Stone Face and grabbed the wooden handles of a wheelbarrow. It was one of those heavy kind like the ones used to move bulk freight between the trains and the storage sheds. Rainwater made a shallow pool inside the wide bucket. Dumping it out, I rolled the barrow back to the countess.

"Impossible," Ivchenko said. "Your arms will give out before we are out of sight of the camp."

"Bet you a gold bar you're wrong. Get in," I told the countess.

"It's wet."

"Countess, the last train is leaving the station. Climb aboard or wait for the red eye."

"Can you dry it first?"

I might have pushed a bit too hard. When she landed in the wheelbarrow, the wind caught the bottom of the sack dress. The three boys gawked at the sight of a woman's bare legs and creamy thighs. For the first time since I started up Gavrilov's tank and pointed its nose towards the depot, I knew what I was going to do.

31

"Mr. Watkins, tell him that horse is lame," the countess said.

I thought of the Cossack riding down the road with Yelena across his saddle. "That horse won't carry you, Ivchenko." I pointed to its foreleg. "It's lame."

The commissar pointed at the wheelbarrow. "You manage your animal and I will manage mine." He slapped the reins against the horse's neck and kicked his heals into its flanks. The horse took a couple of steps.

"Idiot," the countess said under her breath.

Grabbing the handles of the barrow, I lifted it far enough off the ground to make it roll and started pushing.

Ivchenko was almost right. The wheelbarrow and I made it out of sight of the camp before I had to stop pushing, but not much more than that. It wasn't a problem. One of the teenagers practically jumped for the handles. They were just three young boys stuck out in the middle of nowhere for who knew how long. Women were a rare commodity and the countess, short sack dress barely covering her knees and constantly fighting the wind, was an eye grabbing fascination. The opportunity to stare down a woman's top and watch a flimsy sack blow in the wind was irresistible.

Ivchenko rode behind us. Every time I looked over my shoulder, he was doing his best to force the limping horse to carry him a little farther. The horse kept stopping, forcing the commissar to slam his heels into its flanks. Stone Faced Yuri kept pace with the limping horse. I walked a little faster, hoping the boy at the handles would keep up. He did. The teenagers gawking at the woman in the wheelbarrow never once looked back. The horse fell a little farther behind.

Two of the boys had worn themselves out pushing the wheelbarrow by the time we hit the big hill. The third one took over; all smiles as he leaned forward and pushed.

"Watkins, how much farther?" Ivchenko demanded for the fourth time.

"Ways to go yet," I shouted over my shoulder.

Ivchenko and his horse were at the edge of what I guessed was pistol shot range. Yuri, walking beside the commissar's stirrup, had his rifle slung over his shoulder.

"It was dark when I came in this morning. The woods all look alike when it's dark. When we get to the crest, I'll take the wheelbarrow. You and your men drop back a little. If Wilhelm is watching, and you know he will be, if he sees soldiers, he'll mount up and ride for the hills."

"Yuri is an amazing shot with his rifle, Watkins. I have seen him hit a running man at one hundred meters. If you try to run, he will put three bullets in you before you get ten steps."

"Wheelbarrow, Ivchenko. The whole reason I came back is parked in the wheelbarrow. Why would I run now?"

The crest was coming closer. Five more minutes, and we would be on the downward slope. How far back into the surrounding trees had I pushed the Mack? I tapped the teenager providing the wheelbarrow's horsepower. He didn't want to give up the view. Yuri growled something and the boy dropped the handles.

The hill began to level out.

"Countess," I said in a conversational tone. We hadn't spoken since leaving the train yard. Her head half turned to look over her shoulder. She still didn't speak. "Do you miss the music of the Czech's violin?" The wheelbarrow's handles rocked in my hands as she twisted farther around. "Remember that song he played for us when we left the dock?"

"Be quiet, Watkins," Ivchenko said from somewhere behind me. "How much farther?"

She twisted around inside her metal shell to better see the commissar. "I do. I remember every note."

Wind whistled over the hilltop catching the sack cloth. She didn't try to control it as kaleidoscopic flashes of snow white skin came and went in the hard blowing wind.

"Did you keep up your lessons? On his violin?" I asked in a voice only she and I could hear.

I saw it then. It was that same look she had when she stepped out of the shadows of her bedroom in nothing but a blouse. Maybe it was a look in her eyes or a slight tilt of her head, but the look was there. A sharp gust of wind ballooned the cheap cloth around her. A smile, just the tiniest hint of upturned lips touched her face. The leopard was stalking the gazelle again.

"I am very good with a violin." Her voice purred the words. "He was an excellent teacher."

The wind tugged at the dress. Without taking her eyes off me, she made a knot of the fabric with her fist.

"Countess, he left the violin in the truck. In the floorboard."

Ivchenko's horse snorted and refused to take another step. Yuri grabbed at the animal's bridle and started pulling. The boys hadn't noticed anything but a flapping dress since we topped the hill.

"I love violin music. But not long songs," I added.

The countess nodded. "Short songs."

"Some *distracting* music." I stretched the word out and looked at her legs. "Something to appreciate."

"I will not warn you again, Watkins," Ivchenko shouted before turning his attention to Yuri. The Russian shouted at my teenaged escort, then gave the bridle of Ivchenko's horse a solid yank. The nearest teenager slipped his rifle off his shoulder.

The leopard curled herself back around inside her cage and faced the bottom of the hill. "How much longer before we will be able to play music again?"

She pointed one very smooth leg in front of her while working her sore foot around in a circle as cold Siberian wind pushed the sack dress far up her thigh. She had to place a hand over her crotch to keep the thin cloth from blowing as high as her navel. One of the teenaged boys tripped on my foot causing me to stumble. The countess made a feminine sound as she slapped at the hem of her sack. Grabbing for the sides of the wheelbarrow, the dress flapped in the hard blowing north wind. The dress billowed around her transfixing the boys.

"Very soon now." I said it so low, I wasn't sure she heard me.

I steered the wheelbarrow near the edge of the muddy lane. The boys moved with me. I wanted them on the same side of the road as the truck. It would be harder for them to see it from that side. None of them took their eyes off naked thighs balanced on the wheelbarrow's edge.

The horse whinnied and Ivchenko cursed. I glanced behind me. The commissar was slapping his heels into the unmoving horse's flanks while Yuri pulled at its bridle.

The slope steepened and I saw the wheel marks from last night's attempt to climb the hill. The weight of the wheelbarrow pulled me down the slope. Ivchenko said something behind me. The wheelbarrow rolled faster and the distance between us increased.

"Watkins, slow down," Ivchenko ordered.

"Too steep," I shouted. "Can't hold it."

"I am going to play you a wonderful song, Mr. Watkins.

Everyone will dance when they hear my music."

The wind blew, the sack dress rose up creamy legs and teenaged boys stumbled in mesmerized astonishment beside me. The leopard took her time pushing the dress back down. The boys were talking among themselves. Even I watched as the countess twirled her foot and the sack flapped in the cold breeze.

"Watkins," Ivchenko shouted. "You are testing my patience."

I didn't look behind me. We were almost to the bottom of the hill. Any moment now, I knew one of the Russians was bound to look up and see the Mack pushed into the trees. The countess grabbed the sides of the wheelbarrow, forgetting modesty and her flapping sack of a dress as she braced herself. I saw the Mack still sitting where I left it. The countess had already seen it.

"Shall we dance, Mr. Watkins?"

I threw the handles of the wheelbarrow forward. If she hadn't been ready, I would have thrown her face first into the mud. But she was ready. The countess flew out of the upturned barrow at a dead run. If her foot still pained her from her long ago injury, she ignored it. Sliding on the slick ground, she darted to the right and into the trees beside the road.

One of the teenagers shouted as she jumped for the Mack's running board. I spun just as the soldier started to run after her. The hardest punch I'd ever thrown caught the soldier on the nose. His feet flew out from under him as I ran at the second soldier. That's how I thought of them now. They weren't teenagers anymore. They were soldiers. Putting everything I had in it, I drove both of my hands into the second soldier's chest. The blow took him off his feet and sent him sailing backwards. Ivchenko bellowed orders as his horse danced sideways. Yuri wasn't pulling on the horse's bridle anymore. He spun away from the animal as the rifle's sling slipped off his shoulder in a smooth, professional movement. I watched as the Russian brought his rifle to the firing position.

His face was as expressionless as a statue. He looked at me with eyes that said I was finished in this world. Yuri sighted down the barrel. He could hit a running man, the commissar said.

It was the horse that saved me. It danced sideways and bumped him hard enough to make Yuri stumble. As he brought the barrel in line with my chest for the second time, something behind me caught his eye. For the first time that morning, an emotion crossed Yuri's face. The rifle swung past me as the Russian tried to aim at a more important target.

Ivchenko had the Mauser out of his holster with the barrel waving in my direction. He tried to find me in his sights as the horse continued to move under him. When he fired, the bullet went by so close, I heard it tearing the air past my head. The teenaged messenger was backing up while trying to get the rifle's sling untangled from his pack as the soldier with the bleeding nose started to get to his feet. I ducked, then jumped quickly to my right as the Mauser fired again. Ivchenko's gun followed me as the soldier I had shoved onto his back pointed at the trees and screamed a warning. The messenger boy stepped in front of me as Ivchenko fired his third shot. The kid lurched forward as his high peaked hat with its red star flew off his head. He fell at my feet face down in the mud.

In one of those brief, intensely clear moments, I had a sudden thought. What if someone had taken the Lewis while I was away?

"Down!" the countess screamed.

I dropped onto all fours as the countess started playing her song. The first burst from the Lewis was a long rip that tore Yuri's legs out from under him. There was a half second pause before her second burst ran across the chest of Ivchenko's horse. The animal reared on its hind legs and screamed as it died. Yuri never made a sound. The Mauser fired again as the commissar fell with his horse. The third burst from Bohdan's violin caught the Russian soldier with the bloody nose halfway between sitting and standing. The bullets tore across his chest in a series of very loud thumps. Muddy splashes marched a deadly line to the last soldier. He was the one who pointed at the trees and screamed a warning. The bullets twisted him into a ball before sending him rolling into the mud of a cold, Siberian forest road. The silence only lasted for a moment before a second burst swept across both dead men. Their bodies jumped as the bullets struck again and again.

I heard a very loud mechanical click behind me.

"I'm out," an adrenalin soaked voice said from the truck. The dance was over.

Grabbing a dead man's rifle, I sprinted up the muddy road. All my attention was on the dead horse as a foot moved in a stirrup. Ivchenko wasn't dead. I heard the sound of leather moving and a man grunting. The horse's carcass was broadside to me with its unmoving legs pointing downhill. Ivchenko's foot came out of the stirrup. I heard the sounds of a man struggling as I reached the horse. With my bayonet pointing at the little man who had dreams of grandeur in far off Moscow, I looked over the side of the saddle. Ivchenko was stretched out and reaching with all the effort of a hopelessly desperate man. The Mauser lay in the mud just beyond his clawing fingers. With his left leg buried under the horse, his other boot was braced against the saddle. The commissar pushed with all his might. Nothing was moving. Ivchenko wasn't going anywhere. He was trapped by the dead animal's weight.

"Well," I said, as the commissar jerked around to face me. "Aren't you in a pickle?"

The countess limped her way to my side. She had one of the dead soldier's rifles was in her hand. Yuri, a body's length away from the dead horse, rolled onto his stomach. His rifle had careened out of his hands when the Lewis found him and was lying near the edge of the road. The Russian crawled towards it one slow inch at a time. A red smear marked the sodden road like some giant slug crawling across a garden path. He never made a sound. There was no question of his standing. Bohdan's violin had ruined his body below the waist. Crawling was all he could do. Everyone, even Yuri, knew he was never going to make it to that rifle. Once more, the commissar lunged for the pistol stretching his arm out as far as it would go. The arm wasn't any closer than before. Yuri stopped his slow crawl, then laid his head upon his arm. His journey was over.

"Mr. Watkins," Ivchenko said. "I can help you." He looked at the countess as the bag he'd dressed her in flapped and twisted in the wind. "Both of you." He kicked his free leg against the saddle in impotent fury.

"Don't you just hate horses," I told him.

32

"I've never shot a horse before," the countess said. "Its leg was broken, wasn't it?"

I looked at the animal, certain it was the same one I had knocked off its feet during the Cossack raid. The right leg was swollen where I hit it with the rifle stock, but I couldn't see anything that looked like bones pointing the wrong way. The countess watched Ivchenko. I don't think she wanted to look at the animal's leg.

"I'm sure it was. It could barely put its hoof on the ground."

She nodded her chin. "It had to be put down then."

"Watkins, I know very powerful people," Ivchenko said. "I can be useful to you."

The countess walked past me. The rifle was balanced at her waist with the bayonet pointing at the pinned man. The wind pressed at her back lifting the prisoner's rag past her knees.

"Commissar Ivchenko, I am cold. The wind has teeth this morning. May I have my late husband's coat?"

Ivchenko, with eyes fastened on the end of the bayonet's

steel tip, fumbled at the buttons of the leather coat. It took some effort, but he managed to get his arms out of the sleeves. Stepping closer, rifle in one hand, the countess grabbed the coat by its collar and pulled. Sticking the rifle bayonet down in the mud, she snatched the soft wool cap off Ivchenko's head. She used the hat like a whisk broom, slapping it against the soft leather knocking off bits of mud and dirt. When she was satisfied, she draped it over the upturned stock of the rifle.

"He watched, you know." The countess, cap in hand, stepped past Ivchenko. She squatted and picked up the pistol still lying just beyond Ivchenko's reach. Using the cap as a rag, she rubbed and cleaned the Mauser. "When he ordered the whore and that one," she glanced at the corpse of Yuri, "to strip me. He sat there behind his little wooden desk and his neat piles of paper, the bread maker's boy, and watched." She stood slowly, the pistol in her hand.

"Time's wasting, Countess. We need to be on our way."

"That's right," Ivchenko barked. "Twenty men will be coming over that hill at any minute. I left orders to come running if they heard shots."

The countess stopped her gun polishing. She looked at Ivchenko and I almost felt sorry for him.

"Liar, bread maker's boy."

She tossed the cap away. The wind caught it and sent it tumbling towards Yuri.

"I doubt there are twenty soldiers left alive back there, and even if there were, I doubt any of them would have the nerve to come into the woods. Not after what General Semyonov did to them."

Ivchenko ran a nervous tongue across his lips. He looked like he was about to say something when the countess made her next demand.

"The rest," she said. "Take it off."

"What?" Ivchenko said. "Mr. Watkins, control your woman. We, you and I, we can come to an arrangement."

"Not me, Comrade." I touched a finger to my ear. "I've

seen what she can do with that horse pistol of hers. You should probably do as she said."

"Your tunic, bread maker's boy," the countess said, her voice as smooth as Singapore silk. "I'm cold and this rag you put me in isn't decent. No need to be shy. I showed you mine. Now it's your turn." The Mauser tapped a slow rhythm against her thigh.

"Here," I said, starting to unbutton my jacket. "Where are my manners?"

"No, Mr. Watkins. Your clothes are wet and I do not wish to catch my death in this wind." She glanced at the swaying trees. "There will be frost tonight. Besides, I seem to always be borrowing your clothes, don't I." The pistol still tapped against her thigh. "Hurry up, bread maker's boy. I'm starting to shiver."

"Mr. Watkins," Ivchenko said.

The pistol rose in her hand. It stopped with the barrel in line with the commissar's forehead. Ivchenko started pulling at his shirt.

"Here," he said, pulling the tunic half over his head. "Take it."

Like the coat before it, the countess grabbed the fabric and pulled. When it was free from Ivchenko, she snapped it twice in her hand as if she was trying to shake off any remaining bits of its former owner. When she finished, she draped it over the upturned rifle like she had the coat. She glanced around at the three dead teenagers and Yuri.

"No," she said. "They are all much too big for me."

She looked down at the commissar. He was rubbing his arms up and down his bare arms. Drizzle was in the air and he had begun to shiver.

"But you, bread maker's boy, you are only a little man." Her head cocked to one size. "Almost my size, I'd say. What do you think, Mr. Watkins? Isn't he almost my size?"

"Countess," I said. "Tick tock. We could be five miles farther down the road by now."

"Time, yes. I shall not be much longer. Just as soon as I have the bread maker's boy's trousers we shall be on our way."

"I can't take them off," Ivchenko said. He gestured at the horse between his legs as if we had somehow failed to grasp its significance. "Control this bourgeois cow, Mr. Watkins. I can put you on a military express train. Today. Safe passage. Anywhere you want to go. Anywhere at all."

I thought about Bohdan's Greek cholera victim and the waxed envelope in my pocket. "Way ahead of you," I said, as I slid the heavy envelope partway out. "Got mine and the lady's tickets yesterday."

The commissar kicked at the saddle with his free leg, screamed something in Russian, then beat his fist against the horse's neck.

"What's our friend saying?" I asked.

"The bread maker's boy just broke the third commandment."

"Man in your position, Commissar, might want to be careful about offending higher powers at this juncture in his life."

"He will never free himself," the countess said.

"Stuck tight," I agreed. "If he tried digging the dirt away, he'd get out eventually."

"I don't know," the countess said. "A horse is surprisingly heavy." Motioning with a hand like she was explaining a difficult geometry problem, she added, "I don't think the fool pulled his boot from the stirrup when the poor beast fell."

Ivchenko spat something in Russian at the countess. I looked at her.

"The commissar is questioning my parentage," she explained.

I kicked him. Not too hard. Just hard enough to remind him of his manners.

"Can you pull him out?" she asked. "I really do want his trousers. My legs are freezing."

I looked over my shoulder at the Mack sitting pushed in among the trees as the wind screamed and the sky threatened to soak us all. "Not a problem."

The countess followed my gaze.

"Yes, that should work nicely."

"Countess Irena," Ivchenko said. His voice wasn't the demanding all-powerful commissar's now.

She smiled. "Please, bread maker's boy. Call me Bourgeois Cow."

The commissar began to speak in Russian.

"Now, now," the countess said, wagging the long barreled pistol at Ivchenko. "We mustn't be rude. Mr. Watkins only speaks English."

Ivchenko stopped speaking.

"Mr. Watkins says he will use the, what is it called?" she asked me.

"Mack."

"The Mack to drag the horse off your body so I may take your trousers."

"Easier to drag him out from under instead of dragging the horse." I was pretty good at geometry. The countess didn't seem to notice.

"What was it you said to me this morning when you were about to hang me? Do not urinate on your floor? Kindly return the favor and hold your water."

The half clothed woman standing beside me extended her arm and sighted down the barrel of her pistol. Ivchenko's vulture eyes opened very wide. The first bullet hit him just above his left eyebrow. His head bounced against the dirt as the back of his skull erupted in a spray of brains and blood. I didn't see where the next three hit. When the countess lowered her arm, Ivchenko, the bread maker's boy, was unrecognizable with half his head gone. I smelled cordite, horse sweat and blood.

The wind blew and the sack dress flapped against her legs.

"There, Mr. Watkins, you see. I took your advice, after all. Yelena lives and I put a bullet in Ivchenko instead."

So she had. Four of them.

"I'll get the truck," I said, as I shook something unpleasant off my boot. "See if I can't drag what's left of him out from under that hay burner."

"Lovely," the countess commented as, unbothered by the remains of Ivchenko's corpse, she knelt beside the body and began to unbuckle the holster for her pistol.

I had to step over the body of one of the boys who just minutes ago, knew nothing more important in his world than the sight of a half naked woman lounging in a wheelbarrow. A fly crawled across dead eyes. I looked away. The little dirt road squeezing its way through nowhere in a Siberian forest looked like a miniature battlefield. All that was missing were trenches, sandbags and a few coils of barbed wire. I hadn't killed any of them, not even the horse, and yet my plan had killed them all. Some voice in the back of my head told me I should feel something, remorse maybe, but all I felt was relief. I wasn't going to die this day. She wasn't going to, either, and that was good enough for me.

Swinging the Mack's iron crank handle out of its bracket, I braced my feet and gave the bar a spin. Nothing happened. I spun it again with the same results. The Mack was in a cantankerous mood this morning. I spat in my palms, took a double grip and spun the handle as fast as I could manage around and around.

Nothing.

When I stopped to catch my breath, the countess was wearing Alexi Gavrilov's black leather coat. Using the sack dress as a towel, she wiped Ivchenko off her legs. Tossing the prison rag away, she stood there with bare legs slightly apart and gazed at the empty wheelbarrow farther up the hill. She had good legs and the short coat falling just below her rump made her look like she was wearing the world's shortest dress.

Hands on hips, she half turned to look at me over her shoulder. Our eyes met.

"Mr. Watkins."

"Yes?"

"Haven't you seen enough of my body for one morning?"

"Oh, right," I answered, as I looked away from her.

"Perhaps you should focus on our Mack. I would be delighted to hear the sound of its lovely engine running."

I cleared my throat and set my feet to get better leverage on the iron handle. "Wasn't looking at your body," I said, as I spun the crank. The Mack coughed then steadied itself into a rough idle. I pointed at the metal grill in front of me. "Was just catching my breath."

"Right," she said slowly. "Your breath." She tugged at the ends of Gavrilov's coat trying in vain to make the leather any longer than it already was. "Are those my things?" she asked.

I had completely forgotten about tossing the canvass rucksack onto the back of the flatbed before Bohdan stole it. "Thought you might be needing them,."

"Wonderful," the countess said.

She moved as dignified as a woman can when the situation requires negotiating various corpses with nothing on except an oversized leather coat and a dead man's shirt. After her burlesque show in the wheelbarrow, I thought she looked like she was dressed for church. With the truck idling like a showroom model, she pulled the well-worn canvas towards her.

Climbing into the cab, I heard her saying something in her mother tongue. She didn't sound happy.

"Something wrong?"

She held up a mixed assortment of items. "Two stockings, a shoe, spurs, one," she waved something white and flimsy in the air, "and," holding up the other hand, "a half empty bottle of absinthe."

"You packed it," I said, as I put the truck in gear.

"I started to pack it. You threatened me with a saber."

"Cossacks," I reminded her as I eased the truck out of the trees. She said something else, but with the Mack in first gear and my foot on the peddle, whatever it was got lost in the noise of the motor. The reverse gear made the engine whine as I backed the truck towards Ivchenko. I stopped it a few feet from his body.

The horse's bridle and reins were the closest thing I had to a rope. Tying one end of the leather around the corpse and one around the truck's bumper, I climbed back into the cab and eased the Mack forward. The countess, still bare legged, watched from the road as Ivchenko's blood splattered body squeezed its way out from under the dead animal.

"Far enough, Mr. Watkins," she shouted. "He's out."

By the time I jumped from the truck to untie everything, the countess had stripped him of pants, boots and socks. Ivchenko, stretched out in the dirt and wearing only his underwear looked nothing like the fearsome Bolshevik commissar. In death, he was once more just a baker's son. While she was knocking mud off the new additions to her wardrobe, I remembered my sidearm and the dead messenger boy.

The rucksack on his back hadn't stopped Ivchenko's bullet. The shot went straight through, punching a single hole through my raincoat before hitting the boy right about dead center of his heart. Rolling the corpse onto its back, I saw my pistol still stuck in his waistband.

"Sorry, kid," I told his body. I was glad he hadn't been killed by Bohdan's violin. At least he wasn't ripped and torn up like his companions. The drizzle was getting stronger and I wasn't getting any drier. It only took a second to pull my raincoat away from his body.

"Mr. Watkins?"

I stood, dropping the Colt into a pocket. "Countess?"

The countess, slightly muddy pants now safely protecting her modesty from wandering eyes, stood by the dead boy's feet doing a pretty good imitation of a private standing at attention.

"I wish to thank you formerly for coming back for me. If you hadn't," she looked behind her at the dead man stretched out in his underwear, "he would have hanged me."

The countess held a folded over wad of rubles in her hand. It looked like a not unsubstantial amount of money. Probably as much or more than what she pocketed when we sold the *Orca.*

"For a Marxist," she continued, "the commissar was not a strong believer in universal poverty."

I was reminded of Bohdan's words. His kill, his loot. She handed me the gold ingot.

"This was in his pocket."

I took the bar from her hand and wondered if the ingot was now *my* loot? Our fingers touched.

"And," she began to say.

Her shoulders sagged. The illusion of a private standing at attention vanished. Her whole demeanor changed and I was reminded of that night in the cafe. The one where a beautiful woman ran her fingers across my palm and told my fortune.

"I wouldn't have come back for you." She made her confession in a softly spoken whisper.

I thought of the major. Everybody wanted to tell me things I already knew. "Well," I said, "if I hadn't gone back, I wouldn't be able to say I told you so."

She smiled and it was as if the *Orca,* the ordeal on the horses, Cossack raids and the menace of Ivchenko never happened. It was the smile I remembered from the cafe. Her hand tightened in mine.

"I told you not to go chasing after Yelena." I said it good and loud. I wanted to make sure she heard me.

"Please do not shout, Mr. Watkins." She let go of my hand. "Ivchenko's woman hit me with a tree limb and my head is aching. There's a lump. See?"

She leaned forward with one of her fingers gently touching her scalp. All I saw was the chop job Yelena had done to her hair.

I touched the spot and felt her wince. "You're lucky," I told the top of her head. "You should see what she can do with a rock. How's the fit?"

"Ivchenko must have been the runt of the litter." She looked down at her new outfit. "The boots are too large, but the rest fits well enough." Holding her arms out in front of her, she said, "Alexi's coat is closer to your size than mine, but it will do."

She rolled the sleeves up to her wrists.

"Your ingot wasn't all I found."

"You found a map?" I thought it unlikely, but I have paid a lot right then to know where I was.

"No."

She reached inside Gavrilov's coat pocket and produced four golden sovereigns. The coins, I assumed, were the ones used to bribe their way into Vladivostok. I wondered how the commissar managed to get his hands on them. She held one of the coins against the sky.

"Are you a betting man, Mr. Watkins?"

"Roulette wheels have a certain appeal."

"They know," she said. "Ivchenko found four of the coins. Semyonov must have found the others." She lowered the coin. "My bet, it is why the Cossacks attacked. They were looking for me."

"Why would they be looking for you?"

"Because General Semyonov wants his gold. The gold he helped Bohdan steal."

The countess looked at the drizzly sky as finger length strands of red hair whipped in the wind.

"And you're just now telling me this?"

"I think, Mr. Watkins, I mentioned there were hunters. On the *Orca.* Remember?"

"You didn't mention these hunters had their own army."

She shrugged, made a hopeless try at smoothing her new hairdo, then said, "Would it have changed anything if I had?"

"That's not the point."

The countess patted my chest.

"If you say so. Now, what hole has our Czech friend crawled into?"

"I left you a note. Carved it in a stack of ties with a saber. Guess you didn't see it."

"No."

"It was a long shot, but I wanted you to know where I went. Of course, if you hadn't gone rabbit hunting after a Russian prostitute."

She held up her hand.

"When you didn't show," I continued, "Bohdan said Yelena probably killed you. He wanted to go find Ivan while everything was chaos at the yard and go get the gold."

"That sounds like Bohdan," the countess said. "Always thinking about opportunities. His opportunities."

"When I said we were going to wait for you, he pointed that fancy gun of his at me and borrowed the truck."

The countess walked away from me, put her hands into the pockets of her dead husband's coat, and surveyed the trees.

"How did you kill him?"

33

"I didn't kill him." I jerked a thumb over my shoulder at the idling truck. "Wonderful inventions, trucks. Better than a string of mules any day except they won't go very far if you don't fill the tank. That's a lesson Bohdan won't soon forget."

"He ran out of petrol?"

"He did. A few miles farther down the road. Last night, while you were being entertained by the dead guy without any pants, me and a couple of gas cans went for a stroll in the woods. It was all in my carved note you didn't get to see."

The countess tapped her fingers against the holstered Mauser on her hip. "When I shoot him this time, it won't be in the ear. Where is the cockroach?"

"That's a good question." It wasn't a lie. Maybe not the whole truth, but not a complete falsehood. I saw a shadow cross her face. She could tell there was more.

"Look, Countess," I said, "I need to tell you—"

The sound interrupted me. With all our violin playing and corpse looting, I had almost forgotten what was just over the big hill and down the road. The wind took a breather and in the near silence of the forest we heard it again. It was still far away, but the sound sent chills down both our spines. The countess walked to my side as if something bad was about to jump out of the woods. She put her arm through mine and pulled her body close against me.

"That was a train whistle," she said.

"From the direction of the bridge. Not Vladivostok," I added.

"Troop train," the countess whispered.

"Reinforcements," I said just as quietly.

"A pity, that," she added. "I think we should go now, Mr. Watkins. There could be a few dozen Bolsheviks on that train or a few thousand."

I was already jogging for the truck.

"Get their packs," she called after me. "Ivchenko told them to pack rations. And their bandoliers. Don't forget those. The Lewis is empty."

Thirty seconds, maybe forty-five and we were in the truck rolling down the muddy road. I drove while the countess emptied bandoliers and fed loose bullets into the machinegun's magazine. Her hands were shaking as she loaded.

"Will they follow us?" she asked.

"Let's hope they don't and assume they will."

All the bandoliers were empty. The countess pitched the leather and canvas belts into the trees alongside the road. Replacing the magazine drum onto Bohdan's Lewis, she stuck it barrel down on the far side of the seat. "How long before we fight them?"

I'd been thinking about that very question as I tried to nurse more speed out of the truck.

"Who says they are going to catch us? The track's blocked by the freight train and the late commissar's express. The engineer will have to stop before he gets to the depot. Then, whoever's in charge, will have to assess the situation. He'll find the late Colonel Gavrilov dead in the one single building still standing, no next in command since the Cossacks killed him and no Ivchenko. I think it will be awhile before they come looking for us. And even when they do, if they do, I didn't notice a lot of people paying much attention to which way we went this morning. All the ones who know anything for certain are dead."

"Yelena isn't dead," the countess told me. "She will tell them what happened."

"Maybe," I said. "I didn't see her standing around when we left. There's a good chance she doesn't know where we went."

The countess touched the handle of the holstered Mauser. "Too bad she didn't come with us on our morning hike. I could have shot her, too."

"I don't know," I said, as the Mack, running up the side of a hill, slowed to a crawl. "If Yelena was with us, your dancing dress routine wouldn't have been so universally distracting."

"Were you distracted, Mr. Watkins?"

"Me most of all."

The Mack kept climbing. More than once, I was afraid the wheels were going to slip, and we weren't going to make it up the grade. The countess didn't seem to notice. She spent most of the climb looking behind us, making sure Russian cavalry wasn't about to swarm over the slow moving truck. As we made the crest, the countess opened one of the dead soldier's packs and pulled out a loaf of bread and something covered in white cloth.

"Are you hungry?"

Inside the cloth was a fine looking sausage; a twin to the one I shared with the messenger boy. My stomach grumbled loud enough to be heard over the engine's exhaust.

"I'll take that as a yes," the countess said. Using a bayonet, she cut off a mouth sized piece.

The Mack needed two hands to keep straight on the muddy road.

"I'll pull over."

"Do not pull over."

Leaning towards me, my traveling companion put a piece of sausage in my mouth as I fought to keep the truck pointing in the right direction. By the time I swallowed, the bayonet was ready with the next bite. We finished the sausage and bread, then washed everything down with water from a dead man's canteen. If my clothes had been dry and I wasn't worried about Russian horsemen in hot pursuit, I might have enjoyed our little motorized picnic.

The countess slid closer. "Mr. Watkins, sooner or later you are going to have to tell me about Bohdan."

I started to talk. The countess touched my lips with a finger.

"Not yet. I have something to say first. When we were trapped in the city, I told Bohdan he was wrong. He needed to find someone else but the cockroach said you were the one. He knew it, he said. Imagine my disappointment in you when I offered my bribe and you said yes."

"About that," I said. Again, she touched my lips.

"Bohdan gloated when you agreed. He said he was a professional and knew how to pick his recruits. He had done it many times. I was so disappointed in you. You deserted for money. But when we were alone in my bedroom, after what I did in front of you in that tub."

I looked at her and saw a soft blush on her cheeks.

"You could have done anything you wanted. You know what I mean."

I knew.

"And I didn't dare stop you," she continued. "Then, that morning, you came back for me. And again today, just when I thought my days were over, there you were."

She touched my chest and felt the golden ingot.

"You gave Ivchenko the gold bar. The whole reason for your being here."

Her hand left my chest.

"The girl," she said, then looked at the road behind us.

I twisted my head around. I hadn't seen a girl. "Where?"

"The one in the hotel the morning we left."

"The window dressing? What about her?"

The countess gave me a head tilted, enquiring look. It was all questions and no words.

"I thought it would be less conspicuous if I had one of the working girls in my room for the night."

"Window dressing," she said. "I see. Why that one?"

"I wanted a view of the waterfront."

"The girl, Mr. Watkins. Why that one?"

"It wasn't like there was a selection of flavors standing outside that flophouse."

She pulled at a strand of hair that Yelena and her bayonet had missed. "Her hair was black."

I nodded.

"Do you like black haired women?"

"Never put much thought into it. They're okay, I guess."

"She was very thin," she added to the description, "and shorter than me."

"Short and skinny," I said agreeably.

The countess touched her hair again.

"I must look awful."

Her lower lip was puffy from her battle with Yelena. One eye had a dark circle under it and there were raw friction burns around both wrists. Her hair was chopped and hacked into ten different lengths. She reminded me of a little girl's doll after the child found her mother's scissors.

"You look good with short hair," I said, hoping my face had the proper reassuring smile. "It suits you."

She patted her scalp. "That bad," she sighed. The wind whistled through the broken windshield. "I loved my hair. The whore knew it. If I see her again, I will dig her eyes out of her skull with a spoon."

It didn't sound like an idle boast to me. "I doubt we'll see her again. She's lost her influence with Ivchenko dead."

The countess moved over the seat until she sat very close to me. Her leg touched mine. I put my hand on her knee. The same one she had removed my hand from with determined patience back in our Vladivostok cafe. She didn't take it away this time. A few minutes later, her head touched my shoulder and I felt her body relax. The countess had fallen asleep. We rode like that together, side by side, for the next two hours. The countess never moved. Even when I shifted gears or had to muscle the wheel around slippery curves, she slept like someone beyond exhaustion. There was a particularly deep hole in the road and I didn't see it until it was too late. The truck bounced hard enough to loosen a filling. I had to grab for the woman sitting beside me to keep her from hitting the floorboard. She stretched, yawned and punched my shoulder a couple of times like she was fluffing a pillow then laid her head on my shoulder once more.

"What if she really is a Chekists?" I heard her say.

"Yelena?"

"What if Ivchenko thought she was just his whore but it was she who was using him?"

"I think she was a peasant girl with a cruel streak as wide as the Missouri River and the morals of a stray cat."

The countess sat up and rubbed her fist in her eyes. "So tired. I could sleep for a week."

"You were out for a couple of hours."

"She liked you," the countess said after a moment.

"So do hungry lions."

"She has legs like a plow horse," my traveling companion said informatively. The countess used her hands to pull at the front of Gavrilov's coat. "And breasts like a cow's udder. One frequently milked." She smoothed the front of her coat. "Did you find her attractive?"

"There was a certain appeal. Horse legs and cow udders notwithstanding."

The countess elbowed me in the ribs. "You are teasing and I am serious."

"I barely noticed her. The only chance I had to really look at her, I had this other woman swimming naked in my fishbowl."

The countess patted my thigh.

"I have sworn an oath," she told me. "I am never touching absinth again."

"Uh huh. Didn't see you pitching that bottle into the bushes earlier."

"An oath," she repeated.

I stuck my hand outside the cab. It felt like the wind was blowing harder. "Going to be cold tonight. We might need that alcohol to keep from freezing to death." I said it as a joke but my clothes were still damp from last night's rain. Now that all the walking and wheelbarrows were long behind me, I was feeling the temperature.

"Are you cold, Mr. Watkins?" There was concern in her voice. "We should have taken one of those idiot boy's overcoats."

She rubbed her hands up and down my arm.

"I wasn't thinking," the countess continued. "Too surprised to still be alive."

"I looked." Nodding my chin at the violin sitting nose down in the floorboard, I said, "That thing ruined anything salvageable."

The countess put her arm over my shoulder and hugged me. "We will have to get you dry soon." She looked behind us again. "We could stop? Build a fire. Get you out of these wet things and get them dry."

She said it but both of us knew there was no way we could stop.

"I'll survive. Ivan shouldn't be much farther. He'll have a blanket or something I can wrap up in while we think about what to do next."

"My, aren't you the clever one," the countess said. "How do you know Ivan is down this road?"

"Tomatoes." The road flattened out and the Mack crawled its way to something close to twenty miles per hour.

"Tomatoes?"

"I'll tell you about it when we find Ivan."

We were coming to another hill and I had to shift the truck into a lower gear for the climb. My driving skills were improving by leaps and bounds. The countess watched me. Maybe watched is the wrong word. Appraised was probably closer. The corners of her mouth turned up in that halfway smile of hers.

"We have made it, Mr. Watkins. You and I. All my enemies are either dead or too far behind me to matter. There is nothing stopping us now. Ivan will take us to the treasure and we will be rich."

She rubbed her hand up and down my arm again.

"You and I," she added.

Then she laughed. Not the disturbing giggle from our night in the bathtub or a vodka induced chuckle. A real laugh, like the ones I'd heard in Vladivostok. A boxcar full of gold. How much would that be worth? I laughed with her. When the sounds of laughter died away into smiling remnants, she touched my ear. The same one she had tried to bite off in the fancy horse trough.

"Does it hurt?" she asked.

"Can't hear you. Got a bad ear." I felt a finger touch the spot where her teeth did their worst. She said something, but the Mack was making too much racket or she wasn't speaking loud enough. I really couldn't hear this time. The truck went around a sharp curve in the road. I saw a church ahead of us. Or what remained of one? The steeple was destroyed with only a porting of the tower still standing. Holes made by two armies shooting at each other marked its sides.

"Soldiers been through here, looks like," I said. Aside from the general emptiness of the area, I hadn't seen a lot of war damage until the raid on the train depot. "I see a road up ahead."

"The crossroad," the Countess said. "The church was untouched the last time I was here. Pity."

"Crossroad? *The* crossroad? Your rendezvous point?"

The countess was paying very close attention to the

churchyard. If she heard me, she made no reply.

Pushed into the weeds on the side of the road, someone had abandoned a smashed up wagon. A man rode a horse around the wagon. The countess jumped. She practically flew across the seat until she was hanging outside the cab. She waved an arm over her head and shouted in Russian. The horseman stood in his stirrups, raised a hand over his head, and waved back.

"Tomatoes," I said, nodding my head at Bohdan's deductions. The countess didn't hear me. The Mack's engine and the wind blowing through the broken windshield swallowed my words. I don't think she would have heard me if we were sitting still in a dead calm. She was too busy shouting and waving at the big Russian sitting on his horse. She stepped out onto the running board.

"Ivan!" Half of Siberia must have heard the shout.

Coming back into the cab, she slid across the seat until she was pressed against me.

"It's Ivan. He's waving. See?"

"I see him," I said as, once again, the Mack's engine drowned my words. The countess put her arm through mine.

"I told you. There's nothing to stop us now. We've made it behind the enemy's lines. Admit it. My maneuver with the *Orca* worked."

"Yes, Countess. Everything went exactly as planned." She pinched my arm then stamped her soldier's boots in a rapid rhythm on the floorboard. I had never seen her so happy.

"Have you ever been to Venice, Mr. Watkins? I long to ride in a gondola."

She laughed and squirmed beside me. Then she planted her lips on my cheek so hard my head was pushed sideways. The Mack swerved nearly clipping a tree before I could get it straight.

"Careful, Countess." I felt her hand on my thigh as Ivan's crossroads drew closer. "What?" The countess had said something I didn't catch.

"Do you remember the day you gave me my lovely present? Back on the *Orca?*"

"The shirt? Special ordered from the finest ship's chandlery on the Pacific Coast."

The truck slipped sideways, causing me to fight the machine to get us back into line. Ivan was still standing in his stirrups; still waving a hand above his head.

"I remember it well," I said.

I could see the house now. It was a simple place with a wood shingle roof and a chimney. A chimney meant fire and a fire meant the odds of me freezing to death were going down. The owners had put up a stone fence down one side of the road and something that looked like a garden plot was coming up on the right. I didn't see any red banners flapping in the wind.

Placing her lips as close to my ear as she could, the woman sitting beside me whispered, "When you gave me my present, I asked you to stop looking at me. On the boat."

I let off the gas and the Mack began to slow. The countess leaned her body hard against mine. The Russian was close enough for me to see the expressions on his face. Standing in his stirrups, he had been smiling through his beard as he waved and shouted at the woman sitting beside me. As we got closer and as the countess slid her body next to mine, the look on his face changed. The smile faltered. The waving hand hung motionless in the air. It was my turn to smile. Ivan had the look of a man recently stabbed in the stomach. The Mack was barely moving when her lips touched my ear. The unhappy Russian sat motionless on his horse as the countess wrapped her free arm around my neck. My arm pulled the brake lever harder than I intended. The countess tightened her grip as the truck jerked to a stop. I could feel her looking at me. I turned to face the woman sitting beside me. Her lips were very close to mine.

"Countess. There's something I need to tell you."

Ivan's horse was beside the cab now. As he leaned down to peer inside the truck, I saw his black coat was open. The grip of the Webley revolver under his arm was plain to see. His eyes first saw the countess in Ivchenko's clothes, then the hand on my thigh and her arm around my neck.

There was murder in his eyes. Ivan's hand moved towards his weapon.

The countess traced a line along my thigh with her finger. Ivan saw it all.

She used her finger to turn my face towards hers. I saw Ivan over her shoulder. He was still sitting on his horse and still kept the revolver under his arm. His mouth was open and his head moved almost imperceptivity slowly from side to side. I looked into the blue eyes of the woman sitting beside me. She was smiling like she had in our cafe when she traced the lines on my palm and told my fortune.

"On the boat, I said we weren't going to be lovers," the countess said in a voice liquid with pleasure. "Do you remember?"

I nodded, but decided now was a good time to keep my eyes on the big Russian and his revolver. The countess touched her nose to my ear then whispered two words.

"I lied."

My eyes found hers.

Ivan said something in Russian and for maybe the first time since I made the unpleasant Russian's acquaintance, I think I knew what he was saying.

"Now," she purred, "shall we go get the gold?"

EPILOG

The major wasn't sure what part of his body was hurting worse; his hand where the Cossacks' saber had nearly taken off two fingers or the fresh bullet hole in his leg. The way he was strung up, he had just enough slack to let him stand on his toes like a ballerina with wrists crossed and tied over his head. He grimaced and tried to shift his weight to the other side.

It didn't help. It just made the wound in his leg feel like somebody was trying to cauterize it with a hot poker.

"Watkins," the major said to himself, his voice muffled by the feedbag they had pulled over his head, "if you're still alive, I swear I'm going to murder you with my bare hands."

Just as soon as he could use his hands again. His eyes might not be able to see through the hood, but there was nothing wrong with his sense of touch. His mangled fingers had bled down his arm, covering him with sticky blood all the way to his shoulder. He didn't think he'd be strangling anybody anytime soon.

How long had it been now? Two hours? Three? When the Russians hauled him into the barn, it was still dark outside.

Now, through the burlap sack they had over his head, he could just make out fuzzy daylight. The rope creaked and the major tried to ignore the pain. Three hours, he decided. It had to be at least that long.

A hinge squeaked and he heard the sound of a heavy door swinging open. A fresh blast of cold air blew into the barn. Footsteps were coming from his left. He had company.

"Take that off," a voice said in Russian. It was a deep voice. One that resonated with the familiarity of command.

An unseen hand grabbed the burlap and pulled. For the first time in hours, he smelled something other than oats and horse spit. The man holding the makeshift hood was the same one who'd strung him up like a side of beef in a slaughterhouse. He was a big Russian in a white undershirt, blue suspenders and a fur hat. The man had a pair of shoulders that looked like they could lift a beer keg like it was a bar of soap. His arms were covered with enough hair to keep a bear warm through the winter.

"Cut me down," the major said in Russian.

Big Shoulders shoved him in the chest and started him swinging. The rope around his wrists bit like a steel trap. New blood began to ooze from his hand. The major made a mask of his face as the big man eyed a spot about where his left kidney would be, then drew back a fist.

"None of that, Sergeant," the commanding voice said.

Big Shoulders grunted and stepped away. The major tried the ballerina toe balance thing again. He managed to stop the swinging and twist himself around to face the voice. The first thing he saw was Laughing Billy. The Czech didn't look so good. In fact, he looked like a man that might have accidentally fallen down a ravine, a steep one. He was scratched and dirty and his outfit had the occasional rip or small tear. That enormous mustache of his was covered in caked blood and one eye was swollen nearly shut. Like the major, his hands were tied. The voice that called off Big Shoulders stood beside the Czech. He wore the uniform of a

Russian officer. The major didn't recognize the insignias on the man's uniform, but you didn't have to be an expert in the Cossack military to know a high rank when you saw it. Another Cossack had a handful of Laughing Billy's coat collar. He gave the Czech a hard shove. Billy stumbled forward and straight into the hairy armed sergeant. As if he were trying to rid himself of a horsefly, the sergeant made a backhanded swing. The blow caught Laughing Billy on the chin, sending the Czech into a pile of straw that looked like it had been mucked out of a horse stall. The fancy uniform didn't check the sergeant this time. Instead, he used his gloves to slap dust away from his sleeve as the second man who had shoved Laughing Billy helped him out of a fur lined cloak.

"Is that him?" he asked, still swatting dust away from his uniform.

"That's him," Bohdan said from his pile of straw. "That's the American major I told you about."

The officer handed his gloves to the soldier holding his cloak, grabbed at the leather belt circling a trim waist and adjusted an expensive looking saber to a better position. He motioned impatiently at Bohdan. "Where are your manners, Colonel? Make the introductions."

Bohdan wiped at his chin with his bound hands, then said, "May I present General Grigory Semyonov, Ataman of the Cossacks and Supreme—"

"That's enough," General Semyonov said. "I said introduce me, not announce me to the czarina."

The major looked at Laughing Billy sitting in dirty straw with a blacked eye and busted nose. For the first time in hours, he didn't feel so bad. "Last time I saw you, Billy, you looked like you were riding hell bent for China."

"I told you," Bohdan said angrily. The ever present laugh was nowhere to be heard in his voice now. "Sakhalin was the way to go. But you had to make for the Amur." Bohdan touched his nose and winced. "My horse gave out on me."

General Semyonov barked out a laugh. "As if a Czech could

outrun Cossacks." He took a step closer to the major. "The report said they shot you out of the saddle."

"They shot my horse out from under me," the major said. "Bullet clipped my thigh or you'd still be trying to figure out where I went."

Semyonov looked at the bloody tear in the major's trousers. He turned to the sergeant with the impressive shoulders. "He was lucky. A little higher and his time with women would be over."

The sergeant smiled, showing a missing front tooth.

The rope creaked and the major wished he had Watkins' nuts in a vise. This was his fault. If he had obeyed orders and pulled Billy out of that shed when he told him to, none of this would have happened. The three of them would be miles away by now. "Cut me down," he said, "and I want to speak to the American consul."

Semyonov raised his eyebrows. "Well, Major, one I might do, but the other would prove difficult. The nearest consul is about two thousand kilometers from here."

"Farther," Bohdan said.

Semyonov ignored the interruption. "I am going to ask you a question, Major, and—"

"I'm not talking," the major said quickly.

"Not that kind of question. I have no interest in learning your secrets." Semyonov drew his saber. He did it slowly, letting the sound of killing steel hum a tune only a sword could make. The general faced an imaginary opponent on the other side of the barn. He took up his stance, feet apart, knees slightly bent, curved blade pointing at a wooden post. Semyonov lunged, recovered and sliced at an imaginary adversary.

The major eyed a slicing blade that was far too close to his ribs for comfort.

"The war is almost over," Semyonov said between slashes at the post. "Anything you could tell me about contacts, orders, operational plans, it would all be useless in a few weeks." The general sliced the air with his saber fast enough to make the steel whistle. "I can lead armies in the field, maneuver tens of thousands of men, execute attacks the Bolsheviks can only dream of accomplishing but the simplest command." Semyonov recovered his stance and looked at the man holding his cloak. "A straightforward order. Attack a defenseless depot. Kill everything you see and while the Bolsheviks are trying to defend one of their precious locomotives, rescue one single woman and bring her here." The general slapped the saber against the side of his boot. "Right here."

The man holding the general's cloak stared at the dirt beneath his feet.

Semyonov looked at the marine still dangling on his rope. His voice low enough to sound almost conspiratorial, he said, "My sister's boy. I still have hopes for him. Is this Watkins the Czech has told me so much about a competent man?"

"No," the major said.

The general pointed the curved blade at the young man holding his cloak. "Because of him, I had to bring the Transbaikal Host much too far east." Lowering the steel, he added, "Three men. Three *good* men he sent to find her and all three turn up dead." The saber made a slow circuit of the barn until it pointed at Bohdan. "I smell your handiwork in that bit of death, Colonel."

"Gut the American," Bohdan said from the dung splattered straw. "He is useless to us."

"Us?" Semyonov spat out the word. "There is no *us*. I do not forgive men who betray me." The general swung the saber in a backhanded arc. The edged steel sliced through the rope holding the major like scissors cutting a thread. The marine fell against the post then sagged to the floor. He tried to stand once, then decided he would sit for a while and contemplate the man standing in front of him.

Semyonov bent over making the tip of the saber rest on the barn floor like an old man's cane as he examined the bullet wound. After a long moment's professional appraisal, he said, "Not so bad. I was cut worse when I was a student at Monsieur LeClair's fencing academy." He straightened. "Can you ride?"

The major used a finger to move the bloodstained fabric away from the wound. Semyonov was right. It didn't look half as bad as it felt. The bullet made a two or three inch cut across the top of his thigh. A few stitches and a clean bandage and it would be fine. It would hurt, but he could ride. "Show me a horse," the major answered. "I can ride." He looked up to find the Russian general staring at his bound hands.

"If I were you," Semyonov said, "I'd be more worried about that hand. If it festers, we'll have to take it off." Semyonov stuck the point of his saber between the marine's legs, sharp side up.

The major slid the knot across the steel's edge. When the rope fell away, he tucked his injured hand against his chest.

Semyonov turned towards his nephew. "If I ordered you to go find the doctor, do you suppose you could at least get that right?"

The nephew didn't answer. He just turned around while still holding the cloak and walked out of the barn. The sergeant grinned his missing tooth smile.

"And find my steward," Semyonov shouted after him. "Something hot for our guest to eat." The general glanced at Bohdan still sitting in the stable's dirty straw. "For the major, you lying Czech. Not you. You go hungry. Now," he said, sliding his saber back into its scabbard, "my question."

"I've already told you. I'm not answering your questions," the major said.

Semyonov waved a dismissive hand. "I admire your resolve," he turned to look at Bohdan, "and loyalty, but as I said, I am not interested in answers you cannot provide. I don't care what your mission was or what you planned to do with that Czech liar and thief. Keep your secrets."

"Shoot him, General," Bohdan said. "He is a dangerous

man."

"But is he a reasonable one, Colonel?" The general looked at the man sitting with his back against a post and cradling his hand. "Are you reasonable, Major?"

The major looked at the big shouldered sergeant glowering at him. That one, he thought, agreed with Bohdan. Laughing Billy looked at him like a man holding four aces against his pair of jacks. "I like to think I'm reasonable," the major answered.

"Good," Semyonov said. "I like reasonable men. My options, you see, grow fewer with each passing day. The Bolsheviks control almost all of Siberia." The general pointed a finger at the barn's wall as he spoke as if all of Siberia was just beyond its timbers. "The White Army is finished and no help to me. No real surprise there. What kind of army puts an admiral in charge of a land battle?" Semyonov swept his arm around the barn's interior. "Do you see any ocean? Admirals," Semyonov said. "What were they thinking?"

The marine nodded his head. He could add a thing or two about admirals.

"I could go south," Semyonov continued, "but to do that, I must have enough men to make the warlords respect me." He looked at Bohdan. "You remember Manchu Wu," he said. "I'm told he still walks with a limp because of you."

"The man tried to cheat me," Bohdan said.

"Manchu Wu is offering ten thousand yuan to anyone who brings him Colonel Wilhelm Bohdan. Alive, of course. Ten thousand yuan and the hand of his second wife's youngest daughter. Or was it his youngest wife's second daughter?"

For once, Laughing Billy found nothing at all humorous in that statement.

"The reward is considerably less for a corpse," Semyonov added. "That is one option. Manchu Wu can keep his daughter, but his favor would go a long way with the warlords. Then there is the coast and my Japanese friends. I could sell the Czech to them."

Bohdan began to speak.

"Not a word," the general said warningly. "They wouldn't offer asylum and a young Manchu virgin. No, for you, Bohdan, the reward is five hundred rifles and ten thousand rounds of ammunition to whichever warlord, Mongol bandit or," he paused, "Ataman of the Cossack Host that finds you. That, I think, is a very reasonable second option. What do you think, Major?"

"Let me go, General Semyonov, and I'll act as a middleman for you."

Semyonov smiled. "I don't think so."

The cloak carrying officer came back from his search for the doctor. "I found him, Ataman Semyonov. They are sobering him up now."

The general turned to the marine. "When my nephew told me of his brilliant failure at the train depot, I told him he was banished from the Host until he made good his mistake. I didn't care if it took until next winter's ice. He wasn't to come back until he had what I wanted. I confess, Major, I didn't have very high hopes. But, last night a messenger found me. My nephew had her." Semyonov smiled. "Like I said, I have high hopes for him." He turned to the sergeant. "Bring in our lost sheep."

The sergeant jumped to attention, then hurried out of the barn. Semyonov removed a sable hat and rubbed his forehead. Replacing his hat, he said to Bohdan, "Do you think this Watkins man succeeded? And Colonel, if you have ever told the truth, you better tell it now."

"Ivchenko," Bohdan said.

"Who is Ivchenko?"

"One of their political commissars. Watkins is most likely a corpse by now. Let me go and I will know before the sun sets one way or another."

The major looked at Bohdan. The Czech had a peculiar look in his eyes. Wheels were turning. Schemes were hatching those eyes said.

"If you stop talking, Colonel, you might survive this day," Semyonov told him.

The big shouldered Russian came stomping into the barn. He wasn't alone. He had a woman with him, a girl really wearing, of all things, English riding boots and pants. The major gave her an appraising look. It was the first time he'd seen her up close. So this was the woman who had made his horrendously incompetent lieutenant forget his duty. He shook his head. He didn't approve of women in pants. It was almost indecent; behavior fit only for actresses and spoiled women trying too hard to be noticed. The woman who most likely got Watkins killed didn't look like an actress or spoiled. She looked feral. "No accounting for taste," the major mumbled in English.

The girl yanked away from the sergeant and the major thought she was about to do something unladylike, but the Russian raised a hairy arm ready for an open handed slap. She didn't cower away from the raised hand, but she didn't try to yank her arm free anymore.

"So that's her," the major said. "All this trouble for a pants wearing female."

Bohdan started to laugh. It wasn't his usual full bellied laugh. This one was more of a seen-it-all-now chuckle.

"Her?" the general said. "No, Major. That is my nephew's understanding of my orders. I told him to fetch the countess from the depot, so he grabbed a girl in English clothes and brought," Semyonov eyed the woman up and down, "this to me."

"General," the nephew began. "She looks like the woman you described. Everyone thought it was her."

"Yelena," Bohdan said so low the major almost didn't hear him.

The major nodded his head in understanding. He recognized her now. It was the pants and boots that put him off. This wasn't the woman Watkins was chasing. The last time he'd seen this one, she'd been rolling around in the leaves with the other woman. Irena.

The big Russian shook Yelena's arm. "Give your curtsy in the presence of the Ataman, girl."

"Leave the Bolshevik be, Sergeant," Semyonov said. He turned to Bohdan. "Did I hear you say a name?"

"Yelena Ilyinichna," Bohdan answered. "Sometimes Yelena Olegovna. It changes from time to time."

"Like yours," the general agreed. "It changes from time to time."

"Call her what you want. She works for the Cheka."

"You know this, Colonel Bohdan?" Semyonov asked.

Bohdan's mustache twitched. "If she doesn't, she should."

"Are you with the Cheka, Yelena Ilyinichna?"

Yelena stopped struggling against the man holding her arm. "No, Ataman Semyonov." Her free hand touched the red scarf knotted at her throat. "I am a woman on my own." Her hand left the scarf and touched her hip. She smiled, showing a flash of white teeth. "Commissar Ivchenko forced me to help him."

Semyonov felt the sleeve of her blouse. "Silk, isn't it?"

Yelena nodded.

"Where are you from, Yelena Ilyinichna?"

"Chita, Ataman Semyonov."

"Chita? Is that so? Sergeant, how long were we in Chita?"

The sergeant blew out his cheeks and thought for a moment. "I think it was thirty months, General."

Semyonov let go of the cranberry colored silk and admired Yelena's boots and trousers. "Did you ever see any of the Chita women wearing silks and trousers like these?"

The sergeant laughed. "Never seen any woman wear pants before. Anywhere."

"Where did you get those boots, Yelena Ilyinichna?" the general asked.

"I bought them, Ataman Semyonov. With my money."

"They belonged to the countess," Bohdan said. "She obviously killed her."

The sergeant tightened his grip on her arm. Yelena

screamed and half sank to her knees.

"I didn't kill her. The commissar told me I could have whatever I wanted. She was going to hang, anyway."

The sergeant relaxed his grip.

"Was going to?" the general asked.

Yelena nodded. "He hung the *kompolka*.

Semyonov looked at Bohdan.

"One of the new Bolshevik army ranks. She means Gavrilov, her husband."

Yelena nodded. "Yes, Gavrilov. The countess betrayed him with Watkin—"

"Knew it," the major said, as he leaned against his post.

"—and the commissar was about to start her trial when Watkin came in."

The major forgot the pain in his hand and sat up straighter.

"The lieutenant you told me about?" Semyonov asked Bohdan.

The Czech nodded.

"Then what?" Semyonov asked.

"I don't know." She screamed again as the hand around her arm began to squeeze. This time, she did go to the ground. "Please. I don't know what happened. Watkin left with his woman and the commissar." Yelena grabbed at the hand squeezing her arm. "You're hurting me."

"Why did Watkins leave with this commissar?" the major said.

Yelena seemed to notice him for the first time. "Something happened. With Commissar Ivchenko. Something Watkin gave him. I didn't see what it was but it made the commissar," she paused, trying to think of a way to describe what had happened. "Something changed," was all she said.

Semyonov glanced at Bohdan. The Czech nodded his head. "Clever, Stick," he said in a low voice. "Very clever."

"And the woman?" Semyonov asked.

"She was fine, Ataman Semyonov. Watkin took her with him."

The major snorted.

The general nodded towards the barn door. "Put our lost sheep somewhere safe while I think about what to do with her."

The sergeant yanked Yelena to her feet and pulled her out of the barn.

"So, Major," the general said. "There you have it."

"There I have what?"

Semyonov swung his arms at the nearly empty barn. "Surely you see the situation? Have I not made everything crystal clear?"

The marine looked at the open barn door, looked at Laughing Billy sitting in squalor and at the severed end of the rope hanging from a roof beam. Finally, he looked at General Semyonov. "No," he said, shaking his head. "You haven't."

The Cossack squatted in front of the marine. "I'm offering you a trade, Major." Without looking behind him, he pointed a finger in Bohdan's direction. "I don't need Japanese rifles and I don't want some warlord's daughter. What I want is for you to get on a horse and go find your missing lieutenant. When you do, you're going to bring the Countess Irena Obolensky to me. When you do *that*, when you bring her to me, I'll give you that lying scoundrel Czech sitting in horse shit over there and wish you both bon voyage." The general placed his hand over his heart. "My word as an officer and loyal servant of the czar."

The major got his good leg under him and, using the post as a support, pushed himself up from the barn's dirt floor. The effort made him dizzy and sent bolts of fire through his hand. He felt in a pocket with his good hand, found his pipe and tobacco pouch and managed to stuff the bowl full with his thumb. Sticking the stem between his teeth, he patted his pockets for matches.

Semyonov patted his own pockets, found a cigar, then bit the end off. He spat the tobacco out before producing a flint lighter. Spinning the wheel, he held it over the major's pipe. After the marine exhaled a cloud of blue smoke, he touched the flame to the end of his cigar. Semyonov extinguished his lighter, dropped it into a pocket, and examined the glowing end of his cigar.

The two men smoked in companionable silence for a few moments. The major spoke first.

"I'm not in the kidnapping business."

Semyonov nodded his head in understanding. "Are you in the exchange of prisoners business?" He looked at Bohdan. "I have yours and your man, he has mine. I'm not going to hurt the woman, if that is your concern."

The major let his gaze drift to the rope hanging from the rafters. "Is that so?"

Semyonov followed his gaze. "Yes, Major, that is so. You were a prisoner. Caught out of uniform, I should mention. Irena is a woman and a countess. These things matter. Decorum and all that."

The major looked at Bohdan smirking at him from his pile of dirty straw.

"A prisoner exchange," the major said agreeably.

"Precisely."

The major looked at Bohdan. The cards had been reshuffled. He didn't have a pair of jacks this time and the Czech wasn't holding all the aces. The marine nodded his head. "I can do that. But first, tell me one thing, General. Why do you want this countess?"

Semyonov tapped ash away from his cigar, smiled a world weary smile then moved a half step closer to the marine.
"Let me tell you a story."

ABOUT THE AUTHOR

A. C. Foster makes his home not far from Galveston Bay. He has seen a good bit of America, about forty states and counting, and has worked and lived in four countries, five if you count a long distance dalliance with Canada. A veteran of the US Navy, he holds a degree in History from the University of Texas at Austin.

His first novel, *The Scarab's Touch,* is a historical adventure thriller set in 1934 in the Pacific Northwest.